FASCINATED

FASCINATED

BERTRICE SMALL

SUSAN JOHNSON

THEA DEVINE

ROBIN SCHONE

KENSINGTON BOOKS
http://www/kensingtonbooks.com

Contents

Mastering Lady Lucinda

Bertrice Small

Chapter One

England, 1750

George Frederick Worth, the Bishop of Wellington, had one elder brother. Lord William Worth was a colonel in the King's Own Royal West Worcester Dragoons, stationed in India. The bishop had five younger sisters, four of whom had married quite well and were nicely settled. Laetitia, the eldest, was the Duchess of Solway. Charlotte, the second eldest, was the Marchioness of Cardiff. The third, Georgeanne, was the Countess of Dee, and the next to the youngest, Julia, was married to Lord Rafferty of Killarney. It was the youngest, however, who was a thorn in the bishop's portly side.

Lady Lucinda Harrington had been wed at seventeen, and widowed at twenty-three. Her husband, an older man, had left her his considerable fortune, which had not been entailed upon his estate. His title had passed to his twelve-year-old nephew, an obnoxious lad, whose mama had not been of a mind to allow Lucinda to remain at Harrington Hall under the circumstances. Lady Margaret had fully expected her son to inherit all of his uncle's goods and chattels. When he hadn't, she had become quite piqued.

Advised by her trusted barrister that she hadn't a snowball's chance in hell of overturning her brother's will, she had done the next best thing and ordered his widow from the hall. As there was no dower house at Harrington Hall, and as her parents were both deceased, it was George Frederick Worth, the Bishop of Wellington, who had been obliged to take his widowed sister into his household. And from the moment she had arrived, the bishop's life had been more difficult than he could have ever imagined.

"I shall only remain until I can find a house of my own," Lady Lucinda Harrington had announced to her brother and sister-in-law upon her advent at the manse. "I think London, perhaps. I have never lived in the city. I believe a small mansion on one of those delightful little squares I have heard so much about should suit me quite nicely."

Lady Lucinda Harrington smiled a brilliant smile at her brother and his wife. She was a very beautiful young woman with rich, chestnut-colored hair and bright, marine blue eyes. Her sisters were all equally stunning. They had been immortalized by one of the foremost portrait painters of the day in a great canvas titled *The Five Graces*. It hung in the bishop's main salon. His guests often commented upon the extaordinary beauty of his female siblings.

"You cannot buy yourself a house, Lucinda," the bishop said.

"Why on earth not, George? I am, to use a most vulgar and common expression, filthy rich," Lucinda replied.

"You are a woman, alone," he answered her.

"Because I am a woman, and alone, I cannot purchase my own establishment? That is absolutely ridiculous, Georgie!" she told him.

"I think, my dear," her sister-in-law interjected, "that what George means is that a lovely, well-born widow, without children, alone in her town house might cause unfortunate gossip. You will, of course, want to remarry as soon as possible in any event. Your new husband will more than likely keep a house in London for the season. It would be imprudent to expend monies for your own house under such circumstances. Wouldn't you agree, dearest?"

"But I do not necessarily want to remarry," Lucinda said quietly. "Remember, I was wed at seventeen, and never really had a season in London as Papa couldn't afford it with Julia's dowry to scrape up."

"*Not remarry?*" The bishop looked scandalized. "Of course you will remarry, Lucinda. You have no other choice."

"Of course I have a choice, Georgie. With my own monies I do not have to be at the mercies of some man. Robert, bless him, certainly saw to that. He advised me himself not to remarry except for love, and love alone. That, he said, was the most valuable advice he could give me. I promised him I should indeed not remarry except for love. You surely would not want me to break a promise I made to my late husband on his deathbed, would you?" She cocked her head to one side questioningly.

"You cannot leave my home except as a bride," the bishop responded stubbornly. "Your reputation would be in tatters almost immediately, and the gossip would reflect upon us all. I know the others would agree, Lucinda. Fortunately your husband was wise enough to leave the management of your inheritance to Mr. Wythe, Senior, of Wythe, Wythe and Smyth, who as it happens are my own solicitors. I shall speak to them in the morning."

"I could also leave your house in my shroud," Lucinda said darkly, glaring at her brother. Georgie could be such a pompous ass.

"You could," he agreed, not in the least intimidated. "She is such a minx," he said later that evening to his wife as they prepared for bed. "She hasn't changed a bit, I fear." He walked across the chamber to where his wife's maid was laying out Caroline's night garment. "You are dismissed, Molly," he told her.

"Yes, yer worship," she said, bobbing a curtsey and hurrying to the door, casting him a coy look over her shoulder as she went.

Opening the door, the bishop gave her bottom a friendly smack and winked. "I'll see you later," he whispered to her, then closed the door behind the serving girl. After walking back across the room he began to pull the pins from his wife's blond hair as she sat at her dressing table. When he had discovered them all, he picked up her hairbrush and began brushing her hair.

"Ummmm," Caroline Worth murmured. She loosened the tie on her chamber robe. She was quite naked beneath.

The bishop watched in the mirror as he stroked her thick, long hair. Finally he set the brush aside, and leaning over he cupped her two breasts in his hands. Caroline had large, pear-shaped breasts with enormous nipples. He fondled the flesh and pulled the nipples out to their full length, one by one. Her breasts felt weighty in his big palms. Their eyes met in the mirror as she pulled her nether lips open, smiling.

"Come, and have a little taste, darling," she invited him.

He grinned. Anyone seeing his elegant, proper wife would never imagine what a wanton she was when the bedchamber door was closed. He released her breasts and knelt between her thighs, bending his head to lick at her and suck her naughty little clit. He knew exactly what would happen, and it did. Caro was quickly aroused by his actions.

"I want to fuck," she moaned to him. "Hurry, darling! I am so very, very hot for it!"

He slid her off her stool, pulling her to the floor where she lay, legs stretched wide, arms open and inviting. The bishop pulled off his own chamber robe and fell upon his wife, fucking her until she came in a great, gusty sigh, her juices crowning the head of his penis generously. He groaned, well satisfied. "Twenty years married, Caro, and I still want you," he told her.

"Me, and half the female servants," she teased him mischievously.

"I cannot help it if I am a man who needs to give love, darling," he told her. "Besides, you always get my best, Caro. You know, this is what Lucinda needs."

"Love?" his wife replied.

"No, a good stiff cock up her cunt," he answered.

Caroline giggled. "Ohh, George, you are really so naughty for a clergyman. Now get off me, and let us get into bed. I'm freezing. Tell me, did you ever . . . well, you know, with your sisters?"

He laughed. "Willy and I had a bit of a go with Laetitia and Charlotte before he went off to India. After he was gone they wouldn't, and we never fucked them. It was just kissing, and sucking, and fondling." He chuckled with the memory. "Their husbands got their cherries, or so I presume. Neither Willy nor I ever did."

Her nightgown now on, and her person comfortably ensconced in their bed, the bishop's wife said, "What are you going to do with Lucinda, George?"

"Well, she is still young, and certainly a beauty. Her pedigree is respectable. She's rich. We'll have a husband for her in no time at all, m'dear. I guarantee it!" the bishop reassured his wife.

A year passed, and Lady Harrington remained domiciled in her brother's house. It had become a battle of wills between the two siblings. Lucinda wanted her own home in London, but the bishop would not allow her bankers to release the necessary funds for such an extravagant purchase. George wanted his sister to remarry, but there wasn't a gentleman who came to call who suited Lucinda at all; and woe to those who engaged her attention for a time and then had the temerity to propose marriage. A second year passed. George Worth decided that a trip to London was absolutely in order if they were ever to rid themselves of his youngest sister.

At twenty-five Lucinda was considered an incredible beauty. The virginal debutantes in that London season of seventeen hundred and fifty paled before her presence. As there were no great heiresses that year, Lucinda, with her comfortable income, became the most sought after female in society, despite her age. The younger of the fortune-hunting lordlings amused her, and she was tolerant and kind to them. The rakes and roués were quickly dismissed with a sharp word and a toss of her chestnut curls. Lucinda had no time for fools, or men who thought all women gullible before their manly presence.

The field surrounding Lucinda finally narrowed itself into the three most eligible men in London. Richard Rhodes, the Duke of Rexford, was tall with naturally blond hair and silver-gray eyes. He was so proud of his hair color that all of his wigs, but the formal ones he must wear to court, were the exact same color as his hair. He was a great horseman, and his home in Kent, Rexford Court, was considered one of the finest houses in the country.

Hamlet Hackett, Marquess of Hargrave, was his best friend. A portly young man of medium height, he was prematurely balding with a fringe of nut brown hair growing around the pink back of his pate. His eyes were a deceptively mild blue. Even with the finest wigs made, he still had the look of a well-fed monk; although it was known in certain circles that Hamlet Hackett had the libido of an amorous alley cat. Not a maid at his home, Hargrave Manor, was safe from his naughty ways. He eyed Lucinda as though she were an especially tasty pastry and dreamed of making love to her. He did not, however, share his thoughts with Richard Rhodes, who he suspected had similar notions.

Lucinda's third suitor was Lord Benjamin Bertram of Bancroft Hall, near Oxford. This gentleman was outrageously wealthy and had been the target of ambitious mamas for the past five seasons. He was a very tall and thin man whose hair and eyes both were a nondescript brown. His face was lean, almost severe. Lucinda Harrington was the first woman he had considered worthy to bear his name, and his heir, for he could trace his antecedents back to the long-ago time of Alfred the Great.

George Frederick Worth was delighted by all three suitors for his sister's hand. Whoever she chose, it would be a triumph, and add sheen to his family's escutcheon. Heeding his wife's advice, he did not champion any of the trio as a favorite.

If the truth had been known, he didn't care which one Lucinda picked, for all three were eminently suitable.

The season was drawing to a close. They would soon be returning to the manse. The bishop was growing more nervous by the day. "Has she said nothing to you, Caroline?" he finally asked his wife. Often women talked to other women before speaking to the men in their family.

Caroline Worth looked uncomfortable. She attempted to avoid her husband's gaze. At last she said, "Lucinda says she has found the perfect house for herself on Traleigh Square, near the park."

"*What?*" The bishop struggled not to shout, but his temples were beginning to throb. He swallowed hard, and drew in several deep breaths to calm himself. Then he demanded of his wife, "Has not one of them declared? God only knows they have monopolized her time enough."

"She has refused all three," Caroline murmured in a tiny voice. "She will have her own home again, George. I do not believe she will remarry until she gets her way. Unless you want her living with us forever, I beg you to give in to her in this matter." Then Caroline Worth burst into tears. "I want my home back, George! I am to have another baby, and I want my home back again! The manse is not that big. Clarissa is too old to be in the nursery any longer, and I need the bedroom your sister inhabits for her."

"*She has refused all three?*" The bishop's face was purple with his outrage. "*And you did not tell me?*"

"It only happened in the last week." His wife wept nervously. "You cannot make her marry if she doesn't want to, George. This is not the middle ages."

"She must be made to reconsider," the bishop said firmly.

"She has publicly insulted them," Caroline told him. "It is quite the giggle of the Ton, George. I am surprised you have not heard the gossip. I doubt they will reconsider asking her again after what she has said about them."

"What has she said?" the bishop demanded of his spouse.

"She said the duke has a face like one of his own horses and not one of particularly good blood lines. And Hargrave reminds her of the elephant at the tower zoo; and Lord Bertram is a stork in too colorful feathers."

George Frederick Worth was almost apoplectic in his outrage. "Damn her for a high-flying filly!" he swore. "By God, she needs a good lesson in manners. It's obvious Robert Harrington had no idea what he was doing when he left her his fortune. Or he spoiled her rotten. Either way I have the problem to contend with, and I must solve it."

"Let her have the house," his wife pleaded tearfully.

"No, damnit, Caroline! I will bring my sister to heel if it's the last thing on this earth that I ever do. She will remarry, and she will remarry well. She will not bring shame upon this family, or her sisters' families, by her outrageous and willful behavior," the bishop declared angrily. Then seeing his wife's stricken face, he put his arms about her. "Another baby, eh? That will be nice, m'dear." He gave her a small hug, then released her. "I am going to the club now, Caroline, to see if I can repair the damage Lucinda has caused. It is not necessary to hold dinner for me, or to wait up for me. I will probably be some time. You must take care of yourself now, my darling. And in a few weeks' time we shall return to the manse. When is the baby due, Caroline?"

"October," she told him. "Oh, I hope it is a little boy. We already have one for the army and one for the church. We need but an admiral now." She gave him a small smile.

"I should not mind another girl," the bishop declared.

"But what if she's like Lucinda?" his wife asked.

"No daughter of ours will ever be like Lucinda," George Worth said firmly. "We will not permit it, m'dear." Then he gave his wife a loving kiss and departed for his club.

At White's he quickly spotted his sister's three suitors huddled together conversing. He hurried over to greet them. "I must apologize for Lucinda," he began. "Caroline was so shocked by my sister's behavior she has only just confided in me. We're expecting another child, y'know, and it doesn't do for her to be upset."

Then to the bishop's surprise, the Duke of Rexford said admiringly, "I have never met such an arrogant wench as Lucinda. By God, she has spirit! Just the kind of woman one wants to sire heirs upon."

"Aye," the Marquess of Hargrave agreed with his best friend. "No namby-pamby virgin for me either. It's your sister, or I shall remain a bachelor."

"She needs, however, to be taught a lesson in the proper deportment of a lady toward a gentleman," Lord Bertram said quietly. He looked meaningfully at the bishop. "She is very beautiful, and her bloodlines are excellent; but she is far too independent. She must be instructed in how to be subservient to her husband. Does not St. Paul mention such conduct in a woman as proper and Christian, my lord bishop?"

"Yes," George Worth said slowly, wondering if Lord Bertram was hinting at what he suspected he was.

"Lady Lucinda needs to be mastered," Lord Bertram said softly.

"My God, Bertie, you aren't suggesting . . ." the duke began.

"I am," Lord Bertram responded. "Never knew a girl more in need of such correction than Lady Lucinda."

"But we ain't never had a lady up before our court," the marquess interjected. "Just serving girls, merchants, and farmers' lasses. An occasional shop girl, or saucy governess. We've never mastered a real lady."

"Which is not to say we can't," the duke said. "Lucinda has insulted us all when all we did was offer her marriage. Did you not tell me, George, that she offended half the country gentlemen round and about the manse? Isn't that why you brought her to London for the season? So she might have a bigger field in which to husband hunt? Well, the wench has had three most suitable and magnanimous offers which she has publicly scorned. That was bad enough, but she has made all three of us a laughingstock. I cannot go anywhere our friends do not neigh, George. Poor Hammie and Bertie have suffered from her mocking tongue as well. I should like that tongue to be taught more pleasant diversions such as licking my cock. Would you gentlemen not agree?"

"Only if it is my cock she licks," the marquess said with a wink.

"Then, my lords, I suggest we bring Lady Lucinda before the court of the Devil's Disciples for judgment as soon as possible," Lord Bertram responded.

"It would be quite unseemly for me to attend that particular session," George Worth said. "Neither my wife, nor Lucinda, could possibly imagine such a secret society as ours, gentlemen. If my sister is to be given over to The Master for correction, I should not be there."

"Certainly not!" the trio agreed with one voice.

"However, George, you must help us make the plan by which we will trap the lady, putting her in our tender charge," Lord Bertram told the bishop.

"And after she is mastered, she will be forced by the very nature of her situation to choose a husband from among the three of us," the marquess concluded gleefully.

"How much time will you need?" the bishop asked his companions.

"I think at least a month," the duke considered, and looked at his coconspirators, who nodded in agreement.

The bishop thought for several long minutes, and then he said, "Only Caroline would be concerned as to where Lucinda has gone. Two of my other sisters are in Scotland, another in Wales, and Julia lives in Ireland. There will be no one to ask embarrassing questions, gentlemen. I believe the solution is to tell Caroline that Lucinda has gone to Ireland to visit Julia."

"Lucinda must appear to be planning such a trip," Lord Bertram said, "else your wife grow suspicious."

"I know just how to get Lucinda to agree to such a visit,"

George Worth said with a grin. "For two years she and I have argued over her desire to purchase her own home in London. She has found a house she likes on Traleigh Square. I shall allow her to buy it and make all her plans for decoration. Then I shall suggest she visit Julia, while it is being done, and be back in London by the autumn. That gives us the summer months should my sister prove more recalcitrant with The Master than we anticipate and he need more time with her. The house, of course, can be quickly resold once she has married again. It will be well worth the cost of the decor to allow us this time. Besides, Lucinda can afford it. She will still come to a new marriage a wealthy woman. Is this plan suitable to you, gentlemen?" the bishop asked them.

"What about her maid?" the duke said. "No lady would travel without her maid, George."

"Polly? A most naughty piece of fluff, my lords. She will certainly go with my dear sister. And when the time comes for Lucinda to make her choice, Polly will, I promise you, offer you all a most charming entertainment along with her mistress. She's a juicy fuck if there ever was one. I shall miss her, but whichever of you gentlemen wins Lucinda will have Polly in your household, too. I envy you. I have had a most enjoyable two years with Polly, and her sister, Molly, who is Caroline's maid. They are wickedly lewd lasses."

"We shall notify The Master, then, my lords. Let us meet here again at the same time next week to coordinate our plans," the duke said. The agreement secured, the gentlemen bowed to one another and sat down to play cards.

The next morning the bishop, his wife by his side, called his sister into the morning room. "Caroline has convinced me that you will not settle upon a second husband until you have your own home," George Worth began. "I do not want you unhappy, Lucinda. Therefore I have instructed your bank to release to you any and all of your funds. You may purchase your house in Traleigh Square, m'dear. I am not convinced this is the best road for you to take, but it is obvious you will not travel mine until you gain your own way in the matter." He smiled a small smile, feeling not the least bit of guilt.

"Ohh, George!" Lucinda cried, clapping her hands together in delight. "I shall send to dear old Mr. Wythe and have him negotiate with the agent. Is there time before we leave London?"

George Worth smiled more broadly. "Of course," he purred. "And, Luci, you must make arrangements for your decor before we depart. The house, I have not a doubt, will need work. We shan't leave London until you have made all of your arrangements, m'dear."

Lucinda flung her arms about her older brother and kissed him soundly on both of his smooth cheeks. "You are, Georgie, the very best brother a girl could have! Even if you are a bit slow," she said.

"*Slow?*" He was offended. "Whatever do you mean, Lucinda?"

"If you had done this two years ago, it would have been ever so much better," Lucinda told him. "But at least now you have listened to reason and come around to a more sensible frame of mind. I am so very glad!" She kissed him again, then turned to her sister-in-law. "Dearest Caro, thank you for interceding for me," Lucinda said.

"I agree with George, Lucinda, but I also realize that you will not be content to remarry until you can have your way. You are not, I fear, at twenty-five, in the first flush of your youth any longer," Caroline Worth noted sharply. "Having refused three such fine offers as you had, it will not be as easy next season to find a husband."

Lucinda bit her lip to keep from laughing. Poor Caro, for whom a man, children, and home were everything. She could not understand anyone who did not have the same ambitions as she had. There she was married to George, a sweet, but dull fellow, with five children, and yet another on the way. She was as content as a sow in warm mud. *I do not,* Lucinda thought to herself, *think I could have stood living with them much longer.* "I believe, upon reflection, that I should remain in London this summer while the house is being refurbished for me," she said.

"London in the summer is a cesspit," her brother pronounced. "Buy your house, and make your plans, m'dear. Then why not go off and visit Julia in Ireland. You and she always got on quite well. You haven't seen her since you married. Or go up to Scotland to see Laetitia and Charlotte, or perhaps Georgeanne over in Wales."

Lucinda thought a moment. Her brother was being very reasonable, and he was right. London's reputation in summertime was foul. "I shall go to Ireland to visit Julia and her Brian," she decided aloud. Julia had always been fun. Her other sisters bored her.

"I shall write to Julia myself," the bishop said to his youngest sister. "When you have concluded your business, m'dear, I shall arrange for your travel. I have been given to understand that Dublin is quite lively even in the summertime."

"You have been so good to me, George," Lucinda said to him. "I am sorry it has taken us so long to come to terms. But now we have, and everything is going to be all right."

"Oh, indeed it will, m'dear," George Worth agreed. Lucinda would be taken in hand by The Master, and tamed. When The Master had concluded his instruction, Lucinda would be an obedient and proper woman. Her suitors were willing to allow it and wait. In the end she would have to pick one of them. There would be no other road for her to take. She would be well married by Christmas just like his other sisters. One day she would thank him for having taken a firm hand in securing her good fortune. The bishop smiled at his wife and his sister, pleased with his own thoughts. "You had best send for Mr. Wythe," he told Lucinda. "You don't want someone else to snap up your house, m'dear."

By the day's end, however, the house at Three Traleigh Square was the property of Lady Lucinda Harrington. The next morning, key in her gloved hand, she entered her new property in the company of her brother and sister-in-law. George Worth had to admit that his sister had an excellent eye. The house, while not large, was charming. It would resell quickly. On the main floor was a morning room, a formal salon, a library, and a dining room. Below the stairs were spacious kitchens opening onto a large back garden with an apple tree. On the upper floors there were several bedchambers and dressing rooms. The attics were light and airy so that the servants would be more than reasonably comfortable. On a corner of the square, the house had more windows than its neighbors'. The previous owners had not left any furniture, and it needed paint and general decor.

"I'm going to do the morning room and the salon in yellow and cream," Lucinda told Caroline. Then she turned to her brother. "I want *The Five Graces,* Georgie. That portrait you had painted of Caro and the children really belongs in the place of honor in your house, not a painting of your five troublesome sisters." She smiled at him.

"It is yours," he replied generously, smiling at her, knowing he had pleased his wife by his answer. *The Five Graces* would be a worthy addition to Lucinda's husband's home. Wherever that was to be.

Lucinda hired an agent to act for her while she was out of London. She spent the next several weeks arranging for her new dwelling to be painted, carefully choosing the colors herself; dealing with the draper for the fabrics that would be made into draperies and curtains for her windows; speaking herself with Mr. Chippendale about the furniture she was ordering from his shop; and choosing the magnificent Oriental carpets that would grace her floors. There was china from Dr. Wall's Royal Worcester potteries to be chosen from a pattern book and all manner of household items that would be needed. A gardener was hired to restore the walled garden behind the house.

"I shall hire the servants when I return," Lucinda told her brother.

"Excellent! Excellent!" her brother replied. "Do you have any idea of when you wish to depart for Julia's, m'dear?"

"I believe I can be ready in another fortnight," Lucinda said, smiling. "You have been so helpful, Georgie. I'm certain you and Caro will be happy to have the manse back to yourselves. I know if it were my house, I should feel that way, no matter how much I love you."

"I shall make all the arrangements, m'dear," her brother said. "I know it shall be a most eventful summer for you, Luci."

Finally the morning arrived for Lucinda's departure. Her trunks were packed and put atop the large traveling coach that stood before the London house the bishop had been renting. George Worth had told his sister that she would travel across country to Cardiff. From there she would embark for Ireland. She would not, the bishop assured her, have to see her sister Charlotte. Charlotte would not even know she was in the vicinity. As her trip would take several days, her accommodations had been booked at respectable inns and were already paid for by her brother. "My little gift to you," he said as he kissed her goodbye. "I shall come to London to see you when you return, m'dear." Then the Bishop of Wellington helped his sister into her traveling vehicle and waved her off with a smile, and not the least twinge of a conscience.

The weather fair, and the roads dry, Lucinda's carriage traveled relatively swiftly over the day. A basket lunch had been provided. The mistress shared it with her maid, Polly. In late afternoon they arrived at the Silver Swan, a delightful inn at Maidenhead. Lucinda was ushered into the building with all the deference she expected. A two-room suite had been booked for her. She was served a light supper of roasted turkey breast with new peas, fresh bread, a local cheese, and a dish of June strawberries. The wine was the most delicious she had ever tasted, but she was quickly sleepy and had to be helped to her bed by Polly.

"Gracious," she murmured as her maid helped her to undress, "traveling has obviously done something to my head." Then falling upon the bed she was immediately asleep, even before her hair could be undone and braided.

Polly put her mistress's clothing neatly away and laid out her garments for the next day's travel. Then helping herself to the remaining wine, she drank it all and was quickly asleep herself on the trundle. An hour later the door to the little suite opened, and several cloaked gentlemen, their faces carefully obscured, entered. Lucinda's possessions were gathered up and removed. Both she and Polly were carried to the waiting coach. In the morning, the innkeeper, well paid in advance, would assume his guest had departed early in the morning. The elegant vehicle slowly and quietly exited the inn yard, disappearing into the darkness.

Lucinda awoke. Her head was throbbing. Why was the bed so hard suddenly? She tried to turn over, only to discover that she could not. Despite the ache in her head, her senses abruptly sharpened. This was not the inn where she had gone to sleep last night. She was in a tiny, cell-like cubicle. A shutter barred the window, but she could make out a narrow ribbon of gray light coming through it. She was not upon a bed, but a straw pallet. *And she was chained by one arm to the wall!* Her eyes swept the little space for Polly, but the maid wasn't there. Lucinda wondered if she had been kidnapped, and where Polly was.

"Hello?" she called out softly, and then as her courage returned, more loudly, *"Hello?"*

She immediately heard footsteps outside her chamber, and the door opened to admit someone. The shutter was flung wide to allow in the bright light of early morning, the fresh country air. She could see the figure of a man. He turned about to face her, and Lucinda was unable to restrain a gasp of both surprise and shock. The man was quite tall, having a beautiful and extremely well formed body. Lucinda stared. He was bare-chested, and wore the tightest fitting breeches she had certainly ever seen. They followed every line of his body, displaying long legs with shapely calves just above his boots, and well-rounded buttocks. She had never seen such a garment before and thought it deliciously indecent. When he had turned, she saw he was masked so that she could not view his entire face. Then she gasped again. There was a narrow slit in the front of the man's breeches, and his manhood was hanging out quite boldly for her to see. It was, she considered, a most healthy and sizeable organ.

"Good morning, Lady Lucinda," he said.

"Who are you?" Lucinda demanded in a most imperious tone, tearing her eyes away from that most fascinating temptation.

He smiled, and she saw a quick flash of white teeth, "I am known as The Master, m'lady," was the reply.

"Where am I? I demand to be returned to the inn. Have you any idea of who I am? My brother is the Bishop of Wellington," Lucinda said angrily. She lifted her arm and rattled her chain. "Take this restraint off at once, sir! My skin is already chafed from it."

"Impossible," he replied. "Your wristband is lined in lamb's wool. It is not my intention to harm you in any way."

"Then, why am I here? And what the hell is this place?" she demanded of him.

The Master knelt next to Lucinda. "You have, my dear, offended several gentlemen with your sharp words and your less-than-gentle feminine behavior. You are, I fear, too independent, my Lady Lucinda. Tonight you will be brought before the court of the Devil's Disciples where you will be judged for your bad conduct. I am told you will be put into my hands then for mastering. When I deem you suitably trained, you will return before the court, where you will display your new attitude to all the gentlemen present. The three suitors you have so scorned will then each have their way with you. Afterward you will choose the one you favor best. Only then will you be returned to your own world where your engagement will be announced, followed by your wedding."

"I have already told that trio of fools that I should not have any of them," Lucinda said fiercely. "My late husband said that when I wed again, it must be for love and no other reason. I do not love Rexford, Hargrave, or Bertram. There is nothing you can do that will make me love them, sir. Now, unchain me at once. If you release me now, I shall not go to the authorities, but continue on my way to Ireland. If I do not arrive when I am scheduled to arrive, my sister, Lady Rafferty, will inform the authorities. You will be found out, and I shall see you are prosecuted to the full extent of the law, sir!"

The Master burst out laughing. Then as quickly his amusement was gone. He kissed Lucinda hard, his lips forcing her lips apart, his tongue thrusting deeply into her mouth where he caressed her tongue. As suddenly his body forced hers back upon the pallet, lying atop her. "You are going to be a great deal more fun to master than the little governess who was brought to me last time," he told her wickedly. "I am going to enjoy taming you, Lady Lucinda. And you, I promise, will enjoy it, too."

She could feel his manhood rising through the thin fabric of her silk night garment. His body was both warm and hard. For a brief moment she was terrified. Then the feeling dissolved, and she said through gritted teeth, "You, sir, can go to hell!"

With another laugh he stood up. Then looking down at his manhood which was now engorged, he said with a grin, "Until tonight, my dear," and he turned toward the door.

"Wait!" Lucinda cried. "Where is my maid, Polly?"

"In my bed," came the surprising reply. "She's a damned good fuck, your Poll. I'll send her to you after I take care of this," and he gestured to his swollen penis. Then he was gone out the door.

What was going on? Lucinda asked herself. The Devil's Disciples? Her brother would have been shocked to learn that Lucinda had already heard about them. Just bits of gossip, whispered secretly in hushed tones by the ladies at various social functions. They would shiver deliciously and roll their eyes at the mere mention of this group. It was a secret gentlemen's fellowship, a rival to the Hellfire Club, where the men were alleged to sport themselves in all manner of debauchery with women both willing and unwilling. *And there had, indeed, been talk of Lord Meldrew's governess this season past.*

From what this man who called himself The Master had said, she gathered that her three rejected suitors had arranged for this kidnapping of her person. They were indeed as big a trio of fools as she had ever known. When George learned of her disappearance, he would certainly raise a hue and cry. They were going to pay dearly for this outrage. Thank God she was not some little virgin whose lily white reputation could be destroyed by such actions. And while they might brag on seducing a governess, they would certainly not dare to boast of kidnapping and ravaging a lady of quality. If she could not escape them, then she intended seeing that the gentlemen of the Devil's Disciples were taught a stern lesson for their presumption.

The door to the little room opened again, and Polly crept in, bearing a tray of food. "Ohh, m'lady," she began, but Lucinda cut her quite short.

"Do not play the innocent with me," she said. "That bandit who has us in his power says he has bedded you. Is it true, you little bawd?" Lucinda fixed her maid with a fierce eye.

"I couldn't stop him," Polly wailed.

"You were a virgin?" Lucinda said. "The truth, you shameless trull, for I shall ask him, and he is not loath to brag upon it."

"I weren't no virgin," Polly admitted, sniffling as she put the tray down.

"Did you ever . . . with my husband?" Lucinda demanded.

"Never, my lady! Lord Robert were a real gentleman!" Polly cried indignantly.

"My brother, then?" Lucinda probed further.

Polly flushed, and hung her head.

Lucinda laughed. "I thought I heard Georgie creeping about in the night. You know I am a light sleeper, and the floorboards on the stairs to the attics creak. Is he a good lover, my brother?"

Polly shrugged noncommittally.

"In other words as dull as his sermons," Lucinda noted. "A swift kiss-me-quick, and a poke, and Georgie's finished, eh?"

"*M'lady!*" Polly's pretty cheeks were quite scarlet now.

"It was never that way with Robert Harrington," Lucinda said. "He was a man who knew how to love a woman, Polly." Then Lucinda's eye turned to the tray. Upon it was a beautifully poached egg surrounded by a delicate cream sauce flavored with dill, a little slice of pink ham, a slice of warmed bread, already buttered, a dish of honey, and a beaker from which rose the aroma of fine India tea. Lucinda ate it all, asking Polly to cut the ham for her as she had not the use of both of her hands.

Polly departed, returning in midafternoon with another tray. This one contained a slice of capon's breast, another slice of buttered bread, a dish of tiny strawberries, and a goblet of wine. It was the very same wine she had had the evening before, and while Lucinda knew it was probably drugged as the previous beverage had been, she drank it anyway. Then she slept. Sleep was better than sitting about with her thoughts as she had all morning. When she awoke again, she could see the summer twilight was upon the land.

The door to her chamber opened, and The Master entered the room. Bending, he unlocked the manacle about her left wrist, freeing her from her chain. "Come, Lady Lucinda. It is time for you to greet your accusers and face the judgment of the Devil's Disciples."

"Very well," Lucinda answered, allowing him to help her

to her feet, "but you men are really quite ridiculous with all your secret societies and old-fashioned ideas."

"You are brave as well as bold, m'lady," he told her. Reaching up, he pulled the pins from her chestnut hair, tossing them carelessly away. "We shall see how you feel when to-night's festivities are over and done with." He loosed her thick, heavy hair, combing it with his fingers. Then taking her arm The Master led Lady Lucinda from her prison.

Chapter Two

Stepping out into the summer twilight, Lucinda saw they were deep in the countryside. Her prison had been a room in a garden shed. Now they traversed a large, very overgrown garden. The smell of roses was overpowering. Ahead of her she saw a well-proportioned, ivy-covered brick house. It was obviously quite old, possibly dating back to the reign of the great Elizabeth, Lucinda thought. But before they reached the house, he turned aside, leading her down a narrow, winding path and through a small orchard. Exiting the trees on the far side of the orchard, Lucinda saw before her the ruins of a round stone structure. It was roofless. As they entered, she thought the building reminded her of a miniature coliseum, for it was similar in design to the arena she had seen in Rome with Robert when they were on their honeymoon trip.

The scene was very well lit by torches that barely flickered in the warm June night. Above in the twilight sky the stars were beginning to twinkle. The stone benches were peopled by gentlemen in dark, hooded cloaks. An excited murmur arose from the crowd as The Master led his captive into the center of the arena. It was all wonderfully dramatic, Lucinda thought, vastly amused. The poor girls these men brought here for seduction must have been terrified. She, however, was not.

"Here is the female, Lady Lucinda Harrington, my lords, come to stand before your judgment for her crimes," The Master said in his cultured, but rough voice. "What say you, my lords?"

A gentleman arose. "This woman has flirted her way through the season, enticing and discarding the men who courted her," he began. She didn't recognize the voice. "She has made a vulgar mockery," the gentleman continued, "of her three worthy suitors, calling one horse-faced, the second an elephant, and the third a stork in fine feathers." A faint but restrained chuckle arose from the audience. "And what, I ask you, had they done to deserve such unkindness at this arrogant woman's hands? Each had, my lords, done her the supreme honor of asking her to become his wife. A gentleman might accept a polite refusal, my lords, no matter his disappointment, but to be publicly reviled, ridiculed, and derided? It is inexcusable!

"My lords. This woman, a widow once wed to a fine man whom we all knew, is unmanageable. Even her good brother, another gentleman we know and respect, is unable to control her bad behavior. Lady Lucinda Harrington has forgotten her place in the scheme of things. She has forgotten that a woman is an inferior being when placed alongside a man. It is therefore the judgment of the court of the Devil's Disciples that this lady be placed in the custody of The Master for a period of three months to be retrained in her proper duties as a woman. We will reconvene on the night of the September full moon, at which time Lady Lucinda will yield her person in a sweet and docile manner to her suitors, apologize for her past sins, and then choose one from among them to be her husband. Are we agreed upon this punishment, my lords?"

"Aye!" the gallery cried with one voice.

"You are ridiculous, all of you!" Lucinda shouted at them. "Am I supposed to be frightened by all your absurdities and silliness? I am not some shop girl you lust after who can be terrified into abject obedience."

"She condemns herself with her wicked words," the speaker cried. "If any of you were previously reluctant in this matter because of her station, my lords, you surely cannot be now."

"Stool!" snapped The Master, and it was immediately brought. Placing one booted foot upon it, he reached out, yanking Lucinda over his knee. Flipping up her silk night garment, he said in a loud voice, "Gentlemen, how many?"

"Ten!" came a voice.

"No, twenty!" came another voice.

"Aye, twenty good ones! Make her saucy bottom smoke!" the assemblage roared.

Surprised by his quick actions, Lucinda shrieked as a hard hand descended upon her pristine flesh. She wasn't hurt. The blow merely stung her. "How dare you!" she cried, and she attempted to squirm away from the punishing hand that continued to rain spanks upon her hapless bottom as the gallery counted out each blow aloud. *"Oh! Oh! Oh!"* Lucinda howled as she struggled.

"Seventeen!"

"Eighteen!"

"Nineteen!"

"Twenty!" the gentlemen shouted out, and then it was over. "Is she wet?" a voice called from the gallery. "Her little peach is as pink as a full-blown rose."

"Let us see," The Master said. He set Lucinda upon her feet before him and sat down upon the stool. A rough hand ripped her garment off.

Dizzy, Lucinda found herself at a great disadvantage as his big hand reached out, pushing itself between her thighs to examine her. Then pulling her forward he drew her down hard, his penis propelling itself past her nether lips and straight up her cunt. "Wooooo!" Lucinda gasped, taken utterly unawares.

The Devil's Disciples cheered enthusiastically, calling out encouragements to The Master.

"Give her a good fucking, sir!"

"Make the vexatious bitch howl!"

"You devil!" Lucinda groaned in his ear.

"How long?" he demanded boldly.

"Too long!" she countered as their bodies writhed and thrust.

"How long?" he repeated.

"At least four years," she admitted, her blush evident.

"Then I shall, for both of us, and for our rather salacious audience, make you come, my Lady Lucinda."

"Never before these beasts!" she cried, but his probing and nimble weapon was already, despite her best efforts, beginning to have its effect upon her. "Oooooooo!" Lucinda sobbed.

"I am going to tame you, you delicious little wildcat," The Master whispered in her ear, his tongue foraging about the whorl of it. "I am going to turn you into a sweet little house kitten, Lucinda."

"Never!" she hissed in his ear, biting the lobe hard. Then she let herself go, and the orgasm rolled over her, rendering her almost unconscious with the pleasure.

He came in a great explosion of juices, and he hadn't wanted to—not just yet. He groaned. She was going to provide him with a summer's worth of challenges, and the knowledge of it excited him. It had been a long time since he had enjoyed his work. Remembering himself, and where they were he lifted her off his lap and stood her on her feet.

Lucinda swayed, but barely conscious. Then she felt him fasten something about her neck, and opening her eyes she saw the delicate-filigreed gold chain which he attached to a thin leather leash. She looked questioningly at him.

"One final bit of theater," he murmured so that only she could hear him. "You will obey me, Lucinda, or I will cane you before these gentlemen who so very much desire your mastering. I know you can bear a spanking, but you will not be able to withstand a caning. Your cries of anguish will but give them pleasure. Certainly you do not wish that. We will leave the arena now, and you will lift your legs high, trotting like a well-schooled pony for the gallery as we circle the ring. I may once, or twice, flick my crop at your bottom as we go, and a tiny shriek will greatly please the Devil's Disciples. Do you understand me, Lucinda?"

She nodded.

"And you will cooperate? I do not want to hurt you, but I will if I must."

"It is degrading," she whispered.

"It is," he agreed. "But is it any more degrading than being fucked before them and enjoying it? Are you ready?"

She sighed, but then nodded again.

"Now, my lords, we bid you *adieu* until the September moon," The Master said to the assembled gentlemen. "Hup!" He tugged lightly upon the thin braided-leather leash and smacked her bottom with his crop.

Giving a little cry, Lucinda began to trot smartly by his side, her slender, well-shaped legs pushing high, her head up. To her embarrassment she found her ample breasts were bouncing as she trotted. She unfocused her gaze as she ran around the ring at his side, and then they were gone, out the entrance to the sound of appreciative cheers. Lucinda slowed to a walk. "What will they do now?" she asked her companion.

"Spend a glorious summer's evening drinking my wine and fucking the local girls I have brought from the village for them. Your Polly will join the festivities. She is of a mind to see which of her future masters pleases her the best," he told her.

"And what are we to do?" Lucinda wondered.

"We are going to get to know one another better, my pet,"

The Master told her. "I have only three months in which to turn you from an independent, outspoken wench into an obedient and meek lady."

"It will not happen," Lucinda warned him. "You are wasting your time if you think you can change me, sir. I have always been thought self-centered, and I probably am. Where are we going?"

"To my house," he said, leading her back through his orchard and gardens to the ivy-covered brick structure.

"Where is this place?" she asked him.

"All I will tell you is that you are in Oxfordshire," he replied. "The nearest village is seven miles away, and I have no near neighbors. When I am not going about my duties for the Devil's Disciples, I raise and train racing horses." He opened a small door, ushering her into the house. Then he led her into a hallway and up a flight of stairs. "I believe you will find your quarters far more comfortable here than the ones you had last night."

"Where are your servants?" she asked him.

"I have few, and before you query me further, they are used to my ways. Indeed, they often assist me in my endeavours."

"Will you continue to wear your mask, sir?"

"I will. Afterward we might meet in polite society. I should not like you to be embarrassed, Lucinda, by such a meeting, nor your husband either." He opened another door, and they entered into a large bedroom.

The walls of the room were paneled. The large bowed window opened out onto the gardens. The casements were lead-paned. There was, to Lucinda's relief, a big fireplace on the wall facing the great oaken bedstead with its red velvet tapestried bed hangings. There was a standing chest on another wall and an upholstered chair by the hearth.

"Where is Polly to sleep?" Lucinda demanded.

"There is a little chamber next to this room that Polly may call her own. She will spend many nights, I expect, in other beds," he said.

"Yours?" she replied scathingly.

The Master laughed. "Nay, my pet. I shall be spending my nights in your bed, teaching you how to be a good and obedient woman."

"I want a bath," Lucinda said. "I am sticky with your sweat and your juices, sir."

"Of course," he said pleasantly. "I shall have my servants arrange it, and they will help you as Polly is otherwise occupied. I must go back to the amphitheater to make certain the lasses from the village have arrived and all is as it should be." He bowed, and then was gone from the bedchamber, leaving Lucinda standing naked, and not just a little angry.

She gazed about her, shivering, for the evening was growing cool. The door to her bedchamber opened. She looked desperately about her for something with which to cover herself. She did not find it. A bare-chested, liveried footman in a white wig hurried into the room, going immediately to the fireplace to light the fire already laid there. He then rose and, turning, smiled at Lucinda, who was attempting to strategically hide behind the bed's draperies. The footman bowed.

"The bath is being brought, m'lady. Is there a particular fragrance that you prefer?"

"Lavender," Lucinda managed to say.

"Very good, m'lady," he said. "My name is John. My companions and I will be servicing you. Ahh, here is the bathtub. It's probably a bit old-fashioned to a London lady, but we can bathe you quite nicely in it," John assured her.

"I am quite capable of bathing myself," Lucinda said haughtily.

"We have our orders, m'lady," John said quietly.

She stood silent as the round oak tub was filled by two other footmen. John disappeared from the chamber for a brief few moments, returning with a vial he poured into the tub. Immediately the scent of lavender filled the room. With a smile he held out his hand to Lucinda as the two other footmen fussed about, laying towels across a towel rack they placed before the fire. Taking the footman's hand, she allowed him to settle her in the tub. What else was she to do?

John pinned her thick hair up, then took up a large sponge. After rubbing a cake of hard soap across it, he began to wash her back. The sponge swept down the length of her back several times. It was followed by warm water laved over her skin until it was soap free. One of the other footmen placed a small goblet of cordial in her hand. "The Master has ordered it, m'lady," John said. "Please do drink it down while I continue to bathe you."

Lucinda sipped at the liquid. It had the flavor of ripe strawberries and was absolutely delicious. She drank it down as John washed her arms and neck. Now, as his hands moved to her breasts, Lucinda wondered why she wasn't distressed, but she wasn't. The sponge moved quite impersonally about the full mounds of flesh, brushing the nipples carelessly. He smiled at her as they thrust forward. Then his hands moved beneath the water to sponge her more private parts. Lucinda stiffened, but his actions while intimate seemed harmless enough.

"Please stand," he said, and when she had been helped up, he continued his careful bathing of her buttocks, pushing the sponge between her twin moons to cleanse there also.

Lucinda felt her face grow warm. In fact, her entire body was growing warm. The rinse water trickled down her skin and was strangely arousing. She tried to concentrate upon anything else and noted that the three footmen all had thick bulges in the groins of their blue satin knee breeches. John lifted her from the tub. At once the other two young men were wrapping her in warm towels, drying her, their hands moving sensuously over her body. She attempted to move away from them, taking the toweling in her own hands.

"Now, m'lady," John gently chided her, "you must not hinder us in our duties. We have our orders, and we never disobey The Master. We should lose our places if we did, and frankly our employment here is most pleasant. Please allow Dick and Martin to finish."

Her hands fell away, and the young footmen began to towel her again. When they had finished, they brought her to the bed, indicating she should lie down. "Where is my luggage?" Lucinda asked John. "I should like a night garment."

"The Master forbids it, m'lady," he replied, "but on his instructions, we shall soon have you warm." His hands moved to his breeches, and he released his penis. His companions did likewise, and the three young men drew her down onto the bed.

"I do not think . . ." Lucinda began nervously.

"Nay, you must not think," John said. "You are only to experience the pleasure we will give each other, m'lady." He was a pleasant-looking man of medium height with a stocky build.

"Until tonight," Lucinda said, "I have known only one man."

"That is as it should be, m'lady, but now you are in The Master's charge. This lesson we will give you while we await his return is a lesson in *pleasing*. You will learn to give as well as take. Do you believe your husband was a good lover, m'lady? Even virtuous women have an instinct for such knowledge."

"He was tender, and he was kind," Lucinda said. "I believe I grew to love him. I certainly respected him."

"But he was not particularly exciting, was he?" John said. "Here in The Master's house, m'lady, we will teach you excitement. Then when you choose your next husband, you will be able to enslave him with your skilled erudition. I think you will like that, m'lady."

"Indeed I will," Lucinda agreed, "although the three fools who have arranged for these lessons will not benefit from my new learning." Lucinda suddenly realized as she was speaking with John that her other two companions had arranged themselves on either side of her and had begun to play with her breasts. Her eyes met John's mild gaze, and he smiled.

"Is that nice, m'lady?" he asked her. His fingers began to massage her thigh.

Lucinda closed her eyes for a moment. The hands on her breasts and the hand on her thigh were indeed very nice. She stretched slightly, giving a little purr of appreciation. A mouth fastened itself upon her nipple. "Ummmm," she murmured. The second nipple was engaged. Both of her breasts were being suckled at the same time. It was quite a delicious sensation. One such as she had never before experienced. Fingers kneaded at her. Tongues and teeth teased at her sentient flesh. John's fingers brushed her dark bush. She let her eyes follow his hand, her thighs opening for him as he cupped her.

"Your mons is sweetly plump," he said. "I like a woman with a pillowy mons." His fingers pushed themselves between her nether lips, and he began to play with her sex. "Do you like that, m'lady?"

"Yes," Lucinda said with a small smile.

"You are getting nicely moist," he told her, his fingers working her harder, pressing into her love sheath, rubbing.

The door to the bedchamber opened, and The Master entered. He smiled at the lascivious scene before him and immediately began to undress himself. "Can you two greedy lads leave the lady's titties long enough to take my boots off?" he demanded of Dick and Martin.

They immediately jumped from the bed and went to his aid. Then he dismissed them, and with a wave to Lucinda they left the room.

The Master joined the two remaining figures upon the bed, saying, "Come, Lucinda, and play with my cock like a good girl."

"You didn't say please," she taunted him. "Ohh, yes, John, that is quite nice."

His eyes narrowed behind his mask. "I see, Lucinda, that you need a first lesson in obedience," he said. "John, turn her so she lays across the bed the other way, her head on the edge. Then you know what to do."

"Yes, m'lord," the footman said, and pulled Lucinda about protesting. Then John mounted the woman beneath him and thrust deep into her love nest. "Master thinks you need a good fucking, m'lady, and I am most happy to oblige," he said with a grin.

"Ohhhh," Lucinda cried out, and then she gulped as The Master pressed his love lance between her open and surprised lips.

"You can take two, my pet," he told her. "And you will rouse it one way or another!" He caught her hands to prevent her thwarting his desire "Suck, Lucinda! Suck, or I shall punish you."

Her head was spinning with myriad sensations. The man atop her pumping her fiercely. The male organ in her mouth that had entered relatively soft and manageable, but with each tug of her mouth was growing hard and very long. She choked slightly, struggling to contain him between her lips, fighting not to gag because while she and Robert had often discussed this manner of passion, they had never had the opportunity to attempt it. She concentrated on relaxing, and sure enough her throat opened to embrace him deeply.

"Ahhhhh, God!" The Master cried out, genuinely surprised by her compliance. There was no surrender in her actions. She was enjoying it all every bit as much as they were.

John gave a shout, and his juices spilled themselves into her. He rolled away from her almost immediately, panting with his exertions.

"Release me!" The Master's deep voice grated harshly.

Lucinda opened her mouth and was quite astounded to see the size of his engorged organ. She had practically swallowed him, and yet she had believed she could have taken more. "Ohh," she said as he first mounted and then thrust deep into her with a groan. "Do not come, you devil," she murmured, "until I have had my pleasure of you first!" Then she surprised him by pulling his head to her and kissing him.

Her lips were fragrant; her tongue teased at his. She sucked upon it hungrily. He could taste himself in her mouth, and it excited him even more. He pushed her legs up, gradually pressing them over her head, kneeling as he screwed himself slowly and deeply into her love sheath. Lucinda moaned, the sound a most distinct little noise of pleasure. He withdrew from her as slowly, and then plunged quickly back into the soft, wet heat of her body.

"Ohh, God, yes!" Lucinda encouraged him intensely.

His member was absolutely throbbing with excitement. "Bitch," he growled in her ear, "are you not yet satisfied?"

"A little more, Master, and I will be content," she murmured. "Ah! Ah! *Ahhhhhh!*" Her body shuddered with its release.

The Master let his climax burst forth in a torrent of hot love juices. He could not, it seemed, stop coming, his big body jerking with the discharge until finally he shivered one last time. After a moment he said, "My dear Lady Lucinda, I do not know when I have had a better fuck. You are indeed magnificent, my pet!" He rolled off of her and onto his back.

Leaning over, Lucinda whispered in his ear, "Send John away. You and I need to talk, my lord."

"I do not think talking is your strong suit," he replied.

Lucinda laughed. "Why is it that men think with their bodies and not their brains, sir? Send John away. *Please.*"

"You and the lads are dismissed for the night, John," The Master said to the footman. "I will call you in the morning."

John rose from the bed, bowed politely, and left the room.

"Well?" The Master asked Lucinda when the door had shut behind the servant "What are we to talk on, my lady?"

"Revenge, sir. Sweet revenge," Lucinda told him. "You do not appear unintelligent, and I have already ascertained you are a nobleman. You must certainly understand by now that I cannot be brought to heel like some animal you are training."

The Master was silent, and so Lucinda continued.

"I will not under any circumstances wed any of the three gentlemen who tendered me offers this season. I love none of them. My late husband advised me to marry for love the second time."

"Was it not love the first time?" The Master asked her, curious.

"No," Lucinda answered him frankly, "it was not."

"You married him for his money, then?" *How typical of a woman,* The Master thought, half-angry.

"No, I did not marry Robert for his money," Lucinda responded.

"Then, why did you wed him?" Now he was truly curious.

"My late father, Lord Worth, of Worthington Manor in Worcester, was a rich man at one time, but not a *very* rich man. He married for love. Mama brought him a small, but respectable dowry. Then they went and had seven children, all of whom needed to be provided for if they were to make their way in the world. My brothers, William and George, were first- and second-born. They had to be educated at Eton and Oxford. George, as you know, chose the church for a career, but William had always loved playing at soldiers, and so Papa purchased a commission in the King's Own Royal West Worcester Dragoons. Papa said providing for the boys was straightforward. It was when it came to his girls things grew more complicated."

"What happened to your parents?" The Master asked her.

"Mama died when I was twelve. Papa shortly after I married Robert Harrington," Lucinda explained. Then she continued on with her narrative. "Finding husbands and providing dowries for five daughters proved to be more expensive than my father had anticipated. Each of my elder sisters went up to London for a season. The first three came back with a duke, a marquess, and an earl. It was when Julia went up to London for her season, the year she was seventeen, that Papa realized the difficulty of his situation.

"My sisters always stayed at Papa's aunt's home. She is Lady Dunstan and adored launching my sisters, as she so quaintly put it. But that year after Papa had provided Julia with her wardrobe and the other fripperies she would need, he discovered he had barely enough monies left for a modest

dowry for Julia, and that there would be nothing left for me."
Lucinda sighed deeply. "It was then," she said, "that my father
did a most reckless thing. He took Julia's dowry and went to
White's to gamble. And at first he won. His luck was incredible that night. Everyone said so, but then his fortunes turned.
His friends advised him to take his winnings and leave the tables, but poor Papa foolishly gambled on. Finally he had lost
my sister's dowry, and he was desperate. Julia had already met
Lord Rafferty and was madly in love. While our great-aunt,
Lady Dunstan, was against poor Rafferty because he was
Irish, she and Papa knew he was going to ask for Julia's hand
in marriage. He might be Irish, but he possessed a respectable
fortune and was the best my sister would do. There were far
too many very wealthy heiresses seeking husbands that season.
Papa knew that Rafferty would accept Julia's modest dowry.

"Julia isn't like my three oldest sisters. Position means
nothing to her, as it does to Laetitia, Charlotte, and Georgeanne. She was in love. He was in love, and that was good
enough for our father. Now he had gone and lost her dowry.
While I believe Lord Rafferty would have accepted her without one, it was a matter of honor to poor Papa that he provide
his daughter with her portion. So my father did the absolute
unthinkable."

"He cheated at the cards," The Master said.

Lucinda nodded. "In one fell swoop he won back Julia's
dower and a bit more. He thought that no one had noticed,
and indeed he was congratulated all around for his skill and
daring in playing that one last hand. He had even wagered our
home as collateral because he had not had enough monies in
hand. It was a terrible thing he did, but he was so desperate.
As no one seemed to have realized what he had done, he took
his winnings and bid his friends good night. The next morning
Robert Harrington came to call upon my father."

"Ahh," The Master said. "He saw what your father had
done, eh?"

Lucinda nodded. "Father had been playing against him

alone. While Robert had more than enough money, and would have publicly exposed anyone else, he was curious as to why my father, a man of impeccable honor, had cheated. He spoke fairly and honestly with Papa. My father, of course, was overcome with shame, not just for the deed done, but that he had been found out by his opponent. He told Robert the truth of the matter, and Lord Harrington was most sympathetic. Then he made Papa a most unusual offer.

"He told him that he should not expose him, and that Julia should marry Lord Rafferty. In return he said he wanted Papa's youngest daughter, namely me, for his wife. I was not to have a London season. Instead I would be married to Robert Harrington immediately after my seventeenth birthday. I had just turned sixteen when all this transpired. I was not to be told of this arrangement until three months before my marriage, and I would not meet Lord Harrington until the week before we were to be wed. My father, of course, quickly agreed. He had no other choice."

"And so you saw your sister, Julia, married to her sweetheart, then went home to the country to dream of your own London season," The Master said, smiling up at Lucinda, who was now leaning over him as she spoke.

"Precisely," Lucinda replied. "For over a year I envisioned how I would take London by storm. Then I should outdo my three eldest sisters by marrying not a duke, not a marquess, not an earl, *but a prince!*" She laughed aloud. "You can only imagine my chagrin when I learned that not only was I not to have my longed-for season, but that I was to marry a man who was forty-two years older than I was! Oh, how I cried, stormed, and pleaded to be released from my father's promise. He would not tell me the truth of the matter, of course, but George did. And then my churchly brother went on to say it was my Christian duty as a good daughter to obey my surviving parent; to save Papa and the rest of the family from the disgrace exposure of his sins would surely bring."

"And so you cooperated," The Master said.

"Yes," Lucinda replied, "but I was very fortunate, unlike many girls put in similar positions. Robert Harrington was a wonderful man whose only lack was an heir of his loins. His first wife had never been able to successfully conceive and bear him a child. He loved her deeply, and it was a terrible tragedy for them. He had been widowed for a number of years when he decided he must remarry and attempt to father an heir on a young wife. No one really knew how wealthy Robert was, and his family is not of the first rank. He could not manage to contract another alliance with a young woman of his own station. Then when he caught my father cheating, the answer became obvious to him." She ceased her narrative for a moment and, arising from the bed, crossed the chamber to pour herself a goblet of sweet wine. "Would you like one, Master?"

"Yes." He nodded. "Then return, and tell me the rest of your fascinating tale, m'lady Lucinda." He took the goblet she offered him, and she rejoined him to continue her story.

"Robert Harrington was a lovely man. When we first met he at once ascertained my anger and my fears. He attempted to allay them in that week before we were married. It was a simple ceremony, performed in our local church by our ancient vicar. I had no attendants, and my only witnesses were Papa, George, his wife Caroline, and the vicar's wife and elderly sister. A toast was drunk to us afterward at the house. Papa put an announcement in all the London papers. We returned to Harrington Hall immediately that very day."

"Did your husband force your virginity from you that same night?" The Master asked her, curious.

"Nay," Lucinda said. "It was several months before Robert made me a woman. He wanted me to enjoy the sensual experience. He was very skilled, I believe. He said while I might not ever come to love him, he did want our time together to be pleasureable for us both."

"And was it?" The Master queried.

"Yes, it was," Lucinda answered him frankly. "And to my surprise I did come to love him. Not in a wildly passionate way, but in a quiet way. I also respected him for the kind of man he was. Thoughtful. Kind. Generous. I am very sorry I could not perform the only task he required of me, which was to give him an heir. We had been wed several years when he became ill. I nursed him with as much devotion as I could. When he died, no one was more surprised than I was to learn he had left me his entire fortune! The estate itself was entailed upon the next male heir, who also inherited his title."

"Why have you been living with your brother?" The Master's fingers reached out to wrap a hank of Lucinda's thick chestnut hair about his big hand. His gaze was direct.

"There was no dower house at the hall. Robert's nephew, Percy, is a child. His mama, Lady Blythe, was very angry the lad received none of his uncle's monies. She had been counting upon it heavily as she is a widow and, being prone to extravagance, always in debt. Had she allowed me to remain, I would have happily borne the expenses of the estate. In her disappointment she accused me of cajoling her brother into disinheriting her son, and she said it to any who would listen. The lies she told were dreadful. I had used my body in lewd ways to influence Robert. I had stalked him until he had wed me. There are always those willing to listen to such nonsense, of course. I was glad to leave the hall. The bitch even searched my luggage before I went to make certain that nothing belonging to *the estate* was secreted among my possessions. She is really quite an awful woman. Robert disliked both her and her odious brat intensely, but he could not save Harrington Hall for me unless I had a child of his body, and I did not."

"So you came to London to find another husband, eh?"

"I came to London to buy a house of my own," Lucinda said bluntly. "I was forced by convention to live with George and Caro. They dragged every eligible bachelor in the county into my presence; but I am not yet of a mind to remarry, and they refuse to understand it. After I had refused everyone they could think of, Caroline suggested we come to London for the season. I agreed not because I wanted a man, but because I wanted my own home. I have just purchased a delightful little place on Traleigh Square."

He was fascinated by her recital. This was not at all what he had expected to hear from her. She was not in the market for a man. He had been given to understand that Lady Lucinda Harrington was a proper little cock tease, deserving of a lesson in manners, who must be brought to heel. And when she had been, she would be compelled to choose from among her three worthy suitors. But she didn't want to choose.

"You have offended three important gentlemen," he began, "who seek to compromise you so that you must take one of them in marriage. I do not know who they are, for that is not usually important to me. I am employed to do what I do for the Devil's Disciples, and nothing else is of interest to me in these matters. However, they have never put a *lady* in my charge as you know. The story you tell me is vastly different from what I was led to believe. Who do I trust in this matter, madame?"

"Common sense should tell you that, sir," Lucinda answered. "For your own information, I shall tell you the gentlemen I have offended who I believe are responsible for my being here. The Duke of Rexford, the Marquess of Hargrave, and Lord Bertram. I suspect, too, that my brother is also involved in this. The others would not dare to have me kidnapped otherwise. Had I really been meant to go to my sister Julia's in Ireland, a hue and cry would be raised when I didn't arrive. Those villains know that. Therefore I must conclude that my brother stands with them. But then George is a fool, too, I fear."

The Master laughed aloud at her candid remark. Then he grew serious "You have not objected to your treatment at my hands, m'lady. I do not know what to think of it."

"Has it not occurred to you, sir, that I like carnal pursuits? I do not believe that I am a wanton, but I enjoyed my late husband's attentions. It has been several years since we cohabited, as his illness did not permit it in the last two years of his life."

"And now you have been widowed for another two," The Master said.

Lucinda nodded in the affirmative. "Our lovemaking had always, I believe, been most circumspect. Just before Robert grew ill we had spoken on more daring forms of passion such as cock sucking, and arse fucking, but we had never had the time to explore such things."

"So you were not afraid this evening?" His green eyes searched her face for the absolute truth.

"No," Lucinda said. "I found it very exciting to have John atop me filling my cunt while you stuffed your cock into my mouth to suck. At first I thought I would choke. You are not a small man. But then I discovered that by relaxing my throat I could more than contain you. I hope you are not shocked by my confession, sir."

"I am fascinated, madame," he admitted to her.

"You understand now that I cannot be forced into taking one of those three fools for a husband," Lucinda said.

"I am afraid I do, m'lady Lucinda, but the knowledge puts me in a bit of a quandary. The income I earn from the Devil's Disciples helps me to maintain my own small estate and my horses. If I admit to failure with you, I am ruined and could lose everything. What am I to do?"

"Let me see your face," she begged him. She touched the narrow band of black silk across his upper face.

"Nay, m'lady, that I cannot do for the reasons I have already explained," he told her, but his voice was now reluctant.

Lucinda smiled a wicked smile. "I can help you to maintain your reputation, and your income, *if you will help me*," she told him.

"How?" The question was sharp.

"I want revenge upon those three for their arrogance and their presumption that I could be forced to their will like some mindless idiot. Teach me all you can about the erotic arts and how I may please men. When September comes I shall perform before the Devil's Disciples as if I had been tamed, and cowed into genuine obedience. Then you will tell the assembled gentlemen that my dear brother, the Bishop of Wellington, will announce my betrothal at the first ball of the new season, which is being given by the Countess of Whitley." She chuckled mischievously. "It will add drama to the evening, and those three fools will spend the next few weeks wondering which of them I have picked. I shall be seen in public with all of them and encourage each against the other."

"And on the night of the Countess of Whitley's ball, m'lady?"

She shrugged. "My brother will announce my betrothal to the man I love, and no other, sir. If you will help me, Master, you will not lose your vaunted reputation, or your source of income." She paused, and then said, "Why do you do it, sir? You are obviously a gentleman, and yet you allow yourself to be used in this manner."

"We are not all, madame, the possessors of great fortunes," he said. "This estate has been in my family for centuries. I was born here. I grew up here, and I love it."

"Do you have a wife?"

"How could I?" he replied. "I have nothing to offer any woman, and so my line will die with me; but until that time I shall remain in the place I love best, m'lady Lucinda."

"Will you help me?" she asked him again.

He did not have to even think on it. "Yes," he said. "I will help you. I find your plan amusing, and besides, it means that for the next three months I will have you at my mercy, Lucinda. I find the thought a most exciting one. Now, my pet, you had best get some rest, for come the dawn I shall be ready to begin your tutelage." Setting his goblet on the bedside table, he arose. "Good night," he said, kissing the curls wrapped around his hand. Then releasing her hair he walked from the bedchamber.

Lucinda climbed from the bed and went to the now cold bath. Taking a washing cloth she cleaned herself free of the sweat and juices of her lover's exertions. Then getting back into bed she immediately fell asleep. It had been a most interesting day indeed, and tomorrow promised to be even more exhilarating.

Chapter Three

"Wake up, Lucinda! It is time for your morning spanking," The Master said.

Lucinda groaned, and turned over upon her back as he tore the coverlet from her protesting frame. "Is it morning already?"

"Yes. Now come and receive your spanking, wench!"

"Why?" she asked him.

The Master laughed, and sat down on the edge of the bed. "If you are to be totally convincing to the Devil's Disciples, Lucinda, you must practice absolute obedience."

"But am I not to be in charge, sir?" she queried.

"You are," he replied, "but in order to *really* be in command of any situation, you must be perfectly self-disciplined. You cannot be unless you rid yourself of your fears. Instant obedience to a command can only be obtained by two methods: either fear of chastisement if you don't obey, or the knowledge that even in obedience you are in total and full mastery of yourself. Do you understand me, Lucinda?"

"I do!" she exclaimed, truly excited and amazed by this

new knowledge. "I really do, sir! How clever you are. Let us begin again if you please." She smiled at him.

"Good morning, Lucinda," he said. "It is time for your spanking."

She arose, and put herself over his lap, turning over her left shoulder a moment to wink at him. "Yes, Master," she said. And then she wiggled her bottom at him.

"Excellent, you remembered," he approved. Then he spanked her ten firm blows, turning the flesh beneath his hand quite pink, noting that she rubbed herself against his leg after the first few spanks. He slipped his hand beneath her and smiled, well satisfied. "You are nicely wet, my lady, and it took but ten, not the twenty I gave you last night. That is an excellent improvement. Now up, wench, and on your back, legs spread. I have a little surprise for you." He drew an object from the pocket of his breeches and displayed it for her to see.

"What is it?" she asked him, lying back. Then her eyes grew wide. "Ohh! It looks like a big cock! Oh, let me see! What is it made of, sir? It has these little spikey nubs upon it." Lucinda could feel herself beginning to throb with mounting excitement as she viewed the object. It was made of leather, but other than the little nodules that decorated it, it was quite smooth. At its base it had a round ivory handle by which he held it.

"It is called a dildo, my pet," The Master told her. "It is going to give you a great deal of pleasure this morning while I am training my horses. Alas, I cannot amuse myself with you all day." Then drawing another article from his pocket, he wrapped it about her right wrist first, then her left wrist, and attached the two twisted silk cords to two brass hooks hidden high up on the bed's headboard.

Lucinda tested her bonds, then said, "I've never been tied before. Robert and I spoke on it." She was just the tiniest bit afraid, but she fought down her fear as he bound her spread legs to the carved bedposts at the bottom of the bed. Her bottom was still tingling from her spanking, and it was really very exciting. After all, her life was not in jeopardy.

"The ropes are not too tight?" he asked her as he pushed a hard, round bolster beneath her hips so her furry quim was quite visible.

"How long must I remain this way?" she asked him.

He smiled wickedly. "I shall tell you shortly, my pet, but now it is time for you to have a little refreshment." Walking across the room, he went to the tray on the sideboard and poured a small cordial. Coming back to her side, he carefully braced her so she might drink it all down. "It will help to raise the level of your excitement, Lucinda. The Devil's Disciples like to use such methods, for they lack imagination."

"An aphrodisiac? Lucinda asked him.

He nodded.

"I've never had one," she said.

"I should expect not," he chuckled. "It is not usual for respectable married ladies to have access to such things."

"It tastes like strawberries. I had some last night. Is that why I was so uninhibited, sir?" she wondered.

"I believe you would be uninhibited without the benefits of an aphrodisiac," he told her, "but for now it is better you have it."

"When are you going to impale me with the dildo?" she queried, her eyes going to it again. "Will it hurt me?"

"The object is to give pleasure, not pain, my pet," he told her quietly. Then The Master bent over, and his lips met hers. Tenderly at first, but then as his own desires were aroused, his kiss became more passionate. Lucinda's mouth beneath his was warm and sweet. For a brief moment he thought like the man he really was and became lost in her almost innocent passion. Then he caught himself and drew away.

"That was nice," Lucinda said. "I quite liked your kiss. Do it again, Master." Then she saw the look in his eye and quickly said, "No, I think not, but perhaps another time." She smiled at him. "Is that better, sir? Am I more tempting, and quite heartless?"

"Yes, Lucinda, that was quite perfect, my pet," he agreed, but something inside him wished that they had kissed again. He gave himself a little shake. Then crossing the room again, he took a small silver bowl from a cabinet along with a vial of special oil. It, too, was an aphrodisiac. Upon bringing the items back to the bedside table, he poured some oil into the bowl and dipped the dildo into it. "How do you feel?" he asked her.

"I want to be fucked," she told him bluntly.

"Then, you are ready," he said, and lying next to her on the bed, he began to slowly insert the dildo into her love sheath.

It felt . . . it felt very different from a man's cock, she thought, and yet it was incredibly exciting. He began to frig her with the dildo, and Lucinda gave a little shriek of surprise. The tiny nubs teased and irritated her love sheath until she was struggling against her bonds in a desperate effort to obtain release. "Ohhh!" she cried. He worked the dildo even harder, and faster. "*Ohhh!*" Lucinda moaned.

"See how long you can hold out," he instructed her in a careful voice. "The more you can bear it, the better your performance, and the more your suitors will feel they have a mastery over you; but it will be you who obtain this incredible pleasure, Lucinda."

"I can't," she sobbed, and her juices flowed down the dildo, "*Oh God! Oh God!*" Her lithe body shuddered. Then her eyes, which had been tightly shut, opened, and she looked at him. "That was wonderful!" she breathed with a hearty sigh. "Do it again!"

He laughed. "You are truly insatiable, Lucinda." He slowly reinserted the dildo into her body. "It will remain there, my pet, for the morning." Then he stood up. "I must go now and see to my horses. John and the others will come and service you when it is necessary. When the mere sensation of the dildo within you can make you come, Lucinda, then you will have mastered it, instead of the other way around." Bending, he kissed her gently and then departed the bedroom.

He hurried to his own bedchamber, and stripping the leather breeches off, he put on his riding clothes. He needed to get out of the house, and think. Lucinda Harrington had confused his senses. He realized that he didn't want to teach her the erotic arts so she could practice them on other men. But what choice did he have? If he refused to go along with her clever plan, he was ruined. He had not the slightest doubt she would not cooperate with the Devil's Disciples. She would gain her will.

Leaving his bedchamber, he descended the staircase and met John, the footman, at the bottom. "Lady Lucinda will need tending to over the morning, John. You and the others see to it, remembering she is a lady, not one of our usual guests."

"Very good, m'lord," the footman replied.

The Master moved out of the house and went to the stables where his horse was already saddled and waiting. Mounting the beast, The Master rode out of the stableyard and into the countryside. His thoughts were very troubled. For the first time since he had gotten involved with the Devil's Disciples, he had regrets. How overbearing and disdainful of women were its members. And he had been just as bad as they. No one had ever been hurt physically, but a number of young women, reluctant to yield themselves to the nobility, had been seduced into compliance. And most of them had fallen in love with him first. Now fate was repaying him in kind. He barely knew Lucinda, but he was falling in love with her.

He looked about his lands as he rode. The fields were green with summer. His horses were sleek and well cared for, their coats shining. The mares gamboled with the colts that had been born this year. In another field were a half dozen yearlings racing with one another. In the far pasture was his prize stallion, Rhamses, a great chestnut animal which he had raised from a colt. Rhamses had raced for him for two years and had won enough purses that allowed The Master, along with the fees he garnered from the Devil's Disciples, to maintain his small holding.

A few hundred acres remained of what had once been a great estate of several thousand acres. Some of it had been confiscated in the civil wars a hundred years ago. As King Charles had promised not to give back the confiscations to their original owners upon his restoration, those acres had been lost to his family. And then his great-grandfather, his grandfather, and his father had all been gentlemen who believed that their purses could never be emptied no matter how extravagantly they lived. They had, upon the discovery that their funds were low, sold off property.

The women they married came with smaller dowries each generation because his antecedents had less to offer and could therefore not attract wealth. His own mother had not been of noble birth, but rather the daughter of landed gentry. Her portion was small, and his father, a charming wastrel, had gambled it away before his own birth. His mother died shortly thereafter. His father had drunk himself into his grave by the time The Master was thirteen. His paternal grandmother, a kind but stern woman, had raised him with a strong sense of his family's history and honor. She had died when he was twenty, and had been the only woman he ever admired, for she was strong. She had refused to be victimized by either her husband or her son. She had been her own woman, very much like Lady Lucinda Harrington.

His grandmother would certainly not have approved of his occupation as a glorified whoremaster to the nobility. Only one man among the Devil's Disciples knew his identity, its founder, Sir Derek Bowen. He had gone to school with Derek Bowen, who was a few years his senior. Derek had always admired his ability to defuse a situation and bring others around to his will.

"Join us," he had said to his friend.

"I have no taste for rape," The Master had replied.

"Most of these girls are ill-bred," came the reply. "They just need to be persuaded to lift their skirts for their betters. You could be the one to cajole them for us. Get them used to fondling and frigging. Suck their little titties and tweak their little exciters. Then when they are eager for it, bring them to us, and we'll pick their cherries. Many will go on to become mistresses, a far better life than slopping hogs for a brutish husband or sewing until they go blind. The Devil's Disciples give these lasses a chance at a better life. We will call you The Master, old friend. You will be well compensated for your efforts. Think what those monies can do for you. I know you are in debt. You can clear that debt using your powers of persuasion and still have monies to maintain your estate as well. No one will ever get hurt, I swear it," Sir Derek Bowen had promised him.

"I will think on it," The Master had replied. Then he had gone to London to visit his father's former mistress, to ask her advice in the matter.

"They will have these poor girls if they mean to even if you don't cooperate with them," Marianne had told him. "Better someone kind at least prepare them, my dear boy, and God knows you could charm a duck into a roasting pan."

He had laughed. "I will need more than just words," he told her. "Will you help me?"

She had agreed and had taken him to several shops, all located in dark alleys off less-than-respectable streets. There he had been introduced to a variety of sexual toys that might be used, he was assured by the oily shopkeepers, to convince the most reluctant lass to yield herself to her lover. He had also been influenced to design and have made several other articles for his new practice. Afterward he had given Marianne a small piece of family jewelry to thank her. She had accepted graciously, telling him to visit her the next time he came up to London. Her meaning was most clear. The idea of lying with his father's old mistress, who was certainly no longer in the first flush of youth, had appalled him. He had kissed her hand and departed.

Then he had found his friend, Sir Derek Bowen, at White's Club, surprising him.

"I was not aware you were in London," Sir Derek said, calling for a drink for his old friend.

"I have been here for several days," The Master said. "I needed to do some research and, having done it, am amenable to your offer of employment, Derek. Come down on the weekend, and we will discuss the particulars. I have one stipulation, however. No one is to know who I am but you. You may tell your friends only that The Master is a gentleman of good breeding. That is all they need to know else they attempt to treat me as a servant. Do you understand, and are we agreed?"

"We are!" Sir Derek had said immediately. "I shall see you Friday night, my friend."

Sir Derek had traveled to Oxfordshire several days later, and together he and The Master had worked out the ground rules. The Master was to have full responsibility for the women brought to him. Virgins would not be raped. He would simply awaken them to their own sensuality before turning them over to their gentlemen. More experienced women would be treated differently, but with the same end results.

"Find me three footmen who can aid me in these lewd pursuits," he had requested of Sir Derek. "I suspect you know just the right men."

Sir Derek had smiled, and nodded.

"I have an ancient Roman arena on my property. It is quite small, and was probably used by the local patrician family that once inhabited the region. We will use it for our meetings in the summer. You will find us a secure spot for inclement weather nearby. As I will be training these girls in my house, I will want to bring them out to your meetings quickly so they cannot grow fearful."

"There is an old monastary quite near here," Sir Derek had

said. "It has been deserted and ruined for several centuries, but the cellars beneath it are quite habitable and dry. We'll arrange to have it fixed up for our meetings." He had smiled.

"You have obviously been there recently," The Master had noted with a small smile himself.

"It is a very private place," Sir Derek had replied, "and a gentleman likes to have a private place to escape to now and again, eh?"

"Indeed," The Master had acknowledged.

They had then continued to work out a number of small, but important details of their enterprise, and on Sunday afternoon Sir Derek had begun his return journey to London to tell the Devil's Disciples of his progress. Several days afterward John, Dick and Martin, the footmen, had arrived, references in hand and a letter from Sir Derek to The Master. That had been three years ago.

The first girl brought to him had been a high-spirited farmer's daughter. It had taken only a week to master her. She had gone on to give her lustful lordling hours of pleasure, and two bastards, before she was retired to a cottage. There had followed more country girls, shop girls, and several months ago, Lord Meldrew's governess. She had been a most prim young lady who had foolishly resisted her employer's overtures. In The Master's charge, however, she had been developed into a shameless hussy who now ruled her employer by virtue of her big breasts and her nutcracker cunt. The Master had heard recently that Lord Meldrew was looking quite pale and weak as of late.

A rumble of thunder brought his thoughts to a halt. Looking about, he saw the rain coming, and turning his horse about, he cantered back to his stables, arriving barely before the storm. Hurrying across the stableyard and into the house, he met Dick and Martin. "How is her ladyship doing?" he asked them.

The footmen grinned, and then Dick said, "She's taking to the training nicely, m'lord. John is with her now."

The Master ran up the stairs and down the hall to the bedchamber where Lucinda was imprisoned. Entering the room, he saw John bending over her, his hand furiously working the dildo as Lucinda moaned her pleasure openly and encouraged him to continue. The footman turned his head at the sound of the door.

"She's a proper one for passion, m'lord. Yer going to have no problems with this one. Look at this." John opened Lucinda's cunt lips with two fingers to reveal her clit, swollen to twice its size. Taking his hand off the dildo, he flicked the sensitive little organ, and she shrieked, her juices flowing copiously.

"Very good, Lucinda," The Master approved. Then turning to the footman, he dismissed John. Sitting upon the edge of the bed after his companion had departed, he said quietly, "John is correct when he says you are a proper one for passion, my pet. Are you enjoying it?"

"Y . . . yes, and no," Lucinda said. "I have never had such pleasure, even with my dearest Robert, but it is now, I think, too much. I cannot stop coming, sir. I lie perfectly still, but I cannot help squeezing it, and then . . . What is happening to me? I have never before been weak."

"You are not weak," he said. "You are passionate, and it has been several years since you were allowed to indulge those delightful feelings of lust." He worked the dildo gently, and she shuddered. "You are, my pet, a far better woman than any of your suitors deserves, I fear." Then he bent and brushed her lips lightly with his. "We have a great deal of work to do, Lucinda, if you are to have your revenge. When you give your body to each of those three in September, it must be the absolute best passion any of them has ever experienced. It must be so good for each that the mere thought of you choosing one of the others for your husband will drive them to a frenzy. I do not believe that can happen unless I change my method of training. I think, perhaps, you will learn more quickly if we become lovers instead of master and pupil. Would you agree to such a thing?"

She nodded. "Yes," she said, "but only if you tell me your name. How can you be my lover when I do not know who you are."

"I will tell you my first name only," he said to her. "Will that suffice, Lucinda?"

"But you will not take off your mask, will you?" she replied.

"No, and you know that I am right in that. My name is Robert, as was your late husband's name."

"It will certainly be easy to remember," Lucinda said dryly. Then she chuckled. "How deliciously amusing this all is, Robbie."

"I want to make love to you," he told her quietly, and withdrawing the dildo laid it aside. He stood, and pulling off his own boots, quickly undressed. His manhood was already engorged and ready for battle.

"Will you not untie me?" she asked him.

"Your legs, yes, but I should like to keep your arms bound. You will find the sensation of being fucked that way very pleasurable." He loosened the silk cords that had kept her legs spread wide.

"So I am to remain your captive," she said softly. He excited her. He excited her far more than her husband ever had. *Than any man ever had.* He pressed a finger between her lips, and Lucinda sucked thoughtfully upon it. What did he look like behind his mask. It was not, of course, a full mask, only covering his eyes and part of his nose, but it was impossible to tell what a man looked like without seeing his entire face. Did she dare to tear the mask away, but then she remembered her hands were constrained. Besides, if she did not keep to his rules of this game they were playing, she might never learn the truth of who he was. She must be patient. One thing, however, Lucinda did know. Robbie was a real man, unlike those three fools who sought to force her into marriage with one of them.

What was she thinking? he wondered, as she sucked his finger so sensuously. He bent his dark head and began to lick at her throat, kissing it first, then letting his tongue sweep up the column of warm flesh. She stirred in his arms, moving against him so that her silky skin aroused him even more than he was already aroused. His fingers tangled themselves into her chestnut hair, kneading at her scalp.

"There can be no niceties between us at this moment," he said almost desperately, and plunged himself deep into her body. Then he began to ride her, and seeing the look upon her face, he groaned with his own desire. She was so very wet, and so very hot. She excited him by knowing she must struggle a little against her bonds to arouse him even more. Her legs fastened about him, gripping him hungrily. For the first time in his life, he cried out while loving a woman. He couldn't help himself. She was utterly delicious! To his surprise he realized that he was not mastering Lucinda, Instead, it was Lucinda who was mastering him. He kissed her, a deep, passionate kiss, and she shuddered hard beneath him even as his own juices burst forth in a torrent of lust and desire. Rolling off of her, he undid her bonds with his last bit of strength and gathered her into his arms.

Lucinda lay quite aware upon his broad, smooth chest. His heart beat slowly now beneath her cheek. She could smell their passion upon his body. *It was madness!* They had been together but two days, but she knew that this was the man she wanted to spend the rest of her life with no matter who he was. Why had she not met him in London this past season, and would she have even known him if she had? *Yes! Oh. yes!*

"Were you in London recently?" she finally asked him.

"I have not the means to attend the season," he replied. "Besides, as I am not seeking a wife, there is no real necessity for it."

"Then, we have not met, even in passing, before," she sighed.

"No, we have not met until two days ago," he admitted.

Lucinda bit her lip in thought. "But you will come to the Countess of Whitley's ball this autumn, Robbie."

"To see you triumph over your suitors?" he said, a small smile upon his lips.

"Yes," she responded. "To see my triumph."

"I will come," he agreed. "I shall not want to *master* any more females after you, Lucinda. Your suitors have been very generous with your fees. I shall be able to afford one small treat. I shall stay with my friend, Sir Derek, attend the countess's ball, and then return home to my horses." He stroked her thick chestnut hair. "And what shall you do afterward, Lucinda?" he asked her.

"I shall live happily ever after just as they do in the children's stories, Robbie," she told him.

"Without passion when you have such a capacity for it?" he wondered aloud. Damn, why could he not have the means to offer for her himself?

"Oh, I shall remarry," Lucinda assured him, "but the choice shall really be mine, and no one else's. Like my sister, Julia, I care not for position or possessions. Thanks to my late husband I can wed with a pauper if it pleases me. I cannot, I will not, be *mastered* by anyone, Robbie. I will only truly yield to a man who loves me. The man I love. That is what Robert Harrington wanted for me, and it is what I want." She lifted her head off of his chest and looked into the green eyes behind the black silk mask. "Have you ever been in love?"

"Once, years back," he responded. "I wanted to marry the daughter of a wealthy local gentleman. We had known each other since our childhoods. Elise was very lovely. We made love for the first time when I was seventeen, and she, fifteen. After that our passions were unleashed, and scarcely a day went by that we did not meet. I was planning to offer for her when her betrothal was announced to a marquess from Yorkshire. When we next met I asked her if it was what she wanted. I practically wept with my distress. She coolly informed me that her marquess was fabulously rich, and she wanted to be a marchioness.

"'But when he learns you are not a virgin,' I replied angrily, 'what shall you do then, Elise? Your marquess will divorce you and send you back to Oxfordshire in disgrace.' She laughed, and said they had already lain together. 'I cried,' she told me, 'and played the innocent. Then afterward as he slept I smeared my thighs and the sheets with a small skin of chicken's blood my nanny obtained for me.' I was astounded at her perfidy, but then came a worse revelation. She told me she was already with child, although whose it was she couldn't be certain. Mine, or her marquess's, she said. It made no difference as he would believe it to be his and recognize it as his heir. She was married with much pomp the following week. My grandmother and I attended her wedding. We could not avoid it. I was amazed at the dewy innocent she appeared that day," he finished.

"So that is why you dislike women," Lucinda said.

"I do not dislike women!" he protested.

"Then, why do you allow the Devil's Disciples to use you to prepare reluctant lasses for ravishing?" Lucinda asked him politely. "You are, I believe, still angry at this girl for deceiving you, and so, unable to punish her, you punish them."

Her clever reasoning overwhelmed him. "My God," he exclaimed. "What have I done? I did not realize I was still angry, but even now as I spoke on it I felt wrath again at being so deceived. Fury that Elise could have been so heartless as to throw away the love I had for her. Indignation that a title greater than mine and a purse of gold meant more to her than I did. What have I done in my selfish ire?"

"What is done is done," Lucinda said. "Will you allow this woman to continue to control your life by wallowing in remorse over your role as The Master? You have said no one was truly harmed, and you cannot change the past. What you can do is make a better future for yourself, Robbie." She kissed his mouth gently. "We shall spend the rest of the summer being lovers, not adversaries. I will heal all of your wounds. Come September, I shall have my revenge on a duke, a marquess, and a lord. You will have helped me, and certainly that will exculpate your sins." Then she kissed him again.

For the first time in years he felt free, but one thing disturbed him. "You will have to yield yourself to your suitors' lustful desires, or they will not believe your charade. I cannot bear it that you must do this, Lucinda," he said.

"I am not afraid," she told him. "There is no other way I can whet their appetites; no other way in which I may turn them one against the other; no way in which I may have real revenge unless I do this. For the rest of their lives they will remember coupling with me before their companions, crying with their pleasure, hearing me cry with mine, and knowing that never again will they have such delight. Each must marry for his own family's sake. While it may be unfair to the women they wed, no woman will ever again satisfy them like I did. And as the years go by, the memory of that September night will take on greater proportions, growing more vivid in their imaginations. They will suffer as they have made other women suffer."

"You are as fierce as an ancient warrior," he said.

"My father often said had I been a boy I would have, like William, my eldest brother, made a good soldier," Lucinda told him. "Will you agree to be my lover, Robert?"

"Yes," he said, "and I shall send the footmen away."

"Oh, no!" Lucinda said wisely. "The Devil's Disciples sent them to you, and if you send them away now, they will report back to whoever is their true master. Let them remain and help you with my education as they have in the past. I know there is a great deal more I need to learn about sensuality, Robbie."

So began the most wonderful summer of their lives. The Master gathered his three randy footmen about him and explained that Lady Lucinda, being a real lady, must be mastered in an entirely different way. He told them he had gained her cooperation and from now on they would be lovers.

"She will learn more this way," he assured them. "Your part in all of this, I regret, will not be as involved as usual; but this is an unusual case, and we have been well remunerated for our efforts."

"Then," said John, who was the cleverest of the trio, "we are to treat Lady Lucinda as if she were your mistress, and your guest, m'lord?"

"Exactly," he said. "But my identity must still remain a mystery to her. It is better that way should we ever meet socially. She will, however, call me by one of my Christian names, Robert, so do not be surprised if you hear her use it. Her late husband was called Robert. I thought the name would comfort her."

"You are indeed a master, m'lord," John said admiringly. "You could sell King George his own crown, and him none the wiser," chuckled the stocky footman.

The other two footmen chuckled also, but then Dick said, "Will we gets to have a little orgy with her before she leaves us, m'lord? We ain't never had a lady before as you know."

"We must see how things progress," The Master told them. "I will indeed need you for certain things Lady Lucinda needs to learn. She is a most eager pupil. Our employers will be very pleased come September when we meet again."

Polly finally made an appearance before her mistress later that day. She looked tired, and worn. "Well," she said sourly, "I hope you don't really have to choose one of them lordlings who want to marry you, m'lady. The duke howls while he fucks; the marquess almost crushed me with his weight, and his lordship seems to prefer a woman's arse to her cunny. I'm sore all over, inside and out."

Lucinda was sitting up in her bed, looking most fetching. One would have never guessed she had spent the entire morning with a wicked little dildo stuffed up her. "The Master and I have come to an arrangement," she told her servant. "I promise you I shall marry none of them, Polly. Now call the footmen, and have them draw me a bath. I stink of lust, I fear."

"Well, thank heavens for your decision. But what kind of an arrangement has you made with The Master, m'lady, and can you be certain he will keep his word?"

"He will keep his word, Polly. Now, go and tell John I want a bath. I shall then explain to you what I have done."

Polly hurried off, and when she returned, Lucinda elucidated the situation as it now stood. "But what will yer brother say?" was Polly's concern when her mistress had finished her account of her several conversations with The Master.

"My brother, the villain, is involved up to his chasuble in this matter," Lucinda said. "He can do nothing but my will from now on, else I expose him to the archbishop."

"Ohhh, m'lady, you does have the whiphand," Polly replied admiringly. "Then we will live in London?"

"Perhaps," came the answer, and Lucinda smiled mysteriously.

The bath was quickly set up, and with no care for the three footmen, Lucinda stepped naked from her bed and into the tub. "John," she said, "do see the bed is remade with fresh linens immediately."

"Yes, m'lady," he replied, and sent the other two for the lavender-scented sheets. "Shall I do your back, m'lady?" he asked her.

"Ohhh, yer the bold one!" Polly cried, shocked. "I'm perfectly capable of washing my lady without yer help!" She knelt and, taking up the washing cloth, began to soap it vigorously. Then she began to wash Lucinda, muttering all the while beneath her breath about the cheekiness of certain people.

With a mischievous wink at Lucinda the footman crept up behind Polly and, kneeling down, reached about to cup her two plump breasts in his big, rough hands.

Polly squealed, surprised, trying to slap him away.

Lucinda laughed, but then she said, "Let her alone, John. If you are at a loss for something to do, please go and fetch me something to eat. I have not been fed since yesterday afternoon. I do not believe it is The Master's intention to starve me."

John arose, but not before giving Polly's nipples a pinch which caused her to squeak again. "At once, m'lady," the footman said. He hurried out as Dick and Martin returned with the fresh bedding.

"Make the bed quickly, and then be gone," Lucinda told them in a stern voice. Then she said to Polly, "My hair needs washing, too. All that dusty travel two days ago."

"Yes, m'lady," the maid replied, her equilibrium returning.

The two footmen were gone by the time Lucinda stepped from her bath. Polly dried her quickly after wrapping her mistress's hair in a towel first. Then she slipped a scented night garment over her lady, and Lucinda sat by the fire as her maid toweled her thick hair dry, first with the cloth, and then with Lucinda's silver and boar's bristle brush which she had taken from her lady's luggage.

"Am I to unpack everything, m'lady?" she asked as she tied Lucinda's hair back with a blue silk ribbon.

"Of course," came the reply. "It is as if we had gone to Ireland to visit my sister for the summer, Polly. I fear, however, that you shall be required to do the laundry as this house appears to have no servants other than the footmen."

"There's an old lady in the kitchens who is the cook," Polly informed her lady, "and there must be someone to do the linens."

"There well may be, but I doubt The Master wishes his business known to any of the locals. No woman has remained here for more than a week he tells me. You and I, however, will be here for several months. Ask him before you seek any help for yourself. If you must care for me alone, it is only for a short time, eh?"

The door to the chamber opened, and John came in followed by The Master. The footman was carrying a heavy silver tray. He set it carefully upon the table near the fireplace. Delicious aromas arose from the covered dishes.

"Good!" Lucinda said. "I am ravenous!"

"Polly and John are dismissed," The Master said. "I shall serve you myself, Lucinda."

Polly looked nervously to her mistress, but Lucinda said, "While we are in this house, Polly, you will obey The Master. And, John, you may not seduce my servant unless she wants it. Is that understood, you randy billygoat of a mankin?"

"Yes, m'lady," the footman said, but there was a devilish light in his eyes.

Polly curtsied, and the two servants departed the bedchamber.

"Feed me!" Lucinda commanded. "I have not eaten since that delicate little meal I was served yesterday afternoon in your garden shed."

He grinned at her and drew the table nearer, sitting next to her on the small settee by the fire. Lifting a lid from the first dish, he took up a raw oyster and tipped it into her open mouth. She swallowed it down and looked to him for more. He fed her a full dozen, serving himself an equal amount as she swallowed each time. Lifting another of the silver domes, he displayed a small chicken. He tore it in half and took a bite, then offered her one. They alternated bites of the fowl as they had the oysters until it was eaten. The next dish, a long, rectangular one, offered asparagus dripping with a vinegarette. Lucinda picked one up and slowly licked the sauce from the lengthy green stalk. Then her eyes never leaving his, she bit the flower-headed tip from the asparagus and swallowed it down. She sucked upon the stalk, taking the sweetness from it, and then cast it aside. Now she offered him one, but he shook his head.

"They are all yours," he told her with a small smile.

She smiled back and proceeded to eat the vegetable slowly

and sensuously as he watched. She could see the bulge in his breeches with each nibble she took. At one point she reached out, patting it. When the asparagus were all devoured, Lucinda gave him her fingers to lick. He sucked upon each digit with very explicit meaning. The last item left on the tray proved to be a dish of strawberries. They fed them to each other until their fingers and their lips were stained red with the juices of the sweet fruits. When the berries were gone and they had licked each other's fingers clean, he brought them each a crystal goblet of wine. Together they drank it down.

"Are you satisfied now?" he demanded of her when the tray had been decimated.

"No," she said. "There is one more thing I desire, Robbie."

He laughed. "You are a true vixen, Lucinda," he told her. "Very well, as I am not yet satisfied either, you shall have a second dessert. Come," he said, and pulled her up. Then spinning her about, he bent her over the settee, lifting her night garment.

"Ohh," Lucinda exclaimed, "how deliciously wicked!"

The Master loosened his breeches, releasing his male member, and moving carefully behind her, clasped her hips in his hands while he nosed his love lance beneath her into her hot little sheath. "'Tis you, my pet, who are wicked," he murmured in her ear as he bent over her. "You are all wet, and ready for me." He thrust deep.

"Ahhh," she cried, "I have never before done it this way!"

"There are several ways you have not done it, my pet, but I assure you that before you leave here in September, you shall know them all, Lucinda. Ahhh, that's it, my angel, come back onto my cock!" He pumped her vigorously, his fingers digging into the flesh of her hips.

"Ohh, Robert!" she sighed gustily. "I want to learn everything you can teach me before I return to London. Ohhh, yes! Yes! Yes! *Yesss!*"

Chapter Four

It was, Lucinda thought in later years, one of the loveliest summers of her life. It was, she realized, the first time in all of her life that she had really been free to do as she pleased, and not what someone else wanted her to do. She had a lover. He was intelligent, charming, and amusing. He was incredibly passionate. She was in love with him, and she had known it almost from the first moment they had met. She knew that she must learn his identity, for the man who called himself The Master, or Robert, was the only man she would marry.

His house was delightful, built, as she suspected, in the reign of the first Elizabeth when his family had made their fortune in the beginning of the Indies' trade. Their title, he said, predated their short-lived wealth. It went back to the times before King William, he who had come from Normandy. It was, Lucinda felt, a home before it was a great house. The walls were paneled; the floors, wide boards. Both were black with age. There were fine, but worn, Turkey carpets in the public rooms, a wonderful library and a picture gallery filled with portraits of the ancestors.

"Do you look like any of your antecedents?" she asked him one day, and he had laughed.

"No," he said. "I look like my mother, and there is no portrait of her as there were no monies to pay an artist when she was alive." He tipped her face up to his, and asked softly, "Does it matter to you what I look like, Lucinda?"

"No," she said, "but you cannot expect me not to be curious, Robbie. For two months we have been lovers, and you have been masked the entire time when you are with me. Even when we ride out across your lands. I understand your reasons for keeping your face from me, but I shall never wed a man who inhabits high society. It is unlikely we would meet socially."

"But if we do one day, and you have not seen my face, then you shall not be ashamed or embarrassed," he replied.

He never spent an entire night with her, disappearing after their lovemaking to his own bedchamber next door, which was firmly barred to her, and to Polly. " I must know who he is!" she said to her maidservant. "*I must know!*"

"Shouldn't think you'd care given the skillful way he wields that big cock of his," Polly answered saucily. "I asked John what he looks like, and he says he ain't anything special."

"You and John are rather thick," Lucinda noted.

"He wants to marry me, m'lady," Polly confessed.

"You'd marry a man who practices such a profession as he does?" Lucinda was surprised.

"John's pa wants him to come home to Hereford and take over his smithy, m'lady," Polly said. "He only went into service to better himself, but he says now he realizes he's better in the smithy."

"Do you want to marry him, Polly?" Lucinda asked her maid.

"Oh, yes, m'lady, I do!" the girl said. "I'd have me own house and everything. John's pa is a widower."

"You two seem to have discussed this quite thoroughly," Lucinda said thoughtfully. "When do you plan to leave me?"

"John and me both agree, m'lady, that we won't go till this is over and done with. I explained everything to him, and he thinks you're ever so brave to do what you must do to have your revenge," Polly told her mistress. "He says The Master has been a good master, and he knows he's not going to do this any more after you are gone."

"Do you mean to tell me Robert is retiring as The Master of the Devil's Disciples?" He had really meant it, Lucinda considered, excited.

"Yes, m'lady, he is. He says he is bored and tired of it."

"I *must* learn his true identity," Lucinda said, "but how?" She looked to Polly. "Would John know?"

"He might," Polly said, "but I don't think he'll betray The Master, m'lady. Why is it so important to you? Certainly you won't ever want to meet this gentleman after we have left here. You may not wed the duke, the marquess, or his lordship, but one day you will certainly marry again. What if your husband knows this man? Or you meet him at a ball, or a rout? 'Tis better you don't know, m'lady."

"The Master," Lucinda told her surprised servant, "is the only man I will marry, Polly. He has promised to come to the Countess of Whitley's ball where my brother must announce my betrothal. If I don't know who The Master is, how can George announce my engagement?"

Polly's eyes were big with her astonishment. Finally she regained her voice, and said, "But what if The Master ain't a gentleman, m'lady?"

"I know this house is his. His ancestors hang in the portrait gallery, Polly. He is a gentleman. One, I realize, of small means, but a gentleman nonetheless. There has to be a way of learning his true name and rank. *There has to be!*"

Polly shook her head. "I'll tell John what you've told me, m'lady. He'd like to see The Master happy as we're happy, I know, and he'll keep yer secret if I asks him to keep it."

To Lucinda's surprise it was the footman who approached her several days later. "If your ladyship were to go into the library some day," he said quietly, "she would find a large volume upon an oak stand, where the answers she seeks are to be found."

"When?" Lucinda asked softly.

"He has to be away all day tomorrow negotiating with a prince who wishes to purchase one of Rhamses's ungelded male offspring for his own stud in Turkey. The prince is staying nearby at Lord Bowen's home. Dick and Martin like to sneak into the village when The Master's away. The barmaids at The Frog and Swan are most accommodating, and as The Master ain't let them at you, m'lady, they're right randy. I've had some time of it keeping our Polly safe from them two, I can tell you. When they've gone off tomorrow, I'll send Polly to fetch you. Then it's up to you to find the information you need."

"Can you tell me nothing of him?" Lucinda queried the footman.

John shook his head. "We actually know little more than you do, m'lady We was told when we arrived that we was to call him The Master. We was all in service at Lord Bowen's. Dick and Martin will go back, I'm certain, when this is finished. Lord Bowen only told us that The Master was a titled gentleman, and because of what he would do for the Devil's Disciples, he wished to remain anonymous. We've seen his face, of course, but we had never seen him before we came here. Lord Bowen, you understand, spends most of his time in London. Besides, none of us can read, so it wouldn't do us no good to look in that big book."

Lucinda nodded. "I understand, John, and I thank you for your help in the matter. I shall see you and Polly have a fine gift on the occasion of your wedding."

"I must go over to a friend's this morning," The Master told Lucinda the next day. "I fear I shall be gone for several hours. Do you mind being alone?"

"I should welcome it," Lucinda said. "I know the hardest of my lessons are to come very soon, my darling Robbie. It is already September first, and the full moon will be upon us shortly."

He kissed her tenderly. "If there were another way," he said.

"I know," she told him, and indeed she did. If The Master allowed Lucinda to escape, her suitors would take their revenge on him. Then they would hunt their prey down, and one of them would force her to the altar. No. If she was to have her revenge, she would have to pretend to be mastered and yield herself to the hateful trio.

He left her, and shortly afterward Lucinda, gazing out her bedchamber window, saw Dick and Martin hurrying off down the lane in brown homespun breeches and linen shirts, their livery left behind. She waited patiently until Polly came to say it was safe for her mistress to go downstairs into the library. Lucinda hurried down the stairs. How quiet the lovely old house was this morning. Curious, she wandered about for a moment, opening doors. There was a beautiful little Great Hall with a single enormous fireplace. The tapestries on the wall were dusty, but well woven. It was obvious that the house had never been modernized since it had been built in fifteen hundred and one, for that was the date etched into the fireplace wall. Sunlight filtered through the dirty high windows. The furniture was good country oak. Cleaning, polishing, and some accessories would do wonders, she thought. Then she smiled to herself and went to the library, opening the door cautiously as if she expected to find someone there, but the paneled room was quite empty.

There! There by one of the casement windows was the book stand, and upon it the volume John had spoken of to Polly. There was a simple crest upon it. A crescent moon d'or surrounded by five-pointed gold stars upon an azure field. It was artless, but unique, Lucinda thought. Slowly she opened the book. *A History of the Earls of Stanton,* the title page said. Lucinda wasted no time in turning to the back of the book, and it was there she found it. *Lucian Robert Charles Phillips,* born August nineteenth, seventeen twenty. And after that there were no further entries. His mother's and his father's births, marriage and deaths were registered as was his paternal grandmother's.

It was all she really needed to know, but her curiosity not completely satisfied, Lucinda returned to the front of the book to discover that the Phillipses were a very ancient and honorable noble family. Family deaths matched all major battles fought in the king's name. There were at least two Earls of Stanton who had gone on crusade. Before Lucinda knew it the morning had gone, and the afternoon was upon her. Polly came to seek her out.

"Have you found out what you need to know, m'lady?"

"I have," Lucinda replied.

"Then come and have something to eat," the servant said.

Lucinda followed Polly into the garden where a table had been set up with her luncheon. John was waiting to serve her. He held the chair for Lucinda as she sat down. "I know what I need to know now," she began. "I prefer to keep my knowledge to myself for the interim. When we have returned to London, Polly, I shall tell you both. John, I want you to come with us until after the Countess of Whitley's ball is over. Then I will see you and Polly are transported safely to your father's home in Hereford. I think you should be married as soon as we get to London, however."

Polly was disappointed, but John said, "I understand perfectly, my lady. A London wedding would be most suitable. Your kindness toward us is appreciated, especially considering how we began," he finished with a deep blush.

Lucinda's vivid blue eyes twinkled mischievously. "I believe the less said about that small moment in time, the better off we all are, John. You may serve me now."

"Yes, m'lady," the footman said, all business again.

Afterward when she and Polly were alone, sunning themselves on the camomile lawn, the maidservant said, "You'll tell me now that my John's gone, won't you, m'lady?"

Lucinda shook her head. "No, Polly, I meant what I said. The Master's true identity will remain a secret until we are back in London, but rest assured he is a titled gentleman. But even if he weren't, I should be content."

"Is his name really Robert?" Polly asked.

"It is one of his Christian names," Lucinda replied, with a smile. "He has two others as well."

"He is a real gentleman," Polly said, sounding impressed.

Everyone knew that only *real* gentlemen had several Christian names.

The Master returned from a successful day in an excellent mood. He and Lucinda sat that evening dining at opposite ends of the highboard in the Great Hall. It was the first time she had been invited into the hall.

"As I rode back from Lord Bowen's today," he began, "I had an inspiration, my pet. I believe I can save you from being publicly ravished by those three villains who seek to marry you. I cannot, however, be certain it will work, but I believe, knowing the personalities involved, that I can tweak their pride so that they will not embarrass you."

"How?" she demanded of him.

"I do not want to tell you," he said. "Better it not appear as if you and I are in collusion, Lucinda."

"As much as I should like to avoid having any of the trio use my body, if I do not allow it, how can I have my revenge upon them? I want them always to remember I was the best, and the most memorable, fuck any of them ever had. Each time they couple with a woman after, I want them to remember me and ache with my loss. If you save me from them, then how can I accomplish what I have set out to do?"

"I may not be able to save you," he reiterated. "Their lust for you may overcome their vanity and their hauteur. You may well have to yield to them, but *if* I can rescue you from such a fate, you can still accomplish your purpose. I shall tell the assembled that night that your brother will announce your betrothal the night of Whitley's ball. That ball celebrates the end of the fall hunting season and the return to London of society's most important denizens. Everyone who is anyone will be there, my pet. What a coup for the winner of your fair hand to have your betrothal announced that night. And you may keep your swains eager before that evening. Privately, of course, but if I can keep you from public humiliation, Lucinda, I should like to do it," The Master told her. "And then when no announcement is forthcoming, what delicious public humiliation for the trio, for you may be absolutely certain each will have bragged to his friends that it is he you will choose. Then when they come to you outraged afterward, you can threaten to expose the Devil's Disciples and their wicked ways."

She was touched by his concern. Perhaps she could accomplish her purpose without whoring before an audience. Someday she would have children. Those offspring must eventually be matched with their own peers. If the gentlemen of the Devil's Disciples remembered her most vulgar performances, who would her own children wed one day? "See if you can save me," she said to him quietly.

He nodded, and then said, "But in the event I cannot, Lucinda, there is one more performance you must be taught. We will begin in the morning. In preparation I shall leave you to sleep tonight."

The following day she was led early, and without her breakfast, back into the hall, clothed only in her night garment and house slippers. A device had been placed in the center of the room, the likes of which she had never before seen. It was his own design, he told her, and he called it the Maiden Tamer.

A sturdy pole, adjustable he explained, was set in a heavy marble rectangle of a base. Attached to the pole was a wide rounded bar forming a T shape The bar was well wrapped and padded with lamb's wool covered in black velvet. Lucinda saw the manacles at either end, also adjustable, he said. In the base were foot clamps into which she was to place her feet. It was a rather frightening contraption. Brave as she was, even Lucinda was a bit taken aback by The Master's Maiden Tamer.

"Come, my pet, and get up," he said, taking her hand, and helping her onto the base. "Now, remove your garment so we may make the necessary adjustments." She complied as he lowered the crosspiece just slightly and carefully bent her over it, then raised her up again and lowered the bar a bit more. "Now, try bending over it again," he told her, and when she had done so, he nodded, satisfied. "Stretch your arms out,

Lucinda, and let us see where the manacles are to go." She obeyed, and in short order found herself neatly constrained. The manacles, however, were lined in thick, soft lamb's wool, and therefore did not chafe her. "Lastly," he said, his hand smoothing over her bare bottom, "we must affix your feet into the foot clamps. Spread your legs, Lucinda, wider, wider, ah, that is perfect!"

She felt her legs restrained, but as she was wearing her slippers, and the foot clamps, like the manacles, were lined, there was no pain. The position she had now attained was one of perfect submission to The Master. "Dare I ask what you mean to do now?" she laughed nervously.

"Ah, you are concerned," he said. "This is why I decided we must practice on the chance I cannot save you. You don't have to be afraid, Lucinda. It is just a rather colorful means by which you are prepared to be fucked. First, of course, you will be strapped with a good Scottish tawse. Spanking doesn't do for a lady so restrained. Let me show you the leather." He moved over to a chair and lifted what appeared to be a belt from it, but upon closer examination she could see it was much broader. "It is six inches wide," he said. "It has been split four inches up into half-inch thongs that have been tied with small knots. It will not break your skin, but it will, used properly, heat the bottom nicely, and prepare you to be fucked. Indeed, if you respond as I believe you will, you will be most eager. Shall we begin, my pet?"

"Wait!" she cried. "If I must submit to this before the Devil's Disciples, who will wield the tawse?"

"I will," he assured her. "I should not allow any of them to do so. Men not used to such devices have a tendency to become over enthusiastic in the application of punishment and harm their victims. That is not the purpose of it. The function of the tawse is to arouse, with the intention of making the recipient excited and ready to accept a good sturdy cock up her cunt."

"I see," Lucinda replied, but she thought it really quite unnecessary, and said so to him. "After all, if a woman loves a man, she is eager to make love with him. She needs no stimulus other than her passions."

"I agree," he said. "Out there are those men who don't, either because they need to see a woman humbled by such punishment, or the woman herself is cold, without desire, and needs such harsh excitement to be aroused. The gentlemen of the Devil's Disciples are jaded in their tastes. This sort of drama pleases and excites them. In the event I cannot prevent your ravishment before them, you must be prepared for what I will have to do. Are you ready now, Lucinda?"

She swallowed nervously, and said in a small voice, "Yes." She heard the sound of the leather as it swung through the air to make firm contact with her bottom. It stung her, and she squealed. A second, and a third blow made contact. She felt her flesh beginning to grow warm. The narrow, knotted thongs peppered her hapless flesh, causing it to feel as if it were afire. Lucinda bit her lip to prevent crying out.

"Don't try to be brave," he advised her. "They will like it if after a few smacks you begin to howl a bit." He laid the leather across her bottom again.

"Ohhhh!" Lucinda cried out, half in jest, half in hurt.

"Excellent, my pet," he approved, and gave her two more hard spanks with the tawse. Then he reached beneath her furry quim, pushing a finger between her nether lips. She was already moist, but not yet wet enough. He caressed her buttocks four more times with the tawse while Lucinda sobbed most convincingly. A brief second inspection of her privates now told him she was very ready to be mounted. Tossing the tawse aside, he loosed his male member, grasped her hips, and slid his love lance into her juicy cunt. Her bottom pressing into him was hot, the skin a deep pink. "Ahhh, that is good, my pet," he groaned as he sank into her.

"Ohhh, yes!" Lucinda agreed. "It is delicious, Master!"

"Do you want to be fucked?" he whispered wickedly in her ear. Then his tongue tickled it, and his breath came hotly.

"Ohhh, yes!" she replied. "I want to be fucked, Master!" "And so you shall, my pet," he told her. Then he began to piston her slowly, his big cock pushing deep, withdrawing, then pushing into her once again.

"Faster, you devil!" she cried. *"Faster!"* She could feel the long, hard love lance delving within her love passage. Instinctively she arched her back slightly, the muscles within her hot pathway tightening about his thick cock, holding it prisoner a moment, then releasing him.

"Ahhhh, Lucinda!" he cried out. "You arc killing me with your magnificent sweetness." He relinquished his hold upon her hips as he lay over her and reaching down grasped her breasts in his hands, fondling them most desperately.

It was all too much for Lucinda. The tawsing had brought her to a level of excitement she had never before attained. His hands on her breasts only increased the thrill. The relentless pumping of his wonderful cock set her to moaning. She soared with the most absolute, and perfect pleasure she had ever known. Her body shuddered violently, and she came, her juices seemingly endless in her delight. One conscious thought remained. *He had to save her!*

The Master felt her crowning the head of his hungry cock with her juices. With a cry he released his own, his hands squeezing her breasts hard before moving back to grasp her hips, to piston her a final few timcs before he lost himself in her incredible sweetness. *He had to save her!*

He lay bent over her, panting for a short time before he slowly raised himself up. Lucinda was half-conscious, hung over the Maiden Tamer, in a posture of complete submission. Only her breathing indicated to him that he hadn't killed her. He began to undo her bonds immediately.

"Are you all right?" he asked her anxiously, and pulling her free he picked her up, carrying her across the Great Hall. Seating himself in a chair, he cradled the semiconscious woman. "Lucinda! Speak to me, my pet! Are you all right?"

She sighed a deep sigh of utter contentment and slowly

opened her deep blue eyes. "Of course I am all right, Robert," she told him calmly. "Why would I not be? Ohh, my darling, that was the most marvelous fuck I have ever had! The bar is a bit uncomfortable on the middle, but it was all worth it. You do not, however, have to spank me to arouse me, although I will admit to you that the novelty of it was most stimulating." She reached up and stroked his cheek, her fingers toying mischievously with his mask. "You are a wonderful lover, Robert. Why do you allow the fact you have small funds to keep you from marrying? This estate is a wonderful place. I could live here the rest of my life, never again see London and be happy. Certainly there is some girl you might love who would do the same for you alone."

His heart almost broke. She could be happy here. She was happy here. He loved her, but he could not for honor's sake admit to it. "There is no one," he said stonily, and then he tipped her from his lap almost impatiently. "Put your gown back on, Lucinda. There is nothing more I can teach you. Go, and get dressed, and we will ride."

"When is the full moon?" she queried as she slid the night garment back over her naked body. It had to be near, she knew, for she had been watching the waxing of the moon each night from her window

"In three days' time, my pet," he told her.

Three days. She had three days left with him. Three days of this most glorious summer before she must participate in a ridiculous episode that she was actually dreading. She wasn't fearful of being made love to, but what her three suitors wanted of her wasn't love. It was revenge for making them the laughingstock of London society at last spring's season. She wished now she had never gone, except if she hadn't, she would never have met the man she now loved so desperately that she was almost tempted to admit her love to him. But she couldn't. If she did, and he reciprocated her feelings—and she suspected he might, for why else had he decided to save her— would it not give him great pain if his plan, whatever it was, didn't work? If she had to submit to the duke, the marquess, and Lord Bertram before a leering crowd of gentlemen? Lucinda had never felt nearer to crying in her entire life.

The next few days passed more quickly than she would have wanted. They spent the time together, riding out over the fields, now summer-weary. He showed her the ungelded male yearling that was being sent to Turkey. It was a beautiful young animal the same rich chestnut color as her hair. It snuffled an apple from her hand, its soft muzzle tickling her palm. At night they made passionate love together, but he still departed for his own chamber lest the temptation to see his face overcome her while he slept.

"You swear to me on your honor that you will come to London to the Whitley ball," she said. Then, "You can obtain an invitation, can't you, Robert?"

"My friend, Lord Bowen, will arrange it, my pet," he told her, kissing her brow. "Is it that important to you, Lucinda?"

"It is the most important thing in the world to me, Robert," she told him.

"Why?" he queried her, curious.

"You have played the role of The Master for the Devil's Disciples for several years now," she began. "You have said I am to be your last pupil no matter the consequences. I believe that indicates that you have a conscience of sorts, sir. You know what you have done is wrong. The rich and the powerful have no God-given rights to abuse the poor and the helpless. Not that that has ever stopped them, nor will it, I suspect, in years to come. If you can save me from the lustful desires of my three suitors tomorrow night, even if you cannot, I shall give them a public set-down in London such as they cannot imagine. Would you not like to be there for that, Robert? Is it not a fitting and a just end to your career as The Master?"

"They will find another man to play The Master," he said.

"Perhaps, but perhaps not. I intend using my brother, the good Bishop of Wellington, to dismantle the Devil's Disciples. If he does not, I shall expose him and his cronies to the

Archbishop of Canterbury, even if it means revealing my own shame. The Devil's Disciples shall abuse no more young women!" she finished firmly.

He burst out laughing, and then he kissed her soundly. "Lucinda, my pet, you swore to me that I should not master you, and by God, I have not! I cannot tell you how happy that makes me." Then he kissed her again, tumbling her onto her back with a chuckle. "I want to fuck you, my adorable little firebrand. Would you like that? A final fuck before I must send you back to London?"

"Come here to me, my wonderful master," Lucinda purred at him, drawing him down into the circle of her arms. "Ohh yes! That is very, *very* nice," she encouraged him as his lips and his tongue hungrily mouthed her lips, her straining throat, her breasts.

He suckled upon her nipples. He could almost taste sweetness from the hardened little nubs atop the soft mounds of her bosom. His lips moved down her torso, kissing, licking, nipping teasingly. She murmured encouragement to him. He nuzzled the wonderful dark, curly bush of curls atop her plump mound, sliding his long body down and between her milky white thighs. Her nether lips were already moist, a tiny pearl of silvery cum seeping from between them. He opened her tenderly and looked upon the rosy coral flesh for the first time. He had never used her in this fashion, for this was a lover's privilege, not a master's. Her little clit stood at attention, almost throbbing before his eyes. Bending forward, he began to lick it hungrily, then suck upon it.

Lucinda cried out with undisguised pleasure. Her fingers tangled themselves into his thick dark hair, kneading at his scalp desperately. "Oh, God, yes!" she sobbed. *"Yes!"* She felt his teeth gently grazing her, and she shuddered with delight.

Finally he could bear no more of their love play. Her nails were digging into his shoulders indicating her need, and his need was every bit as great. He pulled himself up and, slipping between her open legs, thrust his cock deep into her hot, wet love sheath, smiling as she sighed deeply beneath him. Slowly at first, and then more quickly he pistoned her, and Lucinda scored his back with her nails in her passion. Her teeth sank into his shoulder.

He was hard. His great cock probed deeply into her soft, yielding flesh. She sobbed with her need for him. This couldn't be the last time. It couldn't be. *She wouldn't let it!* She tightened herself around him as if she could never let him go. He groaned, and she wrapped her legs about his torso, sobbing. She was going to be the best fuck he had ever had, and when her revenge was complete, she would marry him. *And he would want her!* Then they came together in a blinding explosion of sensual delight that left them both half-conscious for several minutes afterward. *I love you,* Lucinda whispered in her heart, not knowing that he was silently whispering the same words to himself as his arms tightened about her comfortingly, and they slept.

When Lucinda awoke he was gone. The pillow where his head had rested was cold, but upon it lay a perfect white rose. She picked it up and smelled its heady fragrance, a smile upon her lips as she remembered their passion the night before. Now, however, it was morning. This night she would face her persecutors. Whatever happened, she would still triumph over them, but she hoped with all of her heart that she could be saved from their lust, which would be like a night jar washing over her and befouling her. But if he could not dissuade those three buffoons, they would live to regret their actions. That, Lucinda promised herself.

"Master says you are to have a nice bath, and then he has picked out the garments you will wear tonight," Polly told her mistress. "Ohh, just think, m'lady. Tomorrow we'll be on our way back to London!"

"Yes," Lucinda replied, "but you'll not be long there, Poll. You'll return to the country by Christmas and be in your new home."

"I won't mind," Polly responded, "but it will be nice to see old Londontown a final time. I'm used to the country, m'lady, and now I've got me John. It's the quiet life for us both."

She took a long, leisurely bath, and Polly washed her hair. Lucinda was very surprised by the garments she found he had chosen. There was a delicate cambric chemise edged in lace on the sleeves over which she wore a small corset of flowered white silk that Polly laced up the back. Next came a silk petticoat, then a hooped underskirt support of bent wood. Over it was a quilted satin underskirt, cream with lavender flowers. Lucinda's gown, its skirts looped up on either side to show the underskirt, was embroidered lavender silk. It had a deep, round scooped neckline allowing her breasts to swell slightly over the top, pushed up by her corset. The sleeves were tight to the elbow, and then a waterfall of creamy lace called *engageants* fell almost to her wrists below the sleeves. Her provocative neckline was edged in lace as well. Three bows adorned her pleated bodice, and there was a matching bow on each sleeve just above the *engageants*. She wore low-heeled slippers of cream silk on her feet and cream-colored silk stockings with rose garters. Her chestnut hair was piled high with several ringlets that tumbled down reaching her shoulders. Polly dressed it with fresh flowers. Pearl earbobs were fastened into her ears, and a filigreed gold cross on a chain was fastened about her slender neck.

Lucinda looked at herself in the full-length mirror in her bedchamber. "I look like the respectable lady I am," she said, and then she turned to The Master, who had just entered the room. "Why? Should I not be half-naked, or in something diaphanous meant to titillate?"

"No," he told her. "Not if my plan is meant to succeed, my pet. Tonight you must look and act the perfect lady. Now, remember to immediately obey every order I give you so it may seem as if you are properly mastered."

"What if your plan doesn't succeed?" she asked a final time.

"Then, my pet, you will find yourself stripped naked and bent over the Maiden Tamer so your suitors may have at you," he replied harshly. "So play your part well, Lucinda, that we may triumph over the Devil's Disciples this night." He took her hand up and kissed it. "One more thing, my pet. Polly, the patches, please." The maid handed him a small open box, and The Master extracted two black, heart-shaped patches which Polly dabbed with glue. The first he affixed to her left cheekbone. The second he put upon the swell of her right breast. "There, my pet, now you are ready," he said with a small smile.

He led her from the house, through the garden and the orchard, reversing their journey the first night she had come here. There was no long summer twilight for it was mid-September. Above them the full moon shone brightly, silvering the landscape around them. The little amphitheater was bright with flickering torches; its stands filled again with gentlemen in their dark, hooded cloaks. The Master wore his tight, dark breeches, his cock hanging boldly out, his white cambric shirt opened at the neck. As he led Lucinda forward, there was a gasp of surprise from his audience.

The Master bowed to them, and then said, "My lords, I present to you tonight, Lady Lucinda Harrington, well-mastered now, and as tamed as any good house kitten should be. Make your curtsey to the Devil's Disciples, my pet."

Lucinda curtsied low, her head bent slightly, but not so low that the gentlemen were denied a tantalizing view of her full breasts. She swallowed a giggle as many of them leaned forward eagerly to view the creamy swell of flesh with its shadowed dark valley. Their hot eyes seemed to be drawn to the little heart patch.

"We will begin, my lords, when you have put your hoods back," The Master announced.

Lucinda kept her face impassive as the hoods were flung back, and the faces, most of them familiar, were revealed. There was her brother, George, the saintly bishop, in the front row next to her three suitors. Oh, George would suffer for his perfidy, Lucinda thought, as eyes lowered, she considered her revenge.

"Why is she not naked?" the Duke of Rexford demanded.

"Aye, and where is the Maiden Tamer?" Lord Bertram called out.

"Hear me out, my lords," The Master said to them. "In the past you have brought me young women of low birth. I have mastered them for you, and you have had your sport. I have never failed you. This woman, however, is a real lady. While I have mastered her for you, I do not think you should use her publicly before our little club."

"And why not?" the Marquess of Hargrave wanted to know.

"Do you each still hope that Lady Lucinda will choose you for her husband, my lords?"

"Aye!" the trio exclaimed with one voice.

"And, my lords, will the one she chooses be content knowing the other two have had her publicly before most of their friends, the cream of society? Or does the lucky gentleman intend keeping the lady down in the country forever? And if her first child is born within the first year of the marriage, can the lucky gentleman be certain that the baby is his?"

"You have had her," the Duke of Rexford said. He sounded a bit irritated.

"That is true, my lord; but you do not know who I am, and the proper precautions were taken. Only one man among you knows who I am. If you met me at White's, or at a ball, you would not recognize me as The Master. None of you would, but for the one gentleman. But you all recognize each other, and know who holds membership in the Devil's Disciples, or the Hellfire. If you three publicly ravish Lady Lucinda tonight before your peers, you cannot stop the gossip that will ensue. The lady's reputation will be ruined, as will that of her husband. I know you do not want that.

"Allow me to suggest another way. The lady has been mastered by me, and you have had your revenge in part. On November fifteenth the Countess of Whitley holds her end of hunting season ball in London. We shall all be there. Lady Lucinda has promised me that at that ball her brother, George, will announce her betrothal. In the meantime she has agreed to receive you all as callers in her home at Number Three Traleigh Square, London. I am willing to accept the lady's word, so I am certain that the rest of you must. No one will be embarrassed by this. No one but the Devil's Disciples will know she has been with me these past three months and not in Ireland with her sister. As for you gentlemen, you will certainly not tell for fear your wives, daughters, sisters, mothers and mistresses learn of your lustful little peccadillos."

He looked to the duke, the marquess, and Lord Bertram. "Will you forgo your immediate pleasure, my lords, for all of our sakes?"

"I want to hear the lady agree to this," Lord Bertram said.

"My pet," The Master said, "will you give your suitors your word that you will announce your betrothal at the Countess of Whitley's ball in November?"

"You have my word on it, my lords, and I will indeed welcome you to Traleigh Square when I return to London. It will be my pleasure, I assure you," she purred seductively, and then she curtsied to them.

"I trust you have arranged suitable entertainment in place of Lady Lucinda?" the Duke of Rexford grumbled. Then he waved his hand. "I will agree to The Master's proposal. I certainly don't want it said that Bertram got to bugger my wife before I did."

"I agree as well," the Marquess of Hargrave said.

"And I," Lord Bertram responded.

"Very well, my lords, then it is settled. John! Escort Lady Lucinda back to the house at once. As for you, my lords, when did you ever visit me that I did not provide suitable entertainment for you?" He clapped his hands, and at once a troupe of bare-legged gypsy girls ran into the arena and began to dance, flinging their skirts in the air to display rounded brown buttocks and dark-furred quims. "For starters, my lords," The Master said with a grin. "And later we will be auctioning off a most willing young virgin from the village. You all know her sisters quite well. We will auction both of her virginities, her cunt and her arse. And, of course, we have both village lads and lasses available for your pleasure. The wine barrels are filled with the finest of aphrodisiacs. I shall rejoin you as soon as I have ascertained Lady Lucinda is safely within the house and my randy footmen are not fucking her poor young maid, Polly, a final time."

He hurried off, leaving the Devil's Disciples to their lustful and bacchanalian revels. He reached the house just behind Lucinda and John.

She flung herself into his arms and kissed him most passionately. "Thank you, my lord," Lucinda told him happily.

"I must attend to my guests," he said. "I shall not see you again, Lucinda. You will leave at first light tomorrow for London. All has been arranged for your journey. I understand that John will go with you. We shall not meet again." He gently removed her arms from about his neck.

"We shall meet at the Countess of Whitley's ball, sir. You have promised me, and I know you will keep your promise."

He kissed her hand, smiling almost ruefully. "I will," he agreed.

"Then, we shall meet again, for I shall find you there," she told him.

Chapter Five

Lady Lucinda Harrington's traveling carriage drew up before the well-scrubbed white marble steps of Three Traleigh Square, on a bright September afternoon. The coach had barely drawn

to a stop when the door to the house opened, and several footmen, clad in dark blue and silver livery, ran out to greet it.
John, seated with the coachman on the box, raised an inquir-
ing eyebrow, for he had been told Lady Lucinda would be hir-
ing new servants herself. The door to the vehicle was opened,
the steps pulled down, and a footman's hand steadying hers,
Lady Lucinda descended from the coach, shaking her skirts
free of wrinkles.

"Who are you?" she demanded of the footman.

"James, m'lady. The bishop and his wife are awaiting you
inside." He led the way.

So, Lucinda thought, George and his better half are here. I
certainly hope they are not thinking of remaining. I am hardly
ready to receive visitors, and certainly do not want house-
guests while I *entertain* my eager suitors. She hurried up the
two marble steps, and into the bright hallway of her house.

"Luci, m'dear!" Her brother came forward smiling. "How
was Ireland, and how is darling Julia?" He beamed approv-
ingly at her.

"My summer was quite enlightening, Georgie," Lucinda responded coolly, moving past her brother to embrace her sister-
in-law. "Caro, you are blooming, dearest. How kind of you to
come up from Wellington. Where are you staying? At your sister's? And should you be traveling at this late date in your con-
finement?"

"Why, Luci, we are staying here," her sister-in-law said nervously.

"You cannot," Lucinda said. "I have not yet hired any servants. I have just my Polly and her intended, John, who acts as
my footman." She turned to her brother again. "Georgie, can
you get a license for Polly and John so they can be married
right away? They will be returning to the country after the
Whitley ball. John is to take over his father's smithy. Isn't it
lovely for our Polly?" She smiled brightly at her brother, who
was beginning to look confused.

"But, Luci, m'dear, the duke sent over enough servants for

your little house," he said. "There is no need for you to be bothered interviewing and employing any others."

"George, I am shocked at you. I cannot take such a generous gift from Rexford. Why, Hargrave and Bertram would think I had made a decision without giving them a fair hearing. No! No! No! No! Rexford's servants must leave my house this very day and return to their master." She turned again, and pinned the attending footman with a sharp look. "James, gather your people up and return to your master's house immediately."

"Ohh, Lucinda," her sister-in-law wailed, "you will insult the duke, I fear."

"It is he who has insulted me by suggesting I would accept such a gift, generous as it was meant to be," Lucinda responded. "I shall make my own decisions as I always have."

"You do not seem much changed, Luci," her brother said suspiciously.

"Why on earth would a summer at Julia's change me, Georgie?" she replied innocently. "I am the same woman as ever." She smiled wickedly at him, pleased to see him pale.

"Your promise, Luci. You do mean to keep your promise, don't you?" He was definitely distressed now.

"What promise?" her sister-in-law inquired.

"I promised Georgie before I left London in June that I would reconsider the possibility of remarrying, and I have. Georgie will announce my betrothal at the Countess of Whitley's ball in November, Caro. I would never break a promise to my dearest and most favorite brother."

"Ohh, how exciting!" her sister-in-law cried. "Who have you chosen, Lucinda? Is it Rexford, Hargrave, or Bertram? Do tell us!"

Lucinda laughed, and shook her head. "I shall tell no one until the night of the ball," she said. "Besides, I have not yet decided. You and Georgie may remain the night, Caro, but tomorrow you must return home to Wellington. I am a respectable widow about to be courted again, and I don't want a family about inhibiting my suitors."

Caroline Worth giggled. "Lucinda, you are truly dreadful! Will you try them all, and make your decision by those means?"

"Why, Caro, what on earth do you mean?" Lucinda said primly, but her eyes were brimming with merriment.

"If you send Rexford's servants away, who is to cook dinner?" the portly bishop demanded

"Dinner is probably already prepared," Lucinda said. "Polly and John can serve us. Caro, you and Georgie have your servants with you, I'm certain. So we shall muddle through nicely. I will write a note to Rexford, thanking him for his generosity, but explaining why I cannot possibly accept it. John, is the luggage unloaded?"

"Yes, m'lady," the footman said.

"Polly, fetch my writing box, and tell James he is not to depart without my note to the duke, his master."

"Yes, m'lady," Polly replied with a curtsey.

"Now," Lucinda said, "let us adjourn into the salon."

In the morning her brother and his wife departed much to Lucinda's relief. "We need servants," Lucinda told John and Polly. "Not a great staff, but a good one."

"What will you need?" John asked her. He had worked in Lord Bowen's London house for six years prior to going to The Master.

"It's a small household," Lucinda considered. "A butler, perferably one who can read, write and keep the accounts," she began. "Six footmen, two footboys, a cook, a housekeeper, two chambermaids, three housemaids, a laundry maid, two scullery maids. Where will you find them?"

"I know plenty of servants in many of the big houses. There's always someone looking to move up the ladder, or unhappy with their position. I'll have us staffed in just a few days, m'lady. I'll pick only the best and bring 'em to you to interview."

John was as good as his word, but her lack of a staff that first week in London allowed Lucinda to avoid her eager suitors for several days, although they all called upon her the very next day after George had departed back to Wellington. Her footman showed the trio into Lucinda's morning room, for they had all arrived at her door at practically the same moment, their carriages drawing up one behind the other. Lucinda greeted them in an embroidered, rose-colored, sackback dress with lace edging about the neckline. They tumbled into the room like a group of unruly puppies in their eagerness to see her, and gain her favor.

"My lords!" Lucinda's hand went to her throat as if surprised. "You take me unawares! I am hardly ready to receive visitors, even such distinguished gentlemen as yourselves. Please do be seated. May I offer you some sherry? John, please pour for our guests." She smiled at them and shrugged prettily. "I fear I am practically servantless at the moment and not able to properly entertain you."

"You should not be without servants if you had accepted the staff I sent you," the Duke of Rexford said sharply.

"You sent Lady Lucinda a staff?" Lord Bertram sounded quite offended by the knowledge.

"She sent them back," the duke grumbled.

"As she should have," the Marquess of Hargrave spoke up. "It was extremely cheeky of you, Rexford. Lady Lucinda has not yet, to my knowledge, made her decision."

"No, my lords, I have not," Lucinda told them sweetly. "Instead of judging you so harshly as I did last spring, I am going to give you all an equal chance to win both my hand and my heart. But I must beg you to accept a few little ground rules I think may help us avoid any dissension or confusion. To begin with, I thank you for coming to welcome me back to London." She smiled, and they all beamed back, each convinced that her smile was directed more at him than at his rivals. "I do not, however, wish to see any of you again until next week. I need time to hire my staff and get my house in order. Why, several of the dinner plates from Dr. Wall's pottery in Worcester arrived broken!"

"How dreadful," Lord Bertram said.

"Allow me to replace them," the duke said.

"Do you think you can purchase Lady Lucinda's favor?" the marquess demanded angrily of the duke.

"My lords! My lords! Please, I beg you, do not quarrel," Lucinda pleaded prettily, "but as you seem unable to be civil with one another, you will understand my next request of you. Each of you will call upon me twice a week. The duke on Mondays and Thursdays. The marquess on Tuesdays and Fridays. Lord Bertram on Wednesdays and Saturdays. Sunday I reserve for myself to attend church and rest. We will begin with a morning call. Then we shall move to afternoon tea, and then, perhaps, an evening party. That way you shall each have an equal chance with me. We shall be seen in public enough so that when my brother announces my betrothal none will think it strange, for they will have seen that we have resolved our former differences of last season." She smiled again at them. "I do think it is a most sensible plan, my lords."

"Very sensible!" the duke agreed.

"Capital." The marquess nodded.

"Practical," Lord Bertram approved.

Lucinda arose from the settee where she had been sitting. "Then, my lords, until next week when we begin anew." She held out her hand to them, and each kissed it as she murmured, "Good day, my lord duke. Good day, my lord marquess. Good day, Lord Bertram." And they were gone.

As Lucinda had come up to town in her brother's traveling carriage, she was now without transport. She purchased a beautiful little town coach that could seat four. It was not new, but had been previously owned by a gentleman who had recently retired to the country. It was in excellent condition. Four matching gray horses were included in the sale, as was the former owner's coachman. The coach and horses were stabled two streets away with the coachman, who lived above the stables. By the end of her first week back in London, her household was in order, and she had even found a fashionable modiste to make her some new gowns. Lucinda was ready to receive her suitors. It was six weeks until the Countess of Whitely's ball.

On Sunday evening Lucinda called John and Polly to her. "I promised you when we arrived in London I should tell you the identity of The Master. It will be *our* secret. The gentleman in question is Lucian Robert Charles Phillips, the Earl of Stanton."

"But what good does it do you, m'lady," Polly said, "if you are never to see him again and must marry another?"

"Polly, did I not say I would not have that trio of villains? You must trust me. I promised my brother he would announce my betrothal at the Whitley ball. I did not say to whom that betrothal would be."

"And will his lordship be agreeable?" John asked, suddenly understanding his mistress's plan.

Lucinda chuckled. "Do you think he won't be, John?" she replied.

Now it was the footman who chuckled. "He'll be surprised, m'lady, he will. You'll forgive me if I say that you're a deep one. But I don't think he'll be unhappy about such a turn of events."

"This does not go beyond this room," Lucinda told them, and they both nodded. "Now, the first banns for your marriage were read this morning in church. Two more Sundays, then you will marry, my dears, and you shall have a hundred pounds from me as a wedding gift."

The two servants thanked her profusely. A hundred pounds was a very, very generous gift.

The following morning the Duke of Rexford arrived at eleven to be ushered into Lucinda's bedchamber. She was sitting up in her bed, a lacy shawl about her shoulders, having her breakfast. She smiled, and held out her hand to him. "Richard, good morning! Is it that late already? I have had such a busy week last week and am exhausted."

He kissed her hand, his eyes lingering at the spot where the shawl's two sides met. He was certain her breasts were bare beneath. "You look as fresh as a daisy, my dear," he said, sitting on the edge of her bed, but careful not to tilt her breakfast tray. "Polly, get his lordship a saucer of tea. I keep an excellent stock of leaf that my brother William sends from India."

"When are you going to cease this game and agree to marry me, Lucinda?" he said.

"Now, Richard, you must not press me. I shall not make my decision until the very night of the Whitley ball." She smiled seductively.

"Yer tea, yer lordship," Polly said, pushing the fragile cup and its deep saucer into his hand.

On Tuesday Lucinda entertained the Marquess of Hargrave in her back garden as she cut roses, the dew still upon them.

On Wednesday Lord Bertram arrived to take her for a ride through the park in his open carriage.

Thursday the duke cornered her in her morning room and, pushing her to the yellow settee, fondled her breasts. She scolded him prettily.

Friday the marquess stole a kiss.

Saturday Lord Bertram attempted to put his hand beneath her skirts and was slapped lightly for his trouble, but she gave him a kiss on the cheek to assure him there were no hard feelings.

Sunday Lucinda arrived at church to discover her three suitors waiting for her in her pew. She did, however, go home alone.

The next week was much the same, but Lucinda did manage to get the gentlemen to appear in public with her more, assuring them it was better that they did. The third week afternoon visits began, and Lucinda liked it a great deal more, for she was able to convince her suitors to take her riding in the park which kept them out of the house. The fourth week, however, each was insistent upon staying for tea after they returned Lucinda home. Only the presence of the footmen serving, and Polly hovering, kept her from their lustful advances.

Four weeks into this most public courtship, Lucinda began appearing at parties with her suitors in tow. Now it was impossible to keep them separated, and she was only able to keep to her schedule by allowing one of them to escort her home each evening.

The carriage rides back to Traleigh Square were passionate. Cooped within the closed coach with the duke, the marquess, or Lord Bertram, Lucinda had no choice but to yield to their overtures. She did so coyly, sighing deeply when she was kissed, murmuring as her bosom was fondled hotly by eager hands. The marquess surprised her one night, getting his hand beneath her gown and its petticoats to frig her quite enthusiastically until she came. Then, despite his portly figure, he managed to kneel before her and, sticking his head beneath her gown, licked and sucked at her until she came again. Lucinda did not hold back or demur. She enjoyed the release he gave her and told him so.

"When we are wed, my dear," the marquess assured her, "I shall give you even greater pleasure."

It was obvious he could not keep his little triumph to himself. Several days later on their journey home from a delightful evening of card playing, the duke directed his coachman to drive through the park. In the darkness of the carriage, he lifted her voluminous skirts, then putting her, spread-legged, upon his lap, fucked her with vigor even as he tongued her nipples. Afterward he praised her excitement as quite stimulating to him and, handing her out of the vehicle, escorted her to her door, kissing her hand chastely.

It was obvious now that Lord Bertram would certainly accost her next, and he did not disappoint. This time in the darkened carriage she was set down on her knees before her swane and instructed to suck his cock until it was dry. She did so, and was praised by the gentleman for her stellar performance. "The Master has trained you admirably," he declared.

To spare herself any more of these evening onslaughts from her suitors, Lucinda began inviting them to dinner. In her dining room, surrounded by the servants, they could not assault her. But she could not always remain at home as it was very necessary she be seen in public with them.

She took to devising ways of avoiding their lust. One evening she insisted they all accompany her home. Another evening she cried off with the headache and remained home. A third she grew ill early on in the evening and, loudly insisting her escort remain at the gambling tables, went home alone. And all the while she smiled, and twinkled, and flirted with each of them until each was convinced he would be the winner of her hand.

The banns having been read the required number of times, Polly and John were married on a Monday morning by a local vicar. Lucinda had given them both the day off. She stood as one of their witnesses, afterward walking back to Traleigh Square with two footmen in attendance, leaving the newly-weds to themselves for the day. Her household was all agog with her generosity and her kindness to the two servants.

"She's a real lady," the cook said that evening in the servants' hall. "We're lucky, we are!"

Several days before the Whitley ball, John told his mistress that the Earl of Stanton had arrived at Lord Bowen's house. They would be at the musicale at Lord Carstairs' this evening. Now was her chance to see what he really looked like, Lucinda thought happily. She had missed him, and she had missed his passion. She dressed carefully that evening, her gown in the latest fashionable hue, a flame color called "Burnt Opera House." With her pale skin and her rich, dark chestnut hair, she was quite striking.

Her escort that evening was the marquess. As he was not the brightest of fellows, she was able to ask him in innocent tones, "Who is the Earl of Stanton, Hamlet dearest? I hear he breeds wonderful horses, and I am thinking of purchasing a mare for myself. My footman, John, said he is staying at Lord Bowen's."

The Marquess of Hargrave looked about the salon. "Stanton up from the country? I don't think he's been to London in ten years. A bit of a recluse, but you're right, darling girl, he breeds good horseflesh. Ahh, there he is, next to Bowen, with that lovely piece of fluff hanging on his every word. Lady Grayson is said to be very generous with her favors. Elderly husband, y'know. Would you like to be introduced, Lucinda?"

"Not really," Lucinda said, sounding bored. "I am not ready yet to buy, and when I am, perhaps it is my husband who will gift me with a mare." She smiled up at him meaningfully and tapped his arm archly with her ivory fan, even as her lashes brushed her cheek. Then after a few minutes she asked him to allow her to sit quietly in the rear of the salon as she was feeling faint.

"Can I get you anything, Lucinda?" he fretted.

"Perhaps a bit of champagne," she told him weakly, and he hurried off. Lucinda scanned the room swiftly, and then she saw him again. She was utterly astounded. He was the handsomest man she had ever seen in her life. His face was angular and sculpted. His cheekbones high, his chin a square. She hadn't noticed when he was masked how square his chin really was. He had a long, elegant nose. His eyebrows were thick and as black as his wavy hair. The forehead high. The seductive mouth she well remembered, but without his mask he was an entirely different man. All his features came together magnificently. What on earth had John meant by saying he was *nice-looking*. Lucian Phillips, the Earl of Stanton, was a God! They were going to have the most beautiful children.

"Here is your champagne," the marquess said, returning.

She waved him away. "Take me home, Hamlet," she told him. "I am much too ill to remain. My temples are throbbing, and Master Bach's music will only make it worse, I fear."

They made their apologies to Lord and Lady Carstairs. Their hostess remarked pithily once they had departed, "I wonder if she's really got the headache or is simply eager to get into bed with her marquess. Like everyone else in London, I can barely wait for the Whitley ball to learn whom she has chosen."

"The betting at White's is phenomenal," Lord Carstairs told his spouse. "It's two to one on the marquess, and even money on Rexford. Bertram is the long shot at ten to one. She's a fine-looking woman, and whoever she picks, she'll bring him a nice fortune. Harrington left her everything. If I'd known how plump in the pockets he was, I'd have let him court our Livinia."

Overhearing his host, Lord Bowen told his friend, the Earl of Stanton, "She has the town agog. She's a clever bitch, I think. She's given no indication of whom she will favor in the end. Was she fun, Lucian?"

"You know I don't discuss such matters," the Earl of Stanton said coolly. His heart had almost burst through his flowered vest when he had first seen her. She was the most beautiful woman in the world. Would she really be able to recognize him at the Whitley ball? He now regretted his decision not to reveal his face to her that last night.

The next morning flowers were delivered to Lucinda, an armful of roses and lilies. The plain card with them said simply, *Robert*. She tucked it in her pocket, smiling to herself as she directed a maid to find a vase for the flowers so she might arrange them for the morning room.

The day before the Whitley ball Lucinda paid an afternoon call on the Countess of Whitley, Lady Anne. Seated in the august lady's salon, she said, "I have a rather unusual favor to ask of you, madame," and then she explained. "It must, however, remain a secret until the last moment," she concluded her request.

"My dear!" the countess exclaimed. "You have a marvelous flair for the dramatic. The knowledge alone that you will have George announce your betrothal at my ball guaranteed it to be the most sought-after invitation of the autumn season. Why, even the king is coming! *This*, however, will have those who don't gain entry tomorrow night fleeing back to their country estates in abject shame." The Countess of Whitley chuckled richly. "Lucinda, my dear, you shall be the *sucés fou* of the year with this amusing coup." Then she leaned closer to her guest. "Will you tell me *who* it is?" she said eagerly.

"Tomorrow night," Lucinda replied, her blue eyes twinkling.

"You are such a naughty puss," the countess chortled archly.

Lucinda arrived home to find her brother and his wife had arrived from the country. Caroline was only just out of childbed, having delivered a third son, Frederick Augustus, three weeks earlier.

"George and I want you and your husband to be Freddie's godparents," Caroline said cheerfully.

"I am certain that can be arranged," Lucinda replied. Then when her sister-in-law went upstairs to rest, she took her brother aside. "I want you to obtain a special license immediately," she told him.

"What's this?" the Bishop of Wellington demanded of her.

"Is it not plain, Georgie? I want a special license so I may be married. Don't you want me married? I thought that's what my summer was all about. To bring me to my senses so I would remarry."

"But I thought . . ." he began to bluster.

"I know what you thought. You thought I should announce my betrothal and then have a large society wedding," Lucinda said.

"Yes, I did," her brother replied. "After all, your first marriage to Harrington was a small and mean affair. I thought this time you would want something more grand, Luci." He actually looked disappointed, his round face downcast.

"It shall be grand, Georgie, which is why I need a special license, and lord knows I am plump enough in the pocket to afford it," she laughed. "Tomorrow night you will announce my betrothal, and then you will marry me to my intended right there at the Whitley ball. I have already spoken with Lady Anne, and she is thrilled. It seems my behavior has made her little do a huge success even before it is held. She is convinced my marrying in the midst of her ball will raise her to the rank of an unforgettable hostess. A special license allows me to marry without the bother of banns, and in any location, as long as a clergyman performs the ceremony."

"But what will your intended say? And who is your intended, Luci?" the bishop wanted to know.

"Any man who wants to marry me will do so when offered the first opportunity, Georgie. As for who he is, I have said I will not tell even you until the time comes. Be satisfied, brother. After all, you are getting what you wanted. *And,* I no longer shall be your responsibility shortly." She patted his arm. "You must trust me, dearest. I can hardly do anything too awful amid London's creme de la creme."

"Well," the bishop reasoned, "it will certainly be talked of for years to come, Luci. Very well, you shall have your special license, my dear. You have, after all, been a very good girl. I was worried leaving you alone here in London these past six weeks, but I am given to understand that your behavior has been exemplary. There has not been even the slightest hint of scandal."

"Thank you, Georgie," Lucinda replied, amused by his comment. "Now I must leave you. I have a final fitting on my ball gown for tomorrow night."

The bishop smiled, well pleased as she departed the salon. She had always been a minx, his younger sister, but her summer had obviously done her good. He had felt a touch of guilt putting her in the hands of The Master, but obviously it had done her no real harm. While she might still be a bit headstrong, she appeared to be far more reasonable in her attitude.

Her plans for her wedding might be a bit eccentric, but she was right when she said any man she wanted to wed would wed her given the first opportunity. Besides, Lucinda had obviously planned this event most carefully. It was best not to argue with her in this instance. All of the most important people would be there tomorrow night. It would be quite entertaining. And, once she was married, there was no going back. Lucinda would be her husband's problem.

The next day the household was very busy preparing for the ball. The ladies' gowns were checked for any last-minute problems. The skirts ironed perfectly, and the dresses hung carefully. The baths were brought after tea, and the ladies began to prepare for the evening's entertainment. The ball wouldn't begin until nine, and to be precisely on time would be unthinkable, for the hostess and her private party might not be finished dining. The guests would be arriving closer to ten.

Lucinda bathed, and then lay down to rest. Polly would awaken her at half after eight. Lucinda's gown was, she thought, a triumph. She had insisted her modiste come to Traleigh Square and work on it so no one else would see it before the ball. The silvery pink quilted underskirt was hand-painted with delicate wild flowers. The silver overgown was embroidered with the same flowers. The neckline was low-cut and square. The bodice, finely tucked, had three silver bows decorating it. The engageants, attached to the tightly fitted sleeves, were of pale pink lace and decorated with one silver bow each. The skirts came just to her ankle, revealing her pink silk dancing shoes with their silver buckles. Her jewelry was simple. Pink diamonds in her ears and a small pearl and diamond cross about her neck.

"Ohh, m'lady," Polly said admiringly, "'tis a beautiful gown."

"It is, isn't it?" Lucinda agreed. Then she patted her hair. "I like what you have done," she told her maid.

"Jessie, her that is replacing me, showed me how, m'lady. She is very clever with hair. She calls this style a Pompadour Hairdress."

"It suits me," Lucinda decided aloud, turning her head this

way and that. It was really a simple style for all it had been named after the French king's latest mistress. Her rich, dark chestnut hair was combed back from her forehead, and a few curls were then displayed on the side of her head, seemingly pinned with a pink diamond fan.

A knock sounded at the door, and George Worth's head popped into the room. "Are you ready, Luci? It's quarter to ten o'clock."

Polly wrapped a rose velvet pelisse trimmed with dark fur along its hood about her mistress and then handed her a large matching fur muff. "Yer painted fan is in it, and a lawn hand-kerchief, m'lady."

"Make certain the bed is remade with lavender-scented linens, and the wine tray on the table," Lucinda told her maid softly.

"John and I will have it just right, m'lady," Polly said with a wink.

Lucinda's town coach pulled into the long line of carriages waiting to enter the Whitley mansion. Finally they arrived at the door and were handed out of the vehicle by footmen in black-and-gold livery.

"You have the license?" Lucinda asked her brother for the tenth time.

He pulled it from his pocket and waved it beneath her nose. "Are you ready to tell me yet who is the fortunate gentleman, Luci?"

"Not yet," Lucinda said as they entered the house. She and Caroline, who looked quite lovely in several shades of blue, had their cloaks taken by a little maid. They then rejoined George and waited to be announced into the ballroom.

"The most honorable George Worth, Bishop of Wellington, and Mistress Worth. Lady Lucinda Harrington," the major-domo intoned.

Every eye in the great ballroom swung in their direction, and for a brief moment there was utter silence.

"My dears," the Countess of Whitley welcomed them, her

eyes twinkling with anticipation. "I ordered extra flowers, Lucinda darling."

George bowed. His two companions curtsied. Lucinda murmured a soft thank-you. Her heart was pounding wildly. As she passed into the ballroom, she looked about her anxiously. *Where was he?* She couldn't see him anywhere. Dear heaven! Had he decided at the last moment not to come? She saw the Duke of Rexford trying to catch her eye. Lucinda turned away and sought the necessary behind the screen in a corner of the room. She didn't need it; she just wanted to escape her suitors. She allowed herself a few minutes, and then emerged.

"Lord Derek Bowen. Lord Lucian Phillips, Earl of Stanton," the majordomo called out.

Relieved, she saw them enter the ballroom. She began to make her way across the ballroom only to be blocked by her three suitors. "My lords," she said in a tight voice.

"It is time for you tell us, Lucinda," the Duke of Rexford said. "You have played this game and held us at bay for long enough."

"*Not yet!*" she snapped at them and, pushing past the three, once again sought the Earl of Stanton. Reaching him at last, she put her arm through his and looking up at him said, "The flowers were beautiful."

"I thought they suited you," he replied.

"I told you I would find you," she responded. God, he was so handsome.

"And indeed you have, Lucinda. *Now what?*" His green eyes were gazing deeply into her blue ones.

"We will be married," Lucinda told him frankly.

"I am not certain I should wed such a lively lass as yourself, Lucinda. After all, I never could master you," he teased her with a grin.

"You are the only man who has even the faintest chance of *mastering* me, Lucian Charles Phillips. Do you not love me?"

"Oh, yes, Lucinda, I love you desperately," he admitted. "But do you love me, my pet?"

"So much that I was ill when I arrived and you were not here," she told him. "So much that my brother carries a special license in his pocket tonight so he may wed us here and now. Then we shall leave this hall and spend the next few hours in a glorious bout of fucking, my darling master."

"I have missed you," he told her, and bending brushed her lips with his. "Your scheme has great merit, my pet. I agree to it. I think, perhaps, it is time I met the worthy bishop."

"What is going on?" Lord Bowen asked of them.

"Come along, Derek, and you will see," the earl invited.

As they made their way across the ballroom to find George, they were accosted by Lucinda's three suitors, angrily demanding explanations.

Lucinda stopped. "You will get nothing more from me, my Lords," she told them in a hard, cold voice. "I said tonight my brother would announce my betrothal, and so he shall. To the Earl of Stanton. The gentleman I fell in love with this summer past *when in Ireland at my sister Julia's.* We will be wed tonight, here and now! If any of you dares to object, I shall expose the Devil's Disciples and your part in that shameless band of lustful men."

"What of *your* part, Lucinda?" Lord Bertram said.

"I would remind you three that you still need wives to carry on your family name. How do you think the guardians of next season's crop of dewy-eyed debutantes will feel about your wicked activities? How do you think they will react to the knowledge that you kidnapped a gentlewoman, forcing her into carnal bondage, in order to make her choose one of you for a husband? You would be wise, I believe, to hold your tongues and accept my decision . . . *or suffer the consequences.*"

Lord Bertram bowed. "I retire from the field defeated, Lady Lucinda," he said graciously.

Lucinda nodded as graciously, then said to the Marquess of Hargrave, "The Earl of Felton's daughter, Louisa, has a tendre for you, Hamlet. You might have noticed her last season but that I came on the horizon. She is here tonight. I believe she would welcome your addresses. A lady likes nothing more than to comfort a worthy loser."

"She isn't as pretty as you, Lucinda," the marquess said forlornly.

"No, but she has a kind heart and would love you if you would let her." Lucinda gave him her hand. "Goodbye, Hamlet."

"*Bitch!*" snarled the Duke of Rexford. "I am fortunate to have seen your true colors in time!" Then he turned and angrily walked away from Lucinda, the earl, and Lord Bowen.

They continued across the crowded room, finally finding the bishop.

"Get out the license, Georgie," Lucinda told her brother. "The name is Lucian Robert Charles Phillips, Earl of Stanton."

Startled, the bishop looked at the earl. "*Luscious Lucian!*" George Worth exclaimed.

"You know each other?" Lucinda said, surprised.

"We were in the same house at Eton, but Lucian was several years younger than I was. We called him Luscious Lucian because he was frankly the handsomest fellow any of us had ever seen. The women were mad for him, even as a lad of twelve. It has been years, sir!" Then the bishop looked to his sister. "This is the man you will marry? What has happened to the others? How did you meet?"

"Why, we met, Georgie," Lucinda said wickedly, "thanks to you, this summer, *at Julia's.* Lucian was there to look over some of Rafferty's hunters. We fell in love, but I didn't want to tell you because you so had your heart set on my giving the other three another chance. Well, I did, but I have decided that Lucian is the man for me. You had best make the announcement and marry us, for we are both eager to leave on our honeymoon."

Caroline Worth, who had been listening, wide-eyed, to all

of Lucinda's explanations, began to weep delicately. "This is the most romantic story I have ever heard. Oh, darling Luci, I hope you will be as happy with your husband as I am with mine!"

"Is it time?" The Countess of Whitley was at their side, looking most arch and very excited.

"It is time," the bishop replied.

"Who is it to be, Lucinda?" the countess demanded. "You must tell me before you tell the others!"

"Madame, may I present my intended, Lucian Phillips, the Earl of Stanton," Lucinda said with a twinkle.

The Countess of Whitley's mouth dropped open, her first chin bouncing off her other two chins. She gasped, and then she burst out laughing. "You minx!" she said. "You have kept all of society guessing between the duke, the marquess, and Bertram, and all the while you had another stud in your stable! Well, good for you, my gel! You have chosen, in my opinion—and here in London my opinion counts for every-thing—the best of the bunch. Make your announcement, George." She signaled to the orchestra, and they played a fanfare.

George Worth, the Bishop of Wellington, walked up to the bandstand and, turning to face the ballroom, said, "I should like to announce my sister's betrothal to Lucian Phillips, the Earl of Stanton."

There was a stunned silence, and then a collective gasp from those assembled. Then the Countess of Whitley spoke up, "And George is going to marry them right here and now! I will wager none of you has ever been invited to a ball and found yourselves at a wedding!"

Lucinda and Lucian stepped up before the Bishop of Wellington.

"I have three formal witnesses," the bishop said. "I shall need a fourth."

"I will be your witness," Lord Bertram said, stepping forward and standing next to Lord Bowen, the countess, and Caroline Worth.

Murmurs of approval arose from the audience.

"Such exquisite manners," a voice was heard to say.

"Damned good sport!" another voice said.

"We will begin, then," George Worth said. "Dearly beloved . . ."

They could not, of course, leave immediately after the ceremony although they certainly wanted to do so. They stood in a reception line accepting the congratulations of several hundred people in the ballroom. The king arrived, heard what he had missed, and laughed heartily.

"A very clever wench," he approved. Then he kissed the bride, giving her breast a little squeeze as he did so.

They danced several dances, and then, although it was absolutely unforgivable etiquette to depart before the king, slipped from the ballroom unnoticed. When they reached Traleigh Square, Lucinda sent the coach back to wait for her brother and sister-in-law. Then she led her new husband to her bedroom where Polly and John were awaiting them.

"I'll send over to Lord Bowen's in the morning for your things, m'lord," John said as he helped the earl to undress.

"Gawd almighty!" Polly whispered to her mistress. "He's gorgeous!" Then she gathered up her mistress's finery and hurried from the room behind her own husband, who was carrying the earl's garments.

They were alone. They were naked. They were eager.

"I believe John has fixed the wine correctly," Lucinda said, offering him a goblet. "To us," she toasted them, and they drank their wine down, setting the goblets aside.

Reaching out, he drew her into his arms and kissed her deeply, hungrily. Lucinda slid her arms about his neck, pressing her full breasts into his broad, smooth chest. Her tongue fenced with his tongue, then ran along his sensuous lips. She could feel his cock against her thigh. It was already hard and eager for her.

"I have missed you," she told him.

"Did you fuck them?" he asked her jealously.

"Only Rexford surprised me once and forced the issue," she told him honestly. "I kept him at bay after that. The others were perfect gentlemen."

"No wonder Rexford was bitter," the earl said quietly.

"Husband," Lucinda said, "all of that is in the past and behind us. I was a good wife to Harrington. I will be a good wife to you as well, my lord. No one has ever had cause to question my honor."

"Do you want to be fucked?" he asked her bluntly. One hand moved to tweak her nipple as he fondled her breast while the other pushed through her nether lips to tease at her little exciter. "Do you want to be fucked, my beautiful, clever wife?"

"Yes, Lucian, my wonderful husband, I most certainly want to be fucked! Are you going to spend the rest of the night just talking about it?" Lucinda demanded.

With a wicked grin he pushed her back onto their bed and, falling atop her, thrust his cock deep into her hot, wet love sheath, "No, my darling, I don't intend to spend the night talking about it," he told her. "I intend to spend the night doing it."

And so he did.

Risking It All

Susan Johnson

Chapter One

Monte Carlo, Easter week, 1896

Felicia Greenwood sat in the kitchen of her villa overlooking the sea, tearing the letter she had just received into shreds, casting aspersions on the writer in brisk, heated accents, then turning at last to her two servants, who watched with sympathy in their eyes. "And that's what I think of Cousin Dickie's advice!" She spoke in French, although her thoughts were still colored with a faint Scottish brogue.

"Your auntie disliked him, too." Her elderly housekeeper cum maid of all work offered in reassurance. "Tell Mademoiselle Felicia what the countess called him," she added, looking up at her husband, who served as the sole manservant in the establishment.

Daniel smiled at Felicia seated across the kitchen table. "She called him Monsieur le Prune and never listened to anything he said."

Felicia's mouth curved into a fleeting grin, the description apt. Her cousin's mouth was always pursed in distaste. "Now, if only Cousin Dickie wasn't about to take Villa Paradise from me," she said with a small sigh, "I could ignore him as well."

"You still have a week to find the money."

Felicia's expression turned stricken. She had been given a year to come up with her cousin's required payment. Without success. "If only Auntie's funds were paying better dividends."

"He's robbing you, mademoiselle. I know he is," Claire asserted. "The countess always had plenty of money."

"I know you don't trust Dickie and his lawyers, and I'm not sure I do either; but at the moment our feelings are incidental to the immediate crisis, so I've decided to sell the tiara. I thought about it all last night. Auntie would understand—I hope . . ." The diamond tiara had been given to the countess by an admirer in her youth, an old love she had never forgotten. Brushing aside her misgivings, Felicia lifted her chin. "Desperate times require desperate measures."

"It still won't be enough, my lady." Claire knew to a sou what jewelry was worth.

Felicia knew she was risking it all, but it wouldn't do to betray her uncertainties before her servants. "That's why I'm taking the money to the casino," she said with what she hoped was convincing assurance. "There, I'll be able to parlay it into a much larger sum."

"I'll pray to Saint Dévote that you win the bank," Claire declared, the local saint her bulwark against all the pitfalls of life.

"Pardon, my lady, but you don't know how to gamble." An archpragmatist to his wife's simple, trusting nature, Daniel questioned the feasibility of Felicia's proposal.

"I'll pray to Saint Dévote *and* the Madonna," Claire firmly asserted, glaring at her husband. "Have a little faith, Daniel."

"*Vingt et un* shouldn't be so difficult to play," Felicia observed with a bolstering touch of nonchalance. "How hard can it be to count to twenty-one? I've quite made up my mind, so don't look at me like that, Daniel. Auntie's tiara is the last piece of jewelry left, so I shall simply have to win the additional sum at the casino. With luck," she realistically added.

"And my prayers," Claire interposed.

"It *is* the season for miracles," Daniel kindly noted.

Felicia brushed her palms over her riotous red curls, a good-luck habit from childhood. "Why not a miracle for me?"

"Why not, indeed, mademoiselle," Claire said with a beaming smile.

* * *

Lord Grafton had noticed the flame-haired woman the moment she had walked into the casino gaming rooms, the splendor of her face and form momentarily silencing the hum of commerce in the room. But he was on a winning streak at the roulette table, and he paused only long enough to imprint her image in his memory. There would be time enough later to make her acquaintance. In his experience, females who gambled generally gambled small stakes. She wouldn't be leaving soon.

He kept note of her in his peripheral vision and of the numerous admirers clustered around her. But she seemed intent on her play, and after standing stud to all the society belles of note since his adolescence, he wasn't overly concerned with his ability to overcome competition. His luck was running hotter than hot tonight, and he concentrated on his game until he took note of the lady's sudden distress. Signaling he was out, he swiftly moved toward her table. He had seen that look a thousand times in gambling hells from one end of the earth to the other.

She was about to lose everything.

The throng of men surrounding her parted as he approached, his colorful reputation well known. Whether exploring the outlands of the world or partaking of the fashionable venues of aristocratic society, he had a tendency to take offense when thwarted.

Coming up behind Felicia, he leaned close to her ear, murmured, "Allow me, mademoiselle," and placed a neat stack of thousand-franc chips beside her few remaining markers.

She half turned in surprise and gazed up at him.

He smiled.

Awestruck, she forgot that a lady should take offense when a stranger offered her money and any number of other principles of protocol having to do with strange men and a lady's honor.

"Might I suggest two cards?" His voice was like velvet, his dark gaze warm, his fragrant cologne reminiscent of her beloved highland heather.

"I shouldn't." She struggled to recall the proprieties.

He had heard that hesitant tone—the one hovering on the verge of capitulation—hundreds of times before. "It's only cards," he said with a faint grin. "Let me bring you luck."

She glanced back at her few remaining chips, at the munificent pile of donated chips beside them and, looking up for an indecisive moment, gazed into the diaphanous clouds painted on the gilded ceiling. Was this her miracle?

"Two cards for the mademoiselle."

A deep voice of command, Felicia thought, no angelic messenger of the divine, the decision already taken from her hands.

Two new cards lay on the green baize.

And her handsome benefactor was smiling at her. "Twenty-one, mademoiselle. Didn't I tell you I'd bring you luck?"

The croupier was pushing a very large stack of chips toward her, and with her heart beating wildly, she began to feel a soul-stirring hope. She might not be turned out into the street after all; she might be able to keep her home. It was impossible to reject the bounty before her, no matter what propriety required. Salvation was within her grasp when only moments ago, she was near-destitute. "I'm very, very, *very* much obliged," she breathlessly offered, elation in every grateful syllable, "Monsieur . . . ?"

"Suffolk. Thomas Suffolk." Flynn sketched her a faint bow, and his dark hair momentarily gleamed in the chandelier light. "If I might suggest"—he deftly organized the increased stack of chips, taking out five one-thousand-franc chips and slipping them into her reticule—"perhaps one card this time."

He played for her from that point, smiling at her occasionally, keeping up a low murmur of inconsequential conversation, adding to the pile of chips before her while she stood next to the intoxicating warmth of his body and forced herself to appear calm in the midst of a wondrous miracle.

"Will that do?" he finally asked.

Another huge pile of chips was being added to her winnings. "Oh, yes, very much so. Without question!"

Flynn signaled an attendant to gather the chips and then offered Felicia his arm.

"You might need a guard," he teased a few moments later as they stood before the cashier, indicating with a nod the large pile of bank notes clutched in her hand.

"I don't know how I can ever thank you enough, Mr. Suffolk," she murmured, a glowing delirium in her voice. "My heart's still beating frantically."

Having a thought or two on how she might thank him, he blandly suggested, "Come have dinner with me next door. A glass of champagne will calm you."

She understood that under normal circumstances she wouldn't go to dinner with a stranger; but these were not ordinary circumstances, and he was far from an ordinary man. In fact, he was the most beautiful man she had ever seen. Furthermore, the Hotel de Paris was perfectly safe with Daniel's brother and cousins in service there. And he *had* saved her from a life of drudgery as a governess or companion. He deserved her appreciation. "I'd like that," she said, smiling.

"Perfect." He held out his hand.

"Are you here for the season?" she asked as they strolled from the room.

"Actually I'm on my way back from Baku."

"Are you in oil?"

He shook his head. "I was visiting a friend. Are *you* here for the season . . . ?"

Chapter Two

She hadn't intended to be so garrulous, or stay so long, or enjoy herself so. But three hours later, she was still talking as though she had known her benefactor for years. She had told him about her disastrous marriage, her widowhood, about coming to Monte Carlo to care for her elderly aunt, and about Dickie hounding her for his share of the property when she had not thought he was given a share. About the dismal earnings on her aunt's funds left to her and in general everything about her life that one would disclose under the influence of a superb champagne and a charming man's interest.

"Oh, dear," she murmured, her hand on her mouth in a small theatrical gesture prompted by a modicum too much of champagne. "I've hardly given you a moment to speak."

"I've enjoyed listening to you."

"Most men don't like to listen. They like to lecture or offer pronouncements or go on for unspeakable lengths about the hunting field or the state of the crops or the newest coat fabric—like Dickie . . ." She giggled. "Or in the case of the hunting field, my obnoxious husband." Her sudden smile was enchanting. "Not that he could help being obnoxious coming from his odious family."

"Why did you marry him?"

"Because he had money and I had none and mostly because my father insisted. Actually, he locked me in my bedroom until I agreed."

"I see."

"You probably don't," she replied, interpreting the reservation in his tone. "Not with your looks and money. But in Aberdeen, my choices were limited without funds to have a season. Even when I came here five years ago, Auntie only took me as a companion on a conditional basis. "

"But she liked you."

Felicia smiled again, and he thought his luck was running well tonight. Not only had he won a goodly sum at roulette, but the most beautiful woman in the casino was seated across from him, smiling, and the very large bed in his suite above would offer them a lovely view of the sunrise.

"We came to be friends. Do you have family?"

He shook his head.

"You just travel?"

"I spend a portion of the year in England."

"Hunting?" she teased.

He smiled back. "Sometimes. Mostly I follow my thoroughbreds on the race circuit."

"A racing stable. Now, that requires a win or two at the roulette tables. Thomas Suffolk," she murmured. "Your name sounds vaguely familiar. "

"It's a common enough name." He had not mentioned his title. He often didn't, preferring anonymity if possible. "Would you like more dessert?"

"Heavens no. In fact," she added, taking note that they were the last diners in the room, "I should be going home. I've probably bored you to tears by now, although I want to thank you once again for simply *everything*." She opened her arms wide in an expansive gesture that mounded her breasts above her decolletage in the most delectable way. "And if there's anything at all I can do to show my appreciation, although appreciation is such a bland word for all you've done for me. You've quite literally saved my home for me and kept me from a life of abject drudgery and in general appeared like some beautiful guardian angel out of the blue—" Taking note of his expression, her rush of words trailed off.

"There might be something," he quietly said.

She laughed in delight. "How wonderfully you say that. So softly—without a modicum of demand. I was tempted to ask you the same thing a dozen times, but you were so polite"— she took a small, sustaining breath because she was about to step onto dangerous new ground—"and I've never actually asked a man to take me to bed before, and I told myself you might say no and embarrass me for asking or you might say yes too quickly and make me nervous." Drawing in another breath, she rushed on. "So the answer is yes, of course, yes, I'd like to, if you don't think me too forward. And yes, please, I'd like to very much considering I haven't slept with a man since my husband died five years ago, and even that doesn't really count because regardless of my novice status, I could still tell he was utterly inadequate." She quickly held up her hands. "I don't mean to put any pressure on you in any way, Mr. Suffolk, in terms of adequacy or inadequacy. In fact, I'll apologize in advance for my own incompetence."

It was his turn to laugh. "I'm not sure I want to anymore."

"There. Now I've ruined everything because I never know when to stop talking, although I think the champagne is entirely to blame tonight. You're incredibly handsome, by the way, although I suspect you know that."

"Thank you and you're extremely beautiful, although I suspect you know that as well. Now, if I could interest you in a short walk up one flight of stairs," he offered, rising from his chair, "we could finish our conversation on the terrace."

"Under the stars. How romantic."

He smiled. "I'm not sure I'm very good at being romantic."

"You needn't *be* romantic," she qualified, coming to her feet. "It's quite enough simply looking at you."

His perfect teeth flashed white in a grin. "Lord, you *must* be tipsy."

Sweeping past him, she threw a cheerful glance over her shoulder. "A wee dram never hurt anyone."

She seemed to know her way upstairs, and when he began to wonder if the young lady was more than she appeared, she came to rest at the top of the first flight and further piqued his interest by saying, "I'd suppose you have Wales's suite." She had seen with what deference he was treated by the staff during dinner. The big winners at the casino always had the best suites.

"Why would you suppose that?" His brows twitched. "Or even know that?"

"That's a yes, I presume," she lightly replied, turning to the left and moving down the corridor in a deliciously provocative stroll that further baffled him. Might she be a courtesan after all? Had he misinterpreted her persona or was she simply that good an actress?

Not that it mattered, he supposed. He followed her swaying form and alluring fragrance to the corner suite that overlooked the whole of the harbor as well as the palaces of Monaco across the bay.

"I do adore the Wales's suite." Waiting for him at the doorway, she smiled at him with the most intriguing innocence.

"Do you do this often?" he softly asked, inserting the key into the lock.

"Win money at the casino or go to men's rooms?"

His glance swiveled to her, an ironic cast to his gaze.

"Maybe that's for you to find out, Monsieur Suffolk," she sportively declared. "Am I a woman of the night or not?" She struck a theatrical pose.

His gaze traveled slowly down her body, and when it returned to her face, he was smiling. "We'll find out soon enough, won't we," he softly said, pushing the door open. "After you, Mrs. Greenwood."

"Miss Greenwood," she amiably corrected, brushing past him. "I prefer forgetting my marriage." She quickly spun around. "You're not married, are you? Because while I understand fidelity isn't a requirement for a man—as evidenced by this suite that has never seen the presence of the Princess of Wales—nevertheless, I'd not wish to be a pernicious influence in a marriage."

"Rest assured, I'm *not* married." He quietly shut the door.

"So emphatic, Mr. Suffolk," she teased. "One might almost think you don't believe in the institution."

"Like you, I prefer my independence."

"My goodness. Have you a conscience, Mr. Suffolk? Most men maintain their independence despite their marriages."

"Might we discuss marital infidelity at some other time?"

"Oops." She quickly placed her fingertips over her mouth and playfully batted her eyelashes. "I'm hardly filling the role of courtesan with competence, am I? I'm here to please and be agreeable and never utter a discouraging word."

"A pleasant thought," he drolly murmured, placing the key on a small table.

"Are courtesans really like that?"

"Could we discuss that later as well?"

"Of course, we can simply discuss nothing at all. I love this suite," she expansively murmured, flinging her arms wide and swinging around in a circle. "All warm yellows and bouquets of flowers and rich damask furniture so soft you sink into it like a downy pool."

He pushed away from the door. "Have you been here often?"

"Only in passing, Mr. Suffolk. My servants' family are in service at the hotel, and I've seen every grand room—thanks to them."

For some bizarre reason, he was pleased with her answer, although he had decided sometime ago that Miss Greenwood was no courtesan. She was a shade too prickly and outspoken. As a rule, courtesans were accommodating in the extreme. And after his recent visit to Baku where his friend kept a harem, he was well aware of accommodating women.

He found the contrast refreshing.

She had moved to the open terrace door and was standing with her back to him. "I'm so incredibly happy," she proclaimed, "I could scream."

"Please don't."

She turned around and grinned. "What if I do?"

"I'd have to find a way to silence you."

Her brows rose. "Really?"

They stood a few yards apart in the most sumptuous room in the Hotel de Paris on a warm spring night with the scent of jasmine on the air.

Expectation palpable.

She opened her mouth.

"Don't."

Her smile was heated and tantalizing and so provocative, he wondered for a moment if he had been mistaken and she was trained to be alluring.

Her jubilant cry exploded into the quiet night and lasted only the brief time it took for the Duke of Grafton to cover the distance between them.

He moved incredibly fast for a large man, she transiently thought, and then his mouth covered hers and everything about him seemed large. She wasn't a small woman, yet his powerful body dwarfed hers, his ungentle mouth engulfed hers, and his large hands easily cupped her bottom, pulling her hard against his enormous erection.

She struggled briefly, perhaps out of shock for she wasn't averse to the bargain she had made, but he only tightened his grip. A tiny frisson shimmered down her spine at the tantalizing sense of helplessness, at the delicious sensation of being overwhelmed by this large, handsome man. He wanted her, not dispassionately like the emotionless couplings in her past, but with urbane gallantry and finesse and an intoxicating blend of virtuosity and ravishment that made her feel scandalously alive.

And wild.

She reveled in the heated pleasure provoked by the silken warmth of his mouth and exploring tongue, by the hard length of his body pressed firmly against hers. His kiss deepened, the taste and scent of him filling her mouth and nostrils, the exquisite feel of him becoming more familiar with each breath, more tempting as if his kisses served as appetizers and when she came to know him well, he would allow her the main course. In her urgency and desire, she slid her arms around his neck, lifted her face to better accommodate his mouth, melted against his tall, muscled frame and began kissing him back.

She kissed him like a woman who had never felt the flame

of passion before, like a woman left in the wilderness for all of her life, her eagerness and hunger, her need to kiss and be kissed, captivating. She offered herself with such ardent intensity and longing, he felt a thrilling response he had not felt in years. Like the breathless gratitude in adolescence.

"This has been the absolute most perfect night," she murmured, pulling away for a moment, gazing up at him with adoration. "I didn't know a person could feel this good."

A half smile appeared. "You're easy to please."

"No one's ever kissed me so—well—so perfectly, so I'm warm clear down to my toes. Do your toes tingle?"

"Absolutely. "

"Are we . . . I mean—do you want to—" Embarrassed, she blushed.

He gently brushed his fingertip over her pinked lower lip. "We are and I want to and strangely my toes really are tingling."

"Oh, good. That's *so* good. I mean in terms of—"

"Sex?"

She smiled. "Yes. That."

"You can say the word, you know. We're quite alone."

"I'd rather not."

He moved against her so the imprint of his erection was clearly felt. "Sex is really a very nice word."

She moved her hips in a faint answering undulation. "I can see how it could be with you. The ladies must love you," she murmured, the grand length of him sending a shiver up her spine. "Don't make me wait," she blurted out.

She was a young ingenue, he realized, in the voluptuous body of a woman. "Of course not."

"I've waited a lifetime," she murmured, her lavender eyes filled with longing.

"That's long enough," he whispered, taking her hand and drawing her toward the bedroom.

Hope and delight sang through her senses. "Do you believe in luck?"

"Always," he replied, smiling at her. A risk taker to the core, he viewed life as a gamble.

"I never did until tonight." She made a small moue. "Probably with good reason."

"The trick is in being open to the possibilities."

"I love this," she murmured, squeezing his hand. "Doing something without thinking too much or worrying about—"

Turning, he swept her up into his arms, curtailing her litany. "You're not allowed to worry tonight." A sparkle of mischief shone in his eyes. "Or even think."

"No thinking?" Wide-eyed, she grinned.

"It's absolutely not allowed. That's an order."

She wrinkled her nose. "I hate orders."

"Then, consider it a suggestion," he quickly improvised.

She laughed. "It would be quite enough for you to be just gloriously beautiful, and you're incredibly sweet besides."

He had not been called sweet in recent memory or ever to be precise. "You're a remarkable woman, Miss Greenwood."

"Please, call me Felicia. After all . . . we're going to be more than acquaintances soon . . ."

"Then, call me Flynn. My friends know me by that name."

"You don't like Thomas?"

"It was my father's name."

"I see."

"No, you don't, but then it doesn't matter much anymore. I've been on my own for a long time."

"As have I. Do you believe in fate? As in our meeting tonight?"

Having reached the large canopied bed, he lowered her to the riotous flower-print coverlet. "I believe in my own good luck."

She ran her finger across the broad width of his hand as he sat down beside her. "I believe in your good luck probably more than you. It brought me my life back."

"Pleased to be of service, my lady." Bending low, he gently kissed her.

"Speaking of service," she murmured, kicking her slippers off. "You really didn't mind my asking you tonight, did you? I mean, you're not just being polite?"

"No man with breath in his body would *mind*, dear Felicia. And I intended to ask you, only you asked first." He began sliding his evening jacket from his shoulders.

"You must do this often, I suppose, considering how handsome you are and . . . all."

He glanced back at her as he tossed his jacket on a nearby chair. "More often than you, I suppose."

"More often than every five years." She slid a garter down her leg.

With the view so fine, it took him a moment to answer. "That would be a safe assumption." Unclasping the diamond cufflinks from his shirt cuffs, he slipped them free.

"You must have lots of women asking you." She lifted her other leg to take off her garter and stocking.

"Not really," he lied, fascinated with the pale expanse of inner thigh before his eyes. Reaching out, he slowly slid his palm over the warmth of her thigh, coming to rest on the simple white linen covering her mons. "Let me buy you some silk lingerie."

"Mine's too plain," she ruefully noted.

"It's very nice. Prim and proper and ever so tempting." Easing apart the two sections of her drawers, he slipped his fingers inside and stroked her silky curls. "Has it really been five years?" he murmured, his middle finger sliding down her dewy cleft.

Her breath caught in her throat, and when she didn't answer, his gaze lifted. She nodded to his raised eyebrow, and he smiled. "Five years is a long time," he whispered, gently sliding his finger in a lingering path from her turgid clitoris down one side of her sleek, plump labia and up the other side. "I'd think you'd be ready to come without much foreplay . . ." Easing a single finger inside her only as far as the first knuckle, he circled the pulsing, wet tissue.

She moaned and lifted her hips to draw him in.

Forcing her back down, he held her in place with his palm and slipped a second finger into her vagina, farther this time, midpoint in depth, two knuckles deep. "Can you feel that?" She was hot and wet and beginning to pant, and the suffocated small sound she uttered brought his head up.

"Say that again?"

"You heard me." Her heavy-lidded gaze held a hint of temper.

"Was that an order?" His voice was incredibly soft, the merest whisper.

"It was."

His gaze narrowed. "I may not want to."

She swiftly reached out and ran her palm up his erection, her fingers closing at the last, squeezing hard.

His eyes shut against the surge of lust, and a suppressed groan rumbled deep in his throat.

"Changed your mind?" she murmured, rising to a sitting position, easing away from his hand. "And I'm sorry I offended you." Lifting her skirts, she slipped her drawers and petticoat down and kicked them aside. "Now, if there's anything I can do to make amends, dear Flynn," she purred, leaning back on one elbow, her silken cleft and pale legs framed by the crushed folds of her skirt, "I'd be more than willing to concede to you." She slid a finger down the slick flesh of her labia. "I've never had a man like you. And I'd very much like to feel you inside me. So much better than this . . ." She eased her finger inside marginally. "I've never, ever had an orgasm with a man."

Her words spiked through his senses, his erection surging larger at the thought of her lush body having been so long deprived of satisfaction. "You've had an orgasm, though," he murmured, forcibly restraining his lust.

"The French have so many books on the delights of the flesh. I've learned. But I doubt it's the same."

"So you read books and masturbate."

"Don't you?"

Not since he discovered women. "Not lately."

"I suppose not. How lucky you are. I've often thought it quite unfair—how men can sleep around and women can't."

"Women do." And he should know, having serviced a great many ladies from every walk of life.

"So I'm simply naive. A shame, then. You'll have to tell me how to meet such—er—partners."

"Walk down the street, darling. Surely, you know you're a great beauty. "

"I've been told flame-red hair is quite déclassé."

"You've been told wrong."

"My husband deplored—"

"He was lying."

A small smile formed on her luscious mouth. "I want to make love to you for your kindness alone."

"While I have quite different reasons for wanting you. Are we done?"

"You're over your pct?"

"Don't give me orders."

"My feelings exactly."

He chuckled and stripped off his shirt. "We're going to have to be damned polite to each other." Standing, he unbuttoned his trousers.

"For that, I could even be polite to Cousin Dickie." The tempting bulge in his trousers was irresistible.

"For this?" He drew out his erection, the heavily veined penis framed by the opened placket of his trousers, the length astonishing, the gleaming crest swollen to gigantic proportions.

"Oh, my," she gasped, the pulsing between her legs responding to the glorious sight, to the tantalizing expectation as he stripped off his trousers and silk underwear. "Help me with my gown. I want to feel you everywhere." Scrambling from the bed, she turned her back to him and, trembling, waited. "Hurry, please . . ."

He heard the tremor in her voice and understood her urgency. He had heard the politesse as well and appreciated her understanding. Although he wasn't sure he wouldn't fuck her, orders or not, in his present mood.

"The buttons are ever so small. I apologize."

But he had done this so many times before, he swiftly unfastened the small covered buttons and slid her green chartreuse gown from her shoulders.

As it fell to the carpet, she was already slipping her chemise off, and short moments later, she stood naked before him, breath held and hopeful. "If you don't mind," she whispered, her thighs clamped together to maintain the most tenuous control over her approaching orgasm. "The sight of your—arousal . . . is very exciting . . ."

She was literally trembling for him, and such helpless need inspired a strange degree of involvement quite apart from his usual lust. It gave him pause, but not for long since fucking was a familiar standard in his life. His body responded automatically to a beautiful nude woman, his intellectual impulses secondary to his libido. "Let's try the bed the first time," he murmured, sliding his arm around her waist and moving forward.

It was too much—the implication that there would be more, the possessive feel of his hand on her hip, her tremulous desires—and with a gasp, she stopped halfway to the bed and climaxed in a series of tiny sobs.

He gently held her while her orgasm shuddered through her body, careful not to intrude on the heated flow, discreetly watching, waiting till the last before he lifted her into his arms and whispered, "Sorry. "

"It's not your fault. I'm not very good at this."

"You've been waiting too long."

"Do you mind?"

"Not if you don't. We've all night."

"All night?" She looked alarmed. "I can't stay all night."

"Why not?" He wasn't about to let her go without exploring the full range of her delights.

"My servants will worry."

He masked his shock. "Send them a note."

"What will they think?"

Sitting down on the bed, he cradled her on his lap. "Darling," he softly said. "They're servants. A note is more than sufficient."

"They're really friends."

"A note's good for friends, too. You write it and I'll ring for a messenger." Lifting her off his lap, he placed her on the bed.

"I'm so sorry."

Ignoring his throbbing hard-on, he said, "It's not a problem."

"I really am sorry," she murmured, her gaze on his erection as he rose and walked away.

"I can wait."

"You're ever so nice."

"See if you feel that way in the morning," he replied with a grin. "I intend to keep you up all night." Pulling open the desk drawer, he picked up a sheet of stationery and an envelope.

"Really? All night? You don't . . . I mean—not actually all night?"

His dark gaze held a hint of amusement as he plucked a pen from the holder. "Actually."

She took a deep breath. "My goodness."

"It should be *extremely* good." Adding a bottle of ink to the items in his hand, he moved back toward the bed.

"Better than my orgasm?"

"Oh, yes. I can guarantee that."

How comfortable he was with his nudity, she thought. "Because you do this often and you know about women?"

"Because you fascinate and intrigue me and I feel like fucking you all night."

"Oh, my." Somehow the blunt phrase didn't offend, the soft promise in his words triggering a liquid heat deep inside her.

"Write," he softly commanded, placing the supplies in her

lap, grabbing a book from the bedside table for a writing surface and handing it to her. All the while she repressed her impulse to reach out and touch his arousal. Moving toward the telephone, he asked, "Do you want one of your servants' relatives to deliver your note?"

She hesitated, not sure she wished to expose her indiscretions. On the other hand, aware of the speed with which gossip traveled below stairs, she knew her stay in the Wales's suite of the Hotel de Paris would be impossible to conceal. Better someone she knew to perhaps mitigate the worst of the gossip. "Ask for Claude." She began to write.

Lord Grafton spoke rapidly in flawless French, the voice of authority resonating in his soft tone, his replies to a series of questions brief yeses and nos. Hanging up the ornate receiver, he turned to her with a half smile. "Apparently Claude has been waiting for your summons. It seems Daniel had been looking for you. Do you have a curfew?"

"Oh, Lord. How embarrassing. I suppose everyone knows."

"I was assured your presence here would be kept in the closest confidence."

"Who are you anyway?" Wide-eyed, she gazed at him, wondering why the staff was so accommodating.

"I spend a good deal of money at the casino."

"You're not going to tell me." She signed her name to the few brief sentences.

"I did tell you."

"It really doesn't matter after tonight anyway," she said, taking note of his evasion. "And I do owe you a tremendous debt."

"Is that why you're here?" One brow lifted in skeptical regard.

"Do you really care?"

He gazed at her for a moment, voluptuously nude, beautiful beyond the general standards for beauty, impatient for her first orgasm with a man. "No."

Her mouth quirked in a faint smile. "I didn't think so."

"Are you finished, then?" He nodded at the note, his momentary cynicism dismissed. "Claude's on his way up."

As aware as he of the reasons that had brought them there, she quickly folded the sheet of paper, slid it into the envelope and handed it to him.

Taking it to the desk, he sealed it. Then pulling a gray silk robe from the armoire, he slipped it on and walked from the bedroom, shutting the door behind him. The knock on the suite door sounded as he was counting out a number of bills guaranteed to buy silence from the staff. If Miss Greenwood lived in Monte Carlo, it would be best if her stay with him were forgotten. When he opened the door a few moments later, he conveyed his instructions to Daniel's brother with a decisiveness that couldn't be misconstrued. And money aside, the soft threat in his voice would have been sufficient to see his orders obeyed.

"Your note is being delivered," the duke declared, reentering the bedroom shortly after, "and I was assured not a hint of your presence here would go abroad."

Lounging against the pillows, she lazily scrutinized him. "You must be dangerous or very rich."

Some might say both, but choosing to disclose as little of his life as possible, the duke said instead, "I gave Claude some of the money I won tonight."

"A lot, no doubt."

"Enough." She was so lush and inviting lying on his bed, he would have willingly spent more if necessary. "Now that your concerns for your servants are alleviated, you no longer need worry." His smile gave evidence of his supreme good humor. "And we can concentrate on pleasure until morning."

"You make this very, very easy."

"I have the most selfish of motives."

She playfully shifted into an odalisque pose. "You're sure I'm worth it?"

"Definitely, and I'm always right."

She laughed, delighted to be the object of such regard. "And modest, too."

"Modesty is much overrated." He untied his robe and slipped it off.

She gazed at his tall, muscled form, bronzed from the sun, honed and taut, exquisitely aroused. "You could never be re garded as modest in any way."

"Nor you." He climbed into bed and settled between her legs with a comfortable ease that bespoke much practice. "Let's begin your first lesson in having an orgasm with a man," he murmured with a smile, guiding his penis to her heated cleft. "Stop me at any time if you have questions."

"I have no intention in the world of stopping you." The feel of him poised to enter her sent waves of pleasure upward from the thrilling point of contact.

"A woman after my own heart."

Her gaze came up, the sentiment oddly put.

"A generic phrase," he quickly noted, mildly confounded himself when he scrupulously avoided romantical utterances.

"Do make love to me," she purred, moving her hips in invitation. "And I mean it in the most generic way."

He moved forward, penetrating slowly, gliding into her heated interior with deliberate languor, wanting to give pleasure, but also selfishly wishing to feel each centimeter of the intoxicating invasion. He couldn't remember when he had had sex with such an inexperienced woman, and her breathless desire brought new dimension to his arousal. "Stop me if I'm hurting you."

"*Au contraire* . . ." Her hands were hard on his back, her hips rising to meet him, the melting heat of her desire flowing around his long, rigid length. "Please . . . more . . ."

As he obliged her, he met a small resistance and, unsure, hesitated .

"It doesn't hurt . . . really . . ."

Gazing down, he saw the entreaty in her lavender eyes, the glowing flush on her cheeks.

"Don't stop . . . I want it all . . ." she implored.

A saint couldn't have withstood such a plea and he had never aspired to sainthood. "You're sure?" he asked when he wasn't sure himself how much longer he could act the gentleman.

"I'm dying," she whispered, desperation in her voice.

So long celibate, she couldn't wait, nor in truth could he, his explosive need controlled only with superhuman effort. With her breathless consent, he gave in to his own rapacious urges and plunged forward, burying himself deep inside her, holding himself immobile against her womb, filling her, stretching her. The pleasure was so intense tears came to her eyes. Then he gently moved, and she moaned, the sleek friction stimulating every sensitized nerve and cell to fever pitch. Inhaling sharply at the agony of restraint, he forced himself to ignore the savage pleasure bombarding his senses. Although it wouldn't be much longer, he recognized. Her thighs opened wider to accommodate him, and her panting cries had reached a new level of need.

Settling into a slow, luscious flux and flow, he gave her what she wanted, what they both wanted, the exquisite rhythm of thrust and withdrawal overwhelming all but stark, finite sensation. She cried out, and he softly grunted each time at the blissful point of deepest penetration when the focus of the world centered on the tremulous imprint of his engorged penis against her throbbing tissue. And then breath held as he withdrew, gliding back to the farthest limit, they waited in sweet, shuddering agony for the next powerful downstroke.

The scent of sex engulfed them, the heated odor of passionate bodies in sleek fusion, the raw, primitive act of mating permeating the civilized luxury and sumptuous decor of the bedroom in the Hotel de Paris. An incongruous concept for a man who viewed sex as a casual game, equally incongruous for a woman who had spent the greater part of her life as pure as a vestal virgin.

But at that moment they existed in their own universe,

joined in a dance as old as time, abandoned to a wild, audacious carnality, body to body, torrid desire to torrid desire, fevered, delirious, ravenous for each other. Until she whimpered and he instantly shifted direction, recognizing how close she was to the brink. Plunging forward, he buried himself so deeply she gasped. And then her low keening cry shattered the night air, the sound rising in soaring exultation as her orgasm tempestuously broke, surged, swelled. With blessed relief, he allowed his own fierce urges free rein. His long withheld climax exploded, flowing downward in such violent ejaculations he shut his eyes against the savage assault.

For reeling moments in the self-contained paradise of the canopied bed, convulsed with rapture, they clung to each other, experiencing a wild, tumultuous consummation so intense the world narrowed to blissful sensation and the heated contact of their bodies. How could she have known, she thought, ravished and saturated and filled with sperm, that sex could be so shockingly good. Was her naivete alone capable of such sorcery? he wondered, his senses still on fire despite his climax.

But resisting the notion of intense feeling on principle, intent on retaining the comfortable habits of a lifetime, he dismissed his errant feelings and, raising his forehead from the pillow, brushed Felicia's cheek with a casual kiss. "That was fantastic."

"And now I know what it's like." Her voice was the merest wisp of sound, her eyes half-shut in languor.

"When the world is perfect," he murmured, adjusting his weight on his elbows and smiling down at her.

"With you, you mean." Her lashes lifted, and contentment shone from her eyes.

"Is it better than alone?"

Her smile appeared, beatific and radiant. "As if you didn't know, you arrogant man."

"Just checking." He glanced at the clock on the mantel. "And I can make it better again."

"Impossible. Really," she murmured. "I couldn't."

"Are you sure?" He moved inside her.

She softly groaned, tremulous rapture in the delicate sound. "Don't do that. I'll expire of bliss."

"This kind of bliss?" He slid forward marginally, his erection seemingly undiminished despite his orgasm.

An exquisite flutter rippled through her vagina, and she purred. "That's not fair."

"Are there rules?" His smile brushed her lips.

"Apparently not for you."

"I can make you come again." Dulcet and sweet, he offered her paradise. "As many times as you want," he added in a whisper.

A flaring desire burned through her senses, and she understood unbridled lust for the first time. "How do you do it? Only seconds ago I was incapable of moving."

"Simple. I slide in like this and touch you—here . . ."

She shivered at the streaking pleasure.

"And your body takes note. Now, if I shift a fraction to the right and lift up just a little . . ."

Shocked, she felt an orgasm begin, and endless, hysterical, screaming moments later when her climax was over and her brain resumed its normal function, she opened her eyes.

". . . I can make you come," he playfully finished.

"How do you know that?" she whispered.

"Years of practice if you don't mind the truth." Slowly withdrawing, he rolled away and sprawled on his back.

Rising on one elbow, she gazed at the beauty of his lounging form. "If it didn't feel so good, I'd be tempted to take issue with your years of practice."

Lacing his hands behind his head, he grinned. "Do you want me to apologize?"

"How old are you?"

"Thirty-five."

She softly snorted. "Years of practice aren't the entire reason. My husband was fifty and he didn't know a thing."

"Sex appeals more to some than others."

"The pleasure of it, you mean."

"No, I mean sex."

"Pleasure is incidental?"

"Hardly. It's the raison d'être. But you can take pleasure in a great number of things outside of sex."

"Do you?"

"Do I look like I'm obsessed?"

"You're awfully good at this."

"I have a great number of things I'm good at."

"And yet you're single. How have you eluded the pursuing women?"

He instantly looked uncomfortable.

"Relax, Flynn. I'm not in the market for a husband ever again."

He visibly relaxed, and she laughed.

"Force of habit," he muttered, "with a question like that. Would you like a bath?"

"Are we changing the subject?"

"Definitely."

"Do I need a bath?"

"Not necessarily. But the tub is large enough for two."

"Hmmm." Her gaze was flirtatious. "Do I detect another lesson?"

He faintly moved his head on the pillow. "No more lessons darling. I dislike the role. I'm just sweaty and sticky." He ran his hand over his chest. "But if you don't mind, I don't."

"How big is the tub?"

"Very. And there's a bottle of champagne in an ice bucket just outside the door."

"Since when?"

"Since I told Claude to bring one up."

"Oh, my God! Do you think he heard me scream?"

"Servants don't hear anything."

"What kind of servants do you have? Mine tell me what to eat for lunch."

He grinned. "Then, you've become much too friendly with them."

"If you recall, my high-and-mighty Flynn, I once was very near their rank myself."

His gaze held hers for a moment. "Were you always poor?"

"Does it matter?"

"Not to me." He spent a good deal of time in the far-flung reaches of the world; he was content with a simple life.

"As a matter of fact, my father was a viscount, although a Scottish laird is almost by definition poor. But we lived on a fine old estate, much the worse for lack of funds until my marriage."

"Why don't you live there now?"

"I don't get on with my brother's wife."

"Ah. A common enough complaint. So you were thrown out on the world."

"I chose not to live there under their sufferance. As it turns out, I much prefer Villa Paradise to the chill of Aberdeenshire. And thanks to you, I can continue to enjoy it."

"It was my pleasure, *chou chou*. And at the risk of offending you, would you mind terribly taking a bath with me?"

"Oh, dear, I smell."

"We both do, although I'm thinking of a cold glass of champagne with considerable relish at the moment."

"In a warm bath."

He smiled. "Our own touch of paradise." Swinging his legs over the side of the bed, he walked around the end and, coming up beside her, held out his hand.

"I'd be a fool to refuse, wouldn't I?"

"I think you'll like it."

"That tone of voice makes your offer even more tempting."

"I was hoping it would. You might like to ride me, I thought."

"Flynn!" She felt her body instantly leap in response.

"It doesn't appeal?" His dark eyes held a touch of amusement.

"Everything about you appeals, as you well know."

He didn't pretend false modesty. "Good," he said. "Then, we'll both enjoy ourselves."

The bathroom was enormous, tiled in gleaming red and gold faience that reminded her of the Provencal countryside. The tub was indeed large enough for two or four or nine, one didn't doubt, the gold fixtures ornately cast, the designs of dolphin spouts and sea shell faucets exquisite. Opposite the sunken tub, three flower-painted porcelain sinks were backed by a mirrored wall. Above the sinks stretched a long glass shelf filled with such a variety of colorful toiletries, the array could have stocked a small boutique.

A balcony lay outside wide glass doors facing the sea while two paneled doors in antiqued yellow punctuated the opposing wall.

"If you'd like to use the facilities," the duke offered, indicating the doors with a wave of his hand.

After drinking so much champagne at dinner, the offer was inviting. "You can't listen."

His brows rose. "It's a bit late for modesty, isn't it?"

She blushed, reminded of all that had passed between them. "I'll begin to fill the tub if you like. Would that be better?"

"Thank you." She lifted her hands slightly in a nervous gesture. "I'm very new at this."

Aware of the unusual desires she evoked, he gently said, "Maybe we both are."

"How gallant." Her voice was less uncertain, her gaze once again composed. Turning to the doors behind her, she opened them both before selecting the room with the bidet. Glancing back before she entered, she sweetly smiled. "I feel terribly grown up."

Alarm tightened his stomach. She was a lush vision of womanhood, but so entirely without guile, that inconsistency could pose a danger. "Don't tell me you're sixteen."

"I wish I *could* tell you I was sixteen and forget I was ever married. In a more perfect world, perhaps—"

"I'm not interested in a long discussion right now." His voice was terse. "How *old* are you?"

"You're nervous," she teased.

Nothing so genial resonated in his voice. "Just tell me."

"Twenty-six."

His relief was so apparent she laughed out loud. "Now *that* was a moment of sheer terror."

"Damn right it was. Men have been forced to the altar for far less."

"Let me assure you, dear Flynn, I'm only interested in your"—her gaze traveled down to his penis, and his libido instantly responded—"ability to perform on command," she purred. "By the way," she added, her gaze coquettish, "I like that I can do that to you."

"Go," he gruffly said, at a loss for an offhand remark when he was taut with lust. As the door shut behind her, he took himself to task, reminding himself that innocents like Miss Greenwood were outside his purview for a variety of reasons that bore recall, like families that might object or notions of accountability and responsibility he didn't care to face. He would enjoy her tonight because he would be a fool if he didn't, but worldly women were more his style. They knew the rules of the game. And with that sensible reminder, he walked to the tub, turned on the faucets and went to the second bathroom. He had every intention of drinking enough tonight to obliterate his disturbing attraction to the artless Miss Greenwood.

Even with the tub water running, Felicia heard him in the adjacent bathroom and found herself listening like a voyeur. How strange, she thought, that she was intrigued with even the most earthy facets of the man when she would have considered such conduct coarse and vulgar before tonight. Why this inordinate interest? she wondered, trying to make sense of the intense attraction she felt.

He was handsome as a god, of course, but that wasn't reason enough to be so fascinated in every detail of his life. His lovemaking was glorious, but sex didn't rule her world, or it never had, she ruefully noted, until tonight. As for his charm, he had that in abundance. But charm alone didn't explain her profound desire to know the intimacies of his life. Did he clean his teeth in the morning or at night or both? What kind of bed did he sleep on at home? Did he like scent on his shirts? Did he whistle? Her mind raced with new and peculiar curiosities.

Was this what happened to every woman Flynn made love to? Did his seductive skills leave every woman wanting more, wanting the whole man revealed? Or was she just overly impressionable like a grass-green maid, easily infatuated by a handsome face, spectacular sexual skills and a cock like the rod of empire?

That last indecorous image brought a smile to her face even as she chided herself for such shameful thoughts. She knew very well it would never do to become bewitched. She should regard this brief interlude of pleasure as nothing more than a delightful quid pro quo. Flynn was her angel of mercy tonight in more ways than one, and her amenability would perhaps repay him for his generosity. Or at least marginally, her inexperience a possible deterrent to a man of his sexual expertise.

Moving toward the door, she was suddenly stunned by her nude image in the mirror. Somehow she had forgotten she was unclothed. Perhaps one had to be removed from Flynn's heated embrace to begin thinking clearly again. Dear God, she nervously reflected. How exactly did one enter a room when one was stark naked? Averting her eyes from the disconcerting sight, she glanced about the small room for a garment. Although, maybe it *was* a bit late for prudishness as Flynn had so recently pointed out. And yet . . . she didn't know if she was sufficiently dégagé to face him with equanimity. It seemed as though she were about to walk out on stage.

This intermission, as it were, from heated passion had restored a modicum too much reason to her brain. And since no shred of clothing had materialized, her options were limited. Drawing in a fortifying breath, she understood she could either stay in here forever *or* . . . brazen it out. The forever option was unlikely to work, so exhaling softly, she reached for the door latch. Forcing herself to smile, she pulled open the door and stepped out into the bathroom. "Such splendid luxury," she brightly exclaimed, her voice brittle with élan. "A person could get used to this. Piles of monogramed linen, magnificent bottles of perfumes, scented soaps—"

"And champagne." The duke lifted his glass to her from the sunken tub where he lounged, two silver champagne buckets set on a ledge above his head. "The water's warm," he added, wishing to put her at ease, her discomfort obvious. "Are you hungry at all?"

"After that meal?" She hesitated in the doorway.

"If you'd like something, let me know."

He didn't mean it that way, she knew, but the deep tenor of his voice seemed to insinuate itself precisely where she least wished it to insinuate itself. Slowly inhaling, she repressed the ripple of pleasure fluttering through her vagina.

He noticed, both her response and her resistance. "Try some champagne," he softly suggested, understanding a woman of her background wouldn't easily assume the role of doxy. "And I'll entertain you with an account of my world travels."

He made it so easy to like him, she thought, the tension draining from her body. "Only if you tell me of the Taj Mahal first." She began walking toward him.

"Done." Setting his goblet down, he poured her a glass of champagne and placed it on the broad rim of the tub. She reminded him of a shy, skittish kitten, timid but wanting to play. "The first time I saw the Taj," he began, lounging back in the water, "I was eighteen and in love with a beautiful Irish girl who wouldn't leave her husband for me because my father had cut me off without a farthing."

"I'll bet she regrets it now." A trace of amusement colored Felicia's tone.

The duke shrugged. "I doubt she remembers me. Her husband was transferred to Calcutta, and I never saw her again."

"And you never found another woman to love." Picking up the glass of champagne, she stepped into the tub.

"She broke my tender heart," he sardonically murmured. Sliding into the water, she leaned back against the smooth tile. "How convenient to have such a romantic excuse. And when your father died did he leave you a farthing?"

"He had to or else leave it to a distant cousin who was living in the Australian bush with his native wife."

"Lucky for you. Now, if only my father had left me a farthing. Although I can't complain. Auntie Gillian did leave me what she had. But tell me about the Taj," she suddenly declared, not wishing to dwell on unhappy thoughts. "Is it as magnificent as it looks in pictures?"

He nodded. "And what they say about seeing it in moonlight is absolutely true." He then went on to describe the monument to love and several more of the wonders of the world that he had seen in his years of travel.

They drank one bottle and then began another, adding warm water to the tub as it cooled, their comfortable rapport restored. He related various anecdotes from his life, editing only those portions that would make him recognizable as one of the wealthiest men in England. And she talked of her youth when her world was still filled with joy. "I used to have my own horses, too," she explained. "A beautiful black and a long-legged bay that could run for hours. Although it seems a lifetime ago. My husband sold them."

He almost said, "I'll give you some," but that would entail a future he was reluctant to envision. So he said instead, "He deserves to be dead."

"I know. It's terrible for me to say, but it's true."

"How fortunate for me that Auntie Gillian invited you down. I don't recall ever being to Aberdeen. And I would have disliked missing this evening."

"As would I." She suddenly blushed, conscious that the nude man sitting opposite her in the large tub had been a stranger short hours ago.

"No one will know." He didn't have to read her mind; her disquietude was patent.

"Only the entire staff."

"They've been well paid to forget."

"Really? Do you believe—"

"I not only believe—I guarantee it."

Something in his tone gave her pause, that soft menace fair warning to the staff, she suspected.

"Has anyone bothered us thus far?"

She visibly relaxed and smiled again. "You're to be commended. Thank you for that as well as the great multitude of your other kindnesses."

Always uncomfortable with praise, he searched for a new topic of conversation. "I still haven't described my trek through Turkestan. Are you getting tired? Would you like to sleep or listen?"

As if anyone could sleep while in close proximity to the magnificent Flynn. "Since your description is the closest I'll ever get to Turkestan, please tell me."

He was careful not to make advances. Clearly she was dealing with a bout of conscience. He spoke of his summer ride through the Takla Makan desert, of the scorching temperatures and the tribes he had lived with, of the Russian garrison at Khotan where the only thing to do was drink, and before his tale was finished, she was once more comfortable—asking questions, adding her own observations, laughing again at his attempts to amuse her. In any event, he wasn't in any hurry, having decided to change his departure plans. There would be time enough for sex, if not tonight, tomorrow.

He asked her about her sojourn in Monte Carlo then—a safe enough subject—and she offered lighthearted accounts of her duties as companion to her elderly aunt as well as thumbnail sketches of her daily life. And much later, when they had finished the second bottle of champagne and the sun was beginning to lighten the horizon, when their conversation had taken on an undertone of expectation, he said, "Would you like me to shampoo your hair?"

She ran her fingers through her unruly ringlets. "Do I need a shampoo?"

"No, I just thought you might like it."

Her gaze minutely narrowed. "I have a question."

"Only one?" he pleasantly said, in excellent humor after the major share of two bottles of champagne and such affable company.

"Have you done that before?"

He feigned deep thought for a moment and then grinned. "Never."

She giggled with delight. "Then yes, please do. Although I warn you, I seem to have developed a degree of possessiveness after all this champagne."

"It must be the Cliquot," he drolly observed, "for I find myself with similar feelings."

"We should stop drinking it, then. Surely it's a most foolish emotion."

"Strange certainly," he casually remarked, capable of ignoring his feelings after a lifetime of cultivating the habit. "So you don't want any more? No champagne for breakfast?"

"Don't say it's morning already!" All the ramifications of her real life flooded her consciousness.

"It's not morning," he lied, tossing a bottle of shampoo at her. "Trust me. And since I'm going to play hair dresser for the first time in my life, you may want to take notes."

It took her only a fleeting moment to be drawn into his play, her anxieties vanquished by his warm smile. "Notes about the shampoo or something else?" she playfully inquired.

"Either, both—neither. Actually, I'd rather keep you busy with other things." Moving through the water, he glided over her and, balancing above her, took the shampoo from her hand, set it aside and touched her mouth with a gentle kiss.

She smiled up at him, his butterfly kiss a residual sweetness on her lips. "Perhaps I *should* take notes. I could sell my memoirs back to you someday and spare you the embarrassment of seeing your sexual exploits in print."

"I've been beyond embarrassment for a very long time, darling, but I might take notes on my overwhelming fascination with you." His body lightly touched hers as he floated above her. "I've wanted you since you first entered the casino tonight, and that persistent craving hasn't diminished."

The imprint of his erection was hot on her stomach. "Good, because I wouldn't wish to be alone in my obsession."

"Have I been patient enough?"

Regardless of the unspecified nature of his query, she understood what he meant. "You've been extremely courteous."

"I can't recall ever lying naked in a tub with a woman and doing nothing—for so long."

"I can't ever recall lying naked in a tub with a man."

"Lucky me." He moved his hips faintly.

"No, me," she murmured, matching his slow rhythm. "And I'm quite sure my shampoo can wait."

"You think so?"

"I know so."

"Is your hot little pussy finally ready," he whispered.

"Oh, yes," she breathed. "I've been wanting to ask you for a very long time; but you were so far away and I'd already asked you so many times tonight and I thought, perhaps, you preferred less aggressive women—so in terms of hotness . . ."

He slipped his finger inside her and felt the drenching heat. "You're way past ready."

"Do you mind if I come right away?"

"Do you mind if I have sex with you for a decade?"

"Please do," she whispered, reaching up to kiss him, her small gasp as he entered her warming the duke's mouth.

The sensation of weightlessness, the velvety friction of their bodies, the gentle lapping of the water as they moved together, the languor induced by the champagne, offered a rare enchantment.

"This isn't the real world, is it?" Her eyes were nearly shut.

"It's better . . ." He eased a fraction deeper, and they both held their breaths, intoxicating pleasure melting through their limbs.

"Bathing with you is . . . enthralling."

"Someday we'll do that, too," he murmured, tightening his grip. He held her up, his arms wrapped around her, his elbows resting on the tub bottom, his feet braced against the tiled wall—for better penetration.

"I don't think I can wait."

"You don't have to."

"I'm insatiable . . ."

"Perfect," he breathed, his own carnal urges voracious. "I should keep you naked in my bed." He pulled her closer so his rigid length rammed deeper. "And then I could have you whenever I wanted."

She whimpered, shamelessly aroused by the licentious image.

"I could make you come before breakfast and *during* breakfast, before you dress in the morning—if I let you get dressed. You could lie naked in the sun on the terrace in the afternoon, and I could have sex with you there . . ."

Gasping, she climaxed, the flagrant, thrilling rapture ravishing all her sensory receptors in a fierce, flame-hot rush, his words unspeakably carnal, his erection filling her, impaling her, pouring into her.

And yet long moments later with post-coital bliss warming their senses, beneath the contented glow, unquenched desire still stirred.

"I'm afraid I won't let you go," Felicia murmured, her arms still wrapped around his back.

"Good idea." His reply initiated no alarms in his brain, and were he less consumed by covetous need, he might have noticed.

"We're probably both tipsy."

"Speak for yourself." He never got drunk.

"I am speaking for myself," she said with a delicious giggle. "I've found the path to true bliss."

"Definitely nirvana." He moved faintly inside her as though testing the limits of paradise.

She arched her back and purred, and he wondered at the degree of fate involved that he had found such a perfect fit for his cock.

"I could wash *your* hair." She slid her hands up his back and ruffled the damp, dark curls on his neck.

"Or you could stay right where you are." He lazily glided forward.

In perfect accord, she sighed, wrapped her legs around his back, and lifted her hips to accommodate him more fully.

They made love leisurely, the languor of their recent orgasms adding a drowsy sensuality to the lazy rhythm of their bodies, the water in the tub flowing in faint waves, washing against them, warming their heated flesh. All thought was displaced by sensation. Time disappeared. The centered pleasure, the matched rhythm, the ultimate expression of sexual harmony converged in their blended bodies.

She climaxed first because she was wildly tasting the splendors of lust while he believed in the merits of waiting—a requirement perhaps for a man who was known for pleasing women. Nor was he as famished; he had not gone a lifetime without sex.

He gently kissed her when her fevered rapture had faded, and rolling over, he slid upward and lifted her onto his lap. "It's my turn now," he playfully murmured.

"No . . ." She buried her face in his shoulder.

"You always say no." He brushed a gleaming fall of red curls from her face and met her gaze. "You never mean it."

"I do right now."

"Sure?" His smile was cheeky. "And here I thought you'd like to ride me."

"Do I have a choice?" She took issue with the damning fact he was probably right.

"Of course you do," he pleasantly said, raising her enough to meet the crest of his erection.

She pushed at his chest. "I dislike undue prerogatives . . ." Her words trailed away as he eased her down his engorged penis.

"And so you might if you weren't so wet," he whispered, gently stroking her hips, thrusting upward in slow, measured degrees.

"You can't—just do—whatever—you want," she protested, breathless at the deliberate, thrilling invasion. Her last bit of scruples jettisoned as he intensified the pressure on her hips, when he made it clear who was doing what to whom, when he penetrated to the very deepest depth and whispered, "You'll be keeping my cock warm until I decide otherwise."

"No." But her denial ended on a whimper.

"Sure you will," he softly repudiated, holding her in place so they both felt the excruciating rapture.

"I should slap you," she whispered.

She wouldn't, and if she didn't know it, he did.

"Please me, darling," he murmured, "and I'll see that you get what you want."

"Or I you." The heat in her voice wasn't exclusively anger.

"Now, if only you had the patience. But your sweet pussy is always hot and wet and waiting for this"—he ground into her—"and you can't even think beyond your need to climax. Can you?" he whispered, watching her try to stem her imminent orgasm.

"Maybe I don't want to," she heatedly retorted, arching her back against the exquisite pleasure. "Maybe . . . I don't . . . want to at all," she panted, a faint smile curving her mouth as her climax flared, crested, washed over her in flourishing splendor.

Brought a new degree of meaning to the word gratification.

And a new degree of satisfaction to a man who was contemplating an extended holiday in Monte Carlo. Restraining his own desires until she was lying calm and passive in his arms, he gently lifted her unresisting body upward and then as leisurely downward, his erection undiminished, his senses still in flagrant rut.

Pliant, tractable, she neither resisted nor participated, her passions subdued, her hands resting on his muscled shoulders, the rippling movement beneath her palms counterpoint to the smooth motion of his powerful arms. In a gentle, exquisitely relentless rhythm, he raised and lowered her with effortless strength and an eye to sensation, until she was predictably, feverishly panting once more, until he felt as though his body might dissolve from unsatisfied lust. Until he hoped she would come soon because he couldn't wait much longer.

Suddenly, she caught her breath, shut her eyes, and shuddered under his hands, and gratified, he plunged in that last distance more so they both felt the sweet agony begin.

Their climax lasted and lasted in prolonged, endless wonder, all the hyperbole, all the brandishing magnificence of soul-stirring passion pulsing, throbbing, screaming down their nerve endings. His ejaculation jolted his brain, his body, the hot-spur, out-of-control spasms brutal, jarring, sublime. She was shaking, shaken, scandalized by the power he had over her and, in due course, gloriously replete.

He didn't know where he was for a second when he regained his grasp on reality, and then he saw her and felt her. And with a whimsey that would have seemed far-fetched prior to his visit to the casino, he began to contemplate the existence of miracles. She was truly a gift from the gods.

"You're cold." His transient flight of fancy was overcome by the sudden realization his companion's skin was cool beneath his hands.

"Am I?" Overwrought, she was simultaneously hot and cold, shamed and shameless, existing in the flagrant wonderland of shock and wonder, uncertain of all but the pleasure he gave her.

"Let's get you under the covers." He spoke in the authoritative tone she had come to recognize. Shifting her into his arms, he rose and stepped from the tub, pulling a towel from a heated rack on the way out of the room. Placing her on her feet near the bed, he wrapped her in the warm toweling and briskly rubbed her dry. Then he tucked her into bed, covering her with several layers of comforters.

Leaning over, he dropped a kiss on the slender bridge of her nose. "Better?"

Gazing up from her warm cocoon, she wrinkled her tingly nose. "It would be if you were here."

He raked his fingers through his wet hair, pushing it back in sleek waves. "You're going to wear me out. Although," he added, grinning, "I'm not complaining."

"I feel terrible for hounding you." Her voice was small-girl apologetic, but her smile was the flamboyantly seductive one he had come to adore. "And also horribly sexy."

Surely there was a god, he thought. "In that case, I'll hurry." He began moving toward the sitting room.

She felt instantly bereft. "What are you doing?"

"Getting you something you'll like."

"Oh." Her expression brightened. "For me?"

"For you." He winked, and she was flooded with jealousy for all the women who had been the recipients of that roguish glance.

But even in her pink-clouded bliss she knew better than to take issue with his past or future. His entire persona was distinctly profligate, and such men never stayed long. But she had him now, and she had every intention of enjoying the pleasure. And with him, pleasure was guaranteed. She snuggled deeper into the downy comfort of the enormous bed, intent on ignoring the cold reality of tomorrow. Today he was with her, and all was warm enchantment.

When the duke returned, he was carrying a tray with a coffee service. "I had selfish motives for this," he explained. "I didn't want to fall asleep. Not that it's possible with you," he teased. "And before you ask," he added, interpreting her puzzled look, "I ordered this last night."

She glanced at the tray he set on the bed. "How sweet. Two cups."

"I had no intention of letting you leave."

"How flattering. Even last night?"

"Directly after I saw you enter the casino. You've changed my plans."

"Plans?"

"I intended to leave Monte Carlo today, but if you're not busy, Miss Greenwood," he declared, his faint bow exquisite, "I'd prefer entertaining you for a time."

After all the trials and tribulations of her life, she didn't question the equivocal designation "time." When one was offered paradise, one didn't quibble over details. "I'd like that very much, indeed."

"Thank you, Miss Greenwood," he said with punctilious good breeding and a teasing smile. "And this is for you," he offered, lifting a small package from the tray and handing it to her before he sat down.

She couldn't remember when she had last received a gift; she felt like a child at Christmas. Coming to a seated position with a helpful hand from the duke, she carefully eased off the beautiful magenta silk ribbon, set it aside and opened the indigo-colored wrapping. The embossed gold box was from a well-known confectioner. A smile lit up her face. "Chocolates!"

"Look inside." He began pouring coffee.

"I adore *any* kind of chocolate." Lifting the cover, she opened the crisp parchment and went utterly still. A diamond bracelet glistened from the midst of the chocolates.

"I thought it might go with your gown," he casually said.

Or any gown or a royal diadem, the array of large diamonds was so dazzling. Her gaze came up, her eyes bright with tears. "I don't know what to say. No one's ever given me anything . . . like this . . ." Her voice faltered for a moment. "Diamonds . . . my goodness . . . they're magnificent, but—

that is . . . I'm not sure I can keep it." A tremulous uncertainty quivered in her words. "It would make me—"

"No, it would not." Quickly setting his cup aside, he leaned over and took her hands "It's a gift between friends. It doesn't make you anything; it doesn't make me anything. I've plenty of money, and I wanted to give you a gift." He almost said, "Women don't refuse these," but knew better. She was already uncomfortable with the role of paramour.

"I've never done this before . . . I mean . . . coming here with you—"

"I know." He gently stroked the backs of her hands with his thumbs. "Look." His tone was conciliatory. "I had no intention of making you uncomfortable. If anyone should ask, tell them it's Aunt Gillian's."

"I don't actually know anyone who would ask."

"There. You see?"

"But I'd know," she murmured.

"Please . . ." His voice was soft and low, his gaze tender. "Do you know how fortunate I feel for having been in the casino last night?"

"Not as fortunate as I," she quietly said. "You saved my life."

He traced a lingering path down her middle finger. "Repay me by keeping the bracelet."

A playful light appeared in her eyes. "Now, *there's* a bargain."

"I was the one who gained the most, darling." And for once in his life, he wasn't uttering a charming phrase to please a lady.

"So *you* owe *me*."

"Exactly."

She wrinkled her nose in indecision.

"Take it, darling, or I'll cry."

Her laugh bubbled up. "When was the last time you cried?"

"I was probably two." In truth, he had no memory of ever crying. Indulged by his mother, ignored by his father, his world had been perfection until his mother died when he was twelve. And by that time, he knew full well to never show emotion before his father.

"So you feel that strongly."

"It's only a bracelet, darling, not the crown jewels of England."

"Scotland."

He rolled his eyes.

"If I decide to keep it, I need three things from you."

"They're yours."

"No caution?"

"You can have whatever you want." A staggering statement from a man who habitually viewed intruders into his life with suspicion.

She grinned. "That's the third thing."

His brows flickered in amusement. "And my favorite, I warrant."

"First, I'd like some café au lait."

"I've never met a lady so easy to please." He poured her a cup, glanced up with a spoon poised over the sugar bowl, poured in two when she held up two fingers and added hot milk until she said, "Stop."

"And the second?" he asked, handing her the cup.

"Where did you get the bracelet in the dead of night or do you keep a supply in your luggage for the ladies you bed?"

"I ordered it when Claude came up for your note."

"The shops were closed."

"The shops are always open if you want them to be."

"Really. And how many times have you opened the shops?"

"On several occasions. My cufflinks were from Cartier here."

"Was this?"

He nodded. "They know me."

"I don't think I want to hear any more. You probably do this all the time, and—"

"I *don't* do this all the time." It was the most honest statement he had ever uttered. He had never been obsessed before. And he had had numerous opportunities in the last twenty years to experience the phenomenon.

"Then, we're both tyros," she quietly observed, "because I've never slept with a stranger or any man other than my husband. I've never enjoyed myself so. I've never been given chocolates for breakfast—or diamond bracelets—*anytime* at all. So thank you for—this rare glimpse of heaven."

"You're very welcome, and once we—shall I say—engage in the response to question number three, you may thank me again."

She cast him an assessing glance. "Such confidence."

"In the not-too-distant future, I expect you can tell me if my confidence is warranted." He pointed at her cup. "Now, drink your coffee and eat some pastry," he softly commanded, "because you're going to need your strength."

"There are times, although don't let it go to your head," she said with a provocative smile, "when I adore that voice of command."

"How fortunate, since I have these inexplicable urges to possess you. Would you like to be mastered, darling?" His dark brows faintly rose in query. "I could tie you up."

"No!" But a thrilling frisson fluttered up her spine.

"Or I could initiate you into *droits de seigneur.*"

With anyone else she would have taken fierce offense; but his dark gaze was scandalously wicked, and the thought of being dominated by his strength and power quickened her ready sexuality. "What exactly would that entail?" she hesitantly inquired.

An iniquitous smile curved his mouth. "A good deal of pleasure for us both."

"How exactly would that occur?"

"Are you taking notes?"

"The concept makes me marginally nervous, although not with you—I think . . ."

"Trust me, darling," he assured her. "It's only for fun. Now eat something," he added, handing her an almond pastry. "I wouldn't want my dairy maid to be hungry when I lift up her skirts and put my stiff prick in her."

His words ignited a flame deep inside her; she could almost feel the thrilling invasion. "You make certain aspects of a dairy maid's life sound tantalizing," she murmured, a heated tremor in her voice. "And perhaps the dairy maid could order her master about as well . . ."

His gaze went shuttered. "No."

"Why not?"

"Because I don't allow it."

"Because?"

"You don't have enough time for the answer, nor do I care to discuss it. You had your husband, and I had"—his eyes went utterly cold for a moment—"other people in my life I prefer to forget."

"Except you can't forget everything, can you?"

"It depends what you're doing," he softly said.

"Is that why you travel the world?"

"I don't want to talk about this."

"And that's also why you're so good in bed."

"That's why," he brusquely said. "Are we done?"

"Certainly. I know how to be polite."

"I'm not interested in politeness."

"Actually, I'm not either."

His gaze held hers for a potent moment, and then they both laughed.

"I'm interested in sex with you," she said in well-bred accents.

"I'm interested in *protracted* sex with you." His boyish smile lit up his eyes.

"That's pretty simple."

"It can be."

"If I don't grill you on your feelings."

"You're intelligent in addition to being one of the world's most beautiful women."

"And you should know."

"And I should know. Are you warm now?" he gently inquired.

The discussion was over

"Very warm. It must be these quilts." Her glance was playful.

"I'm sure," he softly drawled, pulling away the fold of quilt that covered her breasts. "Although your nipples look like they're cold." They were hard, peaked, provocatively long.

"Your reference to prolonged sex took their fancy."

"And they became hard for me?" Reaching out, he slid his fingertips around the taut crests, the imprint of his silken touch instantly registering in the pit of her stomach, a delicious heat streaking downward like molten pleasure.

"We've been so busy seeing to your orgasms, I've been derelict in my attentions to these large, lovely breasts." Softly gripping her nipples between his thumbs and forefingers, he tugged them, pulling them one way and then the other, her plump breasts swinging, quivering, the fleshy contours compressing and swelling—the coffee in their cups on the tray rippling with the gentle movement of the bed.

"Do you like that? Do you like me to squeeze these?" His fingers tightened their grip.

A convulsive heat liquefied between her thighs, and she softly moaned at the carnal pleasure.

"I can't hear you. Should I squeeze them harder?" The pink tissue compressed between his fingers, and bending his head, he licked one constricted tip.

She could feel the touch of his tongue in every taut nerve in her body, and shuddering, she wondered if she would ever get enough of him.

Relaxing his grip, he slid his palms over the outside flare of her breasts, slipping his hands under their delectable weight, lifting the quivering flesh upward until her breasts were mounded high, until her tingling nipples were conveniently at mouth level. "If you want me to suck on you," he whispered, lightly bouncing the pink globes, "just let me know . . ."

"Please, Flynn," she breathed, anticipation strumming through her body, her need for him overwhelming.

"Who?" he softly queried, gently shaking his head. Releasing her breasts, he leaned back slightly. "Remember you're the maid and I'm . . . ?"

"The master," she whispered, the throbbing between her thighs quickening at the salacious thought.

"And I'll be putting my hard cock in you."

She squirmed against the fine linen sheet, her soft whimper a distinct plea.

"But you have to please me," he softly warned. "Sit up straighter so I can suck on your big breasts more easily."

She instantly responded, her breasts thrusting upward.

"Make your nipples longer for me. Rub them." And he watched as she massaged her nipples, lightly stretched them, diligently obeying. "Look at what that does to my hard-on," he murmured, and when her gaze focused on his upthrust erection, he wondered if she would come before he touched her. She was flushed, panting, gently rocking on the bed, her eyes hot with desire.

"Do you want this?" Lightly grasping his penis, he slid his hand downward, the movement increasing the length, the gleaming crest arching higher.

"Yes . . . ," she breathed, a heated tremor in her voice.

"You have to let me suck on you first."

"Of course . . . please—whatever you want." With her eyes trained on his pulsing erection, submission resonated in her words.

"Lean forward," he ordered. "And hold your breasts up for me."

She instantly complied, the fleshy abundance spilling over her palms, her carnal hunger so intense she was shaking.

"If your nipples are to my taste," he whispered, his breath warming one crest, "I may allow you to fuck me. What flavor are they?"

She shook her head, unsure of anything but her throbbing need for fulfillment.

"I prefer cherry. Do you think you can accommodate me?" He lightly licked the turgid tip.

She moaned, all her senses alert to the merest touch, the grazing imprint of his tongue vibrating throughout her body.

"You have to answer or I won't let you come. There's cherry creams in your chocolate box." He gently nibbled on the pink nipple she held up for him. "Should we flavor these to make me happy?"

"If you wish . . ." She could barely respond, her desire so ravenous.

"Don't *you* wish?" His voice was brusque. "Tell me or I won't ram my cock in you."

"Yes, yes . . . ," she whispered.

"Are you wet enough?" he murmured and waited for her answer.

It took her a moment to recall the question, and even then she was unsure. "I think so."

"You seem to have your mind elsewhere." His tone turned severe. "I'm not sure you'll do for a dairy maid if you can't concentrate on your duties."

"I'm sorry, sir."

"I may not fuck you if you don't better apply yourself."

"I will, sir," she quickly replied. "Forgive me, sir."

"Well . . ." His tone was considering. "Maybe this once I'll forgive you. You're new and don't understand what's required of you. But you understand, you're on probation."

"I understand. I shall listen—truly I shall."

He scrutinized her for a moment as though questioning her sincerity. "Very well," he finally said. "Now then." He lifted her chin so their eyes met. "The question was whether you're wet enough to have sex with me. Do you think you are?"

She took a small breath, forcing herself to concentrate on answering correctly. "I'm sure I am, sir."

"Why don't we see." Easing her thighs apart, he slid two fingers inside her, slowly, delicately, gliding upward, the slick, hot tissue pulsing around his strong fingers. He avoided contact with the most sensitive areas of arousal. She was teetering on the brink, and he wanted to delay her orgasm—or at least try, he thought with a faint smile. Smoothly withdrawing his fingers awash with pearly liquid, he lightly traced a path down the deep valley between her breasts, leaving a glistening trail. "Your sweet cunt is a veritable river of desire," he murmured, holding his scented fingers up for her to see. "Such enthusiasm. Would I be right in saying you're suitably prepared for intercourse?"

It took enormous effort to respond when her entire nervous system was obsessed with voluptuous sensation. "Yes, sir," she whispered in the merest wisp of a voice, near delirious with wanting him, the throbbing ache between her legs so intense she would do anything to have him inside her.

"Soon we'll test your readiness," he promised, sliding his fingers over one plump breast. "But first I want some cherry-flavored nipples." He rested his fingertip on the turgid crest of one breast as though clarifying his statement. "You may service me after that, provided I'm satisfied with the taste. Keep those breasts up nice and high," he added, adjusting her hands under her breasts before forcing them upward. "I don't want to have to bend down too far." As she quickly complied, pushing the ripe weight of her breasts into great, high mounds, he lifted the cover from the chocolate box, took out the bracelet and snapped it around her wrist. "There's no more debate about keeping this, is there?" His voice was silken.

She shook her head.

"You're sure?" He gently stroked one nipple, and the jarring pleasure racked her body.

She nodded, unable to gather breath to speak.

"How amenable you've become," he murmured. "You'll

find it more rewarding. Obedient dairy maids are allowed to serve me in a great number of ways. Would you like to serve as a receptacle for my sperm?"

She softly moaned, imagining the sensation as his monstrous erection entered her, stretched her, filled her.

"You seem like a particularly hot-blooded little piece," he whispered, waiting her gently away against the rush of heat flowing into her vagina. "Have the grooms been fucking you in my absence? Are you suitably primed for sex? Or have you been waiting just for me?" Picking up a chocolate, he held it to her mouth. "Take a bite," he quietly commanded, "and then we'll see whether you've been trained or not."

Her gaze came up and met his for a potent moment, umbrage beneath the smoldering heat. "I wouldn't do this for any other reason, you know."

"I know." His voice was like velvet or more aptly like rich chocolate cream. "Take a bite, darling . . . yield to me and I'll forgive you for fucking the groom."

Sudden temper flared in her eyes, and she bit down hard on his finger.

With a grunt of pain he jerked his hand away and shoved at her. As she tumbled backward, he followed her down, imprisoning her with his body. "You need a lesson in submission," he growled, his dark eyes only inches from hers.

"Maybe I need something else," she snapped, struggling against his weight.

"And maybe you'll get it if you contrive to please me." Curt and resentful, he glared at her. "Understood?" His voice was whisper-soft, his eyes as hot as hers. "Now, let's start over again, and if you're very, very good, I'll put this in you"—he slid the head of his erection just past the sleek lips of her labia, forcing open the engorged, pulsing tissue, holding himself immobile just inside the entrance to her vagina while she shivered with longing—"so you can *really* feel it." Abruptly withdrawing, he sat up while she tried to stop trembling.

"So whenever you're ready to cooperate," he murmured, selecting another chocolate from the box.

"Damn you," she breathed.

"At the moment, the feeling's mutual. I'm waiting," he coolly said. Why did it suddenly matter that he prevail in this ridiculous game? Why did he require submission when it was never relevant before? But his passions were as immune to logic as hers, and no facile answer materialized in the tumult of his brain.

No more did Felicia understand why she was so humbled by desire, having always regarded obsession as a flight of fancy, poetic license at best, but never real . . . until this moment when she was lost to all reason, desperate for what he could give her. And not compliant so much as lustful, she sat up, leaned back on her hands and offered him a seductive smile. "I'd thought I'd make myself available."

"You don't think I could take you if I wanted?"

"It would be a change, at least. You never have to take, do you?"

"Make a selection, perhaps," he insolently drawled.

"But you want me now, don't you? What if I said no?"

"You can't."

"Nor can you."

"A not unpleasant dilemma, I'd say. Are you ready to try this again?" he softly asked. "Because I'm not finished yet."

"Do you often play like this?"

He had no intention of answering. "Do you?"

"You know better."

"Somehow I like being the first," he murmured with a sinful smile, placing the chocolate against her mouth.

She did as well, the blatant beauty of his smile only one of his numerous charms. And she took the candy into her mouth to please herself and him and bit into it while he watched with a modicum of caution she found amusing. As the chocolate coating cracked, a tiny rivulet of cherry cream oozed down her chin.

"How sweet you look with pink cream running down your face," he murmured, lifting the candy away. Leaning forward, he licked a lingering path upward, devouring the sugary trickle. "Definitely good enough to eat," he whispered as his mouth came to rest on hers. "Now don't move," he warned, easing away.

His warning was unnecessary, her understanding clarified, her body taut with longing.

Tipping the chocolate, he dribbled a thin stream of pink liquid over one nipple and then the other, lightly smearing the creamy sweet over and around each tingling crest. Then dropping the chocolate shell back into the box, he sat back to admire his handiwork. "Look, darling. How do you like being my favorite bonbon?"

She glanced down, the rose crests slick with the pale confection, glossy and emblazoned because Flynn required it. "To be your bonbon is my greatest desire." Her voice was low, infused with seductive flattery. If need be, she would paint her body with sweetness to have him.

"How delightfully submissive." A slow half smile graced his mouth. "You learn quickly, my sweet dairy maid."

"If you would look on me kindly, my lord, I await your pleasure."

"I find humility a most charming asset in a servant," he said, his grin as insolent as her statement. "You may win a place in the main house for such deference."

"Would that mean I might warm your bed, my lord?"

"You'd have to take your turn, of course."

"Perhaps," she whispered, delectable promise in her voice, "I could find a way to please you best."

He gazed at her for a breath-held moment, her lush body incarnate female, voluptuous, full-breasted with a narrow waist and curving hips and soft thighs that could only have been made for love. That *were* made for love. "Perhaps you could," he whispered, a sudden, unnerving truth to his words. But as quickly he deflected such perilous sentiment. "I think we're done now," he abruptly said. For half his life, sex had been his entertainment and amusement, a means of keeping feeling at bay. And he reverted to type with ease.

His mouth closed over one frosted nipple, and with delicate concentration, he swiftly sucked first one, then the other clean. No longer interested in play, he was intent on the simple act of fornication, needing the physical gratification and oblivion that only a woman's body could bring. Easing her down on the bed, he slid between her thighs and plunged inside because he didn't want to think or speculate or change his life in any way; he only wanted to feel the seething rapture of an orgasm. Forcing himself deeper, he buried himself in the anonymous female sweetness that had always offered deliverance. But this time at the farthest limit of his downthrust, his throbbing erection rammed against a soft, specific, highly personalized womb.

Perhaps a fertile, life-giving womb.

The terrifying thought almost arrested the powerful rhythm of his lower body, and if not for the mindless urgency compelling him, he might have been able to stop. But he didn't, couldn't, wouldn't, and as he drove into her again, she suddenly came like she was wont to do in a swift, wild delirium that warmed his cock, his lustful soul and oddly his heart.

Heedless of all but his selfish quest for orgasm, he continued his savage hammering into her, ignoring his misgivings, immune to consequences, rash, impetuous, fevered like a callow youth when he had never been imprudent even then. But everything seemed different this time, his nerves raw to the quick, his sensory receptors so vigilant he was conscious of the pulse beats in the hot, sleek tissue of her vagina—in the answering beat of his heart. And familiar lust was overwhelmed by another kind of pleasure, finer, more pervasive, deep-felt, as though a new vista had opened in the sumptuous realm of sensation.

He was selfish when he rarely was, intent on taking, on possessing and owning her—not in play, but in fact. The rhythm of his body was so violent, she was steadily pushed upward. And even when the pillows piled against the headboard arrested his progress, he continued his assault, softly grunting with each powerful downstroke, forcing her thighs wider with each savage thrust, needing to dominate her completely.

He was unaware of her orgasmic cries when he climaxed, conscious only of a shameless sense of mastery and triumph and the panting voice in his ear, growling, "You're mine," as he poured into her.

But he had avoided attachment for so long, he quickly came to his senses and with cooler, post-orgasmic reason, recalled his commitment to personal freedom. Quickly disengaging himself, he rolled away, the consequences of unprotected sex and entrapment suddenly in the forefront of his brain. Raising himself on one elbow, he scowled at the woman beside him. "Why aren't you concerned with protection—condoms or sponges or cervical caps." His precise litany was for clarity's sake, and that he wanted an answer was equally clear.

Felicia didn't stir from her languid pose, nor did a modicum of distress crease her brow. On the contrary, when she smiled he was reminded of sunshine. "Are you accusing me of something?"

"I'm just wondering why you're not worried about conception." Gruff and grumbling, he was already contemplating how much she would want.

"You don't seem to be worried." That same mild unconcern.

"I'm not the one who might get pregnant," he muttered.

One brow rose infinitesimally, and her voice was amused. "You mean it's my problem?"

"You're enjoying this, aren't you?"

"This? This sexual marathon? Yes, very much," she pleasantly added. "Are you?"

"I was."

"Until your lust-filled brain cooled sufficiently to wonder whether I was trying to trap you?"

His scowl deepened. "Are you?"

"Now, why would I want to do that?"

"Some women might."

"You really mean all women, don't you?" She smiled. "But I'll give you the benefit of a doubt. As for myself"—her voice was serene—"let me assure you, my motives are as selfish as yours and as finite. I'm only interested in sex with you, not motherhood or fatherhood. I was married for four years as you know. Did I fail to mention I never became pregnant? So you're quite safe, Flynn. You may discard that black scowl and continue to think of me as nothing more than your current sexual partner. Is that better?"

He slowly exhaled and then ruefully smiled. "I beg your pardon, most profoundly."

"Apology accepted. Might I suggest, though, if you're concerned with some woman trapping you, you should consider using a condom. It would be a sensible idea."

"I usually do."

Her eyes opened the merest fraction more. "But not with me?"

He looked momentarily afflicted, and then he dazzled her with his warm, boyish smile. "I have no explanation."

"And you have no intention of thinking about it."

He grinned. "No."

Her smile this time was well-bred and urbane. "Nor do I. We are neither in a position to think unduly about"—she sweepingly gestured around the room—"this tantalizing interlude at the Hotel de Paris. If we did, we would have to stop this madness."

"And I have no intention of doing that."

She put up her hand. "A small intermission, perhaps, if you'd be so kind. I really *do* have to go home and let my servants know I'm safe."

"Have them come here."

"I'd be embarrassed in the extreme."

"Then, I'll go home with you." He didn't wish to relinquish her, however briefly, for myriad selfish reasons.

She gently shook her head. "Let me go first and smooth the way."

He laughed. "You sound as though you have chaperones."

"I suppose they are in a way, but they've also been of great solace to me, so I shall go ahead, and you may follow me if you wish."

"Of course I wish." His voice was gruff.

Her smile was filled with delight. "I was hoping you might."

"How long do I have to wait?" He felt like an adolescent with his first lover, burning with impatience, filled with longing.

"Give me, say, two hours. Enough time to explain what I can of this"—she grinned—"relationship . . . and I use the term loosely, and time also to allow them to assimilate the good news of our casino winnings." She reached out to touch his hand. "And for that I shall be eternally in your debt."

"As I am for your delightful company," he smoothly replied, facile charm second nature to him. "And if I must wait two hours, I'd be grateful if you left posthaste, so I may see you that much sooner." Throwing his legs over the side of the bed, he quickly came to his feet. "I'll help you dress."

She wasn't entirely sure his haste was sincerely motivated or predicated on the notion he could rid himself of her sooner if he helped her along. A man of his licentious tastes didn't inspire any ideals of genuine devotion. And whether he would appear in two hours was highly moot. But if he didn't, she would have not only wonderful memories, but the necessary money to save her home *and* a new and delightful appreciation for the enchanting congress between a man and a woman.

He kissed her as she stood by the door, once more dressed and presentable, thanks in no small part to his swift proficiency as lady's maid.

"Thank you," she quietly said, "for everything." Wanting one last moment of physical contact in the event he didn't appear, she touched the lapel of his robe in a lingering caress.

Disconcerted by sentiment, by goodbyes, by the disarray of emotions she occasioned, he glanced at the clock on the mantel. "We needn't say more than *adieu*. I'll see you in two hours."

Her heart leaped with joy even as she cautioned herself to be sensible about a man like Flynn. "Then, I'll just say *adieu*."

"Two hours, darling, and you'd better complete your explanations to your servants, because I intend to monopolize you once I see you again."

"How charmingly masterful you are." Her voice was a low, sensuous purr.

"Don't start that," he warned, reaching for the door latch, "or you'll never get out of here." Pulling the door open, he gently pushed her out into the corridor. "Claude has a carriage waiting for you. And I'd escort you downstairs, but I'm sure you'd rather I didn't."

She blew him a kiss. "Thank you again."

"Hurry," he brusquely said.

She floated down the hall and then down the stairs, and when Claude caught sight of her as he waited near the outside door, he repressed the knowing smile that came to his lips. "Good morning, Miss Greenwood," he said as she approached. "It's a beautiful morning, isn't it?"

"The most beautiful, indeed, Claude." She ran her hands lightly over her coiffure—for all the good luck she had experienced. "Quite the most beautiful," she softly added, walking past him to the carriage waiting at the entrance to the Hotel de Paris.

Chapter Three

While Felicia enjoyed her morning drive home, Flynn summoned two shop owners to his suite, and when they arrived, his orders were crisp and concise. Neither asked for clarification. They both understood the Duke of Grafton demanded the very best for his lady loves. His requests weren't unusual in any event. They were, in fact, quite ordinary for the style of man who spent a great deal of his leisure time in ladies' boudoirs.

They both left the suite much richer for their visit.

While Felicia explained as much of the previous evening as she deemed necessary to her devoted servants, and during the happy interval in which they all exalted at the good fortune that had befallen them, Flynn sent new instructions to the captain of his yacht at anchor in the harbor.

In truth, Claire and Daniel were already party to much of what had transpired the previous night, related as they were to a bevy of servants at the Hotel de Paris. They joyfully fussed over their beloved charge, assuring her in the casual way the French had in relation to amour, that they were pleased and happy for her whatever came of the evening she had spent with the man who had won them a fortune.

"You've been too long alone anyway," Claire observed as she helped Felicia into a bath. "You deserve some amusement."

A bland word for the enchantment she had experienced, Felicia thought, smiling at the memories. "He's coming here, you know."

"I suspected as much. You're smiling like a woman in love."

"Nothing so romantic, Claire. But as you say, amusing, certainly."

"You must wear something delicious."

"As if I have anything so risqué."

"We'll find something, and I'll have Daniel bring up the best champagne."

"And perhaps some cognac. I'm not sure what he likes."

"He likes you, my lady. He's not coming for the liquor."

"Do you think so?" It was a delectable thought when her life had been so devoid of happiness.

"I know so." Claire refrained from saying all the servants at the Hotel de Paris had never been so generously bribed into silence. As relatives who could be trusted, she and Daniel had received a full report.

Sometime later, when Felicia had been bathed, toweled off, perfumed and was seated on the terrace in her robe having her hair dried by Claire, two carriages appeared on the steep drive.

"Oh, Lord, is he here already?"

"No, no . . . the carriages are from Boulonge and Madame Denise. See, Henri and Bertram are driving."

Under their curious gazes, the carriages were unloaded of an astonishing number of baskets filled with roses and a lavish array of beribboned boxes in the distinctive periwinkle blue of Madame Denise's exclusive shop.

And in only minutes more, when the gifts had been carried upstairs to Felicia's suite, she found herself surrounded by an overwhelming quantity of various-colored roses and blue boxes. Fluctuating between alarm and joy at Flynn's extravagant gesture, she anxiously surveyed the spectacle. "I don't know, Claire . . ." The scandalous gifts of lingerie were causing her a level of discomfort no matter how much she adored the giver. "Should I send the lingerie back?"

"Of course you won't," her housekeeper repudiated, continuing to unpack the sumptuous finery. "They're lover's gifts."

"I'm not sure . . ." Felicia's expression mirrored her uncertainty. "What will Madame Denise think of me?"

"She'll think you're a very lucky woman to have such a

wealthy lover. And you can't possibly wear your high-necked linen nightgowns for a love tryst."

Felicia plucked at the skirt of her plain linen robe, the sensible garment in sharp contrast to Flynn's beautiful gifts. The intimate attire Claire had put out on display was a veritable flower garden of radiant color: peignoirs and negligees, lacy drawers and sheer corsets, dozens of silk stockings in every imaginable hue with matching satin slippers. She had often admired the magnificent creations in the windows of the exclusive shop, but the frothy confections had been beyond the reach of her modest salary. "I *could* just try one on."

"Try these first." Her servant held up a lilac lace corset adorned with white rosebuds and ribbon rosettes along with a matching lace petticoat so lavishly ruffled, it had the look of a ball gown—a very expensive one.

"If I accept these gifts . . ." Felicia sighed, struggling against her conscience. "They're so highly indecent—completely immodest and—"

Claire's disbelieving snort interrupted Felicia's litany. "They're the most beautiful lingerie you've ever had. You're not in Scotland now, my lady. You're also a widow, not a schoolgirl. You don't even have to worry about cuckolding a husband. It's high time you had a lover. And," she added with pithy emphasis, "a lady always dresses to please her lover."

"High time, you think . . ."

"You're going to dry up and blow away, but if that's what you want?" Claire shrugged, a particularly Gallic shrug, brusque and dismissive.

The stark reminder of her lonely future vanquished the last of Felicia's reservations. "You're right," she quietly said.

"Of course I'm right. Now, let's see that you look ravishing for your Mr. Suffolk."

"He's not mine," Felicia corrected, thinking Flynn was the least likely man to belong to anyone.

"He is today." Claire's smile was conspiratorial. "And who knows, poppet, with your beauty and charm . . ."

"How romantic, but you haven't met Flynn. He's not a romantic."

"He didn't send you gloves or a book now, did he? And your diamond bracelet is the kind of romance any woman would love."

"He does this for all the ladies in his life."

Claire's shrug discounted Felicia's comment. "You're going to be the loveliest woman he's ever seen, and if you have any sense, you'll stop making excuses and enjoy yourself. Now take off that robe and put these on before he arrives and finds you in that plain thing."

Felicia smiled. "You're not going to take no for an answer, are you?"

"Just hurry," Claire briskly replied, shaking out the garments. "He'll be here soon."

Felicia gave herself up to Claire's ministrations and to her edifying homilies on love and lovers, allowing the happiness she felt at the promise of seeing Flynn again fill her senses. And when she saw herself in the cheval glass, adorned in lilac lace fit for a queen, she felt as though she had been transported and transformed and indeed might be some fairy queen bedecked for her lover—on a very warm summer day, she facetiously noted, the sheer corset and petticoat the merest of coverings.

"Now just a light peignoir, my lady. Something to cover but not conceal," Claire added with a cheerful wink. "This white lace is nicely demure."

"It's hardly demure. It's so sheer, one can see right through it."

"He'll love it." Claire held out the lacy robe. "And think, poppet, when have you ever been so happy?"

She was indeed happy, and Flynn would be here soon unless these lavish gifts were intended as a polite goodbye. Although lingerie or certainly *this* much lingerie suggested a shamelessly serviceable gift instead. Felicia smiled. She rather thought Flynn had something in mind. "Tell me again I'm doing the right thing," Felicia murmured, slipping her arms into the peignoir, needing reassurance after a lifetime of dutiful behavior.

Claire rolled her eyes. "After all our struggles? After almost losing the villa? How can you even ask? He's a gift from heaven."

"I'll have memories at least in my old age."

"Life is to be lived every day, child. You'll have memories tomorrow."

Recall of the previous night made her smile. "It *is* rather nice to give in to impulse on occasion."

"Which you should do more often," Claire observed, pleased her young charge had at last tasted the joys of love. "Now eat your breakfast," she briskly ordered. "You need some food after your sleepless night. I made your favorite Savarin chocolate and toasted baba. While you're eating, I'll check that Daniel has the champagne ready—and the cognac," she added, curtailing Felicia's reminder. "And then, I'll be right back."

Too excited to eat after Claire left, Felicia moved from gift to gift, smelling each bouquet of roses, touching each item of lingerie, sliding the fine fabrics through her hands and wondering if all miracles were so incredibly sweet. And she would stop to admire her glamorous image reflected in the mirror from time to time. So must all paramours look, she cheerfully thought, displayed to advantage in scanty bits of lace meant for a lover's eyes only. Even lilac satin, high-heeled slippers had been included, so from the tips of her lilac toes to the top of her ruffled curls she was elegantly attired in wanton splendor.

And if she wasn't so dizzy with excitement at seeing Flynn again, she might take issue with the blatant sexual nature of his gifts. She wasn't sophisticated enough to completely ignore the impropriety, but she was infatuated enough not to care. In the grip of a mad and glorious exultation, nothing mattered but wondrous amour.

At the sound of racing footsteps on the stairs, she spun around and laughed with joy. He was here!

A moment later, the door crashed open and hit the wall with such force the paintings quivered. But no lover met Felicia's horrified gaze.

"So this is how you've earned the money to pay me, you whoring slut." Cousin Dickie's mouth was lifted in a sneer, his obese body seemingly larger than life in the sudden hush. Moving into the room, he surveyed the profusion of gifts with a withering glance. "I always thought you were a tart with your big breasts and cheeky impudence."

"I'm sorry, my lady." Daniel stood in the doorway, his attempts to stop Dickie unsuccessful. "I told him to leave, that you had the money to pay him, but he wouldn't listen."

"Never mind, Daniel. It's not your fault. I'm expecting a guest. If you'd see that he's comfortable in the drawing room, I'll be down soon." Turning to her cousin, she coolly said, "You're not welcome here. Kindly leave or I'll call the gendarmes."

Ignoring her, Dickie picked up a black lace corset and held it between his thumb and forefinger as though it were odorous. "Really . . ." His voice was oily. "And what would you tell them? That you earn your money as a whore? You might wish to reconsider," he unctuously noted. "And I'm not sure such illicit wages will serve as proper payment for my share of the villa. I'll have to check with my lawyer." He dropped the scrap of black lace. "Are you waiting for another customer?" The lechery in his eyes sent a chill up her spine. "Perhaps you could entertain me in the interim."

"I'd rather kill myself." Felicia held her peignoir tightly closed. "Or better yet you."

"How fierce you sound," he murmured, a loathsome smile on his fat face. "I'm intrigued."

"While I'm repelled as always in your presence. You'll have your money by the end of the day, and that's all you'll get. I want you gone now and out of my life."

"Wouldn't you, now?" Dickie's prominent eyes had a reptilian cast. "I was just thinking," he murmured, as though she had not spoken, "with your new-found wealth, I may have to raise my price."

"I have your lawyer's agreement. You can't."

"You have no idea what I can do," he silkily drawled. "What if I were to tell your brother about your new livelihood. How do you think Ann would like a whore for a sister-in-law, dear Felicia?"

"Mind your tongue when you speak to my wife!"

The deep voice slashed through the warm spring air, fury in every syllable.

Felicia's eyes flared wide. Cousin Dickie pivoted, prepared to do battle.

Until he saw the tall, powerful man in the doorway with eyes chill as the grave. His face turned ashen. "Your . . . Grace . . . ," he stammered, his body frozen in place. "I had . . . I mean . . . I didn't—I had . . . no idea."

"And now you do." Harsh, grating words struck like a blow.

"She's your wife?" Dickie blurted out, incredulity overcoming fear. The Duke of Grafton was the most eligible bachelor in the western world.

"You heard me," Flynn growled. "My wife. Now get the hell out of my sight. And if you're still in Monte Carlo twenty minutes from now, I'm going to find you and kill you." Without another glance for the red-faced man making for the exit, Flynn moved toward Felicia. "Forgive me, darling," he gently said, as though he had not just threatened a man's life. "I'm sorry I was late." And like a child rescued from a fiery dragon, Felicia rushed into his arms. Gathering her close, he gazed down at her upturned face, a wicked gleam in his eyes. "Before that rude encounter, I meant to mention you look good enough to eat in those . . . "

"Unmentionables." Her lashes fluttered in demure parody.

"Ah—" Amused understanding sparkled in his eyes. "We must be discreet away from the Hotel de Paris. If I were to take care with the exact wording, might I do—"

"Anything at all . . ."

His grin was sinful. "Then, I hope you have considerable leisure, because anything at all quite boggles the mind."

"I have all the time in the world," she murmured. "Now that you've scared Dickie away." She eased away slightly and surveyed him with a mild gravity. "But you needn't have gone so far, Flynn. Dickie will talk. There's sure to be gossip."

"We could marry and deter scandalous rumor," he lightly proposed.

She gently shook her head. "I appreciate your gesture, but such a sacrifice is unnecessary. I live outside society, no one knows me, my family is distant and unconcerned—"

"Don't you wish to marry me?" A faint frown drew his brows together.

"Be serious, Flynn."

"I am."

"Of course you're not. You were about to leave Monte Carlo this morning. You'd hate to be married."

Her blunt directness forced him to question his motives. "Maybe I wouldn't."

She laughed. "Maybe? There, you see. You'd be out the door and halfway to Asia before a week was up."

"Have you considered *you* might be opposed to marriage?"

"What if I am? I've reason enough."

"This wouldn't be the same."

"Flynn! Stop. You don't know what you're saying. Think for a minute, are you actually willing to give up your freedom?" Her expression sobered. "Because I'd require fidelity."

A sudden silence fell.

And then he smiled. "I'm willing to risk it if you are."

"Losing your freedom, you mean."

He nodded.

"We should be madly in love to even consider this."

"I am." Until that moment, he had not known.

"How can you be sure?"

"Nothing's sure, darling. But if you don't take the risk, you'll never know. And if this isn't love, I don't care, because it's better than all the amusements and journeys in the world."

She grinned. "It is, isn't it! It's even better than cherry creme chocolates."

His smile was pure sunshine. "That might be a draw. But if you say yes, I promise you chocolates for breakfast every day."

"Ummm, tempting."

"You don't really want to live without me, do you?"

His question cut to the core, and the simple truth was she didn't. "Can you tell?"

He faintly dipped his head.

"Because you know women."

"No, because your happiness is mine."

"Before last night, I hadn't known what happiness was."

He smiled. "Nor I."

"Tell me we're not making a huge mistake."

"I can do that. We're not. Marry me and I'll make you happy."

"So sure?"

He was a gambler who always played for broke, and he had never been so sure. "I guarantee it."

"One question more before we leap into the abyss. You're not just Mr. Suffolk, are you, Your Grace?"

"Does it matter?"

"Not to me. I fell in love with Mr. Suffolk."

"And so I'll always remain, although you may be addressed as the Duchess of Grafton on occasion."

"You aren't!" The Duke of Grafton was the byword for vice and beauty and wildness and of course a king's ransom in wealth. "I see why you don't tell women if they don't know."

"I don't tell anyone. So if you don't mind being a duchess, my vanity would be assuaged with a simple affirmative to my one and only proposal of marriage."

"If not for Dickie, you might not have—"

He stopped her words with a kiss, and when he raised his mouth a lengthy time later, he softly commanded, "Just say yes."

Her mouth quirked into a grin. "Convince me."

And he did with finesse and skill and in the end with a wild abandon that destroyed Madame Denise's lilac-colored creation and momentarily stopped the world.

THE PLEASURE GAME

Thea Devine

Chapter One

Sherburne House, Hertfordshire, England
Spring season, 1812

She was spoiled and she knew it, and she wanted what she wanted *when* she wanted it, and she was very well aware of that vice, too.

She had *said* she wanted Marcus Raulton, a careless comment publicly made, even knowing his libertine reputation superseded the attraction of his wealth and station, and now the pitch was in the fire and Drastic Measures were About to be Taken.

Her father had overheard.

Blast it all.

What demon of misfortune had put him within earshot the very moment she was making idle party conversation with her dearest friend, Ancilla, she would never comprehend.

But the end result was a disaster: her father believed she wanted Marcus Raulton, that she was in hot pursuit of Marcus Raulton, and he meant to do everything in his power to stop her.

No wonder he had been in such a tear to return to Sherburne House this weekend. He wanted her out of London, and he wanted to see Jeremy—Jeremy Gavage, of all people. Her father had *not* been in a hurry merely to take care of business as she had just painfully discovered.

No, he had been intent on sticking his nose in *her* business—and enlisting Jeremy's help in the process.

How fortunate she had eavesdropped on him!

Otherwise she wouldn't have known, wouldn't have gotten wind of this crack-brained scheme of her father's to have Jeremy distract her. It was enough to make any woman insensible with rage. It was ludicrous; it was insulting, as if she weren't old enough to know what she was doing.

That was the whole of it: her father still thought her untouched and unsophisticated—still ten years old in his mind no doubt.

Blast the fates.

No wonder he had called upon Jeremy to try to contain her.

He certainly couldn't. She had trained her father well, in the absence of a mother's constraining influence. He knew that she would do the exact opposite of what he wanted. So why should he risk confirming his worst suspicions by *asking* her if her sights were set on Marcus Raulton. He probably wouldn't have believed her anyway, and for him, it was easier to try to restrain her than to dissuade her.

And so his appeal to Jeremy, who had his own ax to grind after his disastrous liaison with that nasty Marguerite deVigny.

She felt herself boiling up again. Jeremy. Tall, dark, elegant, reserved, indulgent Jeremy. Her neighbor her whole life. The boy who had been like a son to her own father. Who had taught her to ride, who had endured her clumsy flirting, who had been the object of her affections when she was twelve. Who had destroyed all her romantic illusions when he had taken up with the Lady Marguerite three years before.

Grown-up, wounded Jeremy, who was perfectly willing to pretend to—what had he said?—*lust* after her to keep her away from Marcus Raulton.

She ground her teeth. There had to be some heavenly retribution for men like that. Men who would letch and leave and count the experience as no more than a roll of the dice.

Ah, forget about heaven when there was a fury right here on earth. It would serve them right if *she* exacted vengeance on *them*. Both of them. Her father and Jeremy.

Jeremy . . . She couldn't even picture him. But that was only natural: she hadn't seen Jeremy in over three years. He had spent three years abroad looking his minute over the oil Marguerite, and now he was back home to see to overdue business concerns and, by the sound of it, meddle in hers.

Well, he ought to mind his own business, she thought testily. But no—he had no compunction at all about pitching himself right in the middle of her business without even trying to see her.

She might be a pudge-pot, for all he knew. She might be totally at her last prayers. The rumormongers were saying so anyway. Out two years, going on three, and no offers. Surely there was something amiss with the beautiful Lady Regina Olney, they whispered, that no man wanted her. Oh yes, she was well aware of the gossip. And the sly little snipes in the society columns of *Tatler:*

> *What Beauty of the previous two seasons, not yet caught in the parson's noose, still fully expects to rope in the Eligibles this season, just to prove she is still attractive enough to do it?*

And so Jeremy too had assumed that she had the sensibility of a turnip, and that she would just gratefully fall into his arms when he came to rescue her from Marcus Raulton.

Because, of course, she had no discrimination whatsoever. About *anything.*

Their faith in her was positively overwhelming. Oh, revenge would be so sweet: she had her pride, after all. It was only a matter of deciding what—and how.

Maybe—a thought occurred to her—just maybe this ridiculous scheme of her father's would quiet the gossips. Maybe they would think she had been waiting all this time for Jeremy to come to point.

Wouldn't that be perfect, to turn the tables on Jeremy and use him to distract her father all the while she pretended to pursue Marcus Raulton?

She contemplated that lovely idea for a long moment. Exactly the thing. Overlay the forbidden with a healthy helping of respectability. Make everyone think it *had* been Jeremy for whom she had been waiting.

And . . . and . . . oh, this was most excellent: somehow put him in the untenable position of aiding her pursuit of Raulton.

How delicious was this?

But she had to think it through and plan it thoroughly and completely.

Wasn't she her father's daughter?

Poor Jeremy. He hadn't dealt with her in years. He had no idea what he was in for.

Oh, God she was as bad as her father.

And the Season had only just begun.

London, Spring 1812

The next big event this early in the Season was the Skeffinghams' ball.

This was the one it was most likely that Raulton and Jeremy might both attend, and so Regina had carefully dressed in her favorite pearl-encrusted jonquil yellow crepe, the matching pearl necklace and earrings that had belonged to her mother, and a lustrous strand entwined in her raven black hair.

But this was too soon, she thought edgily, plucking at a curl. They had been back in Town a mere two days, and they had already been to dinner at the Tatums' the night before, and now this. It was too much, especially on the heels of the tiring trip to and from Hertfordshire and the fact she hadn't yet wholly formulated A Plan.

"You look all the thing, my dear," her father told her, wrapping her shoulders in a matching gauze shawl. "Are you ready for this?"

She was ready for nothing, let alone a crush of dozens and dozens of conveyances crawling up to the Skeffingham house at the far end of the elite enclave, Bromley Close. Its gates were thrown wide now, and an openly curious crowd gawked as carriage after carriage drew up and discharged passengers dressed in the height of fashion who vanished inside the front door of the stately three-story brick residence as if the doorman had waved a magic wand.

They crowded into the reception hall and wound their way down the long hallway lined with gilt-framed portraits of generations of Skeffingham ancestors and into the two-story ballroom.

It didn't seem possible, but the room appeared full to overflowing already, the stuffiness thankfully mitigated by long french windows at either end of the room that were wide open to the cool fresh air.

Candlelight glimmered everywhere, reflected in dozens of mirrors, the light softening every detail and giving the room an intimacy and a most flattering glow. Chairs lined the walls on two sides, and already the matrons who would not be dancing had gathered with their bosom-bows for an evening of exquisite gossip.

Servants hovered, accommodating every request, and on a balcony ten feet above, a string quartet played under the discreet hum of conversation. And ten feet above that, angels hovered, flitting in and out of puffy clouds on the beautiful painted ceiling.

But no angels here on earth, Regina thought irritably, as she and her father paused at the threshold of the ballroom to be announced, *just Jeremy and her father, devils both of them.*

Since there was nothing yet she could do, she moved through the crowd on her father's arm, greeting friends and acquaintances she had seen a mere five days before.

She was grateful, finally, to see Ancilla Hoxley-Marshall, her dearest friend, who was obviously on the lookout for her. Ancilla was the best person, as sweet and self-effacing as a nun, and yet she was always a repository of the most current *on dit,* especially in a gathering this size.

Regina grasped Ancilla's hands which were cold as alabaster. *"Ancilla!* What a crowd. Have you seen Marcus Raulton?" Time to go forward. She had thought of a strategy; it couldn't even be called a plan, but it involved feeding her father's worst fears by making sure she was seen with or near Mr. Raulton as often as possible. It wasn't a perfect scheme, but it was something, and it just might serve for this evening until she thought of something better.

"So many people," Ancilla murmured. "But I say that every year, do I not? No, I have not been aware of Mr. Raulton's presence. Good evening, by the way, Regina. Oh, look! There's a new face. Could that be—could it—? Jeremy Gavage? After *all* this time . . . ?"

Blast it. Regina whirled, and her breath caught. *Blast!* Her heart started pounding. *Jeremy* . . . She hadn't expected him, not this quickly, not this soon and . . . looking so different— and so much the same.

She felt as if she had taken a header. *So much for plots and schemes. How like a man to just show up and throw everything top over tail.*

She couldn't take her eyes from him. Even through the crowd the faint halo of smoke, the water-light music, and Ancilla's sweet voice droning in her ear, her whole attention was fixed on Jeremy.

She didn't expect this reaction to Jeremy. *Oh, God. Jeremy. Father's knight errant. Purged by the battle of loving a woman who loved her sovereigns more. And now willing conspirator to save her innocent self from taking a pounding at the hands of the most notorious bachelor in London. So appropriate. Truly—errant was the word.*

He seemed taller than she remembered, his shoulders broader, his hair longer, his frown utterly forbidding, but that could be the effect of the high ceilings and low light. Certainly the dark look on his face reflected the fact that he was not pleased, not with anything. Especially not her.

But why should he have any opinion in the matter at all? She could not take her eyes off of him.

Nor could he stop staring at her.

He had been thinking all along he would be dealing with the artless child she had been, only a few years older, of course, and instead he was looking at a woman full grown and aware of her power, a woman with presence and passion. A woman old enough to wed.

It was the most stunning revelation.

Reginald should have warned him. Damn him—Reginald should have *told* him. He felt as if he had fallen off a steep cliff, as if everything—every preconception, everything he knew—had been wrenched out from under him.

And to make matters worse, there was Raulton, strutting and preening around the perimeter of the room, accosting the ladies who would speak with him, and commanding *her* avid attention as she seemed to follow his every move.

Damn, damn, damn. Those eyes. As bright and blue as ever he remembered. But not that womanly body, or that beautiful face. He didn't remember her looking like that at all. Damn Reginald. Damn him.

And standing next to that pale blond woman in white, she positively glowed. Did he not see Raulton slide a proprietary look of interest her way?

Damn it damn it damn it . . . .

Thank God he had come tonight; thank God he had seen her before he had started any intervention, because he couldn't trust himself to go to her now, knowing what he knew.

And he couldn't keep his eyes off of her. Or Raulton.

Things could heat up at the instant, he thought, watching the man warily. Raulton meant business, and there was no more beautiful business in this ballroom than Regina.

And from the way she was looking at Raulton, Reginald had it exactly right. Regina didn't care a fig about his reputation or any improprieties. All she saw was the virile cock-of-the-walk.

So like a woman, he thought mordantly. *Never looking beyond the outward appearances or the size of a bankbook.*

And Raulton looked ripe to feed on a frisky virgin or two. But it mattered not. Regina would not be one of them. If Jeremy had been ambivalent before about this ridiculous charge he had undertaken, he was not now. Reginald had not overstated the case. And he had been right to come to Jeremy.

Raulton was the enemy, and he would never have her, not if Jeremy could help it. His mission was perfectly clear: he had her father's full faith and trust, and he knew exactly what he had to do.

"They say she left him because he wasn't rich enough."

Ancilla's words finally registered, and Regina swung her gaze back to her friend, though she would much rather have gazed at Raulton. He was fascinating to watch, the epitome of cool disdain as he circled the room, dropping a greeting here, a word there, a bow to a lady. Perfect. Impeccable. One would have thought he was the most welcomed *parti* in the world, instead of a man who was bent on mending his reputation.

She reached frantically for the topic of conversation. Yes. "Jeremy, you mean."

"Jeremy, I mean. And doesn't he look the brooding hero now, with that deep frown and dressed all in black?"

"Ancilla!"

"No, no, no. There is a man I would not suit, not in the least. I could never get past that woman."

There was always a *that woman*, Regina thought critically. Witness Raulton. And the *that woman* always seemed to have a great deal more fun, too.

"What about Mr. Raulton, then?" Best to keep her attention there; then she could gaze at him with impunity and fuel the fire, which, given Jeremy's complicity in her father's scheme and the way Jeremy and her father were glaring at her she was more than wont to do at the moment.

It was like having two bulldogs nipping at her heels, blast them both.

". . . how much of a man's more primitive nature ought a

woman support," Ancilla was saying. "And yet, the Skeffing-hams had no compunction about inviting him here tonight," she added, voicing what many guests must be privately saying.

Well, yes, there was a consideration, Regina thought. He had been at any number of events already, hosted by persons ages who seemed to be lending their countenance to his efforts to what? reinstate himself in society's good graces? Reform? What did anyone know of Raulton's motives?

Or any man's for that matter?

"Strictly speaking, he is as eligible as anyone," Regina pointed out. "His wealth must make him so. And morality doesn't enter into it once a man is serious about finding a wife. Every man goes off hall-cocked until he gets leg-shackled. You must admit, he's a most intriguing man, and any one of us would be curious if not interested."

"Not *this* one of us," Ancilla said tartly. "And yet—he's so very good about doing the Proper. That is Harriet Soames with him. She's a very great heiress. She need not even consider anyone of Mr. Raulton's station, and yet there she is. She cannot be above sixteen years. Who could have so ill-advised her as to stand up with him?"

Regina's ears pricked up. *Stand up with him?* The thought settled in her mind, light as air. "Are you sure?" *Stand up with him . . . oh, the very thing to make Father go around the bend.*

"Oh, we are no great friends and she is as aloof as a choir stall, but yes, she is among those everyone is watching to see where her interest lies. Oh, but surely it is *not* with Mr. Raulton."

"Do let's move closer to see," Regina murmured. It was a really bad suggestion, verging on ill-mannered, but she had to make sure that he noticed her. For how else would he know she was there? And how else would Jeremy see them when Raulton came to ask her to dance?

"Regina!"

"Come, haven't you a lick of curiosity about Miss Soames?"

"Not even a lap."

"Well, I do. Do come with me, Ancilla. You know you want to."

Ancilla followed her reluctantly. "It is far too noisy," she whispered crossly as they edged their way to the forefront of the onlookers.

"Oh, but do look. You are so right. Miss Soames looks as though she just let down her dresses and put up her hair. What would a man like Mr. Raulton want with such a milk-and-water girl?"

"Oh, these men!" Ancilla muttered disgustedly. "Why is there not some kind of guide, some kind of tutoring for a girl as young as this to deal with a man like *that* . . ."

Regina was only half listening as she watched them, but then Ancilla's words suddenly penetrated, taking shape, and taking on life, and she grasped her friend's hand urgently. "What? What did you say?"

"I said a girl as young as Miss Soames ought to have some kind of guide or tutor so she could learn how to deal with a man as experienced as Mr. Raulton."

"Oh, exactly!" And why hadn't she thought of that herself? Because Ancilla was a genius, and she was a dolt was why. The answer had always been before her. But now, it was a plan, sprung fully formed from Ancilla's trenchant observation, perfect for diverting Jeremy and accomplishing her own ends.

Yes. Once she got Raulton to dance with her. "Women are always the last to know anything," she added roundly, "especially anything having to do with men."

"Well, poor Miss Soames, in any event," Ancilla said dampingly. I don't envy her if it is Mr. Raulton on whom she seeks to fix her interest."

"Oh, nor I," Regina said hastily as the music ended and the dancers bowed to each other. And now, and now—she needed to catch his eye, but he was busy returning Miss Soames to her mother. He did have manners.

But she really really needed just this one more piece of the pie. Mr. Raulton must dance with her before the evening was done, so she could set her Plan in motion.

However, it became apparent that this night, among the Skeffinghams' refined company, Mr. Raulton was after only those girls who were very young, and very pristine, the ones who perched with great sangfroid on the sideline chairs and waited like queens for each escort to humble himself and come to her.

And so it must be, Regina decided. A woman must always wait. It was one of those things. If a man wished to renovate his name and reputation, he must act impeccably, and seem at the outset to require the most chaste, the innocent, who would be uncritical, malleable, and utterly inexperienced in the ways of the world; those he would be able to control and manipulate by their affection and their desire to be wed, for what else was there for a girl, or even a woman? And so, they must wait.

She must wait. Wait for a man to notice, to speak, to come.

But he would come for her, she was certain of it, when he was tired of all those green girls and their insipid conversation, and at a point in the evening when his choices would not be so much remarked upon.

She sat on the sidelines with Ancilla and patiently waited.

"Your Mr. Raulton shows no favorites," Ancilla commented acidly. "He goes to every sixteen-year-old equally. How democratic of the man."

Regina suppressed a smile. Ancilla's observation was not quite true; as Raulton worked his way around the room, Regina had seen his covert looks at others, and the hesitating step he had taken toward her once or twice.

He *had* been watching her, amused that she, too, played the game of propriety by sitting on the sidelines and waiting, always waiting.

"My lady?" And then his voice startled her, because she had been so deep in thought, and she hadn't been expecting him, not just then.

"My lord?" She looked up at his lean face that only now was showing some of the ravages of his excesses. Pleasant enough, up close, but what really attracted her was the humor in his expression, as if he knew what was said about him and didn't care, as if he were tweaking the mores of the very society into which he sought entree, and *she,* at least, was in on the joke.

He took her hand, and she made a moment's show of reluctance before she allowed him to lead her to the floor for the reel. It was perfect for her purposes: there would be minimal conversation, and she could gaze at him as if her heart's soul were in her eyes.

One dance, one intricate interlacing of hands and steps and things unsaid. She couldn't have planned it better. She hoped Jeremy and her father were both watching. She hoped they both felt as powerless as she.

And it worked. She couldn't believe how beautifully it worked. When Raulton finally led her back to her chair, she found Ancilla had gone, effectively voicing her distress and disapproval. Her father was waiting for her, grim as a bear, and the best thing of all was when she finally caught her breath and looked around the room, she saw Jeremy by the door, his expression as black as a thundercloud.

So now the stage was set. She had only to sit back and wait for Jeremy to dance attendance on her, and then pay him back for his presumption.

She dressed accordingly the next day, in simple white muslin trimmed at the bodice and hem with demure pleating, and a matching lace-trimmed cap. Virginal. Innocent. What everyone expected to see.

She made herself comfortable in the library until, as she knew he inevitably would, her father wandered in.

"This season is too fatiguing," he began, dropping into the wing chair opposite the sofa where she sat. "Last night . . . too crowded, too many undesirables. I don't know what the

Skeffinghams were thinking. That Raulton—there is a man who ought not be received at the docks let alone in polite society. What *is* the world coming to?"

"Oh, indeed? He seemed quite the thing to me."

"Well, he ain't. And you should have known better than to take his hand willy-nilly like that," Reginald grumbled.

"I did no such thing," Regina said indignantly. "I just danced with him. A reel, for heaven's sake. We were barely face-to-face throughout the whole. But"—she lowered her voice insinuatingly—"he did cut quite a fine figure. And his manners were impeccable . . ."

"Re-*gina* . . ." Reginald began, but the butler interrupted.

"Mr. Gavage, my lord."

"Thank God," Reginald muttered, rising from his chair and relieved as a ninepence that he didn't have to pursue the question of Raulton one moment further. "Send him in."

And there he was, framing the doorway, glowering.

"Jeremy, my boy—here's Regina."

Jeremy cast a dark glance at her. "So I see."

Well, Regina thought, that wasn't too promising. She had better reconcile with him right now, or Jeremy would never fall for her plan.

She uncoiled herself from the sofa and went to him, her hands outstretched. "Jeremy, it's been ages too long."

"So it seems," he said in that deep burnished voice of his.

Oh lord, he was tall, taller than he had seemed last night; she didn't remember him being that tall. Or those hands being so warm. Or those eyes so penetrating. Nor had his face been that old. She remembered the youth of that face, before the lines now there had been etched that deep.

He wasn't going to help her either.

"Do sit down. Father, go see to something to eat. Or drink. Would you care for . . . ?" She couldn't even think what this early in the morning.

"Tea and toast will do. I assume you've eaten."

"I could eat some more," Regina said staunchly. She wasn't

some faint-away female. And anyway, food in hand helped. She didn't know how, she just knew it would. "I'll take the same. Father!" She had to get him out of the room. "Do see to it."

"I'll ring"—Reginald looked from Jeremy to Regina. Lord, she looked so sweet and innocent this morning. And yet she had danced with Raulton the night before and looked at him as it he were a god.

Jeremy eyed him meaningfully, and Reginald changed course. "Of course, my dear, I'll see to it." Anything to get out of the room and leave her with Jeremy. He could trust Jeremy. Thank the fates Jeremy had come and none too soon.

Regina closed the door behind him and whirled around to face Jeremy.

"Oh, Jeremy. Did I not see you last night at the Skeffinghams'? Why didn't you come to me? Oh, no matter, you're here now. You cannot know how grateful I am that you came."

She came toward him and edged him farther into the room. This was the moment; she could not fiddle around with niceties or building the story up any further than what Jeremy had seen with his own eyes. She had to preempt him.

She had to take action now.

"You must help me." She looked up at him, her eyes wide and beseeching, the very essence of femininity and innocence. *She hoped.*

"Must I?" Jeremy said repressively. "Are we not to have a moment's civil conversation before you beg a favor of me? After all this time?"

Odious, odious man! Anyone else would have been at her feet, promising her the moon if she wanted it. "We could have done so last night," Regina returned tartly, "but *you* chose not to. In any event, I will not ring a peal over your bad manners—today. This is serious. I need your help, Jeremy, and I haven't a moment to lose. You cannot refuse me."

"Oh no? Appearances *are* deceiving: here I thought to bask

in the company of a childhood friend, and instead I find a spitting hell cat. If I hadn't walked in the door, who might you have dragged off the street to abet you—a sniffing tom?"

Blast it. It was as if she was fifteen again and they were back snipping and sniping at each other. "Jeremy! Be serious. Sit down."

"I have a feeling I will want to be standing." This wasn't going quite the way he had planned either. He waited stoically for the ax to fall.

No choice now. She must dive into it and hope she didn't land half seas over. "There's a man."

He hadn't expected that—that she would immediately confess to her interest in Raulton. It undercut everything.

"Isn't there always?" he said dryly, warily.

The bounder! Of course he would make it as difficult as possible. Which made her all the more determined. And besides, hadn't he had enough time to ask her about Raulton? Any man with guts and gumption would have, immediately. *Blast him.* He deserved the torture she was about to inflict on him.

"Jeremy, be serious. Here's the thing. I want you to teach me . . ."

"Teach you . . . ?"

Yes, he was looking a little green around the gills. It was time to toss the bouncer.

"Well," she went on as artlessly as the child he thought she was, "he's an *experienced* man, much more so than any man of *my* acquaintance. Well, I mean—except *you*, of course. But I haven't seen *you* in years. Not that it matters. *He* is the man I would marry. So all I want you to do is teach me everything I need to know—everything a *worldly* woman would know—so I can fix his interest."

"That's *all?*" Jeremy said in a strangled voice.

She was immensely heartened by his anger. she had gotten to him, as she intended, and she felt a wash of triumph that she had scored on the first gambit.

It was a game, after all, even if he didn't know it yet.

She smiled at him brightly. "That's all."

He was thunderstruck. This was the last thing he expected her to say; but he couldn't let her see that, so he turned away from her to collect his thoughts.

This was Regina, grown-up, God help him, beautiful, spirited Regina, handing herself to him on a silver salver, giving him the reason and wherewithal to carry out Reginald's plan, and she didn't even know it.

What man could resist that offer? A man wouldn't even care that he was not the ultimate object of desire. A man was a man, and a willing woman of good breeding was the stuff of dreams that brought him to point at night.

Ah, but she didn't know what she was asking. And he was bound to go forward with Reginald's best interests in mind.

His own didn't enter into it. He had made it plain to Reginald: he wanted no woman, no entanglements, no more being in love. In short, he was the perfect man for the job. No matter what it was, no matter what it took, he was the one who could remain detached, removed, and indifferent.

He turned to face her, his consent to her wild proposal quick and intended to shock her to the point of crying off now. "Very well, Regina. Lock the door. We'll start your lessons *now.*"

Chapter Two

Now? Now? It was too soon, too soon. She hadn't thought he would make a move this soon, blast it.

Oh lord, here he came, stalking her as though he was the fox and she was the hare. Wasn't it just like a man to take advantage? He didn't give her a minute to think.

Blast him.

"Jeremy . . ." Never mind me she wanted, never. Whatever would happen would happen. She was no green girl, after all. She had been housed. She had made this proposition to him. She knew what she was getting into.

"Exactly what did *you* have in mind?" Jeremy asked, when he had her backed up against the door and stood but six intimidating inches away from her.

She raised her chin, diving in head first, and knowing she might crash hard against his obdurate arrogance. "Everything."

"Delightful thought," Jeremy murmured, his gaze fixed on her mouth. *Everything.* She hadn't the faintest idea what *everything* meant. "And *all* for your irresistible mystery man. It seems such a waste."

"*All,*" Regina repeated resolutely, mesmerized by the movement of his lips. They were very nice lips, she noted abstractedly, firm and curved, with just the hint of fleshy curve to the lower that made her want to bite it.

What!?

"If we are indeed to have lessons, I must know everything," he said.

She raised her eyes to him, feeling heat flare up between them. What was this? He was too close, that was what. She had to get used to him being this close. And closer still. That was what *everything* meant. She knew that. She did.

She felt a tremor go through her body. She had asked for this; he had every right to demand some cursory knowledge of her experience if he were going to teach her.

"I daresay you do know everything," she said spiritedly. "But the point is, I know nothing, and why should I be at such a disadvantage when the remedy is at hand."

"Why, indeed? Here is the answer to everything. I have met

my destiny, lived all my life in preparation for becoming a remedy."

Now she felt impatient. The thing was as obvious as glass. "My dear Jeremy. Look at it this way: you just gave your lady-love her congé. You cannot be looking for another liaison this soon. You won't get involved. And I've known you all my life. Who would be safer than you, Jeremy?"

"Probably *not* the person you've known all your life," he said sourly. "You give me too much credit."

"No, I merely want to credit what I must know to deal with a man of experience," Regina said briskly, wishing he would move a step or two back. Jeremy up close was nerve-wracking. Looming. Overwhelming, even.

No. She must get used to this. This was what it was like with a man.

"He will not be easy. And I will be competing with two dozen sweet innocents he will devour like candy. So do let's begin before my father interrupts us."

"Aren't you in a tearing hurry?"

"*Jeremy* . . ."

"Oh, I'm perfectly prepared to carry on . . ." But he wondered if he was. This was not going to be simple. There were no instructions on how to teach the seductive arts while distracting the seductee from the object of that person's desire.

It was going to get complicated. At the very least, he had to convince her that she attracted him, as indeed she might have, were she not someone he had known forever and were he not one and thirty and she twenty. Young, artless heiresses were not his cup of tea. But Marcus Raulton seemingly had acquired a taste for them, and for some ungodly reason, Regina wanted him.

"Well then—carry on," Regina said brusquely.

Time to come to point. He moved a step closer and cupped her cheek. She had the smoothest skin, the bluest eyes, the sweetest mouth. She lifted her head defiantly against his touch, almost as if she were pulling away. But she could not escape him. Subtly he moved closer, simultaneously lowering his head and brushing those soft virginal lips with his own.

It was the barest breath of a kiss; he hovered, waiting, awaiting her response. Her eyes were closed, her lips curved in a faint smile.

She had been kissed then, at least as much as this. Good. Maybe.

He touched her lips then, imprinting himself there, pulling away in a long, slow movement in which he took her lower lip gently between his teeth.

But not kissed quite as much as that. Her eyes flew open. "*Oh . . . !*"

"That," he whispered, "was the kiss of a boy."

She swallowed. "Oh." *Of course, of course—there had to be more to it, or men wouldn't get so stirred up about the whole thing. Or have mistresses for that matter.*

"And this . . ." He lowered his head again pressing her lips, slipping his tongue between them forcefully, and shocking her to her toes.

What was this—this heat, this wetness, this forbidden invasion—ah! She wrenched away from him, her heart pounding wildly.

". . . is the kiss of a man."

"Oh!" She rubbed her hand against her mouth.

"And the least of what you might expect from a man like Marcus Raulton," he added brutally, just as Reginald pounded on the door.

"Open up, open up . . ." he sang out. "I've got tea and toast and hot chocolate and cake."

Jeremy stepped back, and Regina sagged against the door for one revealing instant. Then she turned and unlatched the door and held it wide to admit her father and the maid who was pushing the tea cart behind him.

"Here we go. Sustenance for the morning," Reginald said

brightly, motioning where the maid was to situate the cart and waving her away. "Have some tea, my boy. Regina, you look slightly flushed."

"Flushed out," Regina said tartly, turning her back on them to pour herself some chocolate, her brains utterly scrambled from just that one overwhelming moment of male domination.

Stupid, stupid, stupid, she castigated herself as she sank into a chair in the farthest corner to examine her feelings. She should stop this right now. She wasn't equipped to handle this—either Jeremy or Marcus Raulton. Oh, especially the likes of Raulton.

She took a deep sip of the chocolate and rimmed her lips with her tongue. Dear God, what kind of kiss was that? She felt like a fool. Ancilla was right: why didn't women know anything? Why wasn't there a tutorial for kisses?

She cast a quick glance at Jeremy, who was sitting in the wing chair and jawing away with her father over inconsequentials. Men didn't go all topsy-turvy over a kiss, she thought resentfully, and it made her even more furious. Jeremy was as cool as a cucumber, and she was just as green.

She might just as well get it over with now; confess the whole to the both of them and that would be the end of the game.

She gripped the chocolate cup so tightly, she almost broke it. She just couldn't do it. Looking at the two of them sitting there, Jeremy so smug and unmoved by what to her had been a gross invasion of her person, and her father acting as if nothing had gone on behind closed doors when, in fact, he was probably congratulating himself for engineering it—it made her blood boil.

She could just picture them the day she had overheard them at Sherburne House, toasting the success of their little scheme to have Jeremy pretend to lust after her. High-handed wretches, the two of them.

That memory alone ought to keep her on her course. Jeremy must be punished for his complicity and her father for his presumption, and who cared what indignities she had to suffer.

She would make Jeremy suffer, too. But how—how? What if . . . Another thought struck her. What if. . . . Could she? In spite of that awful kiss? What if she could make Jeremy fall in love with her?

Wouldn't that be too delicious? Oh, it would serve him right. It would be such a triumph, to set her sights on Jeremy, captivate him, and then throw him over.

And all in the course of pretending to pursue Raulton.

What a scheme.

If she could get past that horrible kiss.

And anything else he had in store for her.

Nonsense, she could get past anything. What was a kiss, after all? It was the rest of it that gave her pause—the part about it being the least of what she could expect from Raulton.

What was the most?

Well, she had some idea. She lived in the country, after all. She had been to the barn. Of course, animals didn't kiss so that didn't enter into it. Blast it, would she never stop thinking about that kiss?

Probably not. And maybe it was best to initiate another one, and another so that she would not be so shocked next time. A person could get used to anything, she thought stringently. And how unpleasant could it be after that?

"Well," Reginald said suddenly, loudly, putting down his cup with exaggerated care, "I beg you'll excuse me. I have some letters to write and, of course, Almack's tonight. Have you secured an invitation, Jeremy?"

He slanted a glance at Regina. "Not yet."

"Oh do," Regina urged him. "I fear I am fatigued and will want only to stay home tonight. But every matchmaking mother will welcome you with open arms, dear Jeremy."

"I think," Reginald said carefully, "I will leave now." He got up slowly, as if his bones ached, or maybe it was just his sensibilties, because he was exhausted dealing with his daughter. But sometimes he did look rather small and frail, Regina thought, watching him depart, and even she perceived it was not the burden of the Season weighing him down.

All would be fine in the morning, she was certain of it. Her father was nothing if not resilient. The question to hand now was Jeremy. What to do about Jeremy lounging in the wing chair and looking insufferably arrogant and male, like a lion who has cornered its prey. She felt cornered, constricted, and somehow he made her feel all that while he was still sitting some ten feet away from her.

The power of a man on the hunt was something to be reckoned with, she mused, an excellent lesson for any woman to comprehend.

"And so," Jeremy murmured, "you eschew Almack's tonight, knowing full well Raulton will be there. I would think you would want to put yourself in his way whenever you could."

"Do I? You tell me, Jeremy dear. Does a man like a woman who is obvious? Do I want to look as if I am chasing him? Or would it profit me more to continue on with our lessons so I will have the wherewithal to handle him when the time comes?"

A faint smile played around his mouth. "Yes, yes and yes."

"Thank you for *nothing*," Regina snapped. "You are of no use this morning whatsoever. Perhaps you ought to go." And in fact, she hadn't expected him to stay. So now what?

"I'm very comfortable where I am, thank you. And *we* have a long way to go. I don't think I've ever seen such aversion to my kisses. Obviously, I have much to learn myself. Or perhaps I should present some testimonials next time I want to kiss you . . . ?"

Her chin went up. "You took me by surprise is all. And how many women *have* you kissed, by the way?"

"Enough to know not to confess my sins to you," he said, his voice laced with amusement.

Oh, and now he was laughing at her. She had never felt at

such a disadvantage before. Blast him. Blast the strictures of a society that kept a woman ignorant of everything.

The real question was how far she would go in her spurious quest for carnal knowledge. She eyed Jeremy consideringly over the rim of her cup. That kiss notwithstanding, there was nothing dislikable about Jeremy except that he knew her too long and too well. Not a disadvantage, except—that kiss. And maybe that was why it had shocked her so. If she had feelings for him, it probably would have been wholly different.

So, it was just a matter of getting used to it. A woman could get used to anything. At least, that was what her father kept telling her, and this was obviously what he meant.

He meant the forbidden things. The things no one talked about, except men in their clubs late at night as virgins slept and mistresses waited and anticipated.

Her instinct was utterly right about that: even to pretend to tame a man like Raulton, any woman had to know things. *Carnal things. Forbidden things. Things that mistresses knew.*

Well, here was she, with a man at her beckoning who was willing and ready to show her everything she needed to know. And Jeremy was not unattractive, in his cocksure way.

So there could be no more shriveling up at his kisses—because for all she knew, he had a new mistress, so she must be every bit as eager and responsive to even keep him interested enough to continue with her plan.

How hard could that be?

She bit her lip. Deuced hard, when a woman didn't know what she wanted or how to ask for it. No, she had asked for it, and then she had gone and reordered the rules, forgetting there was another component of the game: her father's scheme to circumvent her pursuit of Raulton.

And he had just gone and left her and Jeremy alone.

So, she thought, new gambit and Jeremy's move.

"Well, at least you didn't faint dead away at the word *sins,*" Jeremy commented dryly, watching her intently. "Perhaps you can be educated after all."

That fired her up. "I'll have you know I had an excellent education," she retorted indignantly. "Just not in the more—carnal—things in life. You are supposed to give me the . . . the *Grand Tour.*"

"Believe me, I'll love to give you the grand tour," Jeremy muttered, "but that's neither here nor there to your desire to attract Marcus Raulton. Which, by the way, is totally incomprehensible to me."

"Truly? But it is so simple: he's rich, well-favored, romantic, and interesting. A woman of spirit and intelligence could never be bored by him. Which is as reasonable a basis for marriage as any other I know. Do you not think, Jeremy?"

"I think I don't want to think," Jeremy said with teeth-clenching restraint. "It's enough to know that you are the veriest innocent and you are playing with fire when it comes to Raulton."

"Then I will get burned. But I will have him, by hook or by crook. And if you won't help me, I warrant he can teach me to kiss as well as anyone else." She slanted a derisive look at him. "Certainly as well as you."

And there he was, between the devil and the dawn, with his honor at the sticking point. How easily her taunting words rolled off her tongue. He could think of better things to do with it than just sit and listen to her. But he couldn't just take her. So it was time for some decisive action.

It was a calculated risk, granted, but he knew how to handle skittish virgins who were too full of themselves, in spite of what she thought.

"Fine," he said, levering himself out of the wing chair.

Immediately she was up and on her feet. "What do you mean *fine?*"

"I mean, make your proposition to anyone else—or Mr. Raulton, if you must. It is nothing to me."

This was not going the way she had thought, and how was it that Jeremy was giving up on Reginald's scheme already? Blast him.

But perhaps he wasn't. Perhaps he was playing the opposite field to bring her up to the fore. What *was* this game? Was she not in charge? He couldn't just change the rules. Blast it, she *would* be in charge.

"Jeremy . . ."

He held up his hand. "Don't play at cross purposes with me, Regina. I'm not some choice spirit you can wind around your little finger."

"So I see," she murmured.

"Perhaps we know each other too well," Jeremy went on, ignoring that. "Perhaps it was ill-considered of me to consent to such folly."

He was leaving, he was leaving. Blast, blast and blast. How would she, how could she stop him . . . ?

She swallowed, hard. "Perhaps we should try again . . ."

He stopped in mid-step. "Excuse me?"

"I said, perhaps we—I—should try again."

"Try . . . ?" He wanted to make this as hard as possible for her.

". . . kissing . . ."

"Kissing. Kissing? You who quaked and trembled and rubbed your lips as if you had kissed a frog, you want to kiss me—again?"

"Jeremy—don't . . ."

"My lady wants to humiliate me yet again?"

"Jeremy . . ."

"You don't know your own mind, Regina. If you can't bear to kiss even me, however are you going to deal with Raulton?"

How, indeed, Regina thought mordantly, watching him warily. She couldn't tell just which way his sentiments lay or how he would react if he knew Raulton was beside the point altogether.

"*That* is what I want you to teach me," she said, reasonably, she hoped.

He wasn't feeling reasonable—or responsible, even. He was feeling primitive, brutal. *Male.* "High-strung virgins don't appeal to me—or to any man," he growled. "You wonder why men keep mistresses. Here is a case in point. Mistresses freely want a man, and never shrink from any sensual experiences with him. A mistress welcomes him and offers herself to him for his pleasure.

"Why would any man waste his time and energy coaxing and coddling a cowering innocent when his mistress will willingly give him everything he wants? Things you can't even imagine, my *lady*. Things that would put you in a dead faint for a week if they were demanded of you."

Oh, that was cold-blooded. He had shocked her, as he had intended, and more than that, even. She was as still as a statue, her eyes blazing, and some devil in him pushed him to elaborate further.

"And that's the reality of it, and something that can't be taught. Raulton must keep a half dozen mistresses with whom you cannot hope to compete. Give it up now, and eventually some dandy with exquisite sensibilities and no animal desires will ride up on his white horse and carry you off and immure you in the castle where no one will ever have to touch you—or kiss you."

She felt as if she had turned to stone. She hated him. She hated the game. All she wanted in that fraught moment was to be a mistress, a woman who was versed in the erotic arts, and who knew exactly how to fascinate and keep a man.

"Do you have a mistress?" she asked tightly.

"I think that is none of your business."

"Do you?"

He turned away. This was the last thing he thought he would have to confess. "What if I did?"

"And yet you consented to teach me . . ."

"A game, my lady. Men play it all the time."

Didn't they just? she thought furiously. They did the dirty with some delicious and willing woman, and they put every other woman up on a pedestal. But not her. *Not* her.

"Then let's play, Jeremy." Her voice was strung as taut as a bow. "I have too much at stake and too little time. I want you to kiss me."

"Do you take me for a fool?"

Kiss me, Jeremy.

Was he a fool? What man would turn down Regina, even at the cost of some wounded pride?

But then—there was his promise to Reginald to distract and divert, and they were at a convergence of wants and needs. It was just amazing how a man could find an excuse to do anything he wanted to do.

"Then come to me, Regina."

She almost thought she couldn't move. Her body felt stiff and awkward, but it was fueled by a new unexpected resolve, one that had nothing to do with Raulton or revenge. And so she put one foot after the other and went toward him, at his command.

"And now what, Jeremy?"

She looked as though she was going into battle with her blazing eyes and challenging words. He had a latent urge to conquer her, to subdue her, and make her beg.

Could he? The thought intrigued him. *Would he?*

He reached out and cupped her chin. "You're very beautiful, you know."

"That's not what I want to know," she said sharply.

"No. You want all the secrets, now. Things learned through my life's experience bedding women. You had better lower your sights, my lady. You can't know everything and you can only take one step at a time."

But she wanted to jump in headfirst and mire herself in a swamp of sensuality. "Then take the step, Jeremy," she said, her voice husky. "I'm waiting."

The magic words. *I'm waiting.* She could see it in his eyes. A man liked to have a willing woman waiting. One secret to stash away and examine when she was alone.

He tilted her head, holding her head immobile between his hands. Big hands, she noted distractedly. Warm hands.

202 / Thea Devine

He lowered his head. "It's more elegant this way; we won't bump noses. And then, as I approach you, you must open your mouth to receive me." He came closer and closer still, his gaze hooded, watching her response and reaction, and the emotion warring in her eyes.

I'm waiting. Every part of her must be waiting no matter how she felt. Another secret. Oh, how quickly these secrets revealed themselves in the heat of the moment. Another thing to analyze when she was alone.

She closed her eyes, opened her mouth, and felt him swoop down into her, the movement even more shocking for the total domination of it.

His tongue enveloped her, probing, seeking, stroking. She felt inept under the onslaught, but at least she held her own; she didn't recoil at his touch. She didn't pull away. She leaned into him, inviting more.

But she hated her own passivity. How did a woman respond to such a kiss? What did a woman do?

A mistress knows what to do.

Hadn't he made that oh so clear?

A mistress welcomes a man and freely offers herself to him for his pleasure.

A mistress willingly gives him everything he wants. . . .

Secrets.

Mistresses never shrink from any sensual experiences. . . .

More secrets.

Her body constricted. *Never shrink. . . .*

Offers herself. . . .

Her body arched; she moved her tongue against his and felt the faint jolt of his body.

Another secret.

Willingly gives. . . .

This isn't so bad.

Her body seemed to be responding all out of proportion with the observations of her mind. She liked this kiss. She liked the feel of him deep in her mouth, eating away at her. She

liked dueling with him, and discovering that she could nip and
lap and play with him. She liked holding on to his strong hard
hands as she moved into the kiss.

The casual primal, muted sweet. He was by turns gentle and
masterful, and she found she could meet him halfway, either
way.

Amazing where a little determination could take one.

Another secret.

He nipped at her tongue, before taking it between his teeth
and sucking at it.

She almost swooned at the pulling sensation, giving herself
to it willingly. *Freely, willingly. . . .*

All she could do was hang on and offer him all he wanted . . .
all he could take . . . for his pleasure—

He sucked at her more insistently, harder, deeper, harsher.
She felt a deep twinge in her vitals, felt as if she were melting
somewhere between her legs.

*A mistress willingly gives a man everything he wants.
Things you can't even imagine. . . .*

What things? A mistress knows.

Everything.

This?

She felt him tense, his hands tightened, and then the gorgeous heat of his mouth slowly, slowly, slowly eased away
from hers, erotically pulling at her lips before he finally disen-
gaged from her.

She made a little sound at the back of her throat. Don't. . . .

Don't what?

Don't leave me . . . ?

No—

Don't stop.

Her body contracted somewhere deep within. *I want more.*

More.

He did too.

Her breathing constricted. They could be alone in the
house for all Reginald would interfere with them. He could

204 / *Thea Devine*

stay with her and kiss her like that all day. The whole long, long day.

Yes. . . .

Stay with me.

He read every emotion in her eyes, every nuance of her body. The virgin in bloom. There was no more dangerous flower, no more poisonous dew than an innocent newly aroused.

He was susceptible, too. Just for a moment, he forgot who she was and where they were, and he had lost himself in the erotic heat of her mouth, and pushed aside all caution, all restraint.

Oh, a luscious mouth could positively destroy a man.

But not him. He understood the dangers now that she had tasted her power. It was merely a matter of harnessing his, and mastering her long enough to keep her away from ruin.

He was the man for the job. And the tightness in his groin—well, any woman could arouse him to that kind of pitch. It wasn't Regina; it was the driving heat of a succulent kiss. Any man would respond to that.

And yet, as he gazed at her soft mouth and shimmering eyes, all he could think was, *I want more.*

Not so indifferent, he thought wryly. But then, what was the harm? He would teach Regina what she wanted to know, enjoy what little she would give, and keep her out of Raulton's bed.

And in my own.

He shied violently from the thought. This wasn't what it was about, damn it. It was about obstructing her pursuit of Raulton. And teaching her a few things. That was all. Nothing more, nothing less.

The fact he was still breathing hard had nothing to do with anything. But if he stayed any longer, it would.

He could not make himself move. The tension escalated, along with her expectations. He wanted to, he did, and she wanted him to. It was just another step, and he could take her.

He could do anything with her he wanted; he saw it in her eyes. Willing. Waiting. Mirroring everything any man could want, everything a man could desire.

Damn damn damn . . . he couldn't let this get out of hand. He thrust her away. "Enough, my lady."

She shook her head. "Let us take the next step."

"My next step is out the door, Regina."

"Why?"

"Because my taste does not run to foolish virgins," he snapped, out of patience with her—with himself.

She stiffened. How could he? After that voluptuous connection between them, how could he?

But that was a man. That was what he was trying to tell her, and what she had already seen: it was nothing to him and everything to her.

And that was the reason why she must cultivate a different sensibility. A man did not like to be tethered and cobbled. A man wanted to walk away and never regret anything—but who was to say a woman couldn't feel the same? It was just a matter of learning how.

Oh, it was making so much sense, so much sense. But she had to ensure he would not go back on his promise to teach her.

Blast him. "We *will* continue with our lessons," she said, keeping her tone expressionless.

"If you will," he answered in kind. God, it was getting complicated. If only Raulton were not in the picture.

"Excellent. Do remember, Jeremy, it is not you in my *lowered* sights: it is for Mr. Raulton that I must be on the mark."

His body tightened, just thinking of it. "As you say."

"And today, I performed well, did I not, for a *foolish virgin?*"

"No man could complain." And no sane man would walk out on her either without taking advantage of what she so obviously wanted to give. How did that first lesson take so well?

"Then we are all right and tight, and we will go on."

"I said we would."

"When?"

"When your delicate sensibilities dictate, my lady."

Oh, but her sensibilities were delicate no longer. She knew what she wanted now and exactly what she had to do.

"Do you go to your mistress now?" She had to know, and she would know, if not today, then tomorrow or next month, but she would know.

He grit his teeth. "I fail to see how it is your business."

But it will be, dear Jeremy. It will be.

"Friday will do," she said insolently, dismissively, ignoring his sharp tone.

He cringed. Lady of the manor now. She knew how to play that role very well. What had Reginald gotten him into? What had he gotten himself into?

"Friday, then," he agreed curtly, and she turned away from him to hide her triumphant smile.

She followed his progress out of the room by his footsteps, through the hall, a pause for his hat, the slam of the front door, and she watched him covertly from behind the library curtains as he took the front steps and signaled for his horse.

Dear, dear Jeremy . . . you've taught me so much already. You have no idea. In one afternoon, you have turned everything I thought I wanted inside out. And now, I will keep up the pretense of chasing Raulton for one purpose and one purpose only: as the means to get what I want.

And what I now know I want is to be your mistress.

Chapter Three

So this is the secret to enslaving a man. think like a mistress, act like a mistress. Know what a mistress knows.

All the carnal secrets. All the feminine tricks. All the male vices.

She mentally ticked off the points one by one as she stared at herself in the bedroom mirror.

Be welcoming. Be willing. Every part of you must be willing with all that means. Offer yourself freely for his pleasure. Never ever shrink from anything he wants of you. Act as if you crave it, too. Be determined you will do whatever he asks of you.

An excellent bargain for the reward of a man's loyalty and carnal fidelity, and wealth and freedom besides.

Who was Jeremy's mistress? Who among all the beauties had attracted him and even now was giving herself to him willingly? The thought was not to be borne. Not after that kiss.

She would find out. Tonight, at Almack's, among all those women there would be seductive mistresses, known only to the lovers who kept them. She would try to discern who they were and how they behaved to better understand what she must do to take Jeremy away from his mistress.

And she would further the pretense that Raulton was her mark.

There was a full plate for one evening, she thought, and she must dress the part besides.

Nothing pleased her. Every dress she took out of her closet seemed insipid and virginal, and for this evening, this moment, she wanted something much more daring.

She might be turned away because of it—it didn't do to

cross the patronesses at Almack's—but tonight was one night she would take the chance.

She pulled out a dress of blue satin with an extremely high waist and low-cut neck and blond lace trim at the hem and sleeves. Here was some sophistication. And she liked the way the knots of cream-colored flowers on a rouleau of blue ribbon fitted tightly to her midriff, shaping and emphasizing her breasts. There were matching faux flowers to entwine in her hair, which was styled a la Grecque, and matching shoes, gloves and shawl. To finish, she chose to wear a pair of pearl earrings and a long pearl necklace.

She motioned her maid to one side, and stood away from the mirror.

Ah, this was more like it. This was not the reflection of a green girl. This was a woman, whose body tantalized from beneath the sensual drape of her dress, who was covertly, seductively on the hunt.

Was she really this daring, this foolhardy? Or was it just the game?

"Time to go, Regina." Her father knocked at the door. "You look lovely. New dress? Very becoming. I'm so glad you changed your mind."

"No one should miss a moment at Almack's if they have the entree," Regina murmured. "I was remiss not to have considered my good fortune this afternoon." The irony was lost on her father, who believed every social event was a command to attend.

He was just as happy to have her company, particularly during the long wait to debark from their carriage at the door, and then again inside during that first awkward moment of greeting friends and acquaintances.

Everyone was there. The crowd was six deep by the velvet cordon. Regina could barely pass, and she felt a distinct irritation that she wouldn't be able to see, or to carry forward her plan. And she was hoping Ancilla had chosen not to attend because she did not need a Greek chorus naysaying her every move.

But that was a faint hope, blast it. There Ancilla came, In her usual turnout of white muslin, long white gloves, and, a new fashion trick, a marching demimondan in her hair confin ing her pale curls.

"Always a crush," Ancilla murmured. "How *are* you?"

"I'm well to do given we saw each other only yesterday," Regina answered in kind. "And you?"

"As ever. Marking time. Observing the absurd behavior of those around me. No, no, not you. But take note that your Mr. Raulton is here already and in fine fettle. I daresay he has his dance card down and is busily deciding which of the Untouched he will touch tonight. I do wish you would give over your fascination with him. He is not worthy of your con- sideration."

"He is still the most interesting man here."

"And what about Jeremy Gavage? There he is, scowling as ever."

"Does he look our way?" She hoped.

"He scowls our way."

"I ought to greet him, even if he had the bad manners not to come to me last night. Do you wish to come with me?"

"No. There is nothing for me there. But do you go ac- knowledge him."

Perfect. Now it remained only to find Mr. Raulton. Tonight she did not want to dance with him. She wanted, rather, to be seen talking with him, or perhaps pretending to follow him to the garden for a private moment.

Which meant he must always be in her sights, and she must try to be sure that Jeremy was watching. Although how she would manage that, she did not know.

Blast it. Why couldn't a woman control these things?

"Well, don't you look—different tonight?" Jeremy was be- hind her, where she least expected him to be.

She curtsied. "Do you like it?"

"I think your father should not have let you out of the house wearing such a dress," Jeremy said feelingly. He didn't know quite what it was: the low-cut bodice that molded her breasts, or the way the dress shimmered against her body with her every movement.

Or the look in her eye. He didn't like that the most.

"Is your mistress here?" she asked, all wide-eyed and innocent.

"Dear God . . . !" Jeremy exploded under his breath. He grabbed her arm and pushed her to a corner where they could have more privacy. "And just what is your interest in my mistress?"

Her chin went up. "I'm fascinated. Especially since *you* brought it up. And they know *so* much about love and men. I've been thinking that I would be one."

"*WHAT?*"

His anger was something to behold. This was a good tactic, an excellent ploy. "I . . . would . . . be . . . one," she repeated succinctly.

"God in heaven . . . what is this new thing?"

"I want you to teach me."

"I'm teaching you." God help him, he hoped no one was listening. What was he doing arguing such a thing with her here in public where every comma was food for gossip by morning. "And I won't talk about this nonsensical idea of yours here. You don't know what you're saying. You don't know what you want. First it's Raulton, then it's this . . ."

"Well, I reconsidered that. I think it would be much more interesting to be his mistress than his wife. He'd be generous and kind . . . and he's so experienced. A woman really must prefer a man with experience . . . and so, by the same token, ought not a man? Prefer a woman with experience, I mean."

Jeremy blanched. "I'm getting you out of here. You have lost your mind or you have a fever. *Stay here* until I inform Reginald . . ."

She felt a bubble of triumph well up. She had totally confounded him, and the more agitated he got, the more enam-
ored she became with the idea of him teaching her the erotic
arts of a mistress.

Now, if she could only find a way to have that moment
with Raulton, it would just set the cake.

She couldn't believe that it turned out to be a simple matter
of following him discreetly and seizing the moment. She
slipped into the crowd and edged her way around the room,
nodding to acquaintances, and feeling a spurt of resentment
when she was detained to listen to a morsel of gossip or a tid-
bit of news. It was a chore just keeping track of Raulton, with
all the distractions around him.

Ah, there he was, presenting another of his limp young
things with some lemonade. Nasty stuff, but the girl didn't
know it. She looked awestruck; this was probably her first go-
round at Almack's.

And Raulton had had obviously enough of her, too. He ex-
cused himself quickly thereafter, heaving a thankful sigh as he
withdrew and headed for the refreshment room.

She scanned the crowd for Jeremy, caught his eye as he
searched for her and, quick as a cat, went after Raulton.

Nothing could be better. She could make up any story
about her supposed assignation with Raulton. But Jeremy's
speculations would be a lot more pungent. Well, so it should
be, blast him. He deserved to suffer.

He wasn't that far behind her, and he didn't scruple to grab
her and haul her back from whatever folly she was about to
commit. "Damn it. Damn you. What the hell do you think
you're doing?"

Raulton suddenly appeared as if by magic, a glass of ratafia
in hand, and Regina almost fainted at the sight of him. Now
what? She was cooked; her deceit was about to be exposed.

But she should have known: Raulton of all people was
not behindhand about anything to do with subterfuge. He
took in the scene with one lightning look, and then he held

Regina's eyes meaningfully, handed her the drink, and murmured, "There, my dear Regina. A reward for your forebearance. I trust you will be all right?"

He was saying, *I'll play. You play.* It was so perfect. She bent her body toward him. "Quite, Marcus."

"I wish there were more time." He took her hand, he kissed her palm. Her breath caught as his tongue swiped her palm. "There's never enough time."

"Marcus . . ." Who was a better actress than she? "Can't we . . . ?"

"This is the only way," he murmured, and then he was gone.

"Jesus," Jeremy muttered. "You are a menace." He took her arm, as she stared after Raulton, barely able to contain her glee at the scene he had just wittingly played out with her. "Tell me you didn't breathe whisper of that bird-brained scheme of yours to him."

"What scheme is that, Jeremy dear?"

"To become his mistress."

She looked horrified. "Never yet, Jeremy. I'm not nearly skilled enough. But you're going to remedy that, aren't you—and soon."

There was that word again: *remedy.* As though he were castor oil or something. "I'm taking you home."

"There's nowhere I'd rather go with you."

And that tone—he did not like that tone of voice. It was too reasonable. Too rational. So he kept silent during the ride back to Green Street and said not a word as they entered the house.

Here was the moment he ought to leave. He knew it. He felt trouble brewing in his bones if he took one step farther into that house with her.

"Would you like a brandy?" Regina asked.

"I would *like* an explanation."

"Well, it's all your fault. You're the one who started gabbling about mistresses and how you hate to coddle and coax reluctant virgins. And frankly, any woman who thought about it would much rather know about those things than not."

"Get in the library. We're not going to discuss this where print *************** **** ***********"

"I should think not. The brandy's in there; that should calm you down." She waited until he had entered the library and closed the door before she rang for the butler. "Ah, Bertram. That will be all tonight. My father will see to himself when he returns."

"Very good, my lady."

Better than good, dear Bertram. Jeremy is all in a twist over this mistress business. Nothing could be better.

But still, she paused a moment before she entered the library and latched the door behind her. This was the biggest step, the place where she must be willing to relinquish every inhibition, every stricture she had believed her whole life. She had to give herself over to him, no matter how scared she was, no matter what he demanded of her.

This was nothing romantical. And now that she was on the cusp of carrying through, she had to be certain she wanted to cross this threshold. If she entered that room and offered herself, she could never come back again whole and intact. But who would know?

Who would know?

Indeed, who *would* know?

I would know. I'd know everything, every mystery, every question answered, every feminine secret revealed.

And she could still live her life, and no one would ever have to know.

So how serious was she? Blast it. This was no turn of the cards, and ace takes the trick. This was no small thing: she would become no better than a queen of hearts, and in the end, she might wind up the fool.

No one has to know.

No one would look. How would anyone know?

It was the most tantalizing thing. Beyond that door, she would enter the alluring world of the forbidden, the world he had described to her so seductively she hungered for the experience of being a kept woman. And it was Jeremy, not a stranger. For all her fear, she trusted him. And at the very least, he did seem to care about her.

And no one would ever know.

The thought made her breathless. She girded herself and swung open the library door.

He was sitting in the wing chair, staring moodily into his brandy snifter, immovable as a king, and she wanted to play.

"Now we are alone. So tell me, Jeremy, if you were with your mistress tonight, what would you do now?"

"I'd tell her she's a damned fool," he said roughly, "and that she's as green as glass and twice as fragile, and a man would crush her to pieces just with his hands, she's so breakable."

"Well, we keep coming back to the main purpose: teach me."

"You don't know what you ask."

"Then tell me. Hold nothing back."

"And how honest shall I be?" he demanded violently. "Where they list you in *Whoremonger's Guide* depends on who is paying how much to fuck you. And for all that money, you have no life. You belong to your lord every minute of the day, even if he never comes to you. You must be willing to spread your legs at *his* will and whim, and he'll fuck you every which way he can think of, and ten more ways besides. He owns your naked body, every inch of it, and he's paying for what's between your legs. He'll make sure no one else can have you, and you hope to hell he never tires of you. *That* is the life of a mistress, my lady who has never been touched, barely been kissed, and knows nothing about anything. And there is nothing romantic about it in the least."

But there was, there was. Every word made her body twinge; every image made her shake with excitement.

"But you will show me how to please a man," she whispered, and his eyes darkened as his mouth thinned. She licked her lips, and the movement arrested his attention. She saw ░░ he didn't, he couldn't, how could he not—and she shrugged and turned away. "Or someone else will."

He jacked himself out of the chair in one explosive motion and grabbed her shoulders. "You do love using that threat, my lady. You'd come crawling home in a day, your innocence pounded to a pulp and so sore between your legs, you'd never want to leave your father's house in this lifetime."

"Then you do it. You. Teach me everything I need to know."

"Goddamnit . . . !"

She squared her shoulders and thrust out her breasts. *And where did that come from?* "Pretend, then. Pretend I'm your mistress. Do to me what you do to her."

He slammed his hand down on the nearby table.

"I want you to do *everything* to me that you do to her."

"You don't know what you mean," he growled.

"I do know. I understand perfectly." She did, she did, and here was the moment she must make a commitment and back up her bold taunting words. "I'm saying I will be naked for you. Willing. Welcoming. You will own my body, every inch, to do with what you want. And all you have to do is show me everything you do with a mistress and everything a mistress knows."

Oh, God, she had said it, she wanted it, and she was stunned at her audacity and that her own words aroused her to such a fever pitch.

She wanted him to stop talking and start *doing* and bury his conscience when he knew he wanted to do to her all that he had described.

And that she wanted him to.

"You—or another man," she whispered, her body taut with her burgeoning desire.

"Goddamn hell . . ."

"Another man touching my naked body, another man between my legs . . ." Oh, this was so dangerous, and that insinuating voice she used was like setting a match to tinder. He was morally so much stronger than she ever imagined, but she had set the stage, she couldn't go back, and she needed him. *Now.*

She waited, shivering with excitement.

Nothing.

"Fine," she whispered, turning away.

Two steps, and he had her, pulling her up rough and hard against his chest. "It is not fine, do you hear? It is *not* fine, but if you're aching to be fucked, then goddamn, I will fuck you to a faretheewell. I'm not a patient man in this arena, my fancy lady, and you'd better learn to please me quickly, because as of this moment, I hold you to every promise you made to me in this room."

"Yes," she whispered, her body shaking uncontrollably. "Yes."

He pushed her away. "Until then, well—I can handle two of you."

She stiffened. "*Two* of us?"

"Two."

Her excitement escalated again. "One, Jeremy. Just one."

"You don't know enough yet," he said harshly.

"So I practice with you and you spend yourself on her? No."

"I have enough juice, if that's what you're worried about."

"I have yet to find that out. So, one only."

"I'm hard, hot and juicy right now." He waited a long moment to see what she would do. "That was your first test, fancy lady. You failed. You don't know anything about a man's need. But you can be sure my *mistress* knows exactly what to do about it. So . . ." He turned toward the door. "I'll be back . . ."

Lesson one: he is in control and can do whatever he wants with whomever he wants anytime anywhere.

Lesson two: I must be willing to do anything he wants, anywhere, anytime even if I don't know what it is I'm supposed to do.

"If you leave, you will still have a mistress, but you will never have me." Bold brassy words. Some women didn't have that choice. It was implicit in all he had told her: never challenge the lord who paid for your body. She knew it. And by those words, she was testing him.

But it stopped him, and he turned, bracing himself against the door.

"Oh, the fancy piece thinks she's a lady, making threats like that. It's fortunate I haven't fucked you yet, because I *would* own you, and if you spoke to me like that even once, I would never fuck you again."

"Then we are at an impasse."

"There is no impasse. I have the length, strength and juice for two. Make up your mind if you want it." He turned away, and she heard him unlatch the door.

Bluff called. "I want it."

"Tell me again?" He latched the door.

"I . . . want . . . it."

He turned to face her again. "And again?" He began to pace toward her.

She started shaking again. *"I want it." The length and strength and juice—I want it. Whatever it means, whatever it entails, I want it.*

Juice enough for two. . . .

"A lesson well learned, fancy-piece."

Goddamn, nothing scared her. He cupped her chin, and then slid his hot hand down her neck to rest on her heaving breast. *Not even that.* "I won't make many demands tonight, tempted though I am." He slipped his arm around her and slowly moved her to the wing chair and onto his lap.

She felt it tight against her bottom, huge, hot, hard, flexing and nudging her. It was so big. As though she were sitting on a bar of iron.

And every mistress knew what it looked like and exactly what to do with it.

Why didn't she?

What could she tell from how it felt against her buttocks? That it was long and thick and it moved of its own volition. And it elongated with his escalating male need. She could feel every little spurt beneath her thin dress.

Length and strength and juice.

I want it.

His one hand still spanned her breasts, and he studied her face with the intensity of a scientist before he lowered his head and captured her mouth.

Here was a kiss, dominating, sensual and conquering. And then there was the sensation of his fingers playing across her breast, sliding into her dress and seeking her bare hot skin and one taut pointed nipple.

She almost bolted at the contact where no one . . . no man . . . had ever touched her before.

I asked for this. I want whatever he will do to me, no matter what it is, no matter where it leads.

And she ached for that kiss—first and all, that kiss. And anything he could think to do to her after.

Deep in the kiss, she felt a jolt of streaming pleasure as he squeezed the very tip of her nipple, gently at first and then more firmly. It was the most exquisite sensation, spiraling right down between her legs, molten, wet, wondrous, endless. Unspeakable.

Shamelessly in thrall to the feeling, she mutely begged for more, and he gave it to her. She squirmed, she writhed almost as if she were trying to get away from it, and all the while she arched herself into him so that he did not relinquish the pressure of his fingers on her nipple.

Instead, he broke the kiss, and with his free hand, he tore away the bodice of her dress to bare her breasts altogether. "Luscious nipples." He cupped her other breast and slid his thumb back and forth across the taut nub. "Nipples made to be naked, made to entice a man." He lifted her breast, bent his head and closed his lips around just the hot, tight thrust of it and sucked the pointed nub hard into his mouth.

Her body jolted at the gush of sensation that engulfed her. The pleasure and the heat were unremitting, one long slippery silvery flow that pooled deep in her vitals. She couldn't get enough of his avid sucking. She arched against him, seeking and trying to separate the sensations: his steady pressure on the one nipple, and his firm, rhythmic sucking of the other— too much, too much, too much . . . not enough, not enough, not enough—

She felt his mouth disengage from her nipple and his hot tongue trace circles of wet heat all over the swell of her breast, all the while he kept up that erotic pressure of his fingers on the other nipple.

Her body swooned with a hot yearning. He came back to her lips again and again, grazing them with hot, hard kisses. She couldn't keep still; the feeling of those fingers squeezing her nipple was so voluptuous, so sumptuous, her body began to swell, to reach, to unfurl.

"Maybe you're right," he whispered, lapping at her lips. "Maybe you *were* born for this. I can't get enough of this nipple." His mouth closed over hers, rough, hard, demanding, devouring. His fingers flexed, compressing it harder. "I'm going to make sure you never forget this sensation," he growled into her mouth. "When I'm not here, I want you to feel my fingers fondling your teat, squeezing it, rolling it, making it . . ." He ground down into her mouth. ". . . hot for me . . ." Another rough kiss. ". . . hard for me . . ." Deeper into her mouth he went, bruising her, crushing her lips, grinding into her wildly with his tongue.

Dear God, there was nothing like an untried virgin. You could stoke them and they heated up like a blast furnace. Once you primed them for pleasure, they begged you for it every hour of the day, and they were adoring and uncritical to boot.

And you couldn't scare them off with a goddamn jackhammer. No wonder men paid astronomical sums for them.

He had one in his hands if he wanted it. *If* . . . hell, he *needed* it. He was ready to explode all over her and drown her in the backwash of his thick boiling cream. He wanted to spread it all over the hot thrusting nipple between his fingers and then make her suck the residue off of his rampaging penis.

And that was just the beginning. She couldn't pump the half of all his cream. He had plenty to go around, plenty to ram between her legs and spill into that hot, tight hole.

Goddamn, goddamn hell. I am goddamn crazy for letting things get this far . . . she makes me crazy with all her brazen talk. Who wouldn't want to fuck her? She's so goddamned determined, who knows what the hell she'll do—or who with.

He wrenched away from her mouth suddenly, his fingers still holding her nipple with that same erotic pressure.

The air was tight with tension. Damn damn and hell. He was in control, not his unruly manhood. Not her, with her hard responsive nipples, her lush virgin's body, and her wild untutored mouth.

"You play the pleasure game so well for such an innocent," he said, his voice harsh with his effort to restrain himself.

She closed her eyes as he gently removed his fingers from her nipple and roughly pulled what was left of her bodice over her breasts.

This was it; this was the end for today. She hadn't pleased him. He would leave her now and go to the knowledgeable woman who knew exactly what to do about a man's needs, and whose body he would engorge with all the cream she could pump out of him.

"You're going to *her*, aren't you?"

"Maybe I don't have to if I can get what I need here." *His unruly penis speaking, damn damn and damn.*

"I can give you anything she can."

"But I bought her. She has to."

Her body shifted and squirmed at the thought. "If you have enough juice for two, you have enough money for two," she whispered. "Pay for me, Jeremy. Buy my body. And then I have to."

His groin tightened painfully. He didn't think he could walk out of that room. Never in his life had anyone demanded he buy her. Never in his life had a virgin begged to be fucked like this. Never had he had a woman whose nipples responded like this. How could he resist her?

But he had to. Damn it. He was supposed to be *pretending* interest, not trying his best to get her naked and in his bed. Well, he wasn't pretending anymore, but neither was she.

He had to give it another shot. Maybe if he intimidated her, and laid down the most inflexible rules, the most impossible restrictions, she would give up this insane idea, and tonight would be the end of it.

For *her.*

He had to try, the most demeaning terms and conditions he could think of.

"If I buy you, miss wants-to-be-a-fancy-piece, I buy your life. I dictate everything. I come and go as I please. I fuck you when I feel like it, not when you want it. And if I don't feel like fucking you, it's your bad luck. I don't like begging. I don't like disobedience. The mistress I pay for is welcoming, compliant and always ready to spread her legs. I have a lot of expectations, which, living in your father's house, you will have to manage to comply with somehow—*if* I decide to buy your body. Is that understood so far?"

Her throat constricted. Her body writhed voluptuously as if to entice him to make the decision. She nodded, wholly unable to speak.

"Everything you promised before holds the same. I own you, I own your body, every inch of it, especially what's between your legs. You can withhold nothing. You can never refuse me, no matter what I ask, no matter what you want. This is not your willingness to play at being a mistress. These are the terms to *be* a mistress. This is what a man buys when he buys a woman's body: she is his vessel, his convenience, his toy. And he can take her out and play with her whenever *he* wants."

She licked her dry lips, her body quivering at his evocative words. He knew exactly what she wanted, and she must convince him.

"I want that. I want to be to you everything you said."

Damn and blast. "You still need some priming."

"I don't care. Pay me, and you can play with me." She arched her back so that the tattered bodice of her dress slipped down her breasts and caught on her distended nipples. She shimmied her shoulders, and the bodice fell, baring her breasts. "If I become your mistress, no one else will ever suck them."

His penis jolted and pearled. Damn right no one else would ever suck those lush teats. Goddamn hell, could he not control his damned penis? And what was he teaching her . . . that other men would pay for her? That she could sell her naked nipples to the highest bidder? Oh, she did like to use that bludgeon. And he was not immune to it. The thought of another man even touching her was pure agony, because any other man would have banged her up and down the Thames by now, and here he was, his penis painfully at point, trying to scare the bejesus out of her—and succeeding not at all.

What was wrong with him? He had virgin ass on his lap, two succulent nipples to feast on, barely two layers of material between his hard meat and her hot hole, and she was *begging* him to fuck her, and he was *hesitating?*

She was asking for it. And there wasn't a man alive who

wouldn't give it to her now, as hot and hard as she could take it.

"These are my expectations. Nothing impedes me when I want to fuck you. That means you learn to live without wearing undergarments. That means that when you have no social obligations, you are to expect me anytime of the day or night, and you dress accordingly. Simply put, you are naked and ready to take my penis every minute of your day. That's all I care about, just getting inside your naked body the minute I arrive. And for the privilege of being the only man who roots in you, I will pay you according to how well and how quickly you learn to please me. And when you agree to these terms."

"Have I pleased you so far?"

"Your nipples please me. But *you* are still dressed, and that doesn't please me."

"You haven't bought me yet."

"A mistress on the hunt generally shows the merchandise before a man pays for it. After all, how does he know what he's getting? All I see are your nipples, and your breasts could be your only prime attribute."

"Let me get ready for you, then."

"Learn this lesson, fancy-piece: a mistress lives to be naked for the man who buys her. If you can't strip off your clothes in front of me, well, you still have a lot to learn, and perhaps I don't want to pay for the privilege of teaching you. Unless, of course, you show me that your naked body is worth my attention—and my money."

Big mistake to taunt her like that, because to undress, she had to slip off of his lap, and then he didn't have her tight, round virgin ass undulating against his penis every time she moved.

But he did have a front row seat as she pulled down the sleeves of her dress and let it fall to the floor to reveal the thin silk garment underneath. It was so sheer he could see the thick enticing bush of dark hair between her legs; and for the rest, her stomach was flat, her breasts high and full, her body beautifully curved, and her nipples tight with excitement.

She ripped off the slip and flung it at him; he caught it and held it to his face to breathe in her essence.

Yes, he wanted it. He wanted it more ferociously than she.

She eased herself onto his lap again, naked but for her stockings and slippers, and wriggled against his penis as though she had discovered a place to root.

"Do you want what you see? Jeremy?"

"One part of me definitely wants it," he muttered as he felt another spurt of cream erupt.

She slipped off again and paced the room, circling in front of him, posing for him, enticing him. 'Will you pay for my body, Jeremy?"

"Do you accept my conditions?"

She wet her lips. "I do."

He had taught her too damned well, and now *he* could not back down. "Then, I will buy you." He dug in his pocket for a handful of guineas and tossed them carelessly onto the floor "You are mine now, wholly and completely." He began to unbutton his bulging trousers. "Get on your knees."

She knelt in front of him as he freed his rampaging manhood. A monstrous thing, a wondrous thing. With this, he would own her, and she would enslave him.

She put out her hand to touch it. It was so hot, so hard, so undeniably his life force; and as her fingers grasped it, a little gush of pearly cream erupted from the tip, and she swiped it with her forefinger and licked it

He waited, containing himself, hellaciously hard with those innocent fingers squeezing him and exploring him and . . . and . . . sliding him between her breasts, coddling him there, stroking him there . . . and . . . now rubbing the bulging tip of his penis against her erect nipples, one after the other, again and again and again.

How did she know to do that? Damn damn damn—he didn't want her to stop; he didn't want to stop.

She loved the way the hard rock of him felt against the thrust of her nipples back and forth, back and forth, back and forth, back, forth, back, she caught her breath as he thrust upward suddenly, violently and erupted like a geyser, spurning his thick hot cream all over her breasts.

Not enough cream for two — not tonight . . .

He grasped her shoulders and pulled her up onto his lap and ground his tongue into her mouth, massaging his essence into her breasts, her hot nipples, whatever part of her he could reach. He wanted to envelop her, devour her, contain her.

He cupped her buttocks, pressing her thigh and belly into his sticky wet penis that was still hard and randy as a goat. He could have taken her there, just spread her legs and embedded himself forcefully and possessively into her hot velvet innocence, but he resisted tenaciously.

Still he couldn't stop tonguing her and fondling her; every inch of her aroused him to an unbearable hardness, as if he hadn't shot himself all to hell all over her nipples. And her round, tight little ass—he wanted to mark his erotic possession of every part of her body—hard little bites so she would remember to whom she had sold her body.

And then common sense prevailed; Reginald would be home soon. And then what? His naked daughter in the library and the man he trusted most rooting voraciously in her mouth with his cannon of a penis on display. Shit.

He thrust her away. "We're done."

She wriggled more tightly against his spurting shaft. "Do more to me." She stroked the head, her fingers innocently—maybe not—rimming the tip of him and stroking it just where it would arouse him the most.

He got a firm hard grip on reality. It wasn't just Regina discovering sex in a public place; it was the fact that Reginald could come in the door at any moment. "*My* terms, fancy-piece. You have no wants or desires. You agreed to abide by that."

"Are you going to *her* now?" She refused to move from his

lap, and she held his penis in tightly, lightly, stroking him, stoking him as if she didn't want to let go.

"It's not your business."

"You don't have to spend it on her. You have enough to do more to me."

He removed her hand. "Go upstairs."

"Then, come back."

"Go upstairs *now*."

She slipped off of his lap and bent over to gather up her dress and the money, *of course the money*, which provided him with a tempting view of her ass and the lush tuft of pubic hair between her legs from that reverse position. It was almost enough to make him capitulate to her—but that wasn't the point. The point was to push her and push her until she stopped this nonsense—or until he pushed himself into her tight, hot little cunt.

She turned to look at him, mutely begging for him to come with her even as he began tucking away his still jutting penis.

"I don't care what you want, fancy-piece." Did he not?

"Don't go to her. I can give you what she can give you."

"Not quite yet you can't, fancy piece. You can't accommodate me between your legs."

"When, then? When will you do it to me?" she demanded as she dressed, her body electric with arousal and jealousy of the mistress for whom he still had enough cream that he could go to her after everything they had done this night and still fuck.

"When I feel like it," he said callously. He had to get her upstairs—and soon. He took her by the arm. "You agreed." So tempting. So erotic, her standing there in such disarray. He wrapped his arm around her neck, draping it over her shoulder so that he could just compress her nipple, and he marched her toward the door. "This is what a man pays for. Not for your demands or your desires and wants and needs. *His* desires and needs. And now, *I* don't need you any more tonight." He withdrew his fingers from her breast and turned her to pull her bodice back up to cover her nudity.

He was unspeakable, she thought; a monster to fondle her nipple like that and just leave her. But he didn't care.

"Upstairs, fancy-piece." He opened the door and pushed her through. "I know you'll have sweet dreams."

Chapter four

She lay in her bed, naked, her body hot and taut with desire, her skin meltingly soft, her breasts still faintly sticky with his residue. And she could still feel the compression of his fingers on her nipple; she stretched, languid as a cat, as her body reacted to the sensation.

Why wasn't he here to play with her nipples?

She heard her father come home, not minutes after she went upstairs. She heard the clock strike midnight, one, two, three o'clock.

Blast him. Blast him. He was with that cheap piece of haymarket ware he called a mistress and wasting all that luscious cream on her. It wasn't fair. It just wasn't fair. She could spread her legs as wide as any doxy. And if the only reason he wasn't fucking her tonight was her much vaunted maidenhead, well, she could take care of that easily—and it didn't even have to be with him.

Any cock would do, and it would serve him right if another man deflowered her. There were men who loved to go at a virgin full bang. And just to show him, she wouldn't even charge for the privilege.

And then he would never have a reason to root in that apple-wife's bang-box again.

Yes.

Her body went feverish with a heavy longing. *Yes.* She wanted his thick hot penis right *now.* And his wild wet tongue and devouring kisses. And his fingers constricting her nipple with just the perfect pressure that even the thought of it made her go weak. *Yes.*

She felt molten, liquid, breathless . . . *yes* . . .

She heard a sound, and she turned, startled, just in time to see him slip into her room, carrying a candle that he set down on the table by the door.

He turned the lock emphatically, and slowly he paced toward her, removing one piece of clothing at a time until he was naked and thick and erect, aroused beyond saving. And beside her suddenly on the bed, dangling the house key before her, the triumphant symbol of his power.

"I couldn't get your tight little ass out of my mind, so I came for it."

Her breath caught. *Yes.*

"Turn over."

She rolled onto her belly, and she felt his arm slide roughly under her hips and lift her onto her knees. And then—and then his hands, his big hot hands everywhere on her buttocks, feeling and squeezing and sliding into her virgin crease and exploring there, arousing her there. And then his mouth and tongue, licking, and nipping her curvy bottom, biting, sliding his tongue everywhere, working his erotic way down between her legs to her most secret place where he began a prolonged tonguing and sucking of her luscious slit.

She shimmied her bottom, working herself more tightly against the point of his taut tongue. She felt his stabbing movements coming closer and closer to penetrating her moist heat. She felt his hands on her buttocks, holding her, lifting her, positioning her so that she was canted at just the right angle for his tongue to take her.

Just . . . just . . . *ahhhhh* . . . the shocking moment when he slipped his tongue in, and then the luxurious lapping and sucking and pulling hard hard hard on her nakedness, riding her with his tongue, dissolving her, drawing her insides out . . . until she could do nothing but surrender in a long, low, guttural moan as a bolt of pleasure struck her down like lightning.

Slowly, he eased her down to the bed and turned her over so that she had full view of his nakedness as he bent over her and took her mouth in a hard, hot, possessive kiss that was permeated with the very essence of her.

He caged her with his body, his penis flexing between her breasts, and supporting himself on one arm so that he could take that one lush nipple between his fingers.

Her body jolted as she felt the erotic constriction of that thrusting point. His kiss was endless, harsh and rough with a man's uncontrollable desire, his need to possess her fueled by her pleasure, her nakedness, and by her squirming body enticing him as he played with her rigid nipple.

He couldn't get enough of that nipple. It was so taut, so responsive. He couldn't relinquish it as he pulled away from her mouth, a bare inch, and growled, "I'm never letting go of this teat."

And with those words, he knew there was no going back: he would take her, take her at her word, take her kisses, take her body, take her sex, because this was a battle he never could have won.

She writhed at the words, arching her upper body more tightly to his fingers. "Keep doing it. Harder. Do it to me."

"I intend to, fancy-piece. You've been cock teasing me for a good week now, and my patience just ran out. I paid for you and I'm taking what I want. Tonight. Sit up."

She levered herself up slowly so that she did not dislodge his fingers, and swung her legs over the bed, following his lead. He came around behind her, lightly twisting at the nipple to get his arm around her shoulder, so she was braced against his chest, and he rammed himself tightly against her bottom as he edged over to a small, armless boudoir chair.

He lowered himself into it, with her, back to front, on his

lap, straddling his hot penis with his fingers still holding the point of her nipple.

She arched back languorously into his demanding kiss.

Oh, his kiss, his hot, voracious kiss. Her hands on the bulbous head of his penis, stroking it and playing with it as he suckled her tongue and held her nipples and made her want to surrender every naked part of her body to the mastery of his hands.

Somewhere in that kiss, he relinquished one nipple. Somewhere in that kiss, she felt the fingers of that hand probing her velvet heat, penetrating this way, one two three, twisting that way, one two three. And his fingers playing with her nipple, and his greedy, engulfing kiss . . .

Her body spasmed, seeking surcease, but he only intensified the pressure, the penetration, the kiss. She felt as though she was melting, her whole body just dissolving in his hands. She wanted his fingers to thrust deeper, tighter, harder between her legs, his kiss deeper, harder, hotter in her mouth. And his fingers squeezing her nipple . . . how did he know just the perfect pressure that made her want to run away from it, that made her want to lean into him because it was still not enough.

He pulled a breath away from her lips, as ferociously aroused as she. "I need this nipple. But I need to fuck you more."

"Do both," she whispered.

"You couldn't stop me." He pushed harder against the soaking heat of her cleft. She was wide open to him, her body squirming and writhing on the hardness of his shaft, pushing insistently against the hot penetration of his fingers. "Oh, you do like it when I'm inside you."

She made a little noise at the back of her throat.

"You like it," she whispered.

"I'll like it more when my penis is there." God, who would have guessed she was such an easy piece and ripe for the taking. He had wasted three hours before he came back for her. Three hours and he could have had her primed, and on her knees, and he could have been embedded in her, making her beg for him.

Shit. But he loved her squirming ass against the cradle of his hips, and her innocent fingers squeezing his penis head. That was worth having, too. She wanted it, and she wanted it bad; but he wasn't going to give her the satisfaction—not yet—and he wasn't going to succumb to her virginal blandishments either.

Not till he could fully and completely ram himself home.

Except for the temptation of that nipple. God, he wanted that nipple. He could arouse her to a fever pitch before he even walked in the door because of that luscious nipple.

"When?" she breathed against his mouth.

"When what?"

". . . fuck me . . ."

"You can't wait for it, can you, fancy-piece?"

"If it feels like your fingers inside me . . ."

"But it's much longer and thicker and harder. How do you think it will feel?"

She shimmied against his fingers. "Big, thick, hard."

"That's just how it will fill you."

"Yes . . . ," she whispered. "Now."

"Soon."

"Don't move your fingers . . ." as he began to inch them out.

"Have to . . ."

"Don't . . . nipple . . ."

" . . . never—"

She was so ripe down there, so ready. A moment's distress—if that—and he would possess her fully.

It was a moment to savor. And a moment that gave him pause. He was at the sticking point where, up until now, this had been but a pleasure game willingly played by both participants.

But now . . . now . . . something more was at stake: not only her virginity, but her father's trust in him.

Once he went past that point, he could lose everything, and worst of all, he could never get it back.

She knew enough now, his fancy-piece, he had taught her too damned well. They didn't need to do anything more than they were doing to play the pleasure game. As it was, it was almost too much.

"Jeremy . . ." Her voice was mute, pleading, made him think of a half dozen other ways to carry on.

Shit. Too late for scruples. Or to recover his fifty guineas.

She was too hot, too wet, too irresistible. He caught her up again in a deep dark possessive kiss, shifting her body slightly so that her legs were spread farther apart and he could angle his hard shaft against her nakedness.

Ah . . . ! She felt his penis head then, as he slid it all along her moist cleft, back and forth, and then a little deeper, and a little deeper, deliciously prodding, probing, pushing, pushing, pushing, penetrating inch by slow, hard inch, fingering her hot nipple, mirroring her uncontrollable excitement as he slowly embedded his throbbing penis head in her wet, tight sheath.

Oh my God, oh my God, oh my God . . .

Just there. Just crowning her entry, just the head of him. She felt it so intensely, she wrenched her mouth from his because she had to see the rock rigid shaft of him buried between her legs.

He let her feel it, feel his power, his heat, his possession. She wriggled tentatively, as if she were trying to get away, and he pushed deeper.

Let her wriggle and writhe, he thought, the more she shimmied, the deeper she took him into her. She was so slick, so tight, so hot, he was that near to ejaculating. And the feeling of her undulating ass against his hips, and the vision of his male head rooted in her, didn't help his effort to maintain control.

He couldn't move; she didn't move. He still held her nipple between his fingers. He tilted her head to feed on her lips. The tension was hot between them, explosive.

She lost herself in that kiss. *This* was what it meant to be possessed by a man. He had not lied. It meant this deep, dark invasion of the secret places of her body. It meant his having full carnal knowledge of every inch of her. It meant surrendering her whole body, her feminine mystery, her soul. And it meant power, the power that only sex could confer, and that mistresses had known since time began.

Her instinct had been right; she wasn't going to let him hold back. She couldn't. His magic fingers on her nipple made her wild with excitement. The feeling of him between her legs was unspeakably voluptuous; when was he going to ram himself home? She wanted it, more than ever, every thick, rigid inch of him rooted right where he belonged.

She pulled away from the heat of his mouth to whisper, "You feel so good. I want all of your penis inside me."

His body jolted upward, and he felt himself spurting.

"Who would have thought it would feel so good," she breathed, loving that her words had propelled him to erupt. "I can't get enough of it." He thrust again, feeling himself spinning out of control. "More—harder . . . more—"

And he was gone, his whole body involuntarily jacking upward and exploding his hot spuming cream into her untried virgin body.

It was a wondrous thing, a man's body, that even words could excite it beyond endurance; and his penis, as he withdrew it, still in a high state of arousal. It excited her to see it still rigid and slick with the essence of her.

"Oh, we're not done yet, fancy-piece," he murmured. "I have enough left for you." He levered himself out of the chair, holding her around the waist so that she was not an inch away from him, and tumbled her onto the bed. "Spread your legs, mistress. You begged for this."

She was soaking now, from his semen, from her quivering arousal, and he thrust his penis head hard into her, as deep as he could go without tearing her. She eased onto her elbows to look, to see him deeply embedded in her, joined to her in the most erotic way.

"You want my penis inside you. This"—he thrust at her and she flinched—"is my penis inside you." He drew back meaningfully, thrust just the ridged tip into her, pulled it out, thrust again, pulled it out, thrust again, pulled it out, and this time, with no niceties, no further play, he rammed himself home.

A pinch, a tear—what . . . oh God, he's inside me to the hilt . . . oh my God, oh my God, oh my God . . . it's so naked, it's so hard . . . it's so THERE . . .

"You wanted it," he whispered. "Never fuck with a man in heat."

She had to rally; there was no time to examine what was happening, or how she felt, she wanted to get out from under him *immediately,* and she wanted to stay, and all she could do was react in a way that mirrored this hard-hearted possession that she hadn't quite expected. "You're hard as a bone," she whispered, "so how long do I have to wait for you to fuck me to a faretheewell."

Hell. Bitch. How much money had he thrown at her?

"It would serve you right if I just got up and walked out forever," he growled. "Some mistresses are appreciative of anything they get." It was a game, after all. But he was damned if she was going to call the shots. Virgins were hell after they discovered pleasure. Why hadn't he taken that into consideration? "And the fact this is your first fuck—you should be grateful as hell it's not some stranger! On second thought, I am leaving . . ." Deliberately, he wrenched himself out of her body, so she could see the rock-hard jut of his throbbing sex. "I'll get it somewhere else."

Oh, God, no no no. Never did she think she would feel this empty, this bereft. And the worst was over. He could never hurt her again that way. And the pleasure was too much to give up out of hand. A mistake to bludgeon him with his own words like that; if she wanted to follow through on her own expressed intentions, which she did, she would have to swallow her mistake and beg.

"Don't."

"Don't. Too late for don'ts, my would-be mistress. Remember! You agreed to my terms. My needs, My wants. My pleasure. When I want it, How I want it. If I want it. That's what I paid you for. Your nipples. Your ass. Your cunt. Not when you want it. When I want it."

"Come get it, then," she said softly. "I'm ready for you." And she was. She felt the loss of him keenly, and the power, on every level. Once the initial deed was done, the rest wasn't hard at all. She wanted him, that was clear and true. And everything that implied.

He kneeled back on the bed between her legs. "That's the only thing that's keeping me here—that you're naked and I can take you this minute."

"Good," she breathed. *Oh, good.* She watched through knowing, hooded eyes as he inserted himself up to the rim of his penis head. She loved that, the barest tip of him rimming the folds of her sheath with the promise of all the heat and force behind it. He wanted her to feel it, his power, his strength, his virility. He had more than enough for her five times over, let alone two. He was as hard as a poker, and he wanted her to feel every thick hot inch of him as he slowly slowly slowly pushed himself into her wet tight core.

So slowly. He was so long, so strong as his hips flexed and he thrust himself inside her. And when she thought she had wholly encompassed all of his massive length, he pushed yet another inch tighter inside.

"This is what a mistress does, fancy-piece. This is how her lover likes to see her, flat on her back and dominated by his lust."

God almighty—it was too damned late to shock her. What the hell did he think he was doing? Nothing fazed her, not even his insensitive taking of her virginity. A man had to be made of iron to resist her.

"That's what I want," she whispered—and she meant it. And that was nearly the end—of him. She loved it, every stroke, every thrust, every minute; she moved with it, she begged for it, whispering hot words in his ear, grasping his buttocks, raking his back. She felt him, every juicy inch of him, and she worked him as though she was born to be on her back and at his mercy.

And he gave her none. His control shattered, and all he wanted to do was pound them both to oblivion.

She was insatiable. There never was such pleasure, such feelings, such fullness in her. Her body had been aching for this unspeakable forbidden possession by the most devastatingly potent part of a man.

How could anyone live without it after experiencing that secret pleasure? She couldn't stop taking him. His mouth bruised hers, his body rammed into her savagely, pulling her with him, pummeling her until she was swamped by waves and waves of purling, rolling sensations. Never stop never stop never stop never stop . . . something stopped . . . something broke, and nothing could stop the storm of feeling and emotion that crashed over her, into her, around her, hot boiling pleasure pouring through her body and between her legs. His pleasure, his cream, hot and blasting out of him like a cannon, and he couldn't stop it, he couldn't stop it, he couldn't, couldn't couldn't couldn't—

And then one last mighty thrust—and he pitched mindlessly over and into her arms.

Desire was an insidious thing. It crept up on a man at the least likely times. He thought he was dead exhausted, and a half hour after his forceful possession of her, he was still inside her, stiff as a board, and hot to fuck her again. She didn't have to do a thing. All he needed was a vessel, and she was still soaked, thick with his cream, an image that aroused him ferociously.

He eased himself more against her, burying himself so powerfully and so deep, he could feel her pubic hair scraping against his own. He felt himself contract, and then he spurted, not the full blow, but damn and hell, all he had to do was embed himself in her and he went off half-cocked. Shit. He couldn't control anything, not her, not sex, not his unruly penis.

He rocked against her, pushing, pushing, pushing. Her body was so pliant, taking him deeper and deeper as he ground his hips into hers. He wanted to root between her legs forever.

He had been at her so long, the candle was guttering, burned to the nub and suddenly gone, throwing the room in total darkness.

There was something about the dark. Forbidden things happened in the dark. Things that two people did to each other that did not have to be acknowledged in daylight. Things he wanted to do to her right now while she was naked and still coated with his semen.

He nudged her legs together and straddled them so that she enveloped him even more tightly. She stirred, and her sleepy, futile movements stoked him to the blasting point. He covered that one breast to feel her nipple shaping beneath the flat of his hand. He covered her mouth, thrusting his tongue deep within, concurrent with the sharp, thrusting movement of his penis.

She came languidly awake as she accepted his tongue. Her body arched under him as he fingered her nipple the way only he could, and he followed the movement with a hard thrust of his hips.

This was all he needed: his possession of her turgid nipple, the soft, hot accommodation of her supple body, the hot press of his penis deep inside her, her avid mouth voraciously feeding on his lips and tongue.

He didn't want to move. Couldn't move. *If* he moved . . . he spasmed, he spurted, and he ruthlessly got himself under control. He wanted this full bore possession to go on for hours, for days, for months, with no beginning and no end.

And all he had to do was wholly embed himself in her and *not* move.

He had to move. *Had* to move. His tongue, his hips, his fingers. Just to let her know he was there. Inevitably, indomitably *there*.

And that nipple. That hard, pliable nipple . . . it drove him crazy the way he could play with it, rub it, caress it, the way her hips shimmied and ground into him every time he manipulated it, the way her body got hot, stoked, languid with every erotic touch.

Don't move. Let her move. Let her squirm and twist and try to get away from me. This is my nipple. She will never get away from me.

Something else almost got away from him. The more he tried to contain her, the more she writhed and made hot little pleasure sounds in the back of her throat, and the more aroused he became. A man wasn't meant to feel this explosive, as if every part of him would blow apart if he gave in.

He was desperate to give in. His penis was bone-stiff with his lust to possess her. He thrust into her, short, sharp movements, because any more commitment and he would blast. And he wanted to prolong it, he did. He had all best intentions, just short jabbing thrusts, one two three. Feeding on her lips, one two three; feeling the caress of her tongue against his, one two three; a man had to be made of stone, one two three; well, part of him was, one two three—one last drive home and he burst like a dam, carried away by the gushing geyser of his release. One two three.

Light filtering through the curtains. Movement beyond the door, the maids scurrying to begin the morning. Morning. Damn and hell. Morning.

And here he was wrapped around her naked body and hot and hard and primed to go. Had they slept? He thought so. She had only been half awake at the most during the night.

And now she was this enticing bundle in his arms, her naked body his to do with whatever he wanted. And he wanted. He wanted. He would have to get used to his penis at full staff around her. She would have to get used to it.

He pulled her against him, spoon-fashion, and inserted three fingers of one hand between her legs and cupped her breast with the other.

She was still slick with his semen, still hot, still willing. Her bottom undulated against his hips, she parted her thighs to invite his fingers, and her hand grasped his wrist and pressed them deeper into her cleft.

He was coming closer, closer, closer to something, some pleasure point nestling just within her. *There—oh!—there . . .* her body stiffened. She pressed down hard against his fingers—*oh now . . .* He had her other nipple . . . *Oh no oh no— too much, too much—*

A knock at the door and she swallowed her dismay on a tide of wanton need.

"Good morning, my dear," Reginald called. "Come join me for early breakfast."

"Tell him you're exhausted, you're sleeping in this morning," Jeremy whispered.

She couldn't talk. How could she talk with his fingers doing what they were doing to her. "I—I'm still rather tired," she called back, her voice ragged. "I'm going to sleep in this morning."

"As you wish, my dear. We'll talk later."

Blast, blast, blast . . .

"I'm still here," Jeremy whispered.

"I feel so illicit."

"You're my mistress," he reminded her bluntly. "After last night, nothing"—he drove his quiescent fingers into her cleft— "nothing interferes with *this* . . ."

She felt herself quickening. He stoked her and stroked her, twisting his fingers deep inside her; she bore down on him, seeking that elusive thing that she didn't know what it was, and succumbing to the ribbons of sensation that skeined from the tip of her nipple to the pleasure point between her legs.

There it was, there, nestling just within her, that secret place waiting for a touch, a caress, a certain pressure that would send her spiraling out of control. She felt it coming. She felt her body reaching for it, yearning for it, closing on it— there, just there—*there!* Her body seized up, tightened, and then catapulted into a convulsion of unspeakable sensation that just didn't end.

She didn't want it to end. How could she bear it if it ended? And if Jeremy left, as he must certainly do before the morning ended.

Don't think about that. Think about how rock-hard he is and that he's in a fever for your body. That's all there is. And if you want to keep him in your bed, that's all there ever can be . . .

All, all, all, all, all, all—alllllllllllllllll—

A clock struck somewhere in the distance, and she forced herself to move. She didn't want to move. The morning was perfect, with Jeremy lying beside her naked and asleep, and the wonder of him was that when he slept, that rebellious other part of him didn't.

And what an amazing part it was, all muscle and heat and a life of its own. She touched him, sliding her hand down the long, hard shaft and into the thick thatch of hair at the base.

Soon, soon, he must leave her. And then what? She didn't expect this complication about being—*pretending to be?*—a mistress. She hadn't expected any of the realities, least of all the kind of bone-sapping pleasure of which she was capable.

No wonder coupling like this was forbidden, secret, immoral. It was so powerful, in so many ways, and so hurtful in others. If she even thought she had feelings for Jeremy, for instance, she might be devastated the moment he walked out the door.

It was so much better that she had initiated their intimacy

for her own purposes, and that she was in control of her feelings and could and would play the pleasure game as often as he wanted.

Unless she tired of him.

A delicious thought, but truly, how could anyone tire of being the object of desire? It had all worked out perfectly, she mused, tugging lightly at his hair. He had fulfilled her father's mandate to distract and divert her, and she in turn had taken the best revenge on him by becoming his mistress.

And the game wasn't over yet, she thought. Her supposed obsession with Raulton could still be in play. It couldn't hurt to make Jeremy jealous while she enjoyed what he was willing to give. While she could.

A man wouldn't hesitate. And neither would she, now that he had taught her all the tricks worldly women knew.

The reward for capitulating was enough in itself: pleasure beyond words, knowledge beyond all that was knowable, and the sensual power to make any man come to heel.

Something hot enclosed him. Something wet that pulled at the very tip of his engorged member. Something that felt so good, he didn't want to make a move lest he interrupt the steady sucking of his penis head. And those erotic little noises she was making . . . she loved it. He loved it, and the way her still-innocent hands kept fumbling all over his shaft and his balls. . . .

Damn . . . that tongue would set off a firecracker, the way she was using it on him. No one had ever licked him and sucked him so thoroughly and with so much enthusiasm, not even the lamented Marguerite.

Forget about that.

. . . Forgotten.

He felt himself swelling, his penis distending, his body tightening, gathering, pointing . . . right there, right to the very center of all that heat, all that wet and that rhythmic erotic pull that now compressed just the turgid tip of his penis.

242 / Thea Devine

He wanted to jam himself into her, to see if she could en-
compass his length that way, her way, his way. He followed
the pull of her lips and tongue, his body lifting, grinding,
thrusting toward the pulsing sucking of him. Just that, just
there—never never never . . . it was too much, not enough.

Even he . . . he wanted more more more, just that little
more deep in her mouth, stroked by her tongue—the whole
head, nothing more . . . nothing ever more. And she took him,
right to the ridge, and it was cataclysmic, the fury with which
he came, the way she pumped and sucked it right out of him
until there was nothing left. He spurted. Nothing. Another
gust. Over now. Drained and gone.

No. Not over. Damn and hell, she was not getting it all.
Not by hell. He wrested himself from her greedy mouth and
levered himself up on one arm. Oh, yes, he was still hard and
hot to spume. More than enough to blast inside her. And her
breasts already smeared with his cream. . . . He wanted those
breasts in his hands *now* . . . and her flat on her back.

She looked so smug he wanted to mount her right there and
ride her until the sun went down.

No. He wouldn't last.

Really?

"Lie down." That was about the best he could do at the
moment, and he didn't like that cat-lapping smile she gave
him; but she willingly lay down, and he rolled onto her and
just plunged himself between her legs.

Control. Had to keep control.

He rolled onto his back so that she straddled him, and the
expression on her face was wondrous. He was even deeper
now, pressing against her pleasure point, and her breasts were
there before him, her nipples tight and inviting. She leaned forward to offer them, and he took each one between his fingers
as he thrust into her.

Startled, she ground downward to receive him, her hands
braced against his shoulders. Was there ever such pleasure?
Between his fingers voluptuously compressing both nipples

and the short, heated thrusts of his penis, she thought she
would dissolve altogether.

She looked like a goddess, with her wild tumbling hair, her
pumping hips, her round, taut-tipped breasts, and her responsive nipples that were the only way a mere mortal could contain her.

And *this*—he drove into her with all his violent need—
this . . . her nakedness, his; *this* . . . her nipples, his; *this* . . .
her sex, his; *this* . . . his cream, *his,* discharging explosively between her legs. . . .

This. . . .

He had to cool off. It took every ounce of strength to leave
her, and even then, he wasn't sure he should have. He didn't
like the look in her eye, but she could ignore Reginald no
longer; it was already well after noon.

He was still primed as a pistol when he slipped down the
servants' stairway, and getting in deeper and deeper. He could
have pinned her and popped her until she cried for mercy the
way he was feeling, and it shocked him.

Damn, damn and damn. Taking a vestal vixen like that and
making her his mistress. Was he sane? And because she
wanted it. For how long? And when would the recriminations
start? Could he believe anything she said? Or was his penis totally in control and he didn't care?

God, he needed a drink. He needed to sit by himself and
stew in his own hot blood with a tot of whiskey to tame the
rampant beast.

There was always Heeton's, that bastion of male domi-
nance, the most select club in the whole of London, where
men of influence and wealth conducted the business of the na-
tion in the hushed sanctity of shadowy corners.

That was the place for a man to ruminate on his sins and
excesses. And regain what little sanity he had left.

But it was not to be. He was accosted immediately by the
aging quartet known as The Four Crack Hands, who presided

over the Betting Book and the Calendar, and who dispensed any information about social venues as though they were meting out water torture.

But the Book at Heeton's was the be-all and end-all of the Club. It was infinitely more exclusive than the one at White's, private, secure and sacrosanct; nothing written in the Book ever went beyond the doors of Heeton's for fear of total ostracism, and The Four Crack Hands guarded it as if it were the crown jewels.

Bodley was the Keeper. "Here's a familiar face, gentlemen"—he raised a toast—"and not a wager as to when he might reappear amongst the living after dispensing with the fair Marguerite . . ."

Jeremy blanched as he shook hands all around. *Marguerite? After all this time? Still?*

"How did we slip up on that plum pot . . . ?" This was Berkleigh already calculating guineas lost, a sum that didn't bear thinking about. "When *did* you get back to Town, exactly?"

"Three days ago. I didn't snuff it, gentlemen. I've been rusticating. And now I'm back in full cry. So what's to do?"

"Oh, you're a one," Fallowell now. "You think you ain't chatter broth already? Let me disabuse you of that notion. Even if we didn't know, every matchmaking mother in Town was aware to the instant when you stepped foot back in Portman Square."

It was so true, he had to smile. An eligible man was nothing short of a bon bon, to be savored, chewed over, and eventually swallowed whole by one or another of the beauties of the Season.

It was every man's destiny—when he wasn't being a *remedy;* when he wasn't educating a virgin to be a mistress. When he wasn't being swallowed whole by *her.*

Oh, God. . . .

"Speaking of that," he said, his voice raw, "what's the Book this week?"

"You won't believe it."

"Try me."

"Raulton."

Jeremy lifted a brow. Worse and worse. Damn, damn damn. . . .

"It's true. He's been prowling the sidelines and the *on dit* is he's out to hang up the ladle." The amusement factor was enough to send Bodley into transports. "And there's much interest in *some* quarters. They're pounding deep on this one," he added, patting the Book.

"Who's the front line?" Jeremy asked, casually, he hoped.

Bodley ticked off the names. "Miss Law, The *Honorable* Miss Garland, Lady Olney, Miss Soames. This week anyway."

"A tidy cat-patch," Jeremy commented impassively. Regina's name booked? *Already?* Damn, damn, damn and *hell*.

"Your presence could kick things up a bit," the reticent Rustington suggested

"I daresay it will." Jeremy took a flute of champagne from a passing waiter. God, if he thought he needed liquid sustenance before, it was nothing to how he needed it now. Those bettors were among the highest flyers in the land, Personages who didn't discuss their business in public. Or their vices.

Raulton's matrimonial chances would be fair game at White's within days, by the looks of it. Too many people were talking already, and that inevitably and always led to book.

Damn and hell.

He had no time at all to get Regina out of the line of fire.

"And so how did it end with the fair Marguerite?" Berkleigh asked.

Damn again. They were as insatiably curious as women. Better he dispense the story of his congé than let them speculate. At least *his* version would be all around Town by morning. "As you might imagine, gentlemen. She caught a warmer scent and she rode out of town without a backward glance." That they all understood. Who hadn't been given the mitten by a ladylove whose affection was sold to whomever was plumpest in the pocket?

"Ah, poor Jeremy." Bodley again. "It is ever the way with them dashers. Damned shame, but there it is. Well, welcome back, my boy. And let us toast the indomitable Marguerite, wherever she may be." He lifted his champagne flute. "May she be dished up and dashed down and never make another man miserable again . . ."

Chapter Five

So there it was. She had permitted a man to touch her, to possess her in the most intimate and erotic way, and she saw nothing different about herself when she looked in the mirror.

Maybe a little different. Her eyes were brighter; her skin seemed to glow. Perhaps she stood a little taller to emphasize her breasts. She was tellingly aware of her body and her capacity for sensual gratification.

She felt strong, powerful. There was a world of knowledge in her bearing and in her gaze.

And she felt no shame. Rather, every part of her felt sumptuous, carnal, untamed. Clothed, she felt her body spurt to life at her intemperate thoughts. Jeremy must must must come back to her tonight.

But that was not to the point this morning. She was so late to breakfast, her father would already have ordered his midday meal, and there was no ducking that.

It was just that he would be over concerned about her,

about the pace of their days and their social commitments being too much for her.

And now they were, she thought irritably, as she checked her hem one more time and then made her way downstairs. Now she wanted every evening free for Jeremy, even supposing he would come to her every evening; anything else seemed insipid and banal.

But this game must be played as well. And she must contain her impatience and her clamoring body, which, even as she entered the dining room, was erect to all the possibilities of the day.

"Father." She seated herself and poured a cup of tea.

"Regina. Are you all right, my dear?"

"Oh, yes." She sipped. Easier not to talk.

"And Jeremy saw to everything last night? He said you had a headache."

"He was solicitous as ever you would be, I promise you. I spent the night in bed." Not a lie. Not wholly the truth. "And I'm up to the mark for whatever's on tonight." Yes, yes. She had to be, because she saw clearly she couldn't be lolling around waiting for him. That would be the height of folly and confer far too much power on him and his prowess.

Her body stiffened.

Don't think about it. . . .

"I'm glad to hear it," Reginald said. "It is but a small party at the Petleys'—cards, refreshments, perhaps some dancing. Nothing onerous. Everything amiable and early home. Do you feel the thing? Will you come?"

"I'm happy to," she murmured. Anything to preserve the pretense that nothing had changed.

Everything had changed, and she became more aware of it by the minute, not least her consuming impatience over the trivialities of the day. Receiving guests. The ride in the park. The hour calling on friends and acquaintances. Another half hour shopping for furbishments at Clark and Debenham. Over to Hatchard's for a book that she likely wouldn't read. A nap, fruitless by herself alone. A bath, which only served to heighten her awareness of her body.

And a sense of herself observing, taking mental notes about what she felt, what she did and how her everyday life was impacted by her new knowledge.

She had grown up and, in the course of a day, grown away from virginal pursuits. When her maid laid out her gown, her only concern was whether it was adult enough, revealing enough, something a bold and coddled mistress might wear.

And indeed, where would someone virtuous come by clothes like that? Still, her maid could quickly alter a neckline, pare down a puffed-up sleeve, damp down her thinnest under-slip, find a patch to emphasize her best attributes.

And she had to be careful, so careful, that her father found nothing amiss with her appearance. For the party at the Petleys', she chose to wear a dress of cream-colored glacé silk overlaid with lace and trimmed with silk flowers. Innocent, beguiling. A little daring around the oval neckline which was cut low. Slippers to match, shawl and gloves. Her hair done up in a knot with a ribbon of the silk flower trim banding her curls.

Not too formal, she thought critically, surveying herself in the mirror.

Not too girlish. Not too fast. Passable for a private party. Maybe.

She wrapped the shawl around her swelling breasts. Her father couldn't forbid it if he didn't see them beforehand. And if it was too much, she would just wear the shawl all evening.

And besides, there would be no one at the Petleys' who was not over the age of forty. This wasn't a night for pleasure games. It was simply an evening in which she was accommodating her father's desire to be with old friends.

That notion stood about as long as it took them to get to the Petleys' town house in Westcott Square, where it appeared the Petleys had issued an invitation to everyone in their set. By the time Regina and her father arrived, there were at least seventy-five guests crowding into the refreshment room, the card room and the grand parlor, and more guests coming behind them

"Come, come—" Lord Petley in the entryway, a large, bombastic man whose satin waistcoat strained over his belly, a man with a good heart and an open hand to his friends. "Don't stand on ceremony here; there's plenty to do, food in the anteroom, and we're getting up an orchestra for dancing. Cards? To your left. Regina, my dear. Just your night. There's a game of loo about to start in chips. Mr. Raulton heads the table. I know your fondness for it. Do you join them."

Her heart almost stopped. Raulton, here? The man was everywhere. And it meant Jeremy might show as well. What luck. What good fortune.

"I would be pleased," she murmured. "Father?"

"Don't stay on my account," her father said, too heartily. "I can easily drum up some company or a game of cards." And drum Mr. Raulton right out of this house, but that was not his purview, nor could Regina refuse to join Raulton at the card table now without seeming churlish.

Events were conspiring against him, Reginald thought furiously, as he watched Regina glide into the card room and take her seat at Raulton's table. The man was too damned slimy and ingratiating, because if he weren't, the Petleys never would have invited him for the evening.

Nor could he stay and keep an eye on Regina. It was the most damnable thing. She was out to get Raulton, and like a plump plum, everytime she turned around, he fell into her lap.

He stalked into the refreshment room, not quite sure what he wanted to do, but vaguely planning to bring Regina something to drink and then spill it all on Mr. Raulton's head.

Not too subtle, that. He almost wished Regina had been laid low by her headache of the previous night. He hoped against hope Jeremy would come. He felt as helpless as only a father can feel when his beloved child has walked into a predator's trap.

He took a glass of lemonade and made his way to the card room. There was no way to observe them unnoticed. The honest thing was to present Regina with the lemonade and withdraw.

But when he caught sight of the table, with Regina, Raulton, and six other people besides, and saw that the cards had been dealt, and the first lead was in play, he changed course.

No use upsetting things. Nothing could happen *there*.

He needed a drink and something stronger than lemonade.

Damn, he needed Jeremy.

Jeremy was fighting his worst instincts, the invitation to the Petleys' crumpled in his hand, already a block from their town house and thinking it was the worst idea to spend an evening with all those browseabouts and bagpipes when he could be spending *himself* in his mistress.

But not this soon. Not after he had dressed her to the nines on the duties of a mistress to her keeper. Sheer folly to bend under the weight of his lust and give in to his clamoring penis. A man had to be stronger than that. Harder than that.

Damn hell.

A small card party with supper was just the thing to take his mind off of her. He would have to mind his manners and keep focused because Lady Petley had a great fondness for whist and for him as a partner.

Just the thing.

Maybe . . . ?

He topped the town house steps and entered the hall. What the hell was this? A small, select group of what—a hundred?

And the noise! The music from the far parlor. The laughter in the card room. People playing cap-verses in the dining room, shrieking their clever rhymes above the din.

Typical Petley row. Damn. Hell. Now what?

He turned on his heel to leave, and just caught sight of her out of the corner of his eye. *Regina . . . Raulton . . . shit—*

Damn her to hell.

He eased his way into the card room, every expectation met: there was Regina, sitting across from Raulton, beautiful, breathtaking, sensual, and the bastard couldn't keep his eyes off the swell of her breasts, which, with that abomination of a dress, she of course fully intended should happen.

She knew she would see him here, he thought venomously. Maybe she had even planned it. God knew, she had had the whole afternoon to weave her little web, to convince the Petleys perhaps to include him among the guests. Damn and hell, he never goddamned should have left her.

She was booked at ten-to-one at Heeton's. Hard in the running for that man's hand. Soames was fifty-to-one, even though everyone had seen them together at the Skeffinghams'. It was thought she was a little too green in the grass for him.

But Regina, with her breasts and her protruding nipples that even *he* could see from where he stood—Regina, with her beauty, her wit and her style—Regina with her newfound knowledge—Regina was perfect.

And Regina would never settle for being Raulton's mistress, no matter what she said.

Only his.

Well, by damn, that was enough. That was what they both wanted. He had paid for her, he owned her for as long as HE wanted her, and he would make sure that any other interested male could not mistake it.

He left to prepare, as her laughter rippled across the room.

"I don't like that Raulton," Reginald said, feeling as if he had had this conversation at least ten times already.

"He is an amusing man," Regina said. "Interesting. Excellent at cards. But I'm certain he was gentleman enough to let me win several hands."

"He wants to win your hand," Reginald said sourly, "and I tell you now, Regina, I will never countenance such a match."

She prickled up. This had been quite an evening, with

Raulton's attention all on her and her bosom, and Jeremy nowhere to hand. It made her positively irritable that he had not shown, and that Raulton was on her every moment, as if that little play they had enacted the night before entitled him to liberties. Blast him. Blast Jeremy.

"Is that so, Father? I wonder where you got the idea that any such thing was a consideration."

"Watching that damned popinjay is where. This was the first time in a month he didn't need to pay court to some milk and water miss, and he could seek out a woman of wit and guile. Who wouldn't notice?"

"He likes the cards," Regina said tautly, "and a partner with some gumption. There is nothing more to it than that."

"He may wish for that in a life partner as well."

"So do I," she said waspishly.

"Don't say that."

"I've said it. There's nothing more to say, Father. I heard you."

"I don't think so," Reginald said grumpily. "Not by half." And where was Jeremy when he needed him?

He was almost afraid to bid her good night. It didn't seem beyond possibility that she was capable of sneaking out and meeting Raulton, given how cozy they had been tonight.

The thought struck terror in his heart.

It was the worst thing in the world to have such a daughter; no man could resist her, and as was becoming very obvious, there was one man that she could not seem to resist either.

She climbed the stairs wearily. She had been soundly trumped; it was silly and childish, but nothing mattered when she felt as if she had lost the game.

And the heady moments at the card table opposite Raulton? All for show, did Jeremy arrive. And all of it, time wasted.

Tomorrow, she would end the thing and tell her father for true that she had no interest in Raulton whatsoever.

And then the game would be over, and she would move on.
There was a glimmer of light beneath her door, as faint as
hope. What hope? A man had a choice of a dozen women who
would copulate with him for the price of a carriage, a house
and a thousand a year. Pleasure came cheap for a man of
means at that price. And it was an excellent bargain for his
mistress, who got to keep every pound she earned.

Blast it. What *was* she thinking? Raulton's presence at the
Petleys' had her tied up in knots. It had taken an enormous effort to keep him amused and entertained.

But the end result appalled her: he had looked at her with
new appreciation and new consideration, which a week ago
would have fit into her plans and schemes admirably, and that
was the thing her father remarked upon.

And if he had seen it, how many others had as well? Blast
and blast.

Yet another tangle in the web, and she was far too tired to
unravel it tonight.

"Not too tired for me?" Jeremy said from the depths of the
room.

Blast him. She shrugged off her shawl. "Cards do wear one
out. All that mental calculation. And then, to play with a man
with the finesse of Mr. Raulton—well, need I tell you, dear
Jeremy? It fair kept me in high gig just to keep up with him."

"Indeed, you need to tell me, dear Regina. That dress,
flaunting your breasts, your nipples, what I bought, what I
own, in another man's face so he can salivate over what he
can't have. Do tell me, Regina. What *was* that all about?"

"That was about I have a life and you have a life and sometimes our interests cross, and sometimes they don't," she said
rebelliously. "I didn't expect you tonight."

"Obviously. Maybe you thought Raulton would arrive to
take my place."

"Oh, please . . ." Oh, he is jealous . . . he is—

"Oh, please what, since your express intention all along
has been to attract his notice. Well, let me tell you, he noticed

and he *will* come sniffing around you. Only he will find *me* in your bed, or barring that, he will find irrefutable evidence that someone owns you."

"Truly," she murmured, thrilled to the bone by his possessive tone. "And what will he find?"

He held up his hand, and dangling from his fingers there was a thin gold chain at the end of which was a tiny lock. "You will wear my chain as a symbol of my possession so no other man can penetrate you."

She held out a shaking hand to take it. It was such a fine, thin chain that it was a barrier to nothing, and it excited her beyond all measure because it was a tangible sign that she was his mistress indeed and he wanted her body to the exclusion of any other woman. Who would not enchain her body for the pleasure of the man who owned her?

"I will wear your symbol," she said huskily, "but he will not come."

"He was riveted by your breasts, fancy-piece. By your nipples. I saw him."

"You were there?" She felt triumphant. Not all for naught. Not a waste when it had resulted in this unleashing of his undeniable lust for her.

"Watching you. Watching him. I think this game is over, fancy-piece. I am the only one whose interest you must fix." He reached out his hand and hooked his fingers in the bodice of her dress. "The only one for whom you ever reveal yourself." He pulled, and the bodice gave, freeing her breasts. "The only one . . ." He took her nipples one in each hand as her dress dropped to the floor. "These are mine . . ."

She caught her breath as he took them, expert now as to how much pressure, how light, how tight, and both at the same time which sent her senses spinning, made her molten with need.

She wanted nothing more than this, to be half naked with his fingers playing with her nipples; from pure innocence to pure passion on the tight hot pleasure points of her nipples.

Just like that, *just like that . . . harder,* softer—desire and lust rippled through her body, fusing deep in her core, centering on the skeining sensation from her nipples as he fondled them.

Just her nipples. No where else?

No.

Hot gold now, the feeling, sliding down down down down . . . yes . . . hot and thick and bright—gold—enfolding her, enslaving her, pooling deep deep deep, breaking in the center like stone hitting water, and radiating explosively outward, yes, all that heat, all . . . that . . . thick, all . . . that . . . go-old . . .

She wrenched away from him, covering her turgid breasts with her hands, and she sank onto the bed. *What was that—? What WAS that?*

He lifted her hands and pulled the dress away from her breasts, and then knelt so he could remove all her clothes, one piece at a time. Her dress, her undergarments, her slippers, her stockings, the band in her hair.

"A mistress is always naked."

"When she knows the man who keeps her is coming," she said tartly, to rip the mood. She wasn't sure she could bear any more this evening.

What he had done to her was more than enough. Her nipples felt irritated, used.

"He is *always* coming," he muttered, pushing her on her back and removing her undergarments. "He is always there." He dangled the chain in front of her. "Like all men. Thus, we claim the one we fuck." He slipped the chain around her waist, and it was then she saw that there was another chain hanging vertically from it. And that chain he looped between her legs just tightly enough so it caressed her *there*, and he attached it and locked it at the small of her back.

"Stand up."

She stood, feeling the thin strip of chain keenly. It didn't hurt. It was barely there; but she *knew* it was there, and that was what made the difference. He had the key, and another man could not get to her while she willingly let him bind her body.

He made her walk around the room. The enchainment was perfect, settling just on her hips and encompassing her lightly between her legs and enticingly in her crease. Now she was wholly his, her nipples, her body, her cunt. And when she was dressed, she would feel him, and when she was naked she would feel him, and never would a moment pass that she wouldn't feel him possessing her in some way.

The thought made him wild. He was hard to bursting to get to her. But the excitement was heightened by his restraint and by her submission to his will. The chain glimmered in the candlelight which cast erotic shadows all over her naked body as she paced around him.

And those breasts, those nipples . . . he would never get through an hour without touching her. Without . . . *shit*—he came. Damn and hell. He ripped open his trousers and let it come, let it spume all over to show her just what she did to him with her nipples and her compliant naked body.

She licked her lips as she watched him. Such a waste when he could have pumped it all into her. But he always said he had enough for her and more. And it would dry. By morning, it would dry, and by morning, he would be dry—if she had anything to do with it.

She pushed him onto the bed and began to undress him.

How many times had he fucked her? She couldn't even remember. All she knew was that it was morning, he was gone, and the slender chain was locked just between her legs where he should have been.

This mistress business is wearing. He's not here enough. I can't get enough. And now this. . . .

This was Reginald pounding at her door. "It's nearly noon, Regina. I'm worried about you. You never sleep in."

". . . right there," she mumbled, grabbing for her clothes.

Five minutes later, she was downstairs in the dining room once more pouring tea, as if it were the second night of a play in which she was a performer.

And that was just what she was doing: performing

She left the containment of the chair, and she shivered. Jeremy knew just what he was about. He wanted to make her hunger for him, yearn for him, and what better way than this erotic reminder.

Which she didn't need. She craved him enough already. Her nipples were stiff with wanting his touch just from the memory of him touching her.

Desire was the most insidious thing.

"... theater tonight and ... after ..." her father was saying.

Oh, it was too much. She didn't care a whit what her father was saying, and she felt so disgraceful, she couldn't even look at him.

"What day is it?" she muttered, her voice muffled.

"Friday, of course," Reginald said, thinking that the best course was just to ignore her lapses this morning. Better than censuring her anyway, and he hardly had the heart to do that as it was. "The papers have come, my dear. Do you wish to have one?"

She was scared to death to have one, given the gossip columns, but she took one anyway. Friday. Four days ... five? ... since she had formed her ill-considered plan to wreak revenge on her father and Jeremy. And look at the end result: her father still believed she was interested in Raulton (did she not predict it?) and she had willingly become Jeremy's mistress.

How had this train of events happened? How had she gone from virgin to vixen in the space of less than one week? And how had she ever lived without that explosive pleasure?

It was enough to make her brain burst, to think about it. All of it. Or plan what to do next. Or deal with the fear there might not be a next.

258 / *Thea Devine*

Well, there would be a next because Jeremy had claimed her. But when he tired of her—it didn't bear thinking about. . . . She opened the paper instead.

The morning line had opened at White's, and marriage prospects were all the talk, his, Raulton was amused to see, in particular.

It wasn't as if he weren't aware of it, but the fun was in seeing who made the Book. It was always vastly entertaining.

White's echoed Heeton's line but one. Soames was there— insipid little whelp—and Law, who at least had some countenance if nothing else to recommend her. But the interesting one was the Olney. She who had kept up with him at loo this past evening, and who eyed him with more than passing curiosity whenever he saw her.

She was the only one Raulton would not have predicted. She was too outspoken, self-aware, self-sufficient. And not in the least malleable, or one who would be accommodating to his needs.

But beautiful, yes. The most beautiful among this year's London belles, despite the fact it was her third turnout. And well-spoken, witty, stylish, shapely, with plump full breasts and neat taut nipples that she had practically presented to him on a platter last night.

Olney with her thick dark hair and her knowing blue eyes. Silvery laugh. Elegant hands. Exquisitely dressed. An only child, and her father's heir. Fascinating. A woman *any* man should want to marry.

And the Book made her at ten-to-one.

Why had no one told him about her?

He wasted no time finding out. And he liked what he heard: a productive estate in Hertfordshire waiting for the man she would marry. Money in funds. London town house. Best circles.

The woman was surely a treasure. What was wrong with her?

Why had no one snapped her up heretofore?

Did it matter? If no one wanted her, she must be desperate this third Season, and thus, fair game. And he was as eligible as anyone, and mending his reputation daily. It was time to suck it in and throw his preconceived ideas out the window and sniff around a woman he could actually stand to live with.

One who looked like an excellent fuck, judging by her breasts and nipples. And if she was, so much the better. Things—or at least one thing—were certainly looking up.

Ancilla came to call. "What's to do, my dear Regina? I missed the Petleys' party last night, and apparently it was the place to be."

Regina rang for tea, and they settled in the library. "It was a card party and supper for a *few* friends. A few *hundred* friends, that is. Their house cannot accommodate such a rout. But there we were, and so was everyone else they had ever met in all their years in London. I ensconced myself at loo and did not need to bother with the rest."

"No, just with Mr. Raulton. Really, Regina . . ."

She sighed. "Is that out and about already? You would think these people had better things to talk about." She motioned the maid to bring in the tea cart and set up the table. "Like food, for instance. Well, the Petleys do better than most at table, but where can you find anything like this? She filched one of cook's scones from the cart and popped it in her mouth.

A strategic exercise really so she would not have to answer Ancilla's questions. But Ancilla was never deterred, and if anything she was too patient by half, which was probably the way in which she got most of the good gossip she always seemed to have.

"They've booked his matrimonial chances at White's," she said off-handedly. "Father told me this morning. Which means it's been on at Heeton's for at least a week. Would you care to wager whose names are on the line?"

"Soames," Regina said promptly, because it stood to reason that anyone Raulton had paid that much attention to would instantly come on the line. "Other than that, I couldn't begin to guess."

"Well, for today—Soames, but the odds are off the sheet on that one, Miss Law, Miss Babbage—a dark horse—and a certain Lady Olney."

It took Regina a moment to grasp that last. "*ME?!*"

"Your very self, Regina. Now, how did that come to pass? Did you throw yourself at him last night?"

"I played cards for hours and hours and hours. With six other people alternating," Regina said indignantly. "We had not a moment alone, or a conversation that was not overheard by a half dozen onlookers."

"It must have been *very* interesting conversation," Ancilla said.

Had it been? Or was it just the usual card table rousting and jousting? For the life of her she couldn't remember, and all because she had been so furious that Jeremy was not there.

But he was here with her now. She could feel the light touch of the chain around her hips and between her legs. Her body reacted, stiffened.

She belonged to him. She hungered for him. She wondered where she even got the patience to sit with Ancilla this morning. She didn't care about Raulton's stable or whether sane men were willing to lose massive sums of money wagering on which impeccable innocent he might marry.

But the fact her name was on the line shocked her.

God, if her father found out. . . .

Of course he would find out. One round at the clubs and it was over: his every nightmare come true. His daughter's name on the lips of every gabble grinder in the whole of London, and worse than that, scandal broth for the *Tatler,* too.

"I thought you should know," Ancilla said. "Although what you might do about it, short of leaving Town, I don't know." She bit into a scone. "These are excellent, Regina. I must come to tea more often."

They sipped in silence for a few minutes, Regina's mind racing nineteen to the dozen trying to think of some way to cope with this awful news.

"I never encouraged him." Not really. Only Ancilla and her father had overheard her imprudent and unlearned comment about her desire to marry him. Only Jeremy believed that she would have become his mistress, had she not become his. And now this. Irreparable, irreversible *THIS*.

"I did not want him."

"Well, he now has cause to think just the opposite."

Jeremy would know soon enough, too. And after last night when he had ridden her to midsummer and over. How would it be once he heard this news? All the chains in the world could not bind him to her if he believed she truly wanted Raulton. Worse and worse, she had said it often enough.

"My lady." The butler at the door.

She looked up, hard put to even think of receiving anyone else on the heels of this news.

"Mr. Raulton, if you please."

I don't please. Blast blast and blast. With Ancilla right in the front row, lapping up every word.

She slanted a look at Ancilla, whose pale eyes were avid with curiosity; she blew out a hard breath and bowed to the inevitable. "Have Nellie bring more tea, and send in Mr. Raulton."

And there he was, tricked out for a morning visit, doing the Proper with the requisite bowing and scraping and every attempt to curb his natural cynicism as she introduced him to Ancilla and he seated himself in the wing chair opposite the tea table.

"I hope our sojourn at the card table last night was agreeable to you," he murmured.

"Indeed." She motioned to Nellie to set down the teapot and tray, after which she poured him a cup and handed it over. "I'm very fond of cards, and a whole night at it would barely tire me."

"Ah . . . a woman with stamina—good to know." He sipped as she stared at him, appalled.

Even that innocent comment, he turned into something salacious?

She slanted a look at Ancilla, feeling as if she were drowning. She wasn't half awake even, and she must deal with him? Ancilla shook her head, so no help there. All Ancilla wanted to do was observe him like an insect under a magnifying glass. How comfortable it must be to remain so detached from everything. She could resent it if she did not care for Ancilla so much.

"Does not any woman need a certain amount of stamina just to cope with the rigors of the Season?" she asked lightly, seeking to put a less sexual connotation on his words.

"But you're a woman of experience," he came back instantly, "and familiar with all the ins and outs. Are you not?"

What *was* this conversation about? Her head was spinning. She was not used to speaking in double entendres. And for some reason, he assumed she was.

"Am I not which? A woman of experience, or familiar? In both cases, Mr. Raulton, I am not."

"But you are very clever with words, Miss Olney." He rose then and took her hand. "I look forward to seeing more of you." He bowed to Ancilla and withdrew.

What?

Ancilla was fanning herself. "My dear Regina—he *is* quick off the mark. Complete to a shade. And not too bracket-faced for one of his experience."

Regina bridled. "Do you think so? Well, put yourself on the line for his *experience*, Ancilla, because he will in no way *ever* see more of *me*."

Chapter Six

And that was not the end of it. Ancilla left just as her father came home fresh from his rounds of the clubs, fresh with the news, and a fresh rage over her lack of propriety.

"Everyone is talking about the Book," he fumed, "and the worst of it is, all but one of you were booked at Heeton's this past week as well. The wagering is astronomical, but to hear my daughter talked about like a piece of prime flesh is beyond anything a father should have to bear. And it is too late now to dump the broth, my girl. Why could you not be as restrained and proper as Ancilla? *There* is someone who keeps her counsel, speaks not an ill-advised word to anyone, and is universally loved by everyone."

"Except a man," Regina muttered, and immediately hated herself for even voicing such an ill-mannered self-serving comment. "Then, by all means, I shall certainly try to emulate our saintly Ancilla."

"You may mock me, but there is something to be said for a woman of taste and restraint, Regina. And you have proved you have neither . . ."

Oh, if only he knew. . . .

"And that you cannot be trusted to know your own mind."

That stopped her. "I beg your pardon?"

"Your thoughtlessness, your cavalier dismissal of my wishes and my concerns—well, I had thought that all the product of a high-spirited, but at bottom, properly raised daughter. And here instead is the bottom line: she is the talk of the Town, named on the line in two of the most notorious betting Books in London, and is pursued right into her home by the most debauched man in England, a man she professed she *wanted to marry,* and who now apparently may not be averse to marrying *her,* especially if he can line his pockets in the process. Heaven help me, does everything you wish for come true? And yet you denied the whole straight up and down last night. So what is a father to make of *that?* I ought to lock you in the cellars at Sherburne until this stink blows over."

Was there anything more humiliating than this? Her father's anger, his assumption she had been carrying on secretly somehow with Raulton to cause all this furor with the betting Books . . . what would he do if he knew she *was* living a secret life as Jeremy's mistress?

He would die. He would just die. He looked about ready to pop right now, and on the cusp of meting out some kind of punishment that would surely involve her banishment from London.

She didn't know how to make him believe that she had never had a moment's interest in Raulton. It was past doing: the betting line said it all.

And her father would believe that, sooner than her.

And it was all her fault to begin with. Blast it.

She was so tired. "Just don't send me back to Hertfordshire," she murmured.

"It is exactly where I wish you would go, my girl. You understand all the ramifications of this, do you not? Your name associated with Raulton? Bets being placed on *our* good name as to whether he will offer for you. Who in conscience after his decision is made would even *want* to marry you after this debacle? This is your third go-round with no reliable offers. After this Season, you will rusticate until you die, an unwed spinster. There is no other redemption for actions as careless as yours. And perhaps that is the best punishment of all."

Jeremy came later, and Reginald met him at the door. "So you've heard the news?"

"The news?"

"The Book."

White's had it then, and Reginald was aware of the whole,

damn it. He hadn't been in time to shield him from the worst. "I just heard."

"So our little scheme didn't work," Reginald said snappichly

"My dear Reginald—we barely had any time. It's been three weeks in entiring the thread. A week and a half since we made the decision, and this week did I begin to implement it. Events were out of our control. The card party last night. Everyone was talking about the repartee between them."

"You should have come," Reginald said sourly. "You could have taken her away and prevented this."

He could have prevented nothing, least of all his own wanton secret life with Regina. "No. This was booked at Heeton's last week. There was no way to avoid it after that, Reginald."

"Well, let me tell you—Mr. Jack Smart came to her here in her own home. What do you make of that?"

"The bastard was *here*? She let him *in*?" Damn and blast to hell. If he even breathed the same air, he would kill him. He would.

"Ancilla was here; she had no choice in good manners. But still and all—talk to her, Jeremy. I am at wit's end."

You are not the only one, Reginald.

Reginald stalked out, and Jeremy settled himself in the wing chair to wait for her. He rose restlessly when the thought occurred to him that Raulton might have been in this room, sat in this very chair. Damn damn damn. Why hadn't Ancilla stopped her? But what did Ancilla know? Plenty, probably, knowing Ancilla. Damn and hell.

And where was Regina anyway?

"Ah, and here is my lord to ring another peal over me." And suddenly she was there, standing defiantly on the threshold gowned in virtue and bile. "Father wasn't content to beat me to snuff; he had to summon his great good friend to put me further down-pin. Well, go ahead, Jeremy. I'm all to pieces already anyway."

"He was here."

That brought her up short. "He?"

"Raulton—here, in this room . . ."

"So was Ancilla. It was all perfectly proper."

"He was in this room. With you. Which chair?"

"Jeremy . . ."

He wasn't angry. Well, yes, he was. He was furious, fairly simmering under all that impassivity, and she couldn't tell him anything about Raulton's visit that he wanted to hear.

"Where was he seated?"

Time to divert and distract. "Why does it matter?"

"It matters."

He was too cool, too collected. She ought to run scared. She ought to just run and hide, and lock herself in the cellars at Sherburne House.

But she was already shackled—to his desire—and his fury was nothing to her hunger for that.

"Ancilla and I were on the sofa; he sat in the wing chair."

"In the wing chair. In this room. In your home. I see. And what was so urgent that he must fly to your side the moment the betting line at White's is announced? Do you guess?"

"I—" She hadn't thought for a moment about what he inferred. That Raulton's appearance was not just a social call, and that perhaps he wanted to be seen coming and going from their town house in order to increase speculation as to where his interest lay, and thus manipulate the odds.

So much for vanity. But these were the things men always knew and women did not.

"He has all the tricks," she said finally, "and all the experience to influence everything to his design. I should never have let him in. There is no excuse, because now Father believes nothing I tell him and is ready to send me to Coventry for my deceits."

"Not *all* your deceits," Jeremy murmured, feeling his anger ebb at this uncharacteristic show of humility. He bore some of the blame as well; he had done next to nothing to carry out the original scheme that Reginald had proposed, which, had he done so, might have prevented this Raulton imbroglio.

"Not the most important one," she whispered, her words like flame to tinder. Instantly she wanted him, and she knew he wanted her. In the morning, in the library, together, alone. At the instant, and tonight be damned. Tonight would be another story.

"I need to know you wore my chain."

"I wore it. I felt it every minute in that other presence."

"I need to see."

Yes, yes, yes. . . . "Now? Here . . . ?" *Yes. Yes. To be naked for you now. Dangerous. Thrilling. On the edge . . . yes. . . .*

"Lock the door."

She threw the latch.

"Pull up your dress."

She lifted the hem up and up until she was bare to the waist, dressed only in the thin, glimmering chain that defined what she was for him. What she willingly offered for his pleasure.

Let him take his pleasure. . . .

His chain, binding her hips, her cunt, her sex to him. He knelt down and buried his mouth in her thick feminine hair, kissing and sucking her essence, and the chain that symbolized his possession.

He grasped her bottom and pulled her more tightly against his avid mouth. Just this, not even enough of this. She was wet for him already, open to him unquestioningly, wore his chain of possession in willing submission to his desires. And he had been but a morning without her, and he was hungry, ravenous for her.

Oh, there. There. Inserting his tongue insistently, feeding on her, sucking at her with his lips and tongue. Feeling her grinding and the movement of her ass in his hands. He couldn't take her this way fast enough, hard enough; he found the distended nub between her legs and lapped at it, pulled on it, and pulled her with him into the abyss.

Down she went, down, on the floor, his mouth still voraciously sucking her, down into the sworls of pleasure neverending. Down, on her back, where he drove his aching penis into her still spangling body and, in that one shot, poured every ounce of his cream into the hot wet mystery of her.

Down. Down. Down.

Breathless. More.

He pulled her to her feet and then unlocked the door and turned to her.

Heartless to leave her like this.

"Tonight. All you can take of my penis—and more."

She caught her breath. He was warning her. Her body quickened with anticipation, arousal, hunger.

Already.

Tonight. More. More.

And even more.

Waiting for a lover was the most voluptuous thing in life. In the interim between the time she expected him to come and his actual appearance, her imagination played a dozen scenarios in her mind, each one more carnal and salacious than the last.

She lay in her bed, dressed only in the slender gold chain, her breasts heavy and taut, her body turgid with lust. The hours chimed by; her fantasies grew hotter, wilder and more lascivious until all she wanted was his penis right then, right there, all she could take—and more.

But did not this prolonged waiting heighten her desire? Oh, he knew so well what he was doing to her, making her hunger for the fulfillment of his erotic promise. Making her wait until she was ready to explode.

All you can take. And more.

Her body squirmed with arousal; she had thought of nothing else all day, all night. Her whole consciousness was fixed on the feeling of that chain encircling her body and her sex. His symbol. His possession. And tonight, all she could take— and more.

The waiting only increased her desire, made her wet and hot and greedy to have him rut in her, a mistress to her core.

The door cracked open, and he slipped into the room. He had removed his coat already, and his shirt and trousers were undone. It took but another minute for him to strip himself naked and to pull her from the bed and against his heated, jutting length into his hot, devouring kiss.

"Tonight," he whispered against her lips. "You are all mine."

She shivered.

"This is what I want . . ." He stepped back and showed her his wrists which were tied with a soft material. "Give me your body to do with what I want." He kissed her again, hard, harsh, full of explosive excitement. "Let me tie your hands." Another kiss, deep and wet and rooting. "Let me have your body." He sucked her lower lip. "Let me give you all you can take—and more."

She melted under the onslaught; she wanted it. He was talking too much, and his lusciously hard penis was going to waste rubbing against her belly and midriff when he could be fucking her. Anything he wanted, anything, to get him inside her to keep his erotic promise.

"Anything you want," she whispered, stretching out her arms.

He unwound the one length of material from around his wrist and lifted her arm to the bedpost and tied her wrist. And then her left arm, so that both arms were splayed and bound just above her head and her body with that soft, giving material that would keep her firmly in place without injury.

Now she was completely his; now he owned that incredible body that he had bound in chains. He couldn't get enough of just looking at her.

And she couldn't get enough of him. There was something enthralling about being bound and on display for him. Her body arched toward him, her breasts heavy with lust and excitement. She quivered at the knowledge that he could fondle her, anywhere everywhere, he could fuck her any which way, and she could do nothing to stop him.

And she knew this, too: that by her willing submission, she owned him; her body was everything to him, willing, submissive, greedy, insatiable for his penis to rut in her.

All he could give, all the time.

He was like a caged animal now, ready to pounce. Every inch of her body belonged to him. He wanted to look at her bound and chained this way forever. And he wanted to jam himself deep inside her and never come out.

Oh, and then, her nipples. With her arms spread, and her body arched toward him, her breasts seemed rounder, heavier, her nipples tighter, harder.

He needed her nipples *now.*

He came to her. He reached out and took them, and immediately she spasmed at his touch. Instantly, he reached around her to unlock the chain with the key he had wound around his wrist. A minute more, and he rammed himself home, deep home, the angle of his penis perfect to penetrate her as she stood, and he rocked himself into her so deep he didn't know where she began and he left off. And then they were body to body, hip to hip, with her nipple tips tight against his hairy chest.

Don't move don't move don't move . . . he nipped at her lips . . . *don't . . .* he moved his hands down to her curvy buttocks . . . *don't . . . move . . .* he jammed himself tighter, maybe a mistake . . . *don't . . .*

He kissed her deeply, and felt her body squirm against him as if she were seeking to take him deeper still. . . . *don't . . . yes . . .* his penis was so strong, so virile, he could rule the world—he ruled *her*—and maybe that was his world. . . .

Breathless . . . *don't . . . can't take much more*—all she could take . . . *don't . . .* just tight sharp little . . . *don't move . . . have to . . . have to . . . have to have to have to have to . . .*

. . . have to

And gone. Pounding her like a piston and discharging himself in one blasting cannon shot.

Stay.

More.

Not yet.

Now.

He was still embedded in her in this erotic upright position. He held her tightly against him, tight, tight, tight. He kissed her long, hard, deep. He felt himself flexing, hardening, elongating in her tight, soaking sheath. He felt his strength and his power rising.

He wanted more, but she had wrung him out.

This was the test; this was her power. And the evening was still young.

He liked this the best: he owned her nipples, and he could feel or feed on them however he liked all this evening long. And he could fuck her anytime he wanted all this evening long. He liked the freedom of penetrating her at his will and fondling her nipples whenever he felt like it.

He came to her again and again, to fondle and fuck and sometimes both. All she could take. And more.

She was as greedy as he, ravenous for his penis and his possession, and enticing him to take her nipples with every shimmy of her body.

He couldn't keep away from them. He couldn't keep his hands off of her. He felt up every inch of her body, everywhere he could reach. He made her come with his fingers in her cunt, and at her nipples; and he took her from behind, all the while she stood, submitting to his every desire.

"You need to be locked up, fancy-piece. You're dangerous."

"How so?"

"Those nipples. The way you flaunt them."

"Because I want you to make them harder."

"I'm sucked out, my lady."

"Really? After all your boasts of having enough for two? You hardly have enough for me."

"It sounds like my lady is ready to fuck again."

"You said all I could take. I want more."

It was all he needed, her voracious command.

"I rise to the occasion."

He came to her again, and stood so his jutting penis could root just inside her cunt. She never got tired of watching him at the cusp of penetration. And neither did he. "Ready to take it?"

She drew a sharp breath, and he plunged his hips, plunged himself back into the hot depths of her. God, all night she had been so stoked, so hot, so soaked with his cream. Nothing fazed her, not even this willing submission to him or his binding her arms. It was enough to storm all his defenses. All he wanted was to root in her. They had been at it for hours, and he couldn't even count the number of times.

He was sapped; he had just enough in him to push another explosive ejaculation. Just enough to untie her hands and tumble her into the bed. Just enough to kiss her and pull her against his quivering body. Just enough to cup her breast, and to fall asleep with her nipple shaping beneath his palm. Just enough . . . it was . . . just enough—he needed nothing more.

Voluptuous. Her whole body felt swollen, languid, satiated; she wanted to just wallow in bed with him after her father left for his morning calls. She wanted to lounge in the circle of his body all day, all night, forever. The last thing she wanted was company in the morning or even to leave the house for her usual morning carriage ride.

But there was Ancilla at the door with news of the morning line, and there was no way to turn her away, even knowing Jeremy was in the bedroom above dressing—*blast it*—and slipping down the back stairs.

"They say Mr. Raulton will make his determination within

the month," Ancilla announced as she settled herself on the couch and poured a cup of tea. "The odds on that are twenty-to-one. Father said, anyway."

"You are remarkably well informed on Mr. Raulton's comings, goings and matrimonial propensities," Regina said, barely absorbing this up-to-the-minute information.

"The whole of London is agog at his new diversion. Imagine him desiring marriage at all. He wants a wife who is wealthy, who wishes to be married, who is not carnal, and who will allow him his digressions. That is *not* you, my dear Regina."

"No," she murmured, "that is not me. Whoever wagers on that will go down hard." And what would she wager that her affair with Jeremy would last beyond the end of the month as well? How did a woman sustain a carnal life hour by hour, day by day? After this morning, she wasn't sure she wanted to live that way any longer; only her father's dire prediction of her fate stopped her.

And now the morning line, putting Raulton in church and walking down the aisle in less than a fortnight.

Well, people had very little else to do between private parties and the weekly Assembly Rooms. Why not elevate Raulton's private affairs to public property? It amused everyone and harmed no one, except the innocents whose names were in play.

And she, Regina, was no longer an innocent.

She rang for the carriage and brought with her the books she must return to the lending library, the most innocuous place she could think of where running into Mr. Raulton would not be the prevailing sport of the day.

And yet, there he was, and she could have inferred that perhaps he had been watching for her and following the carriage.

He was all politeness. "What a pleasant surprise. You frequent Hatchard's, then? They do have a fine selection. What authors do you favor?"

And Ancilla watching this all with her skeptical eye. Regina fumbled over every word, her mind wholly on Jeremy and not even attending to Mr. Raulton's attempts to engage her.

She felt crowded, suddenly, and too much the center of attention when he was around.

Not so Ancilla, who was critiquing his manners later that evening when they met at the Weydeanes' house for a sit-down dinner. "He can be very pleasant," she observed as they were being seated. "Come to think, he has been exceptionally pleasant at every function."

But here, Regina thought thankfully, was one place he would not be.

That hope was short-lived. He arrived late, profuse with apologies, somehow having wangled his way onto the Waydeanes' guest list. How, how, how? And yet the answer was almost immediately clear: two eligible heiresses were at table, two whose names were linked with his.

The following Wednesday it was Almack's where he prowled, and eventually came around to Regina, Sally Jersey in tow to give permission for Regina to engage in a waltz.

"Mr. Raulton."

"Come." He smiled at her, held out his arms, and she stepped into them warily as the music began.

"This is outside of enough," she whispered fiercely. "What will the odds makers give on the prospective with whom you waltz?"

"At least another half percent," he answered amiably. "But what do you care, Lady Regina? You're a little bit of the rebel as it is."

Not anymore. Never again. It was too draining maintaining a facade of indifference to all this attention.

"Do not offer for me, Mr. Raulton. I am far too demanding and outspoken for you."

"That is the very thing that attracts me."

On the sidelines, Reginald watched. They were having conversation. Everything she had vowed not two weeks ago was coming true. His reputation mattered not. She would tame him, and she would have him, and there they were, dancing like partners of old, the raciest of dances in which he must hold her. And they were alone enough to talk.

"Reginald," Jeremy, thank heaven.

"Well, there they are, and the Book makers are rubbing their hands with glee. He will offer for her for sure, and then where will I be? There is nothing ahead but ruination and degradation."

Jeremy stared at them as they whirled around the perimeter of the room. It was almost as if Raulton wanted everyone to see them, almost as if he were declaring himself. Or using her.

His hands clenched. Raulton would not have her. Damn him to hell.

"He's using her only. Imagine how deep his wagering against the Book. Come now, Reginald, it's not as bad as it looks."

"It *looks* like she's enjoying every moment, Jeremy, and by damn, I'd sooner immure her in a convent than see her marry him. Hell, I'd sooner see her marry *you* . . ."

And he stamped off, leaving Jeremy utterly at *point non plus.*

Marry her? MARRY her?

He will never marry me . . . here is the endgame of all my folly . . . it is ever as women have been warned: a man will not commit to what he can have for the asking . . .

And there is always a woman waiting to be asked . . .

Even marriage to Mr. Raulton is preferable to being a spinster and alone—

Being a mistress is not all glitter and gold.

The only best part is, no one ever has to know . . .

It colored everything, the whole muddle about Mr. Raulton.

"But you will have everything you said you desired,"Ancilla pointed out. "You *said* you would tame him and then marry him, and here he is, practically on bended knee, and you have reservations?"

"It was but a joke, party conversation, Ancilla. It never occurred to me it would go so completely out of control."

"His attentions to you are marked, now, even though he spreads himself between the two other possibilities. But he comes back to you again and again. There is no doubt he will offer for you."

If he offers for me, I don't know what I'll do.

Marry her?
What if he offers for her?
Damn and hell. Things are perfect the way they are—but blast it, every woman wants to be married. Even her. Damn damn damn . . .
If he touches her, I'll kill him . . .
Or some other man touching her . . . taking all that voluptuous carnality for his own . . . ?
He felt murderous. *Hell and damn, damn and hell . . .*
. . . marry her . . .
. . . have her all the time, any time . . . only his . . . no worry about boring her, wearing her out, or the end of the affair and who would be fucking her next . . . her allegiance, her body, her nipples, her sex would be his, and only his . . .
How could he live without it?
Marry her—the natural continuation of the pleasure game—
Marry her . . .

"If he offers," Regina said tentatively—and there was no great assurance that he would—"I will accept."

Reginald closed his eyes wearily. "I suppose that is the only choice. It is not the one I would have made for you."

"It has all been given too much prominence; I can see noth-

ing else to do, particularly since, as you pointed out, this noto-
riety will not die down anytime soon."

And there it was, out in the open. It was but two days till
the end of the month, and Raulton supposedly was poised to
make a declaration. London was holding its collective breath.

Blast it. That a man could force someone to accept marriage despite her wishes just because everyone expected it . . .
it was by the force of society's wishes—and mores—that she
had come to this pass.

And everything with Jeremy must end.

But if Raulton didn't come up to point? Must she relinquish
Jeremy then?

She paced the library long after her brief conversation with
Reginald. This was a hard-won lesson. The freedom she cov-
eted, sexual or otherwise, was a fantasy of her own devising.
She was not free. She was in thrall to the expectations of her
social peers and to propriety.

And not to her dark, voluptuous nights with Jeremy.

At the end of it all, she still wanted marriage and children,
and she did not want to spend her days and nights worrying
about the hour, the minute that he would tire of her, and what
would come next.

She wanted, she needed a life beyond the bedroom walls.

With Raulton or not. She had not the temperament to be a
mistress, after all. Only the will, the body, the desire, the insatiable need. . . .

But not the temperament . . . she was as prosaic as any
country miss, and as provincial. She could not slough off those
feelings, those fears, and that was the difference between her
and a mistress.

And if it turned out to be Raulton, then so be it. And so she
would tell Jeremy—tonight.

Marry her.
The idea was slowly sinking in, and it suddenly occurred to

him that he was not seeing her as that pesky child he had known for years now that he had been bedding her.

He saw her as a woman, with a mind of her own, and with a spectacular beauty, presence and elegance.

And that was apart from her sexuality. That was a thing all its own that could not be quantified. And so, if just the thought of her aroused him to the point of ejaculation . . . how could he live with the idea of her giving herself, giving her nipples, to another man?

Fucking like that with another man?

Any other man?

Raulton?

By damn hell—NO. . . .

No one else, not her, not that body, not those nipples. . . .

Shit—he was erect, hard as bone. Her nipples got to him every time, even the thought of them in some other man's hands. . . .

NO . . .

No.

Marry her.

And play with her nipples for the rest of your life. . . .

He came, as always, like a shadow in the night, and like the mistress she was, she waited for him, this time for the last time, to savor him, to make indelible memories before she said goodbye.

He needed no foreplay; she was naked and hot for him already. He needed only to slip the key in the lock, and his penis into her heat, to bind her to him yet again.

. . . fuck her . . .

. . . marry her . . .

. . . fuck her again . . .

. . . and again . . .

. . . and again . . .

He spurted, he came, he fucked her again.

And again. And again.
And again.

He fucked her to a foretheewell, and then he fucked her again, forward, backward, on her breasts, on her nipples, in her luscious, endless pleasure hole, he took her.

And when they were both panting, unslaked and utterly worn out, he took her again.

It was almost as if he wanted to imprint himself on her, to fuck her and fill her to the point where no other man could take his place.

. . . *marry her* . . .

Somehow, she thought, in a swamp of luxuriant pleasure, somehow he knew this was to be their last time.

He knew nothing except he never wanted to leave her.

Or leave her to another man.

He wanted to root in her. Play with her. Fuck her to the wall. *Marry her.*

Dawn was coming far too soon.

"Jeremy . . ."

'Not now. I need your nipples."

"You always need my nipples."

"True, and it's something to seriously consider."

Light filtering through the curtains signifying a beginning and an end.

She caught her breath as he rubbed his thumb back and forth across her distended nipple. "Jeremy . . ."

"Shhh . . ."

Now, she had to say it now—but she could barely speak because of those familiar skeining sensations unfurling inside her and causing instant fuck me now feelings . . .

Don't stop, don't stop. . . .

He had to stop.

"Jeremy . . . !"

THUMP THUMP THUMP . . .

"Regina!"

"Oh, God—Father!" She made to cover her breast, but Jeremy would not let her go.

"Shhh . . ."

"Regina, are you there? Wake up! I have news . . . the most incredible news . . ."

"Jeremy!" She pulled away from him. "I have to answer him."

"Answer me first."

"What?" She swung her legs off the bed and grabbed the first thing to hand and wrapped it around herself. "Answer you what?"

And then words didn't come so hard after all.

"Marry me."

"What?"

"REGINA! Hurry . . ."

"What? Jeremy—"

"Just say yes."

"Oh, my God. Just a minute, Father! Are you crazy?"

He pointed his penis at her. "Yes. Say yes."

"REGINA! I'm coming in."

"I'm coming."

"And I'll keep you coming," Jeremy whispered, "over and over and over . . ."

"Yes, Father, yes, yes, yes . . . I'm coming, I'm coming . . ."

Oh, God, I'm coming. . . .

She pulled open the door shakily, shielding Jeremy from view. "Such noise, Father. What's to do? It has to be well before nine o'clock."

"Ha! This. Look at *this.*" Reginald thrust an envelope in her hand which had a notation written on it. *For Regina . . . from Ancilla. I've gone and married Mr. Raulton. See note.*

"Oh, my God." Regina ripped open the envelope and pulled out Ancilla's note, scanned it, and then read it out loud.

Dear Regina, I hope you can forgive me; this made the most sense. I am in want of a husband; he is in need of a wife whose interests coincide with his own, but who is willing in the course of events to let him lead his private life. My nature is such that I will be content to manage his estate and to be called his wife. We will be married by special license by the time you read this, and he is exactly relieved to both be finished with the marriage mart and to reap his reward at the expense of the betting Books. As am I.

Your friend, Ancilla.

She was appalled.

"I'm speechless," she said finally.

"It's over," Reginald crowed jubilantly. "Ancilla has made London safe for all womanhood. We owe her a debt of gratitude. You're not angry?"

"I?" Shocked was more like it. And feeling not a little like the carpet had been pulled out from under her after she had gone through such soul-searching to gird herself to accept him.

But now she had accepted Jeremy—or had she? What had just happened in there?

"No. I'm happy for her. She will run him like a top, despite what she says in her letter, and it will be a better bargain for her than for him. And maybe she will bring him to heel in the process. So, Father . . ." She handed him the letter and made to close the door.

"Oh. Oh, of course." He turned to go, and then turned back. "By the way, is that Jeremy in there with you?"

"WHAT?"

"My dear girl, I'm no greengull. Jeremy—you must marry her now."

"And so I will," Jeremy called back, with no compunction, no sense of her feelings.

"Excellent. It's what I had planned from the start. Everything has worked out right and tight."

Regina sagged against the door. "What you—*planned?*"

"My dear girl—a knight to rescue you, orchestrated from the moment I overheard your abominable desire to engage Mr. Raulton. Of course, I had *thought* Jeremy was a man to practice courtly love . . . but—ah, one can't expect everything, can one? Post the banns as soon as ever you can. I can't countenance what has been going on in my very own house for much longer. Congratulations, my dear. Jeremy is everything I could want for you in a husband."

Husband? Husband? Oh, God. Husband!

She slammed the door and whirled around to find Jeremy sitting upright, *all* of him upright. "I am top over tails here. What is going on?"

"Ancilla has run off with Mr. Raulton. I have asked you to marry me, and your father planned the whole from the start. It's perfectly clear. You were always destined to be mine. You are mine. Be mine . . ."

"You don't . . ."

"I do."

"You don't have to. Not here, not now. You don't have to marry me." She had to say it, and she held her breath. He couldn't want marriage now, not after everything she had given him. He didn't need to marry her. But she needed desperately to marry him.

"I do. *You* do. You know you do."

She was on the thin line, the sharpest edge. Everything would end here, and begin, did she say yes.

He didn't move; he didn't importune. This was the most delicate balance, between her need and her desire. His desire and his need. And there was nothing to stand between them now.

She wanted, oh, how she wanted. This was Jeremy. Well-known, utterly adored Jeremy. She should have no hesitation. And yet she did, because how did she cross the line from mistress to wife?

But he had asked her to marry him; he had no qualms whatsoever.

And he was waiting. Jeremy was waiting.

"Say you do."

"I'll do."

He smiled, "You can do nothing less. Say you do."

It was all right then. She smiled back, and she dropped her wrapper and climbed into the bed next to him, "Only if you do"—she grasped his penis and tugged it and pulled him between her legs—"this . . ."

He did *this*, driving into her meaningfully, passionately, and she took him, she rode him, and she sighed. "I do . . ."

A Man and a Woman

Robin Schone

Chapter One

She wanted a man—if just for one night.

The man who stood before her was willing to pay a woman—just for one night.

He blocked the door, six feet tall to her own five-feet-four-inch frame. His face was harshly handsome; it looked as if his features had been hewn out of sand and sun. Lines bracketed his mouth and radiated out from the corners of his eyes—eyes so dark they appeared to be black.

Muhamed, the innkeeper had called him. Mr. Muhamed.

He was an Arab; she was an Englishwoman.

He was garbed in a white robe and turban; she was shrouded in a black dress and veil.

They had nothing whatsoever in common save for their physical yearnings, yet here they both were in Land's End, Cornwall.

Megan knew what she had to do; it was the hardest thing she had ever done. Slowly, deliberately, she lifted her veil and hooked it over the crown of her Windsor hat.

Bracing her spine, she mentally prepared for she knew not what: rejection, acceptance.

The Arab had ordered the innkeeper to procure him a whore; instead, a forty-eight-year-old widow had knocked on his door.

And he had let her in. As if she were, indeed, the prostitute she pretended to be.

And perhaps she was.

No respectable woman would engage in the charade she now played.

Her chest rose and fell, lungs filling, emptying—she could not draw enough air into her oxygen-deprived body. The harsh wool of her gown chafed her nipples. She did not have to glance down to know that they stabbed her bodice.

His black gaze raked over her face, her breasts—they swelled underneath his perusal, fuller than those of a young girl, heavier—dropped down to study her stomach and hips that with the rest of her body had rounded over the years. Slowly his gaze raised back up to her face and the lines there that owed nothing to sand or sun, but everything to a woman's age.

She clutched the side of her skirt and the pocket within that held the key to her own room just down the corridor.

Now he would accept her, or now he would reject her. . . .

"You are too old to be a whore," he said flatly.

But she was not too old to want a man.

Inwardly, she flinched.

Outwardly, she held his gaze; her green eyes, at least, were unchanged by time. "Some would say, sir, that you are too old to need the services of one."

Faint color darkened his cheeks—or perhaps it was her own shamelessness that colored her vision. "You are naked underneath your gown."

The warm color tinting his angular cheekbones leaped blazing hot into her more rounded ones.

She defiantly tilted her chin. "Yes."

Megan wore no bustle, corset, chemise, drawers nor stockings. None of the apparel that respectable women wore.

Nothing that would impede the purpose of her visit.

She wanted this night.

She wanted to lie naked with this man.

She wanted to experience again the closeness found in an intimate embrace.

Megan was fully prepared for—everything. The vinegar-soaked sponge crowding her cervix burned and throbbed, a reminder of—everything.

Possible pregnancy. Potential disgrace. Purgatory . . .

A coal exploded in the fireplace.

Tension prickled her skin. The rectangular bit of the key jabbed through the wool of her skirt and the silk of her glove.

A muscle jumped at the corner of his mouth. "You are not from around here."

Native west Cornish folk spoke with an unmistakable singsong cadence. During the past thirty years, Megan had learned to speak like a gentlewoman, just as the Arab before her had at some point in his life learned to speak like an English gentleman.

"No, I am not from around here," she acknowledged evenly.

"Have you come from another man?"

Megan fought down a spark of—anger? Trepidation? How would the painted prostitute whom she was a substitute for respond to such a question? "No."

She suspected no man would pay for what she now offered.

His gaze remained colder than a starless night. Searching. Probing. Looking for a remnant of the youth she no longer possessed.

A cold sheen of anxiety broke over her.

How could she have been so naive as to believe that for lack of choice, *this* man would take her?

Megan jerkily offered, "I fully understand if you prefer someone who is young   "

"I am fifty-three years old, madam," he interrupted. His dark, chiseled features hardened. "I do not want to lie with a child; I want a woman. As you said, you are a woman. I will pay you one gold sovereign."

Relief coursed through her. It was followed by alarm. Desire. *Surprise,* that he would so generously compensate a woman for the use of her body.

A gold sovereign was equivalent to twenty shillings. The prostitute whom she had intercepted in the hallway had greedily snatched the double florin—equivalent to a respectable four shillings—which Megan had offered her. A sure indication that she had expected to receive considerably less from her waiting client.

Why would this man—this Arab—be willing to pay more than an Englishman?

Forcibly, she relaxed her fingers around the wool-padded key. "Thank you."

"You may call me Muhamed." His black gaze did not waver; something briefly flickered deep inside his eyes—indecision? Aversion? "What name are you known by?"

"Meg—" She paused.

Robert Burns' poem, "Whistle O'er the Lave O't," rose up from the depths of her conscience in a mocking litany: "Meg was meek, and Meg was mild / Sweet and harmless as a child."

But there was nothing meek, or mild, or harmless about her actions this night.

She was a woman, not a child.

"Megan," she said more forcefully.

He pushed away from the door.

She involuntarily shrank back.

A whirl of white robe and elusive spice swept by her; the tantalizing aroma seemed to emanate from the Arab's clothes.

Darkness abruptly cocooned her—he had doused the oil lamp.

A ridiculous pang of hurt ricocheted through Megan. Obviously, he had no desire to see the naked body of a forty-eight-year-old woman.

Fear chased feminine pique.

She remembered every rumor she had ever heard about Arab men: they were exotic; they were erotic; they purchased women as if they were chattel.

The rustle of cloth alerted her to movement.

"Men use you for their pleasure." His terse voice snaked down her spine—it came from behind her, near the bed. "Do you take pleasure in the men you service?"

Megan swirled around, blood pumping, heart pounding.

An endless white ribbon undulated in the darkness. She realized he was unwinding his turban.

Remembered passion clenched her stomach.

"Yes," she said.

It was not a lie. She had taken pleasure in her husband's arms.

The undulating white ribbon soundlessly floated to the floor. All at once, the man's white robe reared up over his head; it hovered there for a long second like a ghostly specter before it, too, silently drifted downward.

Megan did not doubt that he stood before her naked—just as she was naked underneath her dress. She strained to see an outline or a gleam of skin: she could not. It was as if he had been swallowed up by the night.

A soft creak shot through the darkness, bedsprings adjusting to sudden weight. It sharply recalled her to who she was, where she was at, and what she was doing.

She was Mrs. Meg Phillins, the virtuous widow of a vicar.

She was at Land's End, a place to which she had sworn never to return.

She was about to engage in carnal relations with a man whom prior to this day she had never seen, and whom she would never see again after the night.

Tension swirled about her.

He watched her.

She did not know how he could see her in the darkness, dressed all in black, but she knew that he did. Just as surely as she knew that if she bolted now, she would never again have an opportunity to experience a man's passion.

Megan peeled off her silk gloves and stuffed them into the pocket that contained the key to her solitary room and lonely virtue. Her ring finger on her left hand tingled, as if it called out to the gold wedding band she had abandoned for a night of sexual satiation.

The bedsprings creaked again; the penetrating noise was followed by a dual clank, as if metal rubbed metal, *struck* metal.

Her breath snagged in her chest.

There was no accompanying stir of air, no indication that the Arab had stood up.

She licked her lips; they felt drier than the desert sands he had been born to, but that she had never seen. Her hat weighted down her head, heavier than an anvil.

Megan did not need light to illuminate her actions.

His room was much like hers—no doubt like all the rooms at the small inn. The floor was bereft of rugs; the whitewashed walls bare of paintings. Beside the locked door stood a bureau topped with a pitcher of water and a basin. Opposite the foot of the bed, a cane-bottomed, ladder-back chair guarded a small iron fireplace.

She pictured his narrow sleigh bed with its turned down covers, the man who wore no clothes, and the nightstand that stood between them.

The click of her heels were overloud in the taut silence; the trail of her gown an audible drag; the distance to the night-stand impossibly long. . . .

Megan kicked hard wood. A lancing pain shot through her right toe. Simultaneously, the chimney of the extinguished hurricane lamp rattled, a discordant implosion. Lingering oil smoke stung her nose while embarrassment at her clumsiness burned her ears.

The Arab remained silent.

Or did he?

She could hear breathing, a soft, relentless cadence.

His?

Or hers?

Underlying the primal rhythm was the distant wash of the tide—swelling, ebbing, the eternal pattern of desire.

Awkward as she had not been in many years—not since she had been eighteen and a simple Cornish girl—she reached up and slid the pin out of her hat. The accumulated rise and fall of her breasts matched the rhythmical soughing of air that filled the chamber.

Lowering her arms, she carefully slid the hat pin into the flat felt crown. Extending her left hand for guidance, she bent down, fingers splaying, arms reaching, and encountered . . .

A small, shallow, rectangular-shaped metal box.

Megan frowned. It had not been there earlier.

Or had it?

Prior to this night, she had not known of her whorish tendencies.

Or had she?

Dropping the hat down over the tin, she straightened.

The carved bone buttons lining the front of her bodice were too large; they did not want to slide through the buttonholes. Hours passed, coaxing one button free, two, three . . . and all the while that unremitting breathing cautioned her, cajoled her, became her.

Did Arab men love differently than did Englishmen? she wondered, breath and pulses racing against one another.

Would he kiss her?

Would he caress her?

What would he feel like, this naked stranger, when his body strained against hers?

Would he penetrate her deeply . . . or shallowly?

Would he be rough . . . or gentle?

Would she please him?

Would *he* please her?

She shrugged out of her dress; heavy wool scurried down her back, over her hips, swooshed down her legs and collapsed about her feet. A trail of chill goose bumps followed in its wake.

All that prevented her from joining the man were her shoes. She had prepared for this moment, too.

Using the rounded tip of her right shoe, she dislodged her left slipper. Using the bare toes of her left foot, she dislodged her right slipper.

Megan stepped out of the circle of her gown onto cold, unyielding wood.

The darkness throbbed with sexual heat.

She took one step forward. Her breasts lightly bounced. Would he take pleasure in their fullness?

She took a second step forward. Her hips gently swayed. Would he find them lacking?

She took a third step forward, thigh rubbing thigh, friction building, chest constricting.

The teasing aroma of exotic spice enveloped her. Out of the corners of her eyes she espied the faint, red glimmer of burning coals.

Why couldn't she see *him?*

A grain of dirt gritted beneath her left heel. Her right knee collided with ungiving bone and sinew—a naked leg, a muscled leg, a leg that was far smoother than her own. At the same time her foot came down on—a foot.

Moist air scorched her skin. "You smell of vinegar."

Megan froze, held immobile by the impact of his leg, the weight of her foot on his, the heat of his breath, and the jarring repercussion of his words.

Never had she imagined that a man would notice . . . or comment on . . . a prostitute's use of a prophylactic.

And perhaps an Englishman would *not* have noticed; or having done so, he would have courteously refrained from commenting.

"I . . ." She swallowed, acutely aware of his bare foot underneath hers and her breasts that jutted out from her chest, only inches away from his mouth "I have inside me a . . . a sponge that is soaked in vinegar."

"There is no need for that," he said brusquely. "I have prepared myself with a French letter."

The tin on the nightstand—did it contain more French letters?

Did the prostitute whom Megan had replaced rely upon a man to protect her?

Did she use a solution that smelled more pleasing than vinegar?

Did she use a syringe *after* intimacy, rather than inserting a sponge *before*?

Exactly what did a man from Arabia expect from a woman that an Englishman would not?

"Nevertheless, this is the form of protection which I chose to use," Megan said with a calm certainty that she was far from feeling.

Chill awareness traveled up her ankles. He could yet reject her, this Arab who was as terse as any Cornishman.

Megan nervously shifted her right foot, cautiously lowered it. Her toes butted the tips of his. The wooden floor was icy; the heat emanating from his digits was scorching.

"I have never been with an Englishwoman," he said shortly.

Electricity crackled around them, as if a storm brewed outside.

It did not.

She realized that the ragged soughing of air came not from one pair of lungs, but two. They breathed in unison.

"I dare say women are much the same, regardless of their nationality," she said carefully.

But were men?

Her heartbeat clocked the passing seconds. It pulsated inside her breasts, her temples, her vagina, her toes that bridged his.

Why didn't he touch her, *take* her?

Surely the coupling between a man and a prostitute was no different than the coupling between a man and his wife. He would initiate contact; she would quietly submit.

Wouldn't he?

"I have never been with a woman."

The harsh confession came out of nowhere, yet everywhere. *Never been with a woman* imprinted her chest.

Megan mentally reeled backward.

She had expected him to be experienced; he expected her to be experienced.

He had never been with a woman; she had only ever been with one man.

She was not prepared for this eventuality.

Dim light flashed in the darkness—the white of his eyes. "That is why I procured you."

Suddenly the black veil of obscurity lifted, and Megan could make out the bleached darkness that was the sheet, the ebony crown that was the Arab's hair, and the dusky silhouette that was his upturned face.

She felt as if she teetered on the edge of a precipice, afraid to move, afraid not to move.

Why would a fifty-three-year-old man—an Arab who lived in a country reputed to cloister women in harems for carnal convenience—be a virgin?

Why had he come to Land's End—on this, of all nights—to end his abstinence?

"You procured me to . . . to find physical satisfaction," she managed to say.

"No."

No?

What did he want, if not sexual gratification?

Arabic men trafficked in beautiful, young women, not matrons who were well beyond middle-age.

Didn't they . . . ?

For the first time Megan did not feel protected by the relative proximity of the inn's inhabitants.

"I am afraid I do not understand." She swallowed the fear rising in her throat; her toes touching his continued to throb and pulse. "Why would you procure a"—no, no, she could not call herself a whore, even if others would—"a woman, if not for satisfaction?"

"I want to know a woman's body," lashed the darkness, al-most a sound. A breath blasted her face. "I want you to show me how to bring a woman to orgasm. I want you to show me how to bring *you* to orgasm."

A door slammed shut somewhere in the inn, more a shudder of wood than an echo of sound.

Megan could not have heard the Arab correctly.

"You want me to show you how to bring a woman . . . how to bring *me* . . . to orgasm?" she repeated slowly, heart thundering, toes throbbing.

"Yes." His voice was intractable. Heat licked her spine. "That is why I procured you."

"A woman takes satisfaction in a man's . . . a man's possession," she said shakily.

"You are a whore. You of all women should know that a man's member is not a woman's sole source of satisfaction."

But she *wasn't* a whore.

Dear God. He could not be inferring what she thought he inferred.

"A woman has many places on her body that when touched by a man give her pleasure," Megan countered.

"I have never touched a woman," he said stiffly.

"I have never tutored a man," she said compulsively.

Megan bit her lips—too late, the words were out of her mouth.

"No young boy has ever come to you seeking instruction?" he asked bluntly.

Megan suspected her husband had been a virgin. He had never discussed his sexual experience, or lack thereof.

The back of her neck tingled in warning. She should end her charade now, so that the Arab could find a woman to give him the knowledge he sought.

"Englishmen do not readily admit their inexperience," she heard herself say instead.

"Do you think that a man is less of a man, then, because he admits his inexperience?"

"I think . . ." Her heart slammed against her ribs. "I think it is not a man's inexperience that displeases a woman, but his arrogance in not asking what gives her pleasure."

"Do you think that a man is a man, then, because he asks a woman how to please her?"

The Arab's voice was a curious blend of harshness and vulnerability; his face a dark, unfathomable blur. Only the whites of his eyes were visible.

They gleamed in the darkness.

"I believe that it requires courage for a man to acknowledge a woman's needs, yes," she said more firmly.

"How do you judge a man, madam, if not by his sexual experience? Do you judge him by the number of orgasms he gives you? Do you judge him by the hardness of his male member? By the length of it? Do you judge him by his ability to spurt his seed?"

Pain streaked through Megan—hers, *his*.

It dawned on her that this man was afraid.

But of what?

"I cannot bear children," she impulsively offered. "If I judged a man for his inability to produce seed, then I must also judge myself for being unable to carry a man's seed."

Megan's jaws snapped shut. She could not possibly have admitted to this stranger what now echoed inside her ears.

That she was barren.

That she was alone.

That she had failed as a woman.

But she had.

"Do you?"

The question took her by surprise. It sounded as if it had been ripped from some place far deeper than the Arab's chest.

She did not pretend to misunderstand him.

Did Megan judge herself?

Why did it seem perfectly natural to discuss her personal feelings with this man?

Why had not her husband, in all their years of marriage, asked her what this Arab now asked her?

"No." Her throat tightened. "But others do."

Just as no doubt others judged him, an Arab traveling in a foreign country.

"You do not wonder, sometimes, if they are right in their judgment?" he asked hoarsely.

Yes.

But those thoughts were for another time.

"I think . . . when a man and a woman come together—that the closeness they share—I think *that* is life's true miracle," Megan said shakily.

An ember sparked; red light flared, briefly revealing an ear, a jaw. Human flesh bled into dark shadow.

"You have loved a man," he said flatly.

The tightness constricting Megan's throat spread to her chest. "Yes."

"Yet you are a whore."

She should have expected his judgment; she had not.

Hot emotion erupted inside her, hearing the echo of another man's judgment.

"You think a woman is a whore because she has physical needs?" she flared, forgetting that he rightfully thought her a prostitute. Forgetting that she had come to him out of loneliness, not to debate women's morality. "You do not think that women are entitled to take comfort in a man's embrace?"

"I do not know." His grating honesty shattered her anger; his breath lapped at her breasts. "I do not know what either men or women are entitled to. All I know is what I want."

To know a woman's body.

To learn how to bring a woman to orgasm.

"Surely you must also wish to . . . to experience your own release," Megan said rashly. "Would you not like a woman to touch you?"

"I have no need of a woman's touch."

"We all need to be touched," she riposted.

Surely, all men and women needed the intimacy of touching, of holding, of being touched and held in return.

"There are worse things than physical frustration," he finally said, as if he begrudged her question.

"What?" she asked.

What could possibly be worse than sleeping alone, without even the companionable press of buttocks against buttocks to alleviate the ache of loneliness?

"Knowing that there is no release," he bit out, "is far worse than aching with need."

"But there is always release . . ." Her heart somersaulted at her near confession.

An Englishman was not interested in that part of a woman's body which society did not acknowledge.

An Englishwoman did not admit she possessed a place which brought her release that did not also culminate in a man's ejaculation.

"Do you pleasure yourself, madam?" he asked jarringly, a blatant reminder that he was not English, no matter how much he might sound it.

"Yes." Stinging heat flooded her cheeks, her ears, crawled down her throat. She stiffened her spine, refusing to lie. "Men . . . do they not . . . pleasure themselves?"

The silence was complete save for their breathing and the remote lap of ocean waves, teasing, promising, retreating, never fulfilling.

"There is a difference between a man's hand and a woman's body," he said tersely.

"But do you?" she insisted, suddenly wanting to know, no, she *needed* to know that men required the same release that women did.

"I have done so."

He was embarrassed—she could feel the heat of it against her breasts and in her face, hear the roughness of it in his voice—but like her, he would not lie. *Not tonight.*

"What do you hope to gain from this encounter, Mu hamed?"

His name slipped unbidden from between her lips.

It should sound awkward, an Arabic name spoken with an English tongue. It should be awkward, an Arabic man discussing with an Englishwoman what no man had dared say to her, and what, she suspected, he had never dared say to another, be they English or Arabic.

Why didn't it?

"I have told you what I want."

"No, you told me what you want to know," she said, gaining courage from the anonymity of the night, "not what you yourself want."

For a long second she did not think he would answer.

"I want to know that I can give a woman pleasure."

His voice rebounded off of her breasts. Hot, moist air fanned her nipples.

"I want to know what other men know."

Megan was riveted.

By the raw intensity inside him.

By the passion emanating from him.

"I want to know that I am like other men."

Chapter Two

The air was sucked out of Megan's lungs.

What could possibly cause the agony she sensed inside this Arab?

Men who contracted mumps were sometimes rendered sterile, she remembered. Had he suffered from some illness that had incapacitated him?

She took a steadying breath. "I do not think any woman need demonstrate that you are a man, sir."

"Then do not demonstrate it, madam," he said brutally. "Prove it."

The darkness closed around them. It shrank the distance between his mouth and her painfully engorged nipples.

Megan's heart skipped a beat, galloped to escape the confines of her chest.

There was violence in this man. Born of need. Loneliness. Fear.

Emotions she understood all too well.

If she were wise, she would flee his room now, naked.

If she were wise, she would not now be in his room, naked.

She thought of her past, and the empty bed she had slept in.

She thought of her future, and the empty bed that awaited her.

She thought of this Arab, sleeping alone in his empty bed. *For fifty-three years.*

"I have only ever asked one man to touch me," she blurted out.

"And did he?" he asked intently.

She wanted to lie. She found that she couldn't.

"No, he did not," she said.

"This is the man whom you loved?"

She tensed against the barrage of unwelcome memories.
"Yes."

The pale gleam of his eyes did not waver. "He did not wish
to experience the closeness you spoke of?"

An invisible hand squeezed her heart. "No, he did not."

"His rejection still pains you."

"Yes." Tears pricked her eyes. "It still causes me pain."

"Tell me where you asked him to touch you."

His voice was peremptory; underlying the command was a
masculine plea.

To not reject him, as she had been rejected.

To share with him the special bonding that was a man and
a woman's joining.

Scalding perception rushed through her.

Here, in the dark, with this stranger, she could be the
woman she had been twenty-two years earlier.

He could fondle her breasts, in their current position.

He could kiss them.

He could lick them.

He could suckle them.

He could do all the things she had secretly desired that a
man do, but had been afraid of requesting.

Afraid she would shock.

Afraid she would repel.

Afraid she would be rejected.

By her husband.

By any man other than this Arab.

Megan had never before fantasized about teaching a man
how to touch her for her own gratification. She did now.

It was seductive.

It was Adam offering Eve the forbidden fruit.

It was the promise of far, far more than a quick, anonymous coupling.

She struggled to control her breathing; her breasts quivered
with each intake of air, each outward exhalation. "I asked him
to touch my . . . to touch my breasts."

Megan did not recognize her voice.

The darkness reached up.

She inhaled sharply, cupped by callused hands, right breast, *left* breast, heart pounding, skin tightening. Liquid desire pooled between her legs; her nipples hardened to the point of pain.

"Like this?"

"Yes."

Oh, yes, exactly like that.

Ten fingers pounded in time to her heartbeat. Rough yet gentle. Hesitant yet hungry.

Tears pricked her eyes, receiving now from the hands of a stranger what had been denied her twenty-two years earlier—a man's caring touch.

"Tell me what else you asked him to do," he hoarsely commanded. His voice matched hers.

Heat bridged their bodies: his breath, her breath, his toes, her toes.

His desire.

Her desire.

For one brief moment she stared down at the two of them: she standing above a naked man; he sitting below a naked woman.

Both wanting.

Both waiting.

Both willing.

Just for one night.

There was no time for propriety. No room for shame.

"I asked him . . . to kiss my nipples," she said raggedly.

It was not a lie. In her thoughts, she had begged for him to kiss her nipples. In reality, she had asked him to come to her bed.

The callused heat cupping her left breast dissipated. Seconds later, it grasped her left hip.

He did not seem to mind the softness he found there.

Silken flesh, gentle as the wings of a butterfly, skidded across her nipple.

Lightning shot through her chest and out of her toes. She slammed back into her body, and once again she stared down at one head rather than two.

Megan instinctively reached up—and grasped warm, electric hair. It clung to her fingers, alive as the current of heat that raced through her breasts.

"What else did you ask him to do?" Moist breath seared her breast where the Arab had kissed her, but the man whom she loved had not.

She fought for courage; found it.

"I asked him to lick my nipple," she said. *In her thoughts.* In reality, she had asked him to hold her.

He had not.

A hot, wet tongue tentatively rasped her flesh, there on the very tip of her breast.

Once. Twice. Thrice . . .

He licked her, like a greedy cat licking the inside of an empty milk pail. Top side of her nipple, underside, the very tip again. . . .

Her vagina clenched; hot liquid dribbled down her thigh. She instinctively curved her hands around him, such a personal embrace, cradling a man's head while he laved her with hot, wet swipes of his tongue.

Hot air suddenly serrated her nipple. "What else?"

Megan's heart thumped against her chest; she could hear it, feel it—an internal knocking, an external quiver of her breast. Had Muhamed felt it, when he kissed her, licked her . . . ?

"I asked him to . . . to suckle me," she said. *In her thoughts.* In reality, she had asked him to comfort her.

A hot, wet furnace latched on to her nipple.

Oh. . . .

Megan clutched thick, soft hair and held on while he suckled her, hesitantly at first, then strongly, as if he gained sustenance from her breast.

It was—breathtaking.

It was—overwhelming.

It aroused yearnings she had never before experienced: to be squeezed, bitten. . . .

She arched her body, begging for acts she had no words for.

His hands tightened, squeezing, kneading—her right breast, her left hip. A textured swirl of scalding heat encompassed her nipple; at the same time sharp teeth sank into her aureola. Her womb contracted—in pain, in pleasure.

She leaned forward, fingers fisting in his hair, lost in the erotic sensations he was engendering and the memories he had invoked. . . .

"I asked him to touch me between my legs," she whispered. *In her thoughts*. In reality, she had merely begged him to love her, to need her as she had needed him.

Heat grew inside her breast, there where Muhamed suckled her, an inescapable knot of truth.

He *had not* loved her. *Needed her*.

Warm air feathered her stomach. Gentle fingers touched Megan, a whisper of sensation.

Arabic fingers, not English.

A small, inelegant *pop* pierced the darkness—his mouth releasing her nipple. The shock of cold air was replaced with a gust of hot breath. "Your pubis is covered with hair."

It took a moment for the meaning of his words to register. Every nerve in her body was focused on her fingers that throbbed against his scalp and his fingers that combed through her private hair.

"Yes." Her breathing accelerated—too fast, she would surely faint, she who had never before fainted. "Of course."

Scalding heat punctuated his words. "Muslims remove their body hair."

His leg that had briefly impacted her knee, while hard with muscle, had been silky smooth. . . .

"Do you remove *your* body hair?" she asked unbidden.

"I have done everything that the Muslim law commands," he said rawly.

Scattered thoughts flitted through her mind: did his religion

forbid him to touch a woman? Was that why he was still a virgin at fifty-three years of age?

Was her pubic hare of hair?

"It is written that a woman's vulva grows moist with her
arousal, and that at her moment of enjoyment, her flesh rises
hard like the comb of a cock," he said gruffly. "Are you moist
with need, Megan?"

Moist. Swollen.

She felt as if she were drowning in the scent of spice and the
heat of his body.

"Yes," she said unsteadily. "I am moist."

"And when you reach your moment of enjoyment, does
your flesh rise hard like the comb of a cock?"

"You may touch my vulva"—Meg cringed at the bold words,
a whore's words, surely; Megan spread her legs in brazen invitation, a woman shamelessly opening herself to a man.—"and discover for yourself what a woman's flesh feels like."

Night air rushed up, chilling that part of her body that was
swollen like overripe fruit, the original sin—a woman's sex.
The cold was immediately displaced by pulsing heat.

He cupped her, shaped her, weighed her.

Megan held perfectly still: wanting approbation, fearing
aversion.

Her husband's fingers had grazed her only in passing, when
he guided his manhood to her portal. He had not lingered
when he brushed against her.

What had he thought when he accidentally touched her?

What did *this man* think, now touching a woman for the
first time?

"You're dripping with moisture."

"I'm sorry," she said quickly, defensively, body tensing,
preparing for his rejection of her womanhood.

"Why do you apologize?" His breath branded her stomach—he was looking down, as if he could see her in the dark.
And perhaps he could. "Do you not get this wet when you are
with other men?"

"I—"

A long finger sank between the slippery wet folds of her vulva.

It was hard. Callused.

She abandoned Muhamed's head for the more secure anchor of his shoulders. They were tensed, as she was tensed. Strong. Solid. Utterly masculine.

Megan waited: for his next observation, for his next exploration.

His finger burned her. His breath burned her.

The very air was ablaze with sexual heat.

"The opening to your vulva is very small."

Gently, he prodded.

Steadfastly, her body resisted.

"Is this where you wanted to be fondled, when you asked to be touched between your legs?"

Megan squeezed her eyelids closed, blocking out the darkness that was his hair and the pain of the past. "No," she said, more a sigh than a word.

Slowly, he drew his hand back, parting her, tunneling through her slick nether lips until he touched the very tip of her femininity with the very tip of his finger.

It was hot. Wet.

His heat. Her moisture.

A pulse wildly leaped inside her to greet the pulse of his finger. She locked her knees to prevent them from collapsing.

"Did you ask to be touched here?"

"I simply . . . asked to be touched," she said unevenly.

"You're already hard." His breath matched the pulse that beat inside her nether lips, her toes, her breasts. "It is like a small bud. Is it fulfilling, when a man touches you here? When you are brought to release by the manipulation of your clitoris, is it not a male member that your body yearns to feel, rather than a man's finger?"

Clitoris. Megan had never before heard the word; there was no mistaking what he referred to.

She sank her fingernails into his skin, impervious to the pain she might inflict, completely absorbed in the heat and the hardness of his finger. "I do not know," "I am sure most women appreciate . . ." The truth refused to be denied. "No man has ever brought me to release with just his finger."

He gently defined the hardened kernel of flesh that was the most sensitive spot on a woman's body, measuring its size, outlining its shape, his touch a slippery rasp of sensation.

"But you have gained release when a man's verge penetrated you," he insisted.

White dots danced behind her eyelids; white-hot sensation danced along her skin. "Yes."

"When you touch yourself, here"—he pressed hard on the bud of her femininity; a jolt of pleasure hurtled through her womb—"do you not yearn for more?"

"There is a difference between a man's touch and a woman's hand," she said in a parody of his earlier response.

"Arabic women cut off the genitals of young girls."

Megan's eyes snapped open. All she could see was darkness.

Horror shot through her. Her muscles clenched—denying the truth of his statement, resisting her gathering orgasm.

"Why?" she asked involuntarily. "Why would any woman do that to a young girl. . . ?"

How could a woman survive without a means of gaining feminine satisfaction?

"It is tradition," he replied.

His callused fingertip lightly rubbed first the left side of her clitoris, then the right.

"It is a rite of passage."

Fire ripped through her.

"It makes women subservient to men rather than their own desires."

His finger radiated heat. His voice was bleaker than a winter-shrouded moor.

Megan listened in mounting horror while her own pleasure licked higher and higher, hotter and hotter.

In Arabia, the men who guarded harems were called eunuchs. They, too, were reputed to have their genitals cut off.

So that they remained subservient to men . . . rather than their own desires.

A hard, hot hand imprinted her buttocks. A fine tremor racked her.

He was trembling.

Or perhaps it was she who trembled, poised on the threshold of the most intense orgasm she had ever experienced.

"You are growing harder," he said.

Harder. Wetter.

While he recalled practices she could not even begin to imagine.

His persistent finger slipped and slid, left side, *oh*—the very tip, right side, the engorged tip again.

The pleasure his touch engendered was frightening.

What he had told her was frightening.

"Please stop."

He did not stop.

"Did you lie to me, when you said that no man has ever brought you to orgasm in this manner?"

Megan strained—not to escape, but to get closer. "No, I did not lie."

Her only lie was in allowing him to believe she was the prostitute the innkeeper had summoned.

"Does my touch please you?"

"Yes."

She had not thought such pleasure existed simply from a man's touch.

"Then I will not stop until you give me your release and we both discover if a man's fingers are as good as his verge."

Megan tensed. The night tensed.

What had they done to this man?

Suddenly the darkness exploded; Megan exploded with it, gasping, falling, grabbing. Bed creaking. *Legs straddling his legs.*

A wave of energy swelled over hers, swallowed hers, throbbed with a life of its own.

"I felt your release," Muhannad gasped. A hard hand grasped her left hip, finger wet from her body; another hard hand bolstered the small of her back.

Megan struggled to catch her breath, inhaling the almond scent of his breath and the moist, spicy heat of his body. Her left knee was embedded in thick wool; her right knee indented a coarse cotton sheet. Aftershocks of pleasure rippled through her; cool air bathed her naked, exposed nether lips.

Her vulva was open. Utterly accessible.

Her vagina gaped.

Open. Utterly accessible.

Hard, muscled thighs supported her buttocks; they were not cushioned with hair. A hardness bridged their bodies that owed nothing to a callused digit and everything to a man's tumescence.

It felt like rubber.

A rubber prod with a large, blunt head.

Her fingers convulsively dug into shoulders that were as tautly muscled as the thighs underneath her buttocks.

"Do you miss having a verge inside you?" His almond-scented breath scorched her lips. "Would you be satisfied if touch was all that a man could give you?"

It dawned on her that it was his need that had only seconds earlier swelled over hers, swallowed hers.

He might deny that he needed sexual release; his body told its own story.

"Yes." Megan gulped air. What he had given her was far more than she had previously had. "I would be satisfied."

But *he* would not be.

There was so much pain inside her Arab.

She did not want him to hurt. Not tonight.

Megan had suffered through enough pain in her life, and so, she suspected, had he.

She slowly inhaled, deliberately calming her thundering

pulses so that she could say the words that needed to be said. "I do not judge you, Muhamed."

"Do you not?"

His rubber-sheathed manhood throbbed.

Her womb throbbed.

"No, I do not," she said, and reached between their bodies to gift him with the same pleasure he had given her.

He filled her hand. He overflowed her hand.

He *grasped* her hand.

"Don't!" he ground out.

Everything about him was iron-hard—his voice; his thighs; his shoulders; his fingers holding her right hand; his rubber-sheathed manhood.

Whatever Muhamed suffered from, it was not impotence.

"You said you wanted me to show you how to please a woman," she said, undeterred.

"I did not procure you for this."

"Yes, you did," she countered . . . and wondered what gave her the courage to do so. The pleasure he had given her, or the pleasure he so obviously wanted to experience?

His fingers tightened around her wrist; there would be bruises there tomorrow. "I did not want you to know."

"You did not want me to know . . . how hard you are?" she asked boldly.

Megan could feel his surprise. A gentle power filled her.

Tomorrow she would be mortified at her audacity, not tonight.

She had always wondered if men came in different sizes, as women's breasts were sized differently. Now she knew.

They did.

Slowly she ran her thumb over the blunt tip of him; it pulsed underneath the nippled rubber sheath. "You did not want me to know . . . how large you are?" she asked breathlessly.

"Do not play the whore with me, madam," he said harshly, rebuke a blast of almond-scented breath.

She stiffened. "I am what I am."

"I will not have you lie to soothe my vanity."

It reassured to her that it was not her actions he castigated, but his own body. "I assure you, sir, I do not lie. I have never before held a man as large as you."

Long seconds passed while he assessed the truth of her assertion. His banding fingers pulsed around her wrist: he wanted to believe; he was afraid to believe.

"Do you not find me . . . distasteful?" he asked, plainly finding himself distasteful.

"No, I do not," she said firmly. And forced herself to ask: "Were you repulsed by me?"

"A woman's body is not repulsive."

Relief coursed through Megan.

"Neither is yours," she asserted.

A hiss of air escaped from between his lips. "I do not know if I can satisfy a woman."

"I assure you, I am very satisfied."

"I do not know if *I* can find satisfaction in a woman."

"If you will release my hand, sir, you will soon have your answer."

The sound of their breathing momentarily halted—even the waves bathing the surf seemed to pause.

He released her.

She exhaled; he exhaled. The ocean resumed its relentless rhythm of advance and retreat.

Megan bowed her head and stared down at the long, thick appendage she held. All she could see was the dark chasm that separated their bodies, and her own ineptness.

She had never before put a man inside her. The thought of doing so now was both humbling and empowering.

Carefully, she guided him to her vulva. Heat bumped her forehead—his forehead; it was slick with sweat.

He clasped her hand, hard fingers cupping her softer fingers, helping her, urging her. A callused palm slid down the small of her back. He grasped the right cheek of her buttocks, fingertips wedging deep inside her crevice. At the same time, blistering heat grazed her gaping vagina.

Together, they found her portal. Together, they notched his blunt, masculine flesh into her open, feminine flesh.

Megan couldn't breathe. Couldn't move.

Perspiration dripped down her forehead, her nose, plopped onto her chest. She did not know who it came from—her or him.

In all of her twenty-eight years of marriage, she had never experienced the type of intimacy she now experienced, straddling a man's lap while his breath laved her breasts and his manhood kissed her womanhood, sharing sex, sharing sweat, hands joined, body joined.

"I'm not . . . come closer," he grated.

Steadily he pulled her closer, fingers digging dangerously deep inside the crevice between her buttocks, while with his right hand he directed his rubber-sheathed manhood. Rubbing. Pulling. Prodding.

Megan's knees slowly inched across the covers, thighs spreading wider while her hand followed his motions as if she were a marionette. Rubbing. *Prodding.*

Breaching. Piercing. Spitting.

She threw her head back, voice high and shrill, directed up to the ceiling. "Oh, my God!"

"Allah akbar!" His voice was low and hoarse, directed down to parts that could not answer back.

She instinctively released Muhamed's manhood. Using both his shoulders, she tried to lift up.

Grasping her hips with both hands, he pulled her down and forward until he gorged her very womb.

"I did not know a woman was this small," he gritted.

"I . . ." Megan desperately tried to compose her thoughts when all she could think about was the long, hard, thick, rubber-sheathed flesh that impaled her very heart. "You are penetrating me very deeply."

Hot, almond-scented air gusted against her cheek. "Does it cause you pain?"

Yes.

"No."

But it sounded as if he suffered.

She had forgotten how physically close a man and a woman were in conjugal intercourse. Or perhaps she had never really known.

Her breasts molded his chest; her thighs saddled his hips; her groin locked with his groin.

One breath.

One body.

One heartbeat.

"I have never..." Her internal muscles convulsively clenched around him. "I cannot... move. I do not understand how it can be done in this position."

"Grind your pelvis against mine."

He ground her body down onto his. At the same time he thrust his pelvis up.

He gasped.

She gasped.

The surge of heat that shot through her was far more agonizing than pain. Far more intense than pleasure.

Her nether lips were flattened against smooth skin—he had no pubic hair. The hardened bud of her femininity rubbed bare, naked flesh.

Megan impulsively spanned the short inches that separated their mouths and kissed him.

Lips closed. Eyes open.

He froze.

His lips were dry. Firm. Softer than a sigh.

The heat radiating through her pelvis leaped to her mouth, her breasts that stabbed his muscled, hairless chest, and bolted back down to her vagina that milked his rubber-sheathed manhood.

She jerked back, breathing hard.

"I have never kissed a woman," he said stiffly. He, too, breathed hard.

"Did you like it?" she asked, feeling invaded, feeling vulnerable, feeling as if she were far younger than a woman her age had a right to feel.

"Yes," he said shortly.

Megan was not deterred by his shortness.

Releasing his shoulders, she cupped his face in her hands— his skin felt as if it had been freshly shaved—and deliberately pressed her mouth to his.

His lips clung to hers. And then they possessed hers.

Shocked pleasure washed over her.

He was—probing the seam of her lips with his tongue. As if he wanted her to open her mouth.

Megan opened her mouth.

He touched the tip of his tongue to hers, simultaneously piercing both her upper lips and her nether lips.

A wave of heat ripped through her.

Megan climaxed, mouth sucking in his breath, vagina drawing on his manhood.

When she moved to jerk away, to escape the unexpected jolt of sensation, Muhamed grabbed her by the back of her head and held her in position. A sharp hairpin jabbed her scalp, a distant pain.

He licked her as if he could taste her pleasure, underneath her tongue, the roof of her mouth.

Light exploded inside her head.

Gripping her behind with his left hand, he ground her against him, making her ride out her peak of enjoyment until she could not distinguish between pain and pleasure, or even between an Arab man and an Englishwoman.

She tore his mouth away and rested her cheek against the hot slipperiness of his. Gasping. Still spasming.

"*In sha' Allah.*" The foreign phrase scalded her ear.

Without warning, Muhamed stood up in a crouch, taking

Megan with him. The motion drove him deeper inside her, knocking the breath out of her lungs. Then he turned, and he was slipping out of her, and she was falling.

The bed creaked and groaned coarse wool bit into her buttocks; her head sank into a pillow, unmercifully driving hairpins into her scalp. Megan blindly clutched—with her hands, her knees, and then she had him. Muhamed's hips sank between her thighs; at the same time he surged hard and deep inside her.

Again.

And again.

And again.

The creaking of the bed matched the rasp of his breath in her ear. Their bodies were slick with perspiration. For a terrifying moment she could not tell who possessed whom.

She arched her hips, demanding more.

He gave her more.

A series of feminine cries randomly penetrated her consciousness: "Oh." "Please." "Oh, God." "Love me." "Harder." "Love me harder." "Oh, please." "Don't stop." "Please don't stop."

Muhamed gave Megan her third orgasm. Her forth orgasm. Her fifth orgasm. When he gave her a sixth orgasm, he gasped words she did not recognize. "Allah. Ela'na. LowsamaHt. Mara waHda." And two words she did recognize. "Goddamn you. Goddamn you. Goddamn you."

She dimly realized that it was not all sweat that dripped down Muhamed's face and splattered onto hers; his tears mingled with their combined perspiration. When he bonelessly collapsed on top of her, she held him as tightly as she could—as tightly as she wished she had been held twenty-two years earlier when she had cried in the night.

Chapter Three

The smell of Megan's sex permeated the air: it was more potent than the most expensive perfume.

Light filtered through the drape covering the window, turning faded cloth to luminescent green. Beside him, dark hair threaded with silver peaked out from underneath the covers.

His lips burned in memory of her kiss; his body burned from the contact of hers, shoulder to ankle.

A long, thick braid snaked across his pillow; metal pins glinted in the dim light. Her hair had been secured on top of her head when she straddled his lap; it had come undone during the night.

He thought of the discomfort she must have experienced, sleeping on sharp pins. He thought of the tightness of her vulva, clasping his sheathed verge.

His chest constricted in memory.

She had kissed him, this woman whom he had accused of being too old to be a whore.

She had cradled his head, while he learned the taste and texture of her breast.

She had shared with him the miracle of a man and a woman's joining.

Mingled wonder and shame coursed through him.

He had never felt more like a man than when he had been buried inside her body. He had never felt more vulnerable than when confessing four decades of fear: that he could never please a woman; that no woman could ever please him.

In the end, it had been she who had taken his life in her hands.

Megan's leg rode his upper thigh; her head was pillowed on his shoulder. Flyaway hair snagged his chin.

She slept as innocently as a child, a whore who had offered

comfort as well as pleasure. Her cheeks were pale—from sleep? From exhaustion? From satiation?

Her clitoris had risen against his finger once. Her vulva had clenched about his wrist five times, tighter than his fist. She had reached her peak six times in total.

He watched the stillness of her face, and thought of the man he had nearly betrayed—*El Ibn,* "the son" of his heart, if not his loins.

He studied the fan of her lashes, and thought of the woman he had silently loved—safe in the knowledge that she had loved another.

And knew he would never again be the same.

He had experienced sexual union.

One night. With one woman.

Sexless duty was a pitiful substitute.

His biceps and calves ached. Dull pressure radiated inside his groin.

The first would ease with time and exercise; the latter with simple voiding. All he had to do was find the strength to get out of bed, he who had not lingered between the sheets since he was a thirteen-year-old boy, secure in who and what he was.

Moving slowly, so as not to awaken Megan, he slid out from under her head, her leg, and then the covers.

His toes curled. The wooden floor was icy.

Briefly he stood over the bed and watched Megan sleep. Her echoing cries of pleasure rang in his ears.

She had begged him. To not stop. To fill her more deeply. To love her harder.

Never had he been so humbled, yet felt so powerful.

Her black dress lay in a heap where she had stepped out of it to come to his bed. His white turban and *thobs,* a loose ankle-length shirt, was sprawled on the floor farther away, a visible reminder of the road he had traveled and the distance he had spanned.

Prior to that night, he would have neatly folded his clothes away before retiring.

Prior to that night, he would scoop his clothes up now and fold them away.

Bending down, he grabbed the chamber pot from underneath the wooden slats of the sleigh bed. Crumpled rubber shone in the corner of his eye—the French letter he had used to protect himself from disease. Thin fluid congealed in the bottom of the sheath, proof that even he was capable of ejaculating.

Plucking up the used prophylactic, he crossed the plank floor. Setting the heavy porcelain down on the chair by the fireplace that no longer emitted even a vestige of warmth, he lifted the lid in his right hand.

Chipped black print stared up at him.

Use me well, and keep me clean,
And I'll not tell what I have seen.

A slight smile hitched up his lips. There was a certain bawdy charm about the English.

Dropping the condom into the bowl, he reached down with his left hand to guide himself. For the first time the term *manhood* came to mind.

She had praised him for his size—he who had never thought to receive praise from any woman.

Hot urine arced into the chipped porcelain; it steamed in the chill morning air. Cursorily shaking himself dry, he replaced the lid.

Megan would need to make use of the chamber pot when she awakened; he turned, leaving it on the chair for her convenience.

Shadowy eyes stared up at him from the depths of the narrow sleigh bed. He did not need to see their color to know what it was: they were moss green. Verdant with life as the desert was not.

His first instinct was to hide himself. For the first time in forty years he did not.

His head felt oddly light, with no turban to protect his black hair that was liberally streaked with gray. But it was not his head that snared her attention.

Gaze oddly hesitant, she stared at his groin.

A prickle of heat rushed down his spine.

He stood still, waiting for her to laugh—as women in the harem laughed. Afraid to move, lest he invoke the very laughter that he feared.

"I did not know that men in Arabia shaved their private regions." Megan's gaze skidded up to meet his, danced past him. "Is it not chilly in the winter?"

Her sally fell flat in the chill morning air.

She had not judged him in the dark of night. But she did now in the light of day, else she would not make sport of his condition.

The surge of rage took him by surprise.

"Take another look, madam," he bit out. "It is more than 'private' hair I am missing."

Her eyes widened. With uncertainty? Alarm that she had offended an Arab dog?

He had offered her a gold sovereign. How much more money would it take for her to accept him in the light of day, as she had accepted him in the dark of night?

She glanced back down and studied him for long seconds. Her tongue flecked her lips, a darker shadow in shadowy twilight. "You are not as . . . as large as you were last night, but that is understandable, surely."

Megan's response was naive; it was not manufactured.

His head snapped back.

She was a whore. How could she not see the obvious?

How could she not have felt it last night—that lack of flesh which made a man, a man—when she had grasped him in her hand? How could she mistake him for anything other than what he was, after he had lain between her thighs, buried so deeply inside her vulva that not even the night air had come between them?

Unless. . . .

"Who are you?" he snapped.

Her gaze leaped back to his. The paleness of her face bleached into stark white. "I told you who I am."

"You're not a whore," he said baldly.

No whore could fail to observe what she had apparently missed.

His stomach clenched.

But if she wasn't a whore, why had she come to his room? What was she doing in his bed?

He had cried, when he orgasmed, the tears he had not cried for forty years. She had held him, comforted him, loved him as if she were used to men who cursed and cried while they fought to find release inside a woman's body.

Who was she?

Tense seconds passed. A man's muffled shout for an ostler penetrated the outside hotel wall, a blaring reminder that the night was over and a new day had dawned.

"I am a widow," she said finally, evenly. "A patron of this inn, as you are."

His eyes narrowed, remembering his observation—that she did not sound as if she were from around Land's End; remembering her answer—that she was not. Why hadn't he questioned her further?

"How is it that you came to my room last night?" he bit out.

"I overheard you order the innkeeper to find you a . . . a prostitute." Her breath fogged the air, blurring her face. "I intercepted her in the hallway. I knocked on your door in her stead, hoping you would mistake me for her."

And he had.

A shrill whinny carried on the air; it was followed by a short, sharp, canine bark.

It dawned on him that he should be cold, standing naked before a woman in a chill English inn, but he wasn't. Blood pumped through his veins; vivid memories flashed through his mind like colored sand in a kaleidoscope, changing, shifting. Questions he had asked, thinking she was a whore; reassur- ances she had uttered, encouraging his abandon.

Had she been disappointed by his ignorance . . . or had she reveled in her sexual superiority?

Ten half-moons throbbed to life in his shoulders, the imprint of her fingernails.

Had her flesh clenched around his in enjoyment . . . or frustration?

She had lied to him, no matter that he, too, lied by inadmission. What did the likes of him know about women?

How did he know if he had pleased her?

"Exactly what had you heard about Arabs that incited your curiosity, madam?" he lashed out, masking his vulnerability. "Did you hope that my verge would be larger than that of an Englishman? Arab men are reputed to be masters at pleasuring women. Tell me. What did you hope to gain through your deception?"

She had not cowered from his curtness the night before, nor did she cower before his anger now.

"One night, sir. I hoped to gain one night of pleasure." Her head slid back on the pillow, braid coiling, chin mutinously thrusting forward. "I thought that was what you wished, too, else I would not have taken up your time."

A woman lying naked among crumpled bedcovers, with her hair unkempt and her face shiny with dried sweat, should not manifest dignity. But Megan did.

Unexpected pain ripped through his rage.

This woman had not belittled him. Ridiculed him. Pitied him.

I do not judge you, she had said.

Why not?

She was an Englishwoman, if not of good breeding, at least from a respectable family.

How could she accept what harem women did not?

"I am *hadim,*" he said brutally.

"I am English," she returned.

Literally translated, *hadim* meant hairless; in any other language, it meant only one thing.

He gritted his teeth and forced out the hated word—a word he had hoped not to use with this woman; a word that had haunted him for forty years. "I am a eunuch, madam."

The desert was a place of treacherous sand and shrieking wind; it was also a place of stillness and perfect quietude. He had never before witnessed such stillness in an Englishwoman, but he witnessed it now, in Megan.

Her gaze did not waver from his. "I would say, sir, that your performance last night attests otherwise."

Silently, he cursed the heat that blistered his cheeks. He had not blushed in forty years. Twice now this woman had caused him to blush.

"They cut off my stones," he said crudely, hoping to shock her. To horrify her.

To prove that he was not the man she believed him to be, but which he had felt like for one single night.

She regarded him calmly. "By stones, I take it you mean your ballocks?"

The tips of his ears pricked hotly at her blunt English. "I have no seed."

I have no seed reverberated inside his head—the cry of the thirteen-year-old boy he had once been, irreparably altered. The excuse of the Muslim he had grown up to be, filled with rage.

His heartbeat pounded in his temples and his groin, counting the seconds, preparing for defense.

"My husband was a vicar," Megan said in a clear, dispassionate voice. "When the surgeon told him I was fashioned in such a manner that I would never be able to carry his children, he refused to share my bed. He did not want to endanger my life, he said, by causing me to have any more miscarriages. The local midwife apprised me of certain prophylactics that would prevent conception. My husband refused to use them, even though their use would have allowed us to be together. He said such devices were immoral, and that marital pleasure was solely for the benefit of procreation."

The faint protest of a carriage approaching and the dull clip-clop of hooves broke the stark silence that followed her words; just as suddenly the external sounds faded.

"I would to God that my husband had had no seed—or that I had been barren," she concluded with cool decisiveness. "It would have been far more preferable than the loneliness he condemned us to."

He stood still, remembering her admission that a man had rejected her.

Not a young swain, as he had thought. But a man who had shared with her the sexual intimacy that was indeed one of life's true miracles. A man who had given her pleasure and who had seeded her womb with children she could not bear.

A man who, by her own admission, she had loved.

A tide of emotion swept over him: jealousy, at the depth of her affection for her deceased spouse; envy, at the long years of companionship she had shared with him; uncertainty, at how to comfort a woman whom he had admitted into his life solely for his own comfort.

Anger came to his rescue, that he should feel the need to comfort and, feeling it, did not have the wherewithal to express it.

Eunuchs could not afford softer emotions.

"How long have you been a widow?" he asked curtly.

"Two years."

"How many men have you been with since you were a widow, or were you in the habit of slipping into other men's bedchambers before your husband died?" he asked, cringing at his cruelty, yet wanting to prove that she was a whore in flesh if not profession.

Wanting to destroy the bond that had been forged between them in the night lest she expect more than he could give, eunuch that he was but did not want to be.

"My husband is the only man I have ever been with, save for you," she said stiffly. Her face, framed by her dark hair and white bedding, was ashen. "We were not intimate the last twenty years that he lived."

Twenty years. Two years.

She had been abstinent more than half the number of years he had been a eunuch. Yet she had come to him, a man who was no man.

"It was your husband whom you asked to touch you," he said flatly.

To kiss her. To lick her. To suckle her.

All the things he had done to her last night.

Had she imagined that he was her husband?

"Yes."

"He was the man you loved."

"Yes. I thought he loved me, too, but he could not have, could he? A man cannot love a woman if he does not respect the needs of her body."

She rapidly blinked back tears.

Of pain. Of anger. Of betrayal.

Megan, too, knew loneliness.

Memories of their joining washed over him: the hot core of her vulva; the silky-soft hardness of her feminine bud; the prickle of her pubic hair grinding into his pelvis while she swallowed him whole and did not once judge either his inexperience or his lack of testicles.

"Women in Arabia use vinegar-soaked wool-plugs," he said abruptly.

"I beg your pardon?"

Heat crawled down his neck. "As a prophylactic," he explained shortly.

"I see."

Tension thickened the air.

Any moment now she was going to get up, dress, and leave. Never knowing what the night had meant to him.

He desperately strove to divert her. "Is Megan your true name?"

Even as the words left his mouth, he realized the incongruity of his question. He asked a truth from her that he was not willing to give in return.

"Yes," she said, terse as he had been terse. "If you will allow me a few moments of privacy—"

"Don't," he grated.

He could feel the stiffening of her body. "Don't what?"

Don't leave me.

"I am not an easy . . . man."

Megan's silent agreement was decipherable in any language.

He persevered, as he had persevered the last forty years.

"I do not know how . . . to talk to women." He spoke carefully, trying to soften his severity, to be what she would want a man to be. "I do not know what pleases them—"

"I have told you—"

"But I would please you, Megan," he interrupted, the harshness kicking in to block out her pending rejection. "If you would let me."

Her expression remained inscrutable. "I do not understand what it is that you want from me."

Last night she had uttered similar words.

His needs had not changed.

He wanted to know what other men knew.

He wanted to be what other men were.

"I would have no more pretense or illusions between us," he said, reigning in hope, harnessing fear.

"Are you asking me to . . . to spend more time with you?" she asked guardedly.

He would never have another chance to experience a woman's honest sexuality.

"I am asking you to spend another night with me," he said tautly.

"And if I did?"

His spine felt ready to snap. "I will do whatever you wish."

"My husband . . ." Megan shifted; the squeak of the bed-springs scraped across his skin. "I did not ask him to do the things I said to you last night."

"You did not ask him to touch you?" he asked, heart pounding, verge stirring, hope thickening his tongue.

Megan held his gaze, suddenly seeming far younger than her years. "I did not ask him to . . . to kiss my breasts."

"Did you ask him to touch you between your legs?"

"I did not have the courage to," she admitted.

But she had possessed the courage to come to him. To tell him what she wanted.

A eunuch had no right to feel exultation at hearing that a woman sought intimacies with him that she had not sought from a man. But he felt that rush of possessiveness now for Megan, knowing he could give what her husband had not.

He remembered her closed lips when she kissed him. Her uncertainty at how she should move on his verge when she straddled his lap.

Her blatant curiosity. Her uninhibited response.

He was inexperienced, but he was not ignorant of sexual practices.

She was both ignorant, he realized, and inexperienced.

"Would you like me to kiss your clitoris?" he asked abruptly.

"What?"

Megan's shock was not feigned.

"Men kiss women on their clitoris," he said, deliberately enticing her with the lure of her sexuality. "They lick them. They suckle them."

Until they reached a peak of enjoyment.

Awareness shimmered between them, he standing before her naked, vulnerable, she covered neck to toes with blankets, equally naked and vulnerable.

"You would . . . you would do that?" she asked, not quite as composed as before. More like the woman she had been last night when darkness had been their alibi and she had freely admitted her desires.

"I would," he affirmed.

"How do you know that men do that?"

How did a virgin eunuch who had never touched a woman know that men did that? was what she really asked.

He could tell her that many Arabic treatises described the act of cunnilingus, just as those same books described a woman's arousal . . .

"I have watched them," he replied baldly.

There would be no more sexual deception between them.

"You have watched . . . men and women together?" she asked, trying to conceal her surprise, but failing.

"I have watched women and eunuchs together."

The condemnation he anticipated did not come.

"You said Arabic women did not have a clitoris."

"Many women who are sold as concubines are not Arabic."

She frowned. "These concubines . . . they perform in front of an audience?"

"There is little privacy in a harem."

Not when there were so many men who lusted after the very thing they were denied: the pleasure of a woman's body.

"Other eunuchs . . ." She did not finish her sentence, that other eunuchs had touched women. *Pleased* women. "But you did not."

"I did not," he admitted, anticipating her next question: *Why not?*

"These women you watched"—understanding flickered in her eyes—"did they reciprocate the caresses they received?"

His throat tightened. "No, they did not."

Concubines were slaves, but eunuchs were . . . eunuchs.

A rustling of bedclothes pulled him out of the past.

"I am in a quandary, sir."

For the first time he saw true embarrassment on Megan's face.

"Why?" he asked, dreading her response.

"Either you must dress, or I must. Either way, one of us has to leave."

A band tightened around his chest.

"Why?" he repeated, not wanting to ask, unable to stop.

Clearly, she had had enough of a eunuch, no matter that he would go down on his knees to please her. Clearly, she was ready to return to a safe English world that did not harbor such as he.

Her face darkened, a vivid contrast against the white pillow case. "Because I need to take care of private matters."

"And when you have taken care of private matters?" he doggedly pursued.

"I would very much enjoy having you kiss my clitoris." She did not look away from his gaze. "And then I would like to kiss your manhood."

"You will stay here, in my room, for another night?" he asked, not daring to believe his ears.

"I will stay."

For a second he thought his knees would buckle. The surge of hot blood to his groin stiffened him.

Pivoting, verge swaying heavily, he picked up the chair—carefully so as not to tilt and upset the chamber pot—and deposited the whole by the bed, wood decisively contacting wood.

"I will tend the fire while you tend to private matters," he said peremptorily, afraid to leave her, afraid she would change her mind. "There are tissues in the nightstand drawer."

Without giving her time to debate, he turned and strode toward the cold, iron fireplace. He deliberately made as much noise as he could, knocking the ashes out of the grate with the tong, crackling sheets of old newspaper to use as kindling, pouring fresh coals from the dust-blackened coal scuttle on top of the paper. Squatting down, he struck a safety match and touched it to the newspaper.

And all the while that he performed his chores, he pictured Megan. This was an intimacy he had not believed possible when he had decided to purchase a whore.

Blue flames leaped to life.

Tossing the match into the fireplace, he stood up. Without warning, he turned.

Megan bent over, naked, holding the chamber pot in both hands to slide it underneath the bed.

His heart stopped, witnessing the pale silhouette of a breast, a gracefully curved spine and a rounded buttock. Her braid spilled down her back.

Purposefully, he padded to the water-stained bureau that shared an inner wall with the door. A white stoneware jug, glaze cracked with age, sat in a matching basin. Deftly, he lifted up the pitcher and filled the basin with water. Clumsily, he set it down on top of the bureau inside a previous water ring. The thud of glass on wood dully rang out in the silence.

Quickly, he washed his hands, a quick lathering of soap, and rinsed them before hurriedly grabbing the folded washcloth beside the basin. He dipped it into the water, then wrung it out.

His hand shook.

Holding the wet washcloth to warm it, he faced the bed.

Megan was in the process of standing, back straightening, legs stretching.

Her buttocks were pleasingly round. He caught a glimpse of her sex, of dark lips fringed with even darker hair, and then she stood, spine erect.

He knew the moment she became aware that he watched her. Her vertebrae fused; her shoulders squared.

A whore would not mind that he see her nakedness, but Megan was not a whore. Even when she pretended that she was, he had not thought of her as a whore, he realized. She had merely been a woman who, for whatever reason, had accepted the needs of a eunuch.

Slowly, slowly, she turned.

Behind her, a narrow beam of sunlight highlighted the hair that had escaped her braid, a shock of vivid color in the dullness of shadow. It was neither brown nor auburn, but a combination of both—rich chestnut threaded with silver.

He had seen naked women in the harem; he had watched them at their play, their baths, their sexual games with each other and with other eunuchs. Some had been more plump than Megan, some more slender; some had had larger breasts, some smaller; all had been younger, more beautiful, but none had stirred him like Megan now stirred him.

Small hands clenched into fists at her sides, she silently stood in front of him, awaiting judgment.

From a eunuch.

It felt as if her hands clenched around his heart.

She tilted her chin, denying her vulnerability. "I have heard that women in harems are very beautiful."

"Yes." Water trickled through his fingers, plopped onto the wooden floor. "Concubines are purchased for their beauty."

Her eyes were wary. Wanting his approval, his praise.

What did she see in his eyes when she looked at him? he wondered. Did she see his need for approval, for praise?

"You have very white skin," he said gruffly. "White skin and pure green eyes such as yours are highly prized in Arabia. Your breasts are ample; your hips generous; your waist supple. You would be valuable in Arabia."

"You need not lie to me, sir; I am fully aware of what I am. As you said last night, I am too old to be a whore. I sincerely doubt any man would want me as a concubine."

He had hurt her, he realized belatedly.

But that had not been his intention.

"Last night . . ."

Her chin elevated, preparing to fend off more painful words.

"Last night I was afraid."

An invisible weight lifted from his shoulders.

The world did not suddenly stop at a eunuch's confession of fear and uncertainty.

Megan was not convinced.

He searched for the words to convince her. "Last night, I realized that my need for a woman would not diminish with age, that I felt the same needs when looking at you as I had felt when I was a young man, watching the women in the harem. I realized that I would continue to have the same needs when I am an old man."

Even if he was unable to satisfy those needs.

"I assure you, madam, you are wrong," he said truthfully. "There are many men who would want you for their concubine."

Her chin did not lower. Uncertainty shone in her shadowed eyes. "Land's End is a small village. I came to you hoping that you would think there were no other available women, and that you would thereby accept me."

Would he have considered her as a sexual companion if she had not come to his room?

He would never know.

Neither would she.

"I took out the sponge," she said hurriedly, as if circumventing his response.

He imagined his bare flesh sinking into her bare flesh, and felt his already turgid member grow longer, thicker.

Her gaze unerringly sought him out.

She studied him for long seconds before slowly lifting her eyelids. "I could . . . shave, perhaps, if you would assist me."

His fingers tightened around the wet cloth; the steady drip, drip of water accelerated. "I do not expect—nor wish—you to look or act like a concubine."

"My private hair must . . . tickle you."

"Yes," he said gravely, lips hitching upward. It had been a long time since he had smiled. "It does."

A tiny pulse beat in the base of her throat. "I need to be touched, Muhamed, but I also need to touch. I would please you, too."

His smile faded. "I am a eunuch, Megan."

"I know what you are, sir."

No, she did not know what he was. *He* did not know what he was.

"It was not you I cursed last night," he said shortly, and cringed at his abruptness.

Megan did not flinch at the tone of his voice. "I know."

He drew in a deep breath, smelling her, smelling him, smelling . . . "I would wash you, madam, and cleanse away the scent of vinegar."

"I am quite capable of washing myself, thank you."

"I would cleanse away your pain, Megan."

Her chestnut hair blazed with life; her face went deathly still. She glanced down at the washcloth in his hand and the water that dripped through his fingers, then back up to his face. "Is it just my pain that you would wash away, Muhamed?"

"No."

He would replace the empty barrenness of his life with the scent and the taste and the feel of this woman, and for a little while longer, he would bask in her belief that he was a man.

Megan's face suddenly lit up with a radiant luminescence that was far more seductive than youth. "I would enjoy your ministrations, sir."

Chapter Four

Muhamed was a eunuch; Megan was a widow.

His body was fit, that of a man in his prime; hers was softer, a woman who had reached middle-age.

His manhood blatantly stood out from his body, long, thick, hard. She did not have to glance down to know that her nipples were equally hard.

They stood before each other, naked, with no more lies to hide behind. With no more darkness to camouflage who and what they were: a man and a woman whose lives, for whatever reason, had crossed paths.

Megan waited with trembling expectation. She ached— both from their joining the night before and the need that flooded her anew.

Muhamed stepped closer. The tantalizing scent of musky sweat and tangy spice teased her nostrils, reminding her of the pleasure they had shared the night before, and of the pleasures that awaited them in the light of day.

"Thank you for your compliment, about my . . . my person," she said breathlessly. And returned it. "You are a very handsome man, you know."

A patch of light clearly delineated his left cheek. Dark crimson stained it; denial flashed in his black eyes. He opened his mouth . . . "Thank you," he said gruffly. And cupped her cheek with the wet washcloth. It was warmed by the heat of his body.

The touch was electric.

Or perhaps it was his manhood which prodded her stomach that was electric. It, too, was damp.

The intensity of his gaze took her breath away. She squeezed her eyelids closed and concentrated on the rough-soft caress of the washcloth, cleaning her left cheek, her right, her forehead, her chin, her neck, her chest, her left breast. . . .

Her eyelids snapped open.

Muhamed's eyes were veiled by thick black lashes.

A squire near her husband's vicarage had once purchased a young stallion for breeding purposes. When the stallion had proved to be sterile, the squire had castrated the beautiful beast.

Megan had watched it in a field one day, trying to do what nature had intended it do but which the squire had made impossible.

Or perhaps it had not been impossible.

Perhaps the gelded stallion had been able to gain release, as Muhamed was capable of gaining release.

Perhaps the gelded stallion had also given his mare release, as Muhamed had given her release.

Muhamed diligently washed her right breast, rubbing and rubbing until her engorged nipple throbbed.

She sucked in cool air, needing to know—"Did the concubines . . . did the men suckle their breasts?"

Or was she, indeed, an abomination, to want a man to suckle her as mothers suckled their infants?

He lifted his eyelids. Black eyes pinned her as the washcloth cleansed her. "Yes."

"What else did the"—no, she could not use the term eunuch, not when his member bridged her stomach and his eyes probed her soul—"the men do to the concubines?"

"Harem women possess *phalli;* they use them on themselves, on each other, or else they have eunuchs ply them."

"What is"—pain-pleasure zigzagged back and forth between her nipple and her womb—"*phalli?*"

"Artificial phalluses."

Megan's heartbeat staggered.

Phalluses. Artificial . . . *penises?*

"Sit down on the bed and lie back."

So he could wash her private parts.

So he could kiss her clitoris.

But what if he did not like the sight of her . . . the taste of her?

"It is not necessary that you do this," she said hurriedly. "It is not what you wish."

"I . . ." The cleansing was for him as well as her, he had said. She thought of the pain he had endured in the harem, watching others engage in the pleasures that he was denied. While Megan was not a young, beautiful concubine, she could give him this. "Yes, I wish it."

Megan stepped backward. The backs of her legs hit the mattress.

She abruptly sat down, bed squeaking. Dull pain radiated up through her pelvis, faded at the cold compress of wool blankets and coarse sheet.

The floor would be equally cold and far harder on his bare knees.

Reaching out, she grabbed a pillow and dropped it on the floor. At the same time dark, long, narrow feet stepped forward. The pillow landed on top of them.

She glanced up . . . and froze.

A single eye stared at her.

She instinctively reached out . . . and closed her fingers around warm, pulsing skin.

Muhamed audibly sucked in air, but he did not pull away.

Last night, sheathed inside a French letter, he had felt like rubber; now—"You feel like satin," she murmured, mesmerized by his circumference and length and pure masculine beauty.

Gently, she grazed the engorged tip—it was dusky purple in the muted light. Slippery clear moisture dampened her thumb. A tiny heartbeat pounded inside him.

She looked up in wonder. He tensely stared down at her.

Megan said the first thing that came to mind. "I never knew a man would be so soft, yet so hard."

"Did you not see—or touch—your husband?"

"The English are more concerned with modesty than sensuality."

"I am circumcised."

"You are perfect," she said in all sincerity.

Hearing the words she had spoken aloud, she blushed.

His manhood flexed inside the ring of her fingers.

She had pleased him with her compliment. Such a simple thing to do, when he gave her so much pleasure.

Pride was a little thing to sacrifice if it would give him back the joy that had been taken away from him.

Realizing the opportunity he presented her with, she reached for the washcloth.

Muhamed knew what she was going to do. What the harem concubines had not done for those men who had given them pleasure.

He gave her the washcloth.

Megan carefully washed him, there, underneath his penis where the skin was smooth save for a hard seam of puckered scars. He stiffened; she persisted, washing the root that was darker than the hairless skin at his groin, the stalk that was thicker than the circumference of her fingers, the purple-tinted crown that cried crystal tears.

She kissed him, there on the tip of his manhood.

He grabbed her head, palms stopping her ears so that all she could hear was the beat of her own heart that matched the tiny heart that beat against her lips.

She tasted him.

Slippery salt coated her tongue.

She opened her lips against him—smooth flesh dragging over smooth flesh, mouth opening wider—

Suddenly the heat cupping her ears disappeared, and a hard hand grasped her braid, pulling her head back while the sound of labored breathing surrounded her.

Muhamed's hard features were drawn; his black eyes filled with—what?

Her heart lodged inside her throat. "Did I hurt you?"

"A man can gain release through a woman's mouth as well as her vulva," he gritted.

Megan saw behind his harshness.

He wanted the release he spoke of. He wanted it so much that he was afraid of it.

"I would enjoy bringing you to orgasm in such a manner," she said calmly.

His mouth twisted—a grimace of pain rather than pleasure. "What if I told you that some concubines enjoy it when eunuchs penetrate their back orifices? Would you enjoy that, too?"

Back orifices. . . .

His meaning slammed through her. The image hovered in her thoughts, refusing to fade. It was overlapped by a vivid picture of an artificial phallus.

She had never imagined such acts as he conjured . . . had she?

When she had picked cucumbers from her small garden, she had never imagined the object to which their shape bore a striking resemblance . . . had she?

When she clenched the muscles inside her vulva, she had never noticed that her buttocks also tightened . . . had she?

When his fingertips had plunged into her crevice last night, she had not wondered what would happen if only they had sunk a little lower, a little deeper . . . *had she?*

"I think"—Megan swallowed, the stretch of her neck making it difficult—"that if an act brings pleasure to a woman . . . or a man . . . then surely it is a cause for rejoice, rather than shame. I think it is those who judge the needs of others that are shameful."

"There are acts that are shameful." The beginnings of pain pricked her scalp. "Acts that some men require that are not natural."

His manhood continued to throb between her fingers; a pulse throbbed at the corner of his mouth.

"What?" she asked carefully. "What acts do you refer to? A

man touching a woman . . . kissing her vulva? A woman touching a man . . . and kissing his manhood? You think those acts are unnatural?"

"No." His hold eased. "It is not those acts which are shameful."

What did this man need—or require—that he deemed unnatural?

"I will do anything you wish, Muhamed, so long as you do not hurt me."

"I wouldn't hurt you." Something flickered in the depths of his black eyes. "I have never hurt a woman."

Megan believed him.

"I saw a young girl and boy once."

The words popped out of her mouth before she could stop them. A stillness came over him; only the throbbing pulse inside his manhood was alive, clocking the passing seconds.

Muted sounds drifted up from the side of the inn—they came from another world, a place that had no bearing on a eunuch and a widow.

"The country, like your harem, is not always a place of privacy," she continued softly, remembering. . . . "They lay together in a field. It was in the spring. The grass was newly green. I watched them over a hedge."

"What did they do?" he asked hoarsely.

"The girl sat astride the boy's hips, while he lay back and fondled her breasts. She rode him like a man would ride a horse."

"Did the sight arouse you?"

The very memory aroused her.

"Yes."

His eyes closed, lashes thick against his cheek. "You gave me pleasure last night, Megan. More than I had ever thought possible."

His eyelids opened; his black eyes were bleak. "I do not know if I will be able to share that pleasure with you again.

Eunuchs such as I grow erect, but it is . . . difficult . . . sometimes impossible . . . to obtain release."

She did not want release if he could not obtain his own.

"Then there is no need for you to give me pleasure—"

"There is every need, madam."

"Why?" she challenged.

"Because you are a very special woman, Megan. And I
would know you."

The protest rising inside her throat died.

"I felt your clitoris harden against my fingers last night," he
continued, voice and face strained. "Now I want to feel it
harden against my tongue. Lie back, Megan. Let me learn
your body. Let me give you pleasure. It's all I can offer you. It's
all I can offer any woman."

Her chest felt as if she squeezed it instead of the washcloth.

Silently, Megan handed him the damp cloth and lay back.
The ceiling had leaked at one time; a maze of brown water
stains ringed it.

"Spread your legs."

Firm fingers helped her. Opened her. Exposed her.

Something icy wet touched her—the washcloth.

She tensed—the muscles inside her vulva, the muscles inside
her buttocks.

The cold washcloth warmed to her body, parted her body,
delved inside her body.

He was . . . stuffing the cloth up inside her.

She winced, invaded by his finger, by more washcloth, his
finger again, and yet more washcloth. Just when she lifted her
head and started to protest that she was not a jar which
needed to be cleaned out by swirling a cloth inside, he took her
into his mouth.

Liquid heat. Scalding moisture.

Megan's head banged the pillow of crumpled blankets; the
mattress squeaked in protest. She stared up at the largest
water stain; darker circles rimmed the outer edges, more re-

cent leaks, a part of it yet separate. Just as Muhamed's sexuality had been a part of his nature, yet separate from his life.

Thoughts of Muhamed and images of the circle of water slowly blurred until sight and sensation became one, and that one was his tongue and the washcloth that was tightly packed inside her.

He stabbed the very tip of her, his tongue hotter than had been his fingertip. Wetter. Faster.

A drop of cool water trickled down her vulva and into the crevice between her buttocks. There was no room for air inside her body, yet her lungs independently sucked it in, deeper, deeper. . . .

Her peak of enjoyment hit her with the force of lightning, searing, rending. Dimly she had time to wonder who had coined the term "peak of enjoyment"—there was nothing remotely enjoyable about the agony that rent her body asunder; *was this what Muhamed was afraid of, this pleasure that consumed one's very soul*—then she was crying out. At the same time her body convulsed. It felt as if his tongue were sucking out her insides.

She tightened her muscles—vulva, buttocks—and could not stop it. With each spasm another inch of her was drawn out.

No, not *her* . . . the washcloth.

He was slowly pulling the washcloth out of her even as her muscles clenched down, trying to stay the motion.

Suddenly there was no stopping it, her body bore down and gave up the washcloth . . . gave up her release . . . gave up a part of Megan that she had not known she possessed until an Arabic eunuch had taken the time to show her.

Megan plummeted back into her body, and once again she was staring up at the ceiling and the large water stain that was ringed by smaller dark circles, joined but separate. A hard hand pressed down on her stomach, as if feeling the contractions that continued to ripple through her womb. A facile tongue probed her vulva, as if feeling the contractions that continued to ripple through her vagina.

Slowly the contractions ebbed and his tongue withdrew. Something soft and silky and alive slipped through her fingers— hair.

When had she grabbed his head? she wondered dazedly. "In the Orient, strung pearls are used instead of a cloth." Hot air seared her nether lips, breathing desire back into sated flesh.

"You have seen men," she gulped air, "insert pearls inside women?"

Hard heat abruptly invaded her—a finger. She winced. It was not padded by cloth.

"I have read about that act and many more," he said hoarsely. "In Arabia there are treatises that describe the various ways a man may please a woman."

"And are there treatises that describe the various ways to please a man?"

"It is through a woman's vulva"—he inserted a second finger, a quick shock that rapidly gave way to tantalizing fullness—"that a man gains his pleasure."

Tears burned her eyes. She determined to find a way to give Muhamed the same pleasure he had given her.

"Thank you for improvising with the cloth. I feel quite . . . cleansed."

His fingers inside her throbbed. Or perhaps it was she who throbbed.

"If you could have anything you wanted, what would you wish for, Megan?" he asked unexpectedly.

"I . . . " *This.* This time with him was everything she had ever wished for. "I don't know." Hard pressure pinched her vagina. "What are you—what would you wish for?"

"This, Megan." He pushed inside her—three fingers—it felt like five. "This is what I've dreamed about ever since I can remember."

She sucked in air—consciously trying to relax her body and give him what he needed. The ceiling was superimposed by images: Muhamed relieving himself; Muhamed preparing for condemnation, when he turned and saw her watching him; Muhamed's face growing shuttered when he thought she was not going to stay with him for another day, another night.

Imagery gave way to the sound of Muhamed cursing the night as he found his first release with a woman.

He twisted his fingers.

Electricity shot through her.

She stared blindly at the ceiling, forcing herself to hold still and allow him to explore her. "What did you say . . . in Arabic, last night?"

"I don't remember."

He was evading her again.

His fingers surged more deeply inside her.

Megan bit her lip. "*Ela'na.* What does that mean?"

"'Damn.'" He crooked his three fingers inside her and gently raked the front wall of her vagina. "You have a button inside you."

A button!

Heat shot through her—hotter than fire, more galvanizing than lightning.

"What does . . . *Lowsam*—" She couldn't remember the word, could barely remember how to speak. "What does *mara*—"

Her body independently surged upward. "Oh, my God! What are you doing?"

He repeated the caress. "*Mara wahda* means 'one time.' Does it give you pleasure, with just my fingers inside you?"

Pleasure was not the word she would use to describe what she felt. Agony. Torture. "Yes, it gives me pleasure. Does it bring you pleasure?"

"Your flesh burns, Megan, with the heat of your desire. Yes, you please me. Can you obtain your release like this?"

"I . . . I don't know."

"Then let us find out."

He found the rhythm that her body needed, as if his fingers were his manhood, driving deep, hard, tips curled, so that each thrust, each withdrawal, teased the special button he had found.

Wave after wave of pleasure rolled over Megan.

She thought of the Arabic women who had been altered, and hoped that they were able to experience, thin, at least, the pleasure that accrued from having the inner wall of a woman's vagina strummed. And then she didn't think, she could only feel as a wave of blinding sensation broke over her, and her entire world shrank to the heat of his hand pressing on her womb while the heat of his fingers pistoned inside her.

Her body bowed in a perfect arch. Seeking to escape. Lifting for more.

He gave her more. Deeper. Harder. Always pressing inward against the inner wall of her vulva.

He gave her release. And did not seek his own.

Megan slowly became conscious of his fingers that were a part of her and the tension that surrounded her.

"I have read that a woman is inexhaustible," Muhamed rasped. "That she may reach a thousand and one orgasms in a night."

"I do not think . . ." She took a shallow breath, unable to draw a deeper one. "I do not think I will survive even one more orgasm right now, let alone nine hundred and ninety-nine more."

His fingers curved around her stomach; at the same time they curled inside her vagina.

"There is a well nearby," he said abruptly. "Madron Well."

It was a mile or so above Madron church.

"Yes." Megan raised her head. Sweat glistened on his face. "I know it."

But how did *he* know about it?

"I would see it. With you."

Her heartbeat drummed against her chest; her breast quivered with the force of her breathing. "I would much rather see to your satisfaction."

His mouth twisted. "I have told you, Megan. Eunuchs are not like men."

His fingers throbbed inside her, telling her he lied, either deliberately or unknowingly.

He was a man, and he could gain release. If only he would trust her.

"I need to . . . to return to my room," she said.

"Why?" he asked, his voice suddenly guarded.

"I need to get . . ." How ridiculous it was, to blush over mentioning an innocent thing like underclothes when his fingers filled her and her body still shook with the release he had brought her. "I need to get my cloak."

"We will stop by your room and get it on our way out."

"I would rather you have the innkeeper prepare us a picnic basket to take along with us while I dress."

"You will not"—he prodded her more deeply, fingers straightening, reaching, as if he mapped her vaginal walls—"change your mind?"

"No. I am hungry." He reversed direction. She took a deep breath, internally following the slow withdrawal of his fingers, one knuckle, two. . . . "I did not eat my dinner last night."

His fingers glistened in the dim light, moist with the essence of her release.

Megan glanced up. His gaze was waiting for her.

That slight half smile hitched up the corner of his lips. "I do not want you to go hungry on my account."

"Then I suggest you feed me, sir."

The trace of his smile disappeared. "I did not know that women like you existed."

"I did not know that men like you existed."

His expression immediately closed. "Eunuchs are mentioned in your Christian Bible, Megan."

"But men who value a woman's satisfaction are not, Muhamed."

Muhamed stood in one swift motion; he was blatantly

erect, Bending down, he scooped up the white turban and robe he had discarded the night before

The muscles in his back, legs and buttocks rippled when he walked, He dropped the washcloth across the wooden bar beside the bureau, then neatly pulled the robe on over his head. Opening the top drawer, he took out a wooden-handled hair brush and ran it through his hair. It neatly fell into wavy curls.

A brief pang stabbed her chest, that he should have such a beautiful head of hair when hers was limp and straight. The pang of envy was immediately replaced by a sense of rightness.

It was comforting to watch a man perform his morning toilet.

His habits were the same as those of an Englishman; he dressed, brushed his hair, his teeth, . . .

Bending his head, he spat into the basin.

She bit her lip to stop her protest when he proceeded to wrap the turban around his head. When he opened the second bureau drawer and took out a pair of baggy white trousers, she could not keep her mouth shut. "Please don't."

The back of his white robe stiffened. "Don't what?" he asked, without turning around.

"I rather fancied that Arabic men did not wear anything under their robes. The Scots are reputed not to wear anything under their kilts. It is . . . interesting for a woman to think that all she need do is toss up a man's skirt."

Muhamed turned, white robe flurrying. "You are . . . jesting with me."

He seemed surprised that a woman would do so.

"Not at all, sir," she said whimsically, feeling absurdly young and carefree. "The English have no sense of the ridiculous, especially when they sit naked in front of a clothed gentleman. Or perhaps that is not well-known in your country."

Shadow crossed his face, a trick of light. "Concubines and slaves do not picnic in Arabia."

She had overseen many picnics as the wife of a vicar, but she had never attended a picnic unchaperoned with a man.

"I dare say it would not be a practical custom in a desert land," she said gently.

"What shall I have the innkeeper prepare?"

His uncertainty was endearing.

"I suspect an inn of this size will not have much of a menu to chose from. A meat pie and cheese will do quite well, thank you."

"You will be here when I return?"

Megan felt a flutter deep inside her chest. Muhamed was so very vulnerable underneath his outward gruffness.

"If I am not here, I will be in the second room down to the left of yours," she said calmly.

He turned toward the door, in a soft swish of cotton.

"Muhamed."

Muhamed halted; he did not turn around. "Yes?"

"How did you come to know about Madron Well? It is a local phenomenon."

"How did *you* come to know about it?"

She had not imagined the shadow that had crossed his face and now pervaded the room; it had nothing to do with a passing cloud.

He had said no more pretense.

"I was born in Land's End," she replied evenly. "My mother—like most of the folk hereabouts—clung to many of the old ways. She baptized me in the well waters."

"What would you like to drink with your meal?" he asked in his old brusque manner.

He was not going to answer her question.

Megan fought down a prick of hurt.

"Cider will be fine, thank you."

With a swirl of robes he opened the door and slid out of her sight. A final click of closure followed his departure.

Her heart skipped a beat. Suddenly she felt forty-eight again instead of twenty-six and full of joy.

What had she said to upset Muhamed?

What if *he* did not return?

Standing up, Megan picked up her black wool gown from off the floor and dressed. Hairpins dotted the pillow and sheet. She scooped them up, Slipping into her shoes, she rescued her black felt hat and the hatpin underneath it.

She mused at the small brown tin on the nightstand. There was no advertisement on the outside, nothing at all to indicate what was inside it.

On impulse, she removed the lid.

It was filled with what looked like rolled-up sausage skins. French letters. She had often wondered what they looked like. They hardly seemed large enough to accommodate a man of Muhamed's size.

Megan grabbed a rubber sheath and replaced the lid, a quick click of metal on metal.

The hallway was dark, empty; a worn wool runner tiredly traversed the length of it. An oil sconce guarded each of the six doors, a dull gleam of pewter. She hurried to her room.

A glint of gold greeted her.

Her wedding band waited on the nightstand beside the narrow, neatly made sleigh bed.

The sight of it did not incur the sense of betrayal she had associated with her marriage over the last twenty-two years.

Impulsively, Megan crossed the wooden floor, heels echoing determinedly, and flung open the worn drapes. Blinding sunlight spilled into the sterile room, proof that there was light after darkness. Turning, she plucked the wedding band off the nightstand and dropped it into the top dresser drawer.

Feeling as uncertain as a young girl awaiting her first beau, she washed, brushed her teeth, loosened her braid, and brushed her hair. Rummaging in her trunk, she pulled out a corset, chemise, petticoats, wool drawers—no, she did not want to wear drawers, she wanted to be accessible to Muhamed.

Megan pulled out a black skirt and bodice. She realized with dismay that all of her clothes were black. They belonged to a woman who was resigned to widowhood, not to a woman who planned upon demonstrating to a eunuch that he was a man.

No time now to worry about her wardrobe.

Hurriedly, she slipped into her chemise and rebraided her hair.

A sharp knock splintered the silence.

Megan's heartbeat quickened.

"One moment!" she called out, mouth full of hairpins.

The knock came again. Louder.

Stomach roiling with nervous anticipation, she coiled the braid on top of her head and secured it with pins.

A third knock came, louder still.

The entire inn would know that Muhamed sought entrance to her room if he continued knocking.

She jerked open the door. And perforce had to step back to prevent Muhamed from walking over her.

A black cloak billowed after him. He carried a battered bucket.

"They did not have a picnic basket," he said without preamble.

"Oh." She flushed, suddenly, painfully aware of the sunshine that warmed her back and starkly revealed a patch of chipped paint on the wall behind him. Shadow had cloaked her nakedness before; the thin cotton chemise would not conceal the changes that age had wrought in her body—breasts that were too soft; hips that were too rounded. "If you like, you may wait downstairs—"

"I have never watched a woman dress."

Her flush deepened. "I have never had a man watch me dress."

"You will not wear a corset to our picnic."

Megan blinked at Muhamed's peremptory manner. "I beg your pardon?"

"Corsets restrict a woman's circulation."

"Corsets also support their . . . bosom."

"Your bosom does not need support, Megan."

"That is for me to decide, surely."

"Men, too, have fancies." His black eyes were wary. "I

would like to look at you over our meal and know that it is
you I am gazing at and not a miracle of whalebones."

Megan mentally struggled with the shy, demure wife she had
been for so long and the woman she wanted to be for this
Arab. She had not worn a corset to his room the night before,
but. . . .

She took a deep breath. "When you returned to your room,
did you don trousers?"

"I am as you saw me."

Was he still erect?

Instinctively, she glanced down; his white robe was tented.

He was ready for her; completely accessible if she wanted
to flip up his skirt.

Scalding blood scorched her cheeks and pounded in her
temples.

"I cannot go outside with nothing on underneath my
dress," she said firmly, raising her gaze to his. "I must wear a
bustle and petticoats, or the hem of my skirt will sweep the
ground."

As it had swept the hallway last night.

Muhamed set the bucket on top of her neatly made bed.
"Very well. I will assist you."

And he did.

Megan had never had an abigail. Had not been assisted
with her dress since she was a young child, so young that she
could not even remember having received assistance.

He buttoned up her bodice, fingers lingering at her breasts.

Desire knotted inside her stomach.

"Thank you," she murmured, suffocating on the tantalizing aroma of spice and masculinity that was uniquely
Muhamed's.

When she made to withdraw, he clung to her button.

"You said you weren't from around here." Almond-scented
breath bathed her face. "Why did you lie?"

"I've lived in Birminghamshire for the last thirty years," she
said truthfully. There was no need to lie, not anymore. She was

neither young nor wealthy nor in any way desirable other than to this man. "Land's End is no longer my home."

"Yet you are here."

"Yes, I am here. My husband died penniless. The vicar who replaced him was a bachelor; he was kind enough to let me be his housekeeper. Last month he married. There was not enough work for two women, so I . . . volunteered to retire my position. My parents left me a small plot of land." Pride intervened; she could not bring herself to tell him that it was a plot of land no larger than a matchbox and that the Branwells, in a place of poverty, had been the most poor. "I had nowhere else to come."

"Did you see your parents, before they died?"

"No," she said. Lingering regret flitted through her. "They died of influenza."

"Did you come back for their funeral?"

"My parents never forgave me for marrying a man who was not a Cornishman. No, I did not come back for their funeral. By the time I was alerted of their deaths, they had already been buried."

"Would you have attended, if you had known about it in time?"

"I don't know."

Or did she?

Megan had not wanted to return to the poverty or the grim austerity of the Cornish people.

"Did you like it when I put my tongue inside your mouth?"

Her breath caught in her chest, remembering the dual penetration of his tongue inside her mouth and his manhood inside her vulva. "Yes."

"I, too, found it enjoyable." Bright color circled his cheeks. He dropped his hands. "The gig will be ready."

Megan grabbed her cloak off one of the rusted hooks that acted as a wardrobe, and the Windsor hat off the bed. Rushing back, she retrieved her gloves and the French letter she had put inside the pocket of the discarded dress.

Chapter Five

Ragged pieces of cloth hung from thorns, mothers' last-year votive offerings torn from swaddling cloths to appease the old gods.

He stared at the clear spring water, and wondered why he had brought Megan to Madron Well.

The truth chuckled and bubbled out from underneath the rock.

Hilla-ridden—to have the stag—was a West Cornish term for a man whose life was riddled with nightmares. Legend claimed that a man could be cured if he washed in Madron Well.

He wanted to be cured.

He wanted to wash in Madron Well and bathe the past away.

"It is said that in 1650 there was a cripple named John Trelilie," Megan said. The brim of her hat and the fold of black veiling hid her face from his view. "He dreamed three times that he should wash himself in Madron Well. But he was crippled, and no one would bring him, so he crawled here to wash himself in the waters. It cured him, they say. They say he walked away from the well upright."

"Do you believe the story is true?" he asked neutrally.

"It is certainly less farfetched than some other Cornish legends." Megan looked up; sunlight sharply illuminated her white skin and the network of fine lines that defined it. "Are there similar legends in your country?"

Arabia was filled with legends. Of genies. Of magical oases.

He opened his mouth to tell her of Arabia. "Eunuchs have been known to marry," he said instead.

It was not what he had intended to say.

Her moss green eyes remained calm. "What did you mean,

earlier, when you said that eunuchs such as yourself grow erect? Are there eunuchs who do not . . . grow erect?"

A bird warbled; the spring gurgled.

It all seemed so far away, the years he had been whole and the day he had been altered.

"There are three types of castration," he said, feeling as removed as the bird's warble. "There is the *sandali,* or *castrati,* in which a boy's—or man's—penis and testicles are cleanly cut off by a razor; there are those who have their penis only cut off; and there are those like me, who have their testicles either crushed or removed."

He spoke dispassionately, as if it had happened to someone else other than himself; as if the crimes perpetrated were not monstrous, but were perfectly acceptable.

In Arabia, they were.

The horror he had earlier expected to see in her eyes was clearly visible. "These men who do not have their manhood—how do they relieve themselves?"

"They urinate through a straw. Or else they squat."

Like a woman.

But they did not deserve that analogy—not from a fellow eunuch.

"And so these men—these men who do not have their manhood—they must suffer, without any consolation at all."

"A eunuch's level of desire corresponds to the age he was castrated," he said stoically, unable to lie and tell her that a eunuch never felt desire, because they did feel desire.

Even those who were castrated before the onset of puberty. Even those who were *sandali.*

"At what age were you? . . ." She paused, unable to say the word.

"I was castrated when I was thirteen," he said flatly.

He had matured early. At thirteen he had sported the shadow of a beard and his testicles had dropped.

"But those men who lose their manhood. . . ."

She did not have to finish her observation. Or perhaps it was a question.

How did a man who had no manhood yet who still possessed desire find satisfaction?

"Some eunuchs take consolation in giving women pleasure."

"I cannot imagine always seeing to the pleasure of others without being able to physically share it."

Yet she had loved a man who had not seen to her pleasure.

"Eunuchs who have neither a penis nor testicles marry," he said reluctantly.

She remained silent, her gaze suddenly alert.

Instantly, he regretted his confidence.

He did not want to talk about his past. He did not want to think about his future.

He simply wanted to enjoy the day, and his first—and last—woman.

Even should he have the ability to find release in a prostitute, he would never be content with passionless union.

Reaching up, he slid out her hatpin and plucked off her black hat. Sunlight turned her chestnut brown hair to a blaze of red and bronze, autumn colors streaked with the silver gleam of winter. "You have beautiful hair. Why do you wear it pulled back so tightly?"

Reaching up, up, up, she said, "You have beautiful hair, too. Why do you hide it in a turban?" and pulled free the end of the white cotton that was tucked inside to hold the turban in place.

He held still, staring down at her upturned face and the faint lines that contradicted her youthful impulsiveness. "A Muslim man may not show his hair in public."

She unwound the cloth, breasts thrusting against her black cloak, against his chest, focusing upon his turban rather than his gaze. "An Englishwoman may not wear her hair loose in public," she said, breath caressing his chin.

356 / *Robin Schone*

It smelled of tooth powder.

"We are not in public," he said, more aware of her touch and the unwinding turban than he was of his own heartbeat.

Cool air cocooned his head. She stepped back, triumphantly brandishing his turban. "No, we are not."

"I am hungry, Megan," he said deliberately.

"What did you bring us to eat?" she asked, moss green eyes sparkling.

His breath caught in his chest.

No woman had ever jested with him. Teased him. Engaged him in sexual banter.

"What would you like?" he asked, voice too gruff.

It did not deter her—his voice—his body.

"Meat pie," she riposted.

"Then you are fortunate," he returned. "There is a meat pie in the bucket."

Megan laughed.

It rang out through the thicket of branches and leafing bushes, ricocheted off the stone walls that isolated Madron Well from the intrusion of modernity. Wings fluttered up to the sky—she had startled the warbling bird.

His groin tightened.

He untied his cloak and spread it on the ground. She unbuttoned her cloak and spread it on top of his.

Her nipples stabbed her bodice.

"You will get cold," he warned.

"No colder than you," she rejoined.

He was not cold.

Turning, he walked to the stone fence where he had left the bucket. His loose cotton *thobs* fluttered against his bare ankles, rubbed against his turgid verge. Catching up the thin metal handle, he turned.

Megan sat on their cloaks, black gown primly tucked around her legs, tugging off black silk gloves.

He stalked her.

She glanced up . . . and stared at his groin. His robe was tented.

"Your meat pie, madam," he said. And set the basket down on top of their spread cloaks.

Setting her gloves aside, Megan raised her head. Her moss green gaze snared his black one. "I do not see it."

The heat surging through him owed nothing to sunshine. "Look harder, madam."

"There is a cloth covering it," she returned, "Perhaps you should remove it."

There was no mistaking her inference.

He remembered the press of her lips and the lick of her tongue when she had kissed his verge.

His heart thudded against his chest. "We will both catch our chill," he warned.

Megan reached for the top button on her bodice. "But we will always have fond memories of meat pie, will we not?"

She unfastened one button, two, three . . . and shrugged out of her bodice.

Her breasts, warmed by sunlight, gleamed like alabaster. Full. Heavy.

Perfect.

"Take down your hair," he said in a strangled voice.

He watched the lift of her arms, her breasts, noted the glint of red-brown hair underneath her arms, catalogued each quiver of her soft breasts.

A long, thick braid fell over her shoulder. Laying aside the hairpins, she slowly unraveled it and raked her fingers through it to straighten out the kinks.

The red, bronze and silver that had only glinted in her hair when it had been secured on top of her head, now was a blazing waterfall that cascaded over her right breast and down to her waist.

The thud of his heart shook his entire body—his chest; his knees.

Megan was willing to satisfy a eunuch's fancy; he could do no less.

He jerked the *thobs* over his head, letting it fall where it would, and kneeled down in front of her.

In the dim light of morning with the curtains closed, his condition had been blatant but not the scars. There was no hiding them in the full light of day.

She did not cringe from their sight.

Solemnly, she uncovered the bucket of food. Equally solemn, he accepted in his bare hand the slice of meat pie she offered him.

Sitting down, he crossed his legs, acutely aware that she could see everything . . . his scars, his desire, everything he had spent the last forty years trying to hide.

Pulling out a small jug of cider, Megan filled two glasses, left breast quivering with her motion, nipple stabbing the chill spring air.

He reached out and flicked back her hair, so that he could see both of her breasts.

The meat pie was tasteless, the cider sour. He would never forget them.

When they had drained the last drop of cider, finished the meat pie and licked their fingers clean, she returned the jug, glasses and empty pie plate to the bucket.

Megan stood up and unfastened her skirt, her bustle, her petticoats. Her hair shielded her face. "I would ride you, sir."

Twenty-four hours ago, he would have thought her ridiculous.

Twenty-four hours ago, he had not opened his door to admit a widow who masqueraded as a whore.

Straightening his legs, he kicked her underclothes off their cloaks and lay down.

The sun was hot. Blinding. The weight of her body was more welcome than his next breath.

Kneeling over him, she grasped his verge.

He stopped breathing.

Wet heat kissed him.

His heart stopped beating.

Unrelenting pressure. Scalding moisture.

He concentrated on Megan's face as she determinedly tried to put him inside her. She bit her bottom lip, like a child studying for an exam.

"Take me home, Megan," he said hoarsely.

And wondered where his home was.

He knew where others thought it was, but he himself did not know.

Without warning, her portal opened and she swallowed him.

She moaned.

He groaned.

Her pubic hair prickled his pelvis. The tip of his verge abutted her cervix.

He could feel the pulse of her body frantically beating against him.

Megan stared down at him. "I think I'm too old for this."

He grabbed her hips. "I think not, madam. Ride me," he gritted. "Ride me like you saw the young girl ride the boy."

Show me what it is like, he silently begged, *to be young and whole and carefree.*

Tentatively she lifted up; cool air surrounded his verge while his crown was gripped by molten fire. Her gaze did not waver from his, green eyes moist with sexual need and something more, the need to please him.

It was not her consideration he wanted; he wanted her selfish enjoyment.

He bucked up; at the same time he pulled her down, forcing her to take the hardness that was all he could give her.

Megan threw her head back; a low cry vibrated along the length of his verge.

He did not know who it came from—her, or him.

She had a long neck, white, graceful.

Slowly, she learned the rhythm: up, thighs and vagina

squeezing him; down, thighs and vagina opening. Blindly reaching, she clasped her hands over his.

They were the hands of a woman used to cleaning and toiling.

The sun haloed her head in a crown of red, bronze and silver. He alternately watched her breasts jiggle and the chords in her throat strain. A chorus of ragged breathing blended with the wet impact of flesh slapping flesh. Megan rode him until he could feel the sun on his back and the ground beneath his feet and the wind in his face, together galloping back through the past to a time when they had both been young and innocent.

And then it stopped—the pounding motion, the driving force, the race for freedom. Megan stared down at him, face streaked with sweat and sunshine, hair clinging to her cheeks and her breasts. Her vagina rippled around him in the aftermath of her orgasm, fisting, relaxing, fisting, relaxing . . . about his heart, his verge. *Too much,* not enough.

He fought back a cry of agony. He was not ready to be a eunuch again, not when the blood still sang through his veins and desire crackled up and down his spine.

Megan's panting breath slowly subsided. "You cannot, can you?"

He did not pretend to misunderstand her. "No."

But Allah, God, he wanted to.

"I am going to bring you to release, Muhamed."

She abruptly levered up onto one knee—he slipped free of her, wincing, turgid verge reaching out for her—and stood up.

He gazed up at the beauty that was a woman's sex; it was pink and wet between a dark fringe of damp curls.

Her pubic hair was darker than that on her head and underneath her arms.

Quickly, she lifted her leg and brought it over his groin, so that her thighs modestly pressed together.

"Come with me," she said, every bit as imperious as he could be.

"Why?" he rasped, chest heaving, lungs laboring.

Why could they not stay as they were, just for a little while longer?

"I am going to make an offering," Megan said cryptically. Bending down in a glistening waterfall of hair, she flipped the side of her cloak over and retrieved something from her pocket.

He could not see what it was.

Straightening, she turned and walked toward the well that the spring fed, buttocks gently bouncing, hips swaying.

He followed her.

Megan stood over the baptistery that mothers dipped their babies in. Cupping her right hand, she scooped it into the water, brought it up, filled. Turning to him, she let the water trickle down his verge.

He sucked in his breath.

The water was icy.

What had been hard shrank to escape the cold.

She ignored the results of her handiwork, concentrating instead on unrolling a French letter. Megan stuck the unfurled sheath of rubber onto a bush that housed the remnants of swaddling cloths.

His throat tightened. She had baptized his male appendage, as women baptized their babies. Now she left a condom offering, as countless mothers left pieces of swaddling cloths as offerings.

"You think that the good fortune mothers seek for their children will visit me?" he asked roughly.

"I know it will," she said firmly. "But later. In a room warmed by coal and the comfort of a bed at our disposal."

He had experienced one miracle, last night buried inside her body; he did not expect another one.

He helped Megan dress, dropping her petticoats over her head, tying her bustle in place, buttoning the band of her skirt, the front of her bodice.

Pulling her hair back from her face, he braided it for her. It was warm with sunshine, slippery fine, softer than down.

Megan held perfectly still for his ministrations, as if she were not used to another dressing her, helping her.

What kind of a fool had her husband been, to reject Megan's love? he wondered angrily. Were she his woman, he would see that she never wanted for attention.

But he was a eunuch, not a man.

She secured the braid on top of her head and crammed on her hat and gloves while he threw on his *thobs* and wound his turban around his head.

It felt heavier than a boulder.

They did not talk as they retraced their steps through the overgrowth of thorny bushes to the gig that waited for them. He unhobbled the horse and hitched it to the carriage.

Megan climbed in, unassisted.

He wanted to rip off her black hat and black cloak.

He wanted to eat more tasteless meat pie and drink more sour cider and lie again in the sun, with her naked body riding his own.

"You said that eunuchs who do not have their manhood or their testicles marry," she said, looking straight ahead at the gelded horse instead of him.

His lips tightened in a grim line. "Yes."

He knew what she was going to ask.

Megan turned and stared at him. "They would not marry, would they, if they were not capable of enjoying a woman's attentions?"

He snapped the reins. "No, they wouldn't."

Chapter Six

The journey back to the inn was completed in silence. He could feel Megan's determination to give him satisfaction.

It incited both anger and hope: anger, that she failed to understand a eunuch's limitations; hope, that she prove he could find gratification as surely as any other man could.

A young stableboy held the horse's head while he lithely jumped down out of the carriage. For the first time he was glad that he had to daily exercise to build muscles or else turn to flab as so many eunuchs did.

His strength would allow him to bring Megan many more orgasms.

Turning, he offered her his hand. She glared in the direction that the stableboy stood.

He did not need to look to know that the boy gawked at the Arab who wore a robe like a woman.

"Megan," he said softly.

She reluctantly tore her gaze away from the stableboy.

"I am used to arousing curiosity," he merely said.

Megan gave him her hand. Her frown did not diminish.

The dim interior of the inn was oppressive after the bright sunshine outside; the smell of boiled cabbage and beef nauseated him after the freshness of spring air.

The innkeeper who had greedily procured him a whore was not at his station. Raised voices drifted out of the pub.

A chambermaid had straightened his room while they were gone. The bed was made; the ladderback chair stood by the fireplace; the water pitcher sat inside the stoneware basin.

It was as if he had not pleasured a woman and been pleasured in return.

He locked the door.

Megan waited for him by the bed. "I trust you to give me pleasure, Muhamed."

But he did not trust her to give him pleasure, she did not need to add.

No woman could give him what he ached for.

She would not be satisfied until he proved it to her.

"Take off your clothes, Megan."

Megan did not gaze away from him as she removed her clothing. The color of her eyes was indistinct in the dull light; the fire in her hair doused.

"Sit down on the bed," he said harshly.

She sat down on the edge of the bed.

Silently he removed his turban and jerked his *thobs* over his head. The act was familiar, his intentions were not.

Megan dropped a pillow to the floor; he knelt in front of her.

He did not have to tell her to spread her legs.

Gently he cupped her breasts, swollen and tender, shrouded in shadow instead of sunlight. Hunkering down, he touched her vulva, her clitoris that was still engorged, her nether lips that glistened with moisture.

Untouched by the beauty and the brutality that was Arabia.

She easily took one finger, two . . .

He stared at the taut ring of her flesh and the dark intrusion of his hand. Moisture leaked from her body, a pearly essence. Slowly, he pulled out until just his two fingertips were buried inside her. Carefully, he pressed his third and forth finger into the gap he caused, fluting them to fit her shape, her size.

She winced, but did not deny him.

Megan would not deny him anything, and he did not know *why.*

He glanced up at her breasts he had held and her nipples that he had suckled. And was overwhelmed by need.

Swooping upward, he took her left nipple in his mouth. Her heartbeat pounded against his tongue; a matching pulse throbbed against his fingertips.

A woman's vagina was made to birth a child. A woman's breasts were made to give milk.

But there would be no offspring from their union.

He suckled, giving her the succor she needed. That he needed. That they needed, together.

He pushed four fingers inside her, first knuckles, second knuckles . . . stretching her as a child never would.

Megan contracted around him.

He circled his thumb around her clitoris, savoring her hardness on the outside, her softness on the inside.

A cry spread through Megan's chest, vibrated against his lips and tongue, labored up through her throat and out of her mouth.

Pleasure. Pain.

Her orgasm crushed his fingers, forcing him to share both her pleasure and her pain. A drip of preparatory moisture was squeezed out of his verge.

Cool fingers cupped his ears; heat riffled the top of his head—her breath. She buried her face in his hair, nose and lips pressing against his scalp as he suckled her and milked from her the last spasm of her pleasure, a gentle flutter around his fingers.

They sat for long moments, his fingers inside her, her nipple inside his mouth, connected in a way no erotic treatise could adequately describe.

Reluctantly, he released her nipple. The heat weighting his head lifted; the fingers cupping his ears slid down to his cheeks.

There was no stubble to prick her fingers, nor would there ever be.

He lifted his head and met her waiting gaze.

"I had a son," he said.

Her fingers tightened around his jaws; her vagina nipped his fingers.

"Not of my flesh," he explained harshly, "but a boy who was placed into my care when I was twenty-seven years old.

We"—he would not reveal another's secret exile, it was not his story to tell—"came to England nine years ago. Last week he threatened to kill me if I hurt his woman."

His pain was reflected in her eyes. Or perhaps it was fear he saw, that another man had felt it necessary to threaten him lest he harm a woman.

"Words said in the heat of anger should be forgotten," she merely said.

"They were not said in the heat of anger." He flexed his fingers inside her; Megan reflexively tightened around him. "He would have killed me. I do not blame him. He did what he had to do."

"Were you a . . . a threat to this woman?"

"Yes."

The pulse beating inside her sped up.

"Why?"

"Because I was jealous." Remembered rage and pain swelled over him. "Because I wanted what he had, a woman of my own."

"But you didn't harm her."

"No."

Or had he?

Were the two of them together, or had he irrevocably come between them?

"Does he—do you—live around here?"

"He lives in London."

"Is that why you are in Land's End—to get away from this man and his . . . woman?"

He opened his mouth to tell her the truth.

He couldn't.

"In Arabia, there was a woman in the harem . . . a woman who married a eunuch," he heard himself say. "He had no verge, no testicles. Yet she claimed that he was capable of orgasm. She said that he would go into a rutting fever . . . and she would hold a pillow over his head when he obtained his peak to prevent him from gnashing her breasts with his teeth.

She and the other women laughed, that a eunuch could be reduced to such ignominy."

He heard again the laughter, the jeering taunt.

He wasn't like that, he thought, on a surge of agony.

He would show her he wasn't like that.

He didn't need a woman to bring him release, other than
through her own release.

Megan's flesh sucked at his fingers when he withdrew. He
gave her his verge, sinking so deeply inside her that there was
not room for thoughts of Arabia or eunuchs.

Her gaze held his, accepting him, accommodating him.

Closing his eyes, he pulled back out, and rammed into her.
Again. And again. And again.

Until his skin burned with sweat.

Until his knees ached.

Until his verge throbbed in agony.

Until she cried out, first in pleasure, then in pain, and he
still could not gain release.

Soft arms wrapped around him. Held him. Immobilized
him.

He leaned into Megan, trembling, wanting so badly that he
wanted to howl. Sobbing for air, he buried his face in the
crook of her neck.

Soft fingers feathered his hair, pressed him closer. "Tell me
how," she whispered.

How could he tell her?

It was unnatural.

A man should not need more than a woman's vulva.

"Tell me," she persisted. "Please. Trust me, Muhamed.
Trust me like I've trusted you."

He pressed harder into her neck, her vagina, wanting to
lose himself inside her, unable to do so. *Because of one man's
decision.* Because of an entire culture that perpetrated a practice that destroyed lives rather than desire.

"A man has a gland inside him that can be caressed," he
said raggedly.

Megan stilled—even the pulse that rapidly pounded against his lips seemed to halt.

It had dawned on her that there was only one place that a man could be internally caressed.

"How would a woman be able to identify this gland?" she asked unevenly.

He repeated what he had heard other eunuchs say, creatures who were not supposed to want sexual satisfaction *but they did*. "It is said to be the size and shape of an unshelled nut. They call it the third almond."

"I want to please you, Muhamed. I want to give you the same pleasure you have given me."

He pulled away from the comfort of Megan's arms. "It is not the same," he said harshly.

"You are afraid."

Yes, he was afraid.

He was afraid that the climax she had given him would never be repeated.

He was afraid of losing what little masculinity he retained.

"It is unnatural," he grated.

Why didn't she see that it was unnatural?

"Muhamed, satisfaction is not unnatural. What *they* did to *you* is unnatural. Men loving women only so they can bear their children is unnatural. But not this, Muhamed. You said you receive satisfaction through my pleasure. Let me share yours. Let me know that I can please you, as you've pleased me."

"They laughed," he said harshly.

"I would never laugh at you."

No, Megan wouldn't laugh at him.

Gently, he withdrew from her and stood up, bones creaking, knees aching.

Megan grabbed a pillow. Dropping it to the floor, she kneeled in front of him.

He stared down at the top of her head; her braid hung down her back. She looked like a schoolgirl.

Her hands that wrapped around him did not belong to a schoolgirl, they belonged to a woman.

Air danced along his verge, the caress of her fingers.

Glancing up, she caught his gaze, "This is for me, too, Muhannad. I've never had the opportunity to touch a man's body. I will always treasure the fact that you trust me enough to let me do this."

Head lowering, she circumvented his response by the simple expedient of taking him into her mouth.

He wished he could see her face.

He wished he could hold her body.

His groin tightened.

He blindly grabbed—a woman had such a vulnerable neck—and felt the laving of her tongue deep inside, as if his member did not stop at his pubis, but wound up inside him.

She suckled him.

He slid his thumbs up, simultaneously feeling the hot suction of her mouth and the muscles in her jaws rhythmically contract, expand, contract, expand.

There was pleasure in having a woman suckle a man's member, but there was also uncertainty. In a woman's mouth, he was entirely at her mercy.

She could hurt him, and there was nothing he could do to prevent it.

Had she felt this same sense of vulnerability when he had taken her into his mouth and suckled her? he briefly wondered.

Did all women feel this sense of vulnerability when a man took them—whether with fingers or verge—and they were entirely at his mercy?

Had Megan felt this vulnerability?

Lungs sucking in air, he threw his head back, his whole world reduced to Megan's lips, Megan's tongue, and the sharp threat of Megan's teeth.

He was melting, yet he had never felt more hard.

A gentle pressure nudged his thighs. His heart jumped—in anticipation, in dread.

He did not want what she offered.

He wanted to be like other men, to take his release as other men took theirs.

Trust her, she had said.

He had never trusted anyone, not since he was thirteen. How could he trust this woman?

How could he *not* trust her?

He parted his legs.

She found him, prodded him. Her finger was slippery wet— from her own body?

He squeezed his eyelids together, emotions roiling, muscles clenching. Denying her access. Denying the unbidden thrill of pleasure her touch engendered, probing for entry.

She would not be denied.

He gasped, feeling her become a part of him. And gasped again when she found the gland he had spoken of.

A bolt of lightning shot down his spine and out of his verge. Light flashed behind his eyelids; voices echoed inside his ears.

The son of his heart: *I will kill you. . . .*

The woman he had loved: *Have you never, ever wanted to find love in a woman's body?*

Megan, the woman who through her selflessness was demonstrating that he knew nothing of love, and never had: *I do not understand what it is that you want from me.*

He gritted his teeth to hold back the pressure that squeezed his chest and overflowed into his throat.

This was what he had wanted.

This was all he had ever wanted.

A woman who would not cringe at his body, as he cringed from it.

A woman who would take what he could give her, and not belittle him for what he could not give her.

A woman who cared about the needs of a eunuch.

The flickering lights behind his eyelids coalesced into one

blinding white light. His world shattered, the past that had
been forced upon him, the present that now brought fulfillment to a eunuch, the bleak future that yawned before him.

A hoarse cry splintered the light, and once again he was a
man.

Not a eunuch.

A man.

Megan's gift to him.

Suddenly they were two people instead of one.

A splash of water sounded in the silence; it was followed by
the clink of stoneware on wood—more splashes, silence again.

He strained to hear her next move, to feel her nearness.
Trembling in the aftermath of the pleasure she had given him.

Soft hands cupped his face, lowered his head.

He opened his eyes. Megan's eyes were bright with unshed
tears.

"I was a part of you, Muhamed. I've never felt anything so
powerful, or so beautiful. Thank you for your trust."

His heart double beat.

She deserved the truth.

"Muhamed is the name that was given me by the Arabs.
My English name is Connor. Connor Treffry."

She recognized the name.

The Treffrys were the most prosperous fishermen in West
Cornwall. Perhaps in the entirety of Cornwall.

Megan withdrew: hands, emotions.

"How?" she asked.

How had he come to be a eunuch?

How could he have deceived her, he who had accused her
of deception?

"I loved the sea," he said raggedly, needing her warmth and
her closeness but unable to express emotions he had held in
abeyance for forty years. "I wanted nothing more than to be a
fisherman, like my father. Like my brothers before me. I convinced my father to let me go out with some of his men one
day. There was a squall. We were blown off course. A ship

picked us up. It was a slaver. We were taken to a Barbary port and sold. I never saw my father's men again."

There were no words for the horror he had felt, imprisoned, away from home for the first time in his life with no hope of ever returning.

"But you were . . . English."

A smile twisted his lips; it did not reach his eyes. "The Arab who bought me was not impressed by my heritage. Nor was he impressed by my rebellious nature. In Arabia, there is a saying: take a wife for children, but take a boy for pleasure. He liked young men. When I refused to accommodate him, he watched while his guards held me down and an Egyptian infidel crushed my testicles. Then he sold me to a Syrian trader."

He stared into her green eyes and saw not the verdancy of England, but the barren desert and the thirteen-year-old boy he had been.

"An infection set in. The Syrian trader cut off the useless sac that hung between my legs and buried me in the sand to staunch my blood."

Megan's pale skin turned pasty with shock.

"I do not remember the pain anymore." A muscle twitched at the corner of his mouth. Images of a blazing yellow sun and bright crimson blood flashed before his eyes. "But I remember crying like a girl. I wanted to die; it was not permitted."

"I'm glad you didn't die," she said quietly.

Last night and today he had been glad, too.

"I could not bring myself to tell my family that I lived," he confessed instead.

There was no condemnation in her eyes. "They believe you are dead?"

"I thought it would be best if they believed me dead rather than knowing what had happened to me."

Her gaze did not falter. It ripped the truth out of him.

"*I* did not want them to know what had happened to me."

He still did not want them to know.

"They would not blame you. How could they?"

"I am the youngest in my family; I have three older broth-ers and one sister. I was the pampered son. I've been in England for nine years, yet I did not visit my parents. They died not knowing that I was alive. I did not attend their funer-als.

"Tomorrow, Megan, tomorrow I will find out if my broth-ers and my sister blame me."

"Do they know you are alive now?"

"They know. I sent them a note the day before yesterday."

The day he had decided to procure a whore.

The day Megan had come into his life.

"I will send them another note tomorrow," he said dispas-sionately. "We will meet over afternoon tea, like English do."

"Why are you visiting with them now, if you do not wish to?" she persisted quietly.

Because his hatred had frightened him.

Because he needed to make peace with himself. Cornwall had seemed like a good place to start.

"I am fifty-three years old, and I do not know who I am. I am a eunuch. I have gone by the name of Muhamed for forty years. But I want what Connor would have had. I want a woman; I want children. I want to live among other men, as a man."

"You *are* a man."

"And which man do you think I am, Megan? Muhamed . . . or Connor?"

"I think the man I baptized today is the man you are," she said firmly.

He felt as if a fist slammed into his chest.

"I don't think the gods will be appeased by a condom, Megan."

"Perhaps not, but it will certainly give rise to speculation, come May," she calmly rejoined.

He did not want to think about May. He did not want to think about the decision he would have to make, come the morrow.

"Hold me," he said starkly. And for the first time in forty years, he said one simple English word. "Please. Come to bed and hold me."

Chapter Seven

Pink dawn divided the darkness inside the bedroom. Faint stirrings penetrated the quiet, the sound of other clients rising. Leaving.

Sounds she had not noticed yesterday, the comings and goings of others.

Megan cradled his sleeping head against her breasts and listened to the easy rhythm of his breathing.

Muhamed. Connor.

Which man did she hold?

How would his family react when they saw him?

Would they stare at him, as the stableboy had stared at him?

Would they welcome him?

Would they rebuff him?

Would they hurt him?

His arm tightened about her waist. She knew that he, too, was awake.

"Muh—" She bit her lip.

What did she call him?

"I have to go," she said.

He did not answer.

Her heart felt as though it were being rent in two.

How ridiculous of her, to hope that he would want her to stay.

He did not stop her when she slipped out from underneath his head and his arm.

He did not stop her when she hurriedly dressed, shivering from the cold and the tears that silently dripped down her cheeks.

He did not stop her when she quietly opened the door and slipped out of his life.

Never to know if he found peace.

With his family.

With another woman.

Once in her room, Megan scrubbed her face, her teeth, dressed her hair and packed her clothes.

It was time to get on with her life.

The innkeeper, a squat man with thinning hair greased back from his forehead, leered at her, obviously aware of the time she had spent with the man he knew as Mr. Muhamed.

Meg would have cringed in humiliation; Megan turned her nose up. "I require transportation to the Branwell place."

"Ain't nothin' there, lady."

"Nevertheless, I would like to hire a carriage and a driver."

"It'll cost you six shillings."

It was an exorbitant price, but her only alternative was to walk. Ten miles.

"Very well."

The driver was a taciturn man who slumped underneath a worn bowler hat. He did not assist her with her luggage. Megan climbed into the seat beside him.

It was a rare Cornish day; two days of sunshine in a row.

Megan thought of the French letter, flapping in the breeze. She thought of her hair, hanging loose down her back as if she were a young girl instead of a middle-aged widow. She thought of the man who had allowed her to be free of the restrictions incurred by age and respectability.

She thought of the warm fluid that had spurted against the back of her throat.

A man's pleasure was far more precious than his seed.

Megan jumped out of the carriage and tossed out her luggage.

He laid across the rumpled bed a tailored black English jacket, folded, starched shirt, and black wool trousers. Beside them, he laid out a white *thobs,* baggy white trousers, and a length of white material to create a turban.

Connor's clothes. Muhamed's clothes.

Muhamed's clothes. Connor's clothes.

He was a eunuch, nothing would ever change his condition.

How could he put aside the last forty years as if they did not exist?

How could he ever have any peace if he did not?

How could Megan have slipped out of his arms and his bed and his room and his life as if they had not shared an intimacy that neither had ever before experienced?

He glanced down. And tried to choose.

To live as an Englishman, or to continue as an Arab.

Megan ignored the leering innkeeper. Heart outpacing her feet, she climbed the narrow stairs.

The hallway was a mile long; the worn wool carpet had turned to molasses, sucking at her feet.

He had given her no indication he wanted her to stay. Why was she embarrassing both him and herself by putting him in this position?

Her husband had rejected her.

What if this man did, too?

Thirty-six hours ago she had thought the hardest thing she had ever done was lift her veil and show her age to an Arab who had procured a whore. This was far, far harder.

Megan lifted her black-gloved hand and knocked.

A lifetime passed, waiting for him to answer.

She was overcome with a sense of déjà vu.

Thirty-six hours ago she had knocked in just such a manner. And waited. . . .

Suddenly the door swung open.

Her eyes widened.

The man who answered the door was not the man who had
allowed her entrance the night before.

"You . . . you're wearing trousers," she said.

His answer was not encouraging. "Yes."

Her gaze lingered on the white turban covering his head,
drifted down to his black eyes, his chiseled features.

His face was tense, as if he, too, waited. . . .

For her acceptance?

Or for her to leave?

In his black wool trousers, vest and frock coat he looked
English, but. . . .

"You've covered up your hair," she blurted out.

"There is only one woman whom I wish to look upon it,"
he said shortly, black gaze stoic.

"I do not require marriage," she said in a burst of emotion.

"My family would be shocked if I visited them with a concubine," he replied tersely, very much the man who had
opened the door thirty-six hours earlier.

Her stomach somersaulted. "Are you asking me to marry
you?"

"I am not an easy man."

"So you have said."

"I cannot erase the years I have lived in Arabia."

"I would not have you do so."

"I am a eunuch."

"If you are a eunuch, then I daresay many women wish
their husbands were such."

His dark features tightened.

"I do not know if there is a place for me in Cornwall."

"I would enjoy seeing other parts of England"—could she live in Arabia, where women mutilated women and men castrated men?—"or other countries."

"I do not know if trousers will suit me."

"I prefer you in your robe."

"*Thobs.*"

"I beg your pardon?"

"It is called a *thobs,* not a robe."

"I'm sorry."

"Yes," he said.

Megan blinked. "Yes, what?"

"Yes, I am asking if you will marry me."

How could happiness be as painful as heartbreak?

"Shall I call you Muhamed, or Connor?"

"You may call me whatever you wish."

He might be Connor in public, but in private he would always be Muhamed.

"I want to learn how to speak Arabic," Megan said firmly.

"I will teach you."

"I want to shave off my private hair."

His black eyes suddenly gleamed. "I will shave you."

"In that case, sir, I will marry you."